By the same author

WHAT A FOOL BELIEVES

This book is a work of fiction.

John Gascoigne and his family, Mary-Anne and her family, Thomas Gadsden and his family, Governors Middleton and Johnson, Captain George Anson and all Naval personnel were real people, although I have dreamt up their thoughts, words and actions. All other characters are entirely fictitious and any resemblance to actual persons, living or dead, is purely coincidental. The opinions expressed are those of the characters and should not be confused with the author's.

The Captain's Wife

Nicola Richardson

Author's Note

The Captain's Wife is a work of fiction imagining the life of my 7th great-grandmother Mary-Anne Gascoigne (née Mighells) (1705-1748). The story starts in 1727 when Captain John Gascoigne married Mary-Anne Mighells and sailed to the West Indies. It is based on real people and events discovered while researching my family tree.

The naval logbooks of Captain John Gascoigne are held at the National Archives in Kew and the National Maritime Museum in Greenwich and are available for public inspection. It was reading these logbooks in my genealogical research that inspired this novel. They give a day-by-day account of where the ship was and what was happening onboard. All dates given are of actual events recorded in John's logbooks. Extracts from his logbooks are quoted verbatim and follow the tradition of the nautical day starting at midday and finishing at midday the next day.

The only records of Mary-Anne's life are Church Registry entries for baptisms, marriages and deaths so I have invented a fictional story around these and the account of John's life given in his daily naval logs.

It is impossible to write about Mary-Anne's life between 1727 and 1734 without mentioning slavery. In the 18th century, sugar cane replaced piracy as Jamaica's main source of income. The sugar industry was labour-intensive and the British brought thousands of enslaved Africans to the island.

Charles Town in the 18th Century was also a key port for the arrival of enslaved Africans, not just to work on the plantations in Carolina but to be transported to all other major cities in Colonial America.

I use the term 'slave' within the novel which reflects its use in Mary-Anne's time, but intend no insult to the millions of men, women and children who were enslaved against their will.

A note on place names:

In the 18th century Port Royal was the British naval dockyard at Kingston Harbour in Jamaica.

Port Royal was also the name of the natural harbour south of Charleston in South Carolina where a military base had been established at Beaufort.

Charleston was established in 1670 in honour of King Charles II of England. In Mary-Anne's time, it was called Charles Town and adopted its present name in 1783 after the American War of Independence.

The Captain's Wife

A Naval Brigantine in a Calm Sea' 1752. John Cleveley, the Elder
A square-rigged 10-gun Sloop of War of the same class as HMS Tryall. To the left, three officials are being rowed out to the ship where men on deck prepare to meet them.
National Maritime Museum, London

I

Jamaica

1727-1728

On 30th March 1727, Captain John Gascoigne was given command of HMS *Tryall*, bound for the West Indies.

From the Captain's Log, HMS Tryall
13th April 1727
At the moorings at Deptford, London.

"Yesterday morning I arrived from the Nore where I found HMS Tryall put in commission by Mr John Durell who is appointed Lieutenant officer on 7th instant, but no men enter'd except the officers and their servants. I went immediately to London & this morning recv'd a commission from Rt Hon. the Lords Commissioners for Executing the Office of the Lord High Admiral of Great Britain & Ireland, appointing me to command his Majesty's Sloop the Tryall dated 30th March which I notified to the Hon. Principal Officers & Commissioners of his Majesty's Navy & then went down to Deptford for 9th instant (the day after my discharge from HMS Portsmouth) & having applied for assistance from the Yard to get the Sloop's rigging fitted and the Ballast in, I returned to London to raise men."

John applied for a Marriage Licence on 9th May 1727 and married the next day.

From Crisp's Marriage Licence Index, London, England 1713-1892
9th May 1727

"Approved personally, John Gascoigne of the Tower Hamlett Esq. aged thirty years and a Batchelor, alleged that he intends to marry with Mary-Anne Mighells of the parish of Saint Olave Hart Street London aged twenty two years and a Spinster. And that he knoweth of no lawful lot or impediment by reason of any Procontract Consanguinity Affinity or any other Lawful Modus whatsoever to hinder the said intended marriage of the both of which he made Oath and pray'd Licence to solomnize the said marriage in the Parish Church of St Anne Aldersgate or the Chapel belonging to Guildhall London or St Bennett Paul's Wharf London.

Curator fiat Licentia Gul Strahan
Signed J Gascoigne."

1

Early morning was not the time of day two young ladies should be on the streets of London. At that hour, the pavements in the city were crowded with porters, hawkers and barrow boys delivering their wares to the wealthy homes of gentlemen. In London tradespeople began their day early; the fashionable world stayed home until noon. Scavengers and night-soil men swept the streets. Clerks, lawyers and agents in their ill-fitting wigs and jackets rushed past to their desks. Two ageing harlots, garishly painted, glided down the street like queens, making plain folk step aside to let them pass. Pickpockets kept an eye out for a purse or pocket watch foolishly displayed. Villains skulked home after a night's work, furtively glancing around to see who else was up to no good.

And that morning I was up to no good. Before the household stirred, I crept quietly out of the house so I could elope with my beloved Captain John Gascoigne of His Majesty's Navy. The evening before, John had sent me a note that he had got the marriage licence as promised. He expressed his deepest love and desire to marry me immediately. His ship sailed for Jamaica at noon so he would meet me at the church of St Anne's Aldersgate at eight o'clock in the morning where we could be married without waiting for the banns to be read at church. It was a short walk from our London house in St Olaf's, opposite the Admiralty where Papa worked.

My sister Alice had read the note hidden under my pillow, even though it was a secret, and she insisted on coming with me.

'If it was secret, he would have written it in code,' she said in her defence. I loved all my sisters dearly but I loved Alice the best. Only she would have expected a lover's note to be written in code. 'You'll never be able to do this by yourself, Mary-Anne,' she declared.

She was right, I wouldn't be able to do this by myself. I was the eldest of four daughters and Papa's favourite, so dutiful and obedient. He always called me his good little girl. He wouldn't call me that again.

John's note was an intoxicating invitation to any girl who longed to be married. John loved me and wanted to marry me and take me to the West Indies. How could I not rush to meet him at the church? I was giddy with excitement and prepared to defy my dearest parents.

Still, I was glad Alice was there with me. I was used to sharing my life with my sisters. And if we took a handle each she could help me carry my heavy bag. Everyone pushed and shoved us as they rushed past.

'We should have taken a carriage or at least a sedan,' I said, but Alice took my arm and pulled me onwards.

'Hurry up,' she said, 'or we'll be late.'

'I can't walk any faster with these pattens over my best satin slippers.'

'You should have worn boots like me.' She lifted her petticoats in a very unladylike manner to show me her sturdy footwear.

'I didn't want to get married wearing my boots,' I said, pulling down her petticoats to preserve her modesty.

Maids swept dust out of front doors all over our skirts. I prayed an early morning chamber pot wouldn't be emptied over my head. This was an affluent part of the city but we still had to tread carefully to avoid the rubbish, excrement and other offensive things littering the pavement. A filthy beggar sitting in a doorway suddenly lurched forward and grabbed my petticoats. He stank of decay, his grey hair was matted and his clothes were rags. As I fumbled in my purse for a coin to throw him, Alice pulled me away.

'Come on! You'll be late. John won't wait for you forever.'

'We should help him. Give him alms.'

'Forget him, Mary-Anne. It'll be far worse where you're going,' she said with gleeful relish. 'The streets will be full of beggars and thieves, cut-throats and pirates.'

I stopped dead in my tracks. What was I thinking? I wasn't brave enough to do this.

'Oh Alice, d'you think I shouldn't go?'

'Not go! Why would you not go? This is the most exciting thing that has ever happened to you or any of us. You must go.'

'Mama thinks it's my duty to stay home and wait for John to return in a year or two. Papa said we could be married then.'

Although my parents approved of John's marriage proposal, they expected us to get married when John returned from the West

Indies. I hadn't told them that John had asked me to marry him in the morning and sail away with him in the afternoon.

'In a year or two he'll have forgotten you,' she said, quite definitely. 'You'll die an old spinster. Imagine the humiliation if Betty marries before you.'

Or worse still, Alice.

I was the eldest of four sisters. Betty was a year younger than me, plump, blonde and bossy, like Mama. She was practical and homely, always telling her sisters off. Alice was two years younger than me, brave, fearless and headstrong. She and I were different in temperament but so alike in looks, small and slight, with dark eyes and raven-black hair. We took after Papa in our colouring. Annie was only eight, still to show us what kind of woman she would become.

Alice was right, I couldn't wait for John to return. As the eldest sister, I had to marry first. Mama had been preparing me for this day since I was born. I had all the useful skills needed to attract a husband. I could smile prettily, dance nicely, sing and play the piano, behave politely at the dinner table and hold my tongue if I disagreed. All I dreamt of was to be married and have lots of children. My husband would adore me, my parents would be proud of me and my sisters would be envious of me.

'Still, I admire you heading off to the West Indies with a man you hardly know,' she said.

Did she think I should change my mind, turn around and run home? After the chaos on the morning streets, I was shaking with nerves so it was tempting. It was true that we'd only been courting since Christmas but Captain John Gascoigne was everything I wanted in a husband and he was an Officer in His Majesty's Navy.

'I knew the moment I met John that he was the perfect husband and you know how much I want to get married and have children. I'm twenty-two already, I can't wait any longer,' I told her, as we stepped aside to avoid the fishmonger brushing stinking entrails into our path.

'I wish it was me going,' Alice said, looking away into the distance. 'I shall die of boredom left in Stratford while you are having adventures in the West Indies.'

I wasn't sure I wanted adventures but before I could think on this further, we had arrived at the church. St Anne's Aldersgate was a small, brick chapel, newly built after the Great Fire in a busy side street in the City of London.

I have imagined my Wedding Day since I was a young girl. I would be married in my local parish church in Stratford in the County of Essex where I grew up. The old stone church would be bursting with summer blossoms, the choir would be singing angelically, the bells would be ringing loudly and the pews would be crowded with my family, friends and well-wishers. Everyone I had ever known would be there to watch me walk up the aisle and wish me well on my special day.

It was nothing like that. No flowers or choirs. No bells ringing. No friends or family, except Alice. No beautiful dress. I was wearing my old blue silk gown. The one with lace cuffs to show off my delicate wrists and the stiff bodice to accentuate my slim waist.

We stopped in the open doorway.

'So, this is what you really want?' Alice asked.

'Of course it is.'

She straightened my petticoats and arranged my black curls to fall prettily over my shoulder. As we walked together down the aisle I noticed a few random churchgoers sitting at the back. Leftovers from Matins. I was surprisingly grateful to these elderly strangers for swelling the congregation.

John stood with the priest near the altar. He was smartly dressed as a Naval Officer should be, in his blue frock coat, white breeches and shoulder-length powdered wig. When he turned around and smiled at me, my heart swelled with pride that he wanted to marry me.

He wasn't especially tall or handsome but he had a kind face and he always smiled at me. Alice said he was like a spaniel, watching me with his big brown eyes, wanting my approval, eager to please. She said that as if it was a bad thing. I had not had many suitors and none that smiled at me as much as John did. For that, I loved him dearly.

His brother James stood next to him, acting as the best man. John had told me about his half-brother, three years his younger, a Lieutenant in the Navy but almost a stranger to him. As John had been at sea since he was a boy, he had not had the chance to spend much time with him.

Alice gave me a nudge and I nervously walked forward to stand beside John. He grasped my hand tightly.

'You came, Mary-Anne! I wasn't sure you would.'

'Of course I came, my dearest. Did you doubt me?'

'Well, it was very short notice. I didn't know if you got my letter. Or if your parents would stop you. The *Tryall* sails at noon and I can't bear to go without you. I'm so delighted you're here.'

Alice sniggered at his excitement, but the priest began the service so I ignored her. John was standing so close I could sense everything about him, his strong hand almost crushing mine, his salty smell of the ocean, his promise to take care of me till death do us part.

I glanced up at the ceiling of the church, painted with blue and gold rosettes, and imagined the Good Lord in his Heaven watching me. I silently prayed for his forgiveness for not telling my parents and I assured Him that I would never break my vows and I promised to be the perfect wife to John and a good mother to our children.

I turned to smile at John and he grinned at me. I loved him even more than before.

The priest wasn't familiar with my family name.

'It's pronounced Miles but spelt M-i-g-h-e-l-l-s,' I told him.

'She's the daughter of Vice-Admiral James Mighells,' John added proudly. 'The Comptroller of His Majesty's Navy.'

The priest wasn't interested in my parentage, especially as my father wasn't there to give me away. 'I just want to spell it right in the register,' he muttered.

Once we had confirmed our vows, he duly recorded in the church's Marriage Register:

"1727 May 10th John Gascoigne of Tower Hamlets, London and Mary-Anne Mighells of Saint Olaf, Hart St with a licence."

John donned his hat, I tucked my hand into the crook of his arm and we walked out of the church as man and wife.

Alice embraced me warmly. We both had tears in our eyes. Mine were due to the sadness of our parting but I suspected her tears were more from frustration and jealousy.

She whispered in my ear, 'Now I am stuck at home with Boring Betty and Little Annie. Without you, my life will be so dull.'

'It may not be so dull when you get home and they have discovered what has happened.'

'You're right. Perhaps I will delay my return for a few hours until the fuss has died down. I hope your letter explained everything,' she said. 'I don't want to take the blame.'

My letter was a short note telling my parents that I loved them dearly but I was going to marry Captain John Gascoigne that morning and go with him to Jamaica. I asked Papa for his blessing and I asked Mama to pack up my clothes and send them to HMS *Tryall*. John had agreed his ship could wait at Galleon's Reach on the River Thames for a few days.

What else could I say? No doubt Papa would shout that he forbade it, Mama would probably faint and Betty would shake her head disapprovingly. But it was done. This had been my chance to get married and I had seized it with both hands.

We said farewell to James. Who knew when we would meet again?

John hailed a carriage to take us to Deptford where the *Tryall* was anchored. It was his first command and he told me enthusiastically that she was a ten-gun sloop of war, a square-rigged, two-masted brigantine. When he pointed her out I was a little disappointed. The ship was small and low in the water, with two masts, one row of gunports and a long bowsprit sticking out the front. There were many larger ships on the river, both warships and merchantmen, with two or three decks, riding high in the water, more impressive and safer for a voyage across the Atlantic Ocean.

I knew better than to say anything. Papa had told me many times that a naval officer's first command was a daunting challenge. To the men onboard the Captain was the ultimate controller of their fate. His commands might be the difference between life and death, between a successful voyage and a living hell. So far John appeared calm and confident in his new exalted position, but it had only been six weeks since he was appointed Commanding Officer of HMS *Tryall*.

We waited on the quayside while the longboat was rowed ashore. As it came alongside, the oars were raised and a sailor scrambled onto the dock with a rope. John helped me down the stone steps, slimy with weed exposed by the low tide. I stumbled and was grateful for his firm hand to steady me.

Once my bag was loaded into the boat, the two lines of oarsmen dipped their oars and we left the dock. I was suddenly conscious of the dark river, the inky surface broken by the rhythm of the oars. As we drew close a shout went out from the crow's nest at the top of the mainmast, 'Boat ahoy' and sailors appeared on deck to await our arrival. We passed enormous, plaited ropes straining to hold the ship on her anchors. Closer up the ship was much taller than she looked from the quay. The masts were impossibly tall. I leaned back to gaze up and almost lost my balance.

The boat drew alongside the hull with a bump and the sailor nearest attached his boat hook to the chains. John grabbed the ladder and I watched fearfully as he climbed upward hand over hand, until he was safely aboard. I stood up to follow him and stepped onto the ladder. Please Lord, I prayed, don't let me fail at the first challenge. As I climbed upwards the ship was swaying and I was nervous about falling back into the deep water and drowning. Luckily two sailors reached down and grabbed me under my arms, lifting me onto the deck.

John showed me into the Captain's Cabin at the stern of the ship behind the huge steering wheel and the Officers' Dining Room. I stepped inside a small, dark cave made from wooden planks. This would be my home for the next six weeks or however long it took us to sail to Jamaica. It stretched the full width of the ship, dark and woody, strong and plain. It could have done with a rug or two or some paintings on the walls or curtains at the windows. The space might have been adequate if it hadn't been filled with a huge wooden table in the centre, laden down with books, ledgers, rolled-up charts, navigational equipment and all manner of strange tools.

'I hope you will be comfortable, Mary-Anne. As an Admiral's daughter, you must be quite used to being onboard a ship.'

The ceiling was so low that John had to stoop. I was small enough to stand upright, just. On one side was a small bed, more of a swinging cot, with curtains for privacy. I was too shy to inspect it while John was standing beside me. Above the bed a shelf was crowded with John's books, his journals and his precious theodolite. Along the back wall there were lockers beneath the stern windows that stretched the full width of the ship. Cushions had been placed on top as a makeshift sofa. He showed me the cupboards for my clothes and the curtain to the water closet which emptied over the side of the ship.

The cabin smelled of damp wood, salty sea air, tar and fresh paint, the stink of a man's sweat and the stench of rancid pork cooking in the galley somewhere below decks. I wasn't sure if I could open the window to let the sea breeze blow in and I couldn't ask John. I didn't want to admit that I'd never been on a ship before. Papa disapproved of women onboard Navy ships.

There was an awkward silence as we turned to face each other.

'Did the marriage service please you, Mary-Anne? It probably wasn't quite the wedding you were dreaming of. Perhaps you would have preferred the much grander chapel at the Guildhall?'

'I think the smaller church suited us better,' I said, thinking of the lack of any wedding guests in the congregation.

He nodded and smiled at me. 'Well, it doesn't matter where we were married, does it? You looked very beautiful, my dearest. I apologise for the haste but I couldn't bear the thought of losing you while I was away. If we'd postponed our marriage until my return some other man might have won your heart.'

He put his hand up to my cheek and I could feel my skin burning under his touch. How could I tell him that ever since the night we danced at the Naval Ball my heart had been his?

He leaned forward to kiss me gently on my lips. As I responded he took me in his arms and his kisses became more fervent.

'I have been dreaming of this moment since I first took you in my arms to dance with you,' he whispered. 'Now you are my wife and I am the happiest man in the world.'

My body softened against him and my heart beat faster. I was unsure what I should do next, but I trusted John to make our marriage work. He held me at arm's length to gaze at me lovingly and then he took from his pocket a locket on a silver chain and opened it to show a miniature of his likeness.

'I had this painted as my wedding gift to you. When I'm away at sea, you can keep me close to your heart.' He fastened the chain around my neck. 'Now I must attend to my duties as Captain. We sail with the tide but this evening I'll come back and be with you.' He released me from his embrace and strode out of the cabin.

I wasn't sure what I was supposed to do until he returned. I opened the cupboards, but they were full of John's greatcoats and jackets and breeches, the drawers were full of his shirts and stockings, his hats and his wigs. There was no place for the few clothes I had brought so I abandoned them in the bag. I couldn't expect John's valet

17

to look after me but eloping in secret meant I couldn't bring my lady's maid with me. John said the Master's wife, Mrs Jenny Bishop, would be on board and she would look after me.

I peered out of the window and could see the skyline of London, bright in the noonday sun. Looking out from this dark cavern, it belonged to a different world, a sunlit world I used to inhabit. I wondered what my family were doing now. I missed them already. I sat down wearily on the sofa under the window, touching the locket around my neck and suddenly after all the excitement of the morning, I felt exhausted. Sitting quietly in the small, dark cabin I knew my life had totally changed. it was going to be very different from now on.

Until this moment my life had the constant background noise of my mother and three sisters laughing, arguing, singing, reading aloud, discussing new dresses and whispering midnight secrets. Now the sounds were strange to me, the slap of waves on the side of the ship, the shouts and whistles of sailors on deck, the seagulls wheeling overhead, the wind whistling in the rigging and the constant creaks and groans of the *Tryall* as she lurched from side to side, swinging on her anchors. It was a strange sensation to sit perfectly still yet feel the ship constantly moving beneath me. I was trapped within her like Jonah in the belly of the whale.

There was a timid knock on the door and a young boy entered with a tray. He was a small, skinny lad with greasy hair falling into his eyes. He couldn't be much older than my sister Annie.

'Cook thought you'd want a cup of tea, m'lady,' he said as he placed the tray on the table, head bowed so he didn't have to look directly at me. 'He says if there's anything you want, seeing as how you're the Captain's wife, you're to let me know. Just ask for me, Georgie Buxton, m'lady.'

I thanked him as he left and realised that my new life as The Captain's Wife had begun.

HMS Tryall set sail from Deptford on 10th May 1727, John's Wedding Day.

From the Captain's Log, HMS Tryall
10th May 1727
At noon abreast of Blackwall.
    "Yesterday the prep gang returned aboard. At 11 this morning slipped the moorings at Deptford and got under sail for Galleons Reach. Wind at NW."

3 days later John's father-in-law paid him a visit.

From the Captain's Log, HMS Tryall
13th May 1727
Anchored in Galleon's Reach, River Thames, London.
    "Moderate gales & fair weather. The Carriage & Swivel Guns came on board & this morning fired Nine Guns to Salute the Hon. James Mighells, Esq Comptroller of His Majesty's Navy at his Coming on board."

2

A loud crash on deck woke me suddenly. I turned over in the narrow bed and pulled the cover over my head hoping to snatch a few more moments of sleep. After three nights onboard HMS Tryall, now on anchor at Galleons Reach, I was finally sleeping better, despite the strange sensation of constant rocking.

The previous day the crew had loaded barrels of gunpowder and that morning there was more noise and commotion. I had no chance of sleep so I washed as best I could in a bowl of cold water, dressed quickly and poked my head out of the door. Lieutenant Durell was within earshot so I asked him what was happening.

'The carriages for the swivel guns are being loaded. Just in time to fire the guns in salute when your father comes on board today.'

'My father is coming on board!'

'Yes, m'lady, he sent an express letter to Captain Gascoigne late last night.'

I ducked back into the cabin.

I was shaking but I smoothed down my hair and my petticoats so Papa wouldn't be so cross with me. John hadn't mentioned this letter to me when he came to bed last night. Perhaps he was regretting upsetting my father, his Sponsor and Superior Officer, the Honourable James Mighells, Vice-Admiral of the Blue and Comptroller of His Majesty's Navy.

John came to see me an hour later and told me what I already knew.

'Please don't let him take me home,' I begged, clutching at his sleeve.

'I'm sure we can persuade him that it's perfectly safe and it will be the perfect opportunity to ask for his blessing.'

He sounded very confident and optimistic. He was so enthusiastic about our voyage to the West Indies. On the contrary, I knew that Papa would be extremely angry. Mama had never set foot on a ship so I knew his views on wives on board His Majesty's warships.

'Times have changed, Mary-Anne. And it's not as if I'm going to war.'

He said that as if it would settle all Papa's objections.

I waited on deck watching the longboat approach. John was standing next to me, resplendent in his dark blue coat, bright with gold braid, and tricorne hat. He was the Captain of the ship and I was proud to be his wife. I wanted to hold his hand for support but I was afraid it would embarrass him in front of his officers and crew.

Square gun ports suddenly opened along the side of the ship and cannons appeared in each one. There was a deafening explosion and the ship shook violently. I grabbed hold of John's hand and hid my face in his jacket, terrified we were being attacked.

John laughed at my reaction and escaped from my grasp, but he kept hold of my hand. Nine times the guns were fired to salute a Vice-Admiral at his coming on board and when I looked up to my great surprise and delight, Papa had brought Alice with him. As the cannons roared, she sat calmly in the longboat next to Papa as if it was to honour her arrival as well.

Sailors rushed to help her climb up the ladder onto the deck, but it was Papa who needed help. I hadn't noticed how old he was getting. Despite his infirmity, he'd made that climb a hundred times before and had no fear.

Finally, he was on deck and John introduced him to Lieutenant Durell. Durell was taller than John, with a rugged, handsome face, tawny with sunburn, freckles and curly rust-brown hair poking out from under his hat. His broad smile made Alice look twice.

Luckily before she could say anything to embarrass me, John ushered my family into the Officers' Dining Room where we sat around the large table, Alice on one side next to Papa and me on the other side next to John. We had taken sides and I had chosen allegiance to my husband not my father.

Papa spoke first. His rage could not be contained any longer.

'Have you taken leave of your senses, Captain Gascoigne? You have kidnapped my daughter and propose to take her with you to the West Indies. There is no place for a woman on board a ship in His Majesty's Navy. I have to say, this is not an auspicious start to your new command.'

'Sir, I appreciate your views but Mary-Anne came willingly. We were properly married on Saturday morning at St Anne's in Aldersgate.

And I have served on several ships where the Captain's wife was on board.'

Papa harrumphed as if he might also have heard of such a thing even if he clearly disapproved.

'Do you think it is wise to take my daughter to Jamaica?'

'My wife,' John interrupted, turning to smile at me. I could feel my cheeks reddening under his loving gaze.

'Yes, yes, but let me tell you, her mother has retired to her bed in a fit of nerves. Port Royal is hardly a safe place for a woman of gentle birth and upbringing.'

Every child from a naval family has heard the terrible stories about Port Royal, the naval harbour in Kingston, Jamaica. The wickedest city on earth, full of brothels, taverns and drinking halls run by cut-throat pirates. In 1692 it was destroyed by a massive earthquake and tidal wave, obviously God's punishment. A city so full of wickedness and evil swallowed into the sea was straight out of the Old Testament.

John had told me that since then, the Navy had caught and hung all the pirates and rebuilt the port as its base in the West Indies. It seemed an endless task, as hurricanes kept destroying all their work. There had been another hurricane last November which devastated the harbour and sank some fifty ships.

John knew the dangers better than Papa. He'd spent most of his naval career in the West Indies and he told Papa we'd only be there for a year while he helped to rebuild the naval dockyard.

'Times have changed since I was out there two years ago on HMS *Launceston*. The last pirates were hung at Gallows Point over five years ago. It's an important base for the British Navy now under the command of Vice-Admiral Hosier.'

'By God, I know Francis Hosier. Now you mention it, I did hear he was sent to Jamaica as Commander-in-Chief last year.'

'Yes sir and since he arrived law and order have been restored to Jamaica and it is now one of England's most prized possessions. The British Fleet is in the West Indies to block the Spanish treasure ships and protect the lucrative sugar trade.'

'Yes, yes, I hear all about this sugar trade in the coffee houses. Lately there is talk of little else. We need the sugar from Jamaica. Every genteel person adds sugar to their tea and coffee drinks. It's surely a sign of respectability. The Sugar Barons seem to have all the power in Parliament these days.'

The effort of arguing was already taking its toll on Papa and he caught his breath. He had visibly aged in the three days since he read my note telling him I had married in secret and was sailing to the West Indies. I realised that Alice had come, not just to see me, but to assist him in his journey to fetch me home.

John started telling him of Navy ships out in Jamaica. Papa had never been to the West Indies and encouraging him to talk about naval matters was a good move. The two men discussed which ships were where, and who was in command, matters that Alice and I had no interest in or knowledge about.

I asked her if she would like to join me for a turn around the deck and she gladly agreed.

Once we were out on deck, she turned to me.

'Well, who would have imagined you would cause such a commotion? Mama fainted when Papa read her your note. She blames Papa of course. It's his fault for introducing you to John and then getting him the command of a ship sailing to the West Indies.'

'Papa can't have known John would ask me to go with him.'

'Mama says that naval officers are no longer allowed to call on us and Papa is not to take us to any more Naval Balls. Betty is very upset. Who's going to marry her now? Being an Admiral's daughter was her only attraction.'

I turned away so she didn't see the doubt on my face. Was that my only attraction?

I had met John at a Naval Ball last December when he came over to pay his respects to Papa.

Nine years ago, John had served as a young Lieutenant on HMS *Bideford*, one of the four ships in the squadron commanded by Papa. Papa always referred to this as His Expedition to Vigo. We all knew the story, recounted many times over the family dinner table, of Papa's final moment of glory as Vice-Admiral before he retired and became Comptroller of the Navy. As he told the story, the citadel of Vigo in northern Spain surrendered to his forces and he captured seven Spanish ships and seized cannons, firearms and ammunition which had been stockpiled for a planned invasion of England. When he returned to Falmouth, his Expedition was hailed as a great success.

There was no doubt John was hoping Vice-Admiral Mighells would remember him and put in a good word for him. There was a lot of competition among lieutenants in the Navy and without a patron to speak for you, it could be hard to get a promotion. Papa had introduced him to his three eldest daughters, Alice, Betty and me, all dressed up in our finery, desperately hoping to meet our future husbands. John said I was the one who smiled at him so he favoured me with all the dances that evening.

After that night he visited us at our family home in Stratford, impressing my family with his exciting tales of life on the ocean waves. In quieter moments, as we strolled in the snowy winter garden arm-in-arm, he told me that he was tired of being alone, having been at sea in His Majesty's Navy since he was a young midshipman aged twelve.

Just as he'd hoped, with Papa's support, the Admiralty gave him his first command in February on HMS *Portsmouth* doing its last days of duty in the Channel. Once he had been promoted, Mama got impatient but he soon asked for my hand in marriage and Papa gave his approval. I was overjoyed and back then, they thought he was a suitable catch. True, I didn't know John well but we would get to know each other once we were married. At the end of March he was rewarded with the command of HMS *Tryall*, bound for the West Indies.

I remember well the day he asked me to go with him.

It was a bright morning at the end of April and John surprised me with a visit. He was busy preparing the *Tryall* for its voyage to the West Indies and would be leaving within a week or so. I had accepted that we would be married when he returned. My husband away for a year or two, home for a few months between commands. I would run the household and raise our children. He would write me the odd letter about his brave heroics at sea. That would be my life as a naval wife.

He asked if I would show him the rose garden, which as every girl knew was an excuse to talk privately. As we admired the bare twigs that would in a few months bloom into roses, he seemed agitated. I feared he might be regretting his proposal a month ago and my heart sank as I prepared myself for the humiliation and disgrace to come.

'Mary-Anne, I don't want to spend the next year in the West Indies on my own with you in England. I want to be married and have a family. I've devoted all my life to the Navy but ever since I met you, I want to change all that. Will you marry me straight away and come with me?'

I had been worried that he might not want to marry me! I was so relieved my head started to move until it was nodding up and down quite definitely. I was so overjoyed and eager to be married that I didn't really listen to the bit about going with him.

'Of course, I will John. In truth, I don't want to wait a year or so either. I want to marry you and have a family as soon as possible.'

He squeezed my hand, leant closer and with a wide grin on his face, embraced me in his arms.

'You won't regret it. I will take good care of you and keep you safe. I don't think it will be for more than a year. It depends on how much rebuilding is needed to restore the port facilities. We would return to England next summer, I promise. And we can be together, man and wife, rather than on opposite sides of the Atlantic.'

It was only when he kissed me passionately that I realised I had agreed to go with him to the West Indies.

'You could live in Kingston and I would visit you as much as possible. Many English people keep elegant households in Kingston, naval officers, plantation owners, merchants, traders.'

It sounded so unreal and impossible to imagine, so I didn't say anything. He had promised we'd only be away for a year and it did sound more exciting than staying at home without him.

On 9th of May 1727, John got the Marriage Licence and sent me that secret note that we could be wed the following day. I hadn't told my parents. I knew they would forbid me from going.

'Papa wants to fetch you home,' Alice said, waking me from my reveries, 'but I told him you're a married woman now so you have to do what your husband says. He can't stop you from going. I've brought a trunk with some of your clothes and I've even packed the family christening robe. Maybe if you give Mama a grandson, she will forgive you for running away to marry John.'

She was right. Papa and Mama would forgive me if I gave them a grandson. They would welcome me back next year as a married woman with a babe in my arms. I would no longer have the humiliation of being the eldest daughter, unwed and desperate to find a husband. As a Captain's wife, my standing in Society would be assured.

'Well, I do hope to give her a grandson soon. John is keen to have children. I just hope I don't have four daughters as she did!'

She nudged me hard in the ribs. 'So, you're enjoying married life, then?'

I was not going to share my marital intimacies with my younger sister. From now on there would be secrets between us. No one told me what to expect in my marriage bed. Mama always said new brides should be innocent of such things. And I hardly knew how to put into words what we had been doing these past three nights when John embraced me in bed at night and kissed me with a fierce passion and lifted my nightdress.

'He has a good heart and Mama always said that's the best you can hope for in a husband,' I told her, rather pompously, to stop her questions.

'I'm hoping for a good fortune in my husband.'

'John will be rich enough now he's Captain,' I said.

'Hmm, not rich enough for me, I think.'

'Oh Alice, you don't mean that. Promise me you'll marry for love.'

'It's all right for you to speak so. What prospects have I got? The third daughter! No one ever notices me and who will I meet in sleepy Stratford when Mama won't let us meet Naval Officers in case we all run away to the West Indies. I'll end up an old spinster taking care of Papa and Mama in their dotage.'

It was hard to imagine that Alice would be the choice of all their daughters to stay home and care for my parents but her frustration was palpable. I had no words of advice for her as I had worsened her prospects by defying my parents.

We completed our tour of the deck without discussing husbands any further. As we approached the Officers' Dining Room, she put her finger to her lips to tell me to be quiet. The door wasn't quite closed and she approached quietly to listen.

'Alice,' I whispered, 'come away. It's not ladylike to listen at keyholes. Someone will see you.'

'Oh Mary-Anne, no wonder you never know what's going on. The men always exclude us from the interesting talk.'

'No they don't. It's just that what they talk about doesn't concern us.'

'You are so naïve and innocent.' She looked at me with pity. 'I guess that's why he married you.'

I was about to protest that John married me for love, but I spotted Lieutenant Durell approaching so I pushed her through the door. Papa turned in surprise as we burst into the cabin.

'Well, Mary-Anne, I never thought it would come to this when I gave John my permission to marry you but if it's your decision to go with him to Jamaica, I can't stop you,' he said, clearly exhausted by the effort of arguing. 'You have to obey your husband now. Of course, I'll help you in any way I can. I'll give you a letter of introduction to Vice-Admiral Hosier. We know each other well. He's a good man, brave and true. When you arrive in Jamaica, present the letter to him and he will give you every assistance.'

John smiled, relief flooding his face. 'Thank you, Sir. The Commander-in-Chief is, without doubt, the highest introduction we could hope for and will greatly facilitate our arrival.'

Papa lowered his voice to talk to John in a whisper, although Alice and I could hear every word. 'It will be more convenient for Mary-Anne to stay ashore. Hosier will recommend a suitable family that she can stay with. Better not to have a woman on board,' he said.

'You are so right, sir. I'm sure Mary Anne will prefer to stay ashore, maybe with one of the more respectable families. A house in Kingston or a plantation house might suit her well.'

To stay with a respectable family in a grand plantation house sounded very agreeable. With the help of the Commander-in-Chief perhaps my new life in Jamaica would not be a hardship after all.

Papa handed John a leather wallet but stopped him from opening it. 'Mary-Anne's dowry,' is all he said. They shook hands and I was sold from father to husband.

'Come Alice, we must take our leave. I wish you both a safe and speedy voyage,' Papa said as he struggled to stand up.

The moment of no return was racing towards me. I ran at Papa and hugged him tightly. He kissed the top of my head. His voice was hoarse as he said gently, 'Dearest Mary-Anne, my sweetest child, I hope you know what you are doing. Your mother and I will miss you greatly. Come home soon.'

His words betrayed his doubts about what I was doing and tears started streaming down my face.

Alice, resigned to her fate as the third daughter, dutifully helped him into the waiting longboat. Too late I realised he never gave me his blessing. I rushed to the rail and shouted after him but my words were caught up in the salty sea spray and devoured by the wheeling gulls before they reached Papa. He didn't turn to look back.

Three days later the *Tryall* weighed anchor, hoisted sails and ran down the River Thames. We sailed through gales and squally rain past Sheerness, Deal Castle and Beachy Head until we reached the Isle of Wight. We anchored at Spithead, south of Portsmouth, and there we waited. John persuaded me not to visit my parents one last time as he expected orders to set sail to arrive from the Admiralty any day.

It was two months before orders finally arrived for HMS *Tryall* to proceed to Jamaica. As we sailed past Lizard Point off the south coast of Cornwall, a gentle breeze from the northeast picked up.

'Finally, we can wave farewell to England,' John said as he stood beside me on the deck, watching the sails fill. The ship sailed gracefully into the vast Atlantic Ocean.

The restless sea stretched as far as the horizon, beautiful and terrifying and I went to grab John's hand to reassure myself that whatever happened he would be beside me but he had moved away to fix the course with the Master. I was left alone on the deck to watch England disappear and I realised that I had no idea of what lay ahead.

HMS Tryall waited in the Solent for 2 months until, on 20th July 1727, orders arrived to proceed to the West Indies.

From the Captain's Log, HMS Tryall
18th June 1727
At Spithead, off Portsmouth.

"Little wind & fair weather. At 1PM notice being sent me by Sir Isaac Townsend, Knight, Commissioner of His Majesty's Navy at Portsmouth & Commander on Chief of his Maj. Ships at Spithead & in Portsmouth Harbour, of the Death of His Majesty King George and that King George the Second was proclaimed at Portsmouth. The Sloop's Colours were Struck half-staff & I fired 14 guns by the half minute gaps, upon which the Dutch Rear-Admiral struck his Flag (as well as his Ensign & Jack as did also his Squadron their colours) half-staff and fired one and twenty guns each at a minute's space asunder. We kept our Colours down until the Dutch had done firing their mourning guns, then they were hoisted and all our Extraordinary Colours spread and we fired 15 guns for the accession of King George the Second to the throne of these Realms. The Dutch Admiral and his Squadron spread all their colours and fired one and twenty guns each. PM Discharged the Caulkers & Carpenters."

A month after leaving the Solent, HMS Tryall arrived at Funchal, Madeira.

From the Captain's Log, HMS Tryall
18th August 1727
Anchored in Funchal Road, Madeira.

"Very light airs of wind Sometimes Calm. At 1PM furl'd our sails (being then about 3 Leagues from the Town of Funchal) got our oars out & Row'd into the Road, where we anchored at 5PM in 30 fathoms of water & this morning took in some Wine for the Ships Company & for Better Dispatch in the Watering & for the Safety of our own, I am obliged to hire Portuguese Boats."

3

H MS *Tryall* sailed south in light winds, a wooden hulk creaking and groaning as sails were raised and lowered, rigging tightened and loosened, ropes tied and untied. I'd never seen the ocean before and had no idea of its vastness, a huge expanse of water, constantly moving below us. The calm sea and lack of wind since we left the Solent were frustrating to John who sent a sailor to the top of the mast to look for waves or ripples, anything to indicate a breeze was on its way. If there was the slightest chance of wind, John gave the order to carry all the sail we could.

I was in no rush to reach the West Indies. I enjoyed being on the ship with my new husband. The calm seas and clear windless days gladdened my heart about the whole adventure. It was a peaceful time. John was relaxed. The officers and crew obeyed him as Captain and accepted me as his wife.

It got hotter as we headed southwards. On windless days the hot damp air pressed against my skin and perspiration ran down my brow into my eyes until my vision was blurred and I couldn't see my book or my needlework.

In the warm evenings before dinner, John and I took a walk around the decks, while he pointed to parts of the ship and told me their names. The decks, the sails, the ropes, everything had its own name so that when a command was given there was no confusion above all the noise and commotion of sailing on the high seas. I couldn't remember all the names which made him laugh, but I was happy promenading arm-in-arm with my husband. It was a special time of the day as the sun dipped over the horizon, when I had John's attention and he was not busy being Captain of the ship. We talked about his exciting youth as a lieutenant in His Majesty's Navy and my uneventful childhood as a dutiful daughter in the sleepy village of Stratford. I asked him about his adventures and he wanted to hear about my family life.

We dined with the other officers, Lieutenant Durell, Master Robert Bishop and his wife Jenny, and Mr Oakley, the Surgeon. Some evenings I sat next to John out on the deck and he pointed out the constellations of stars in the dark night sky by which he navigated the ship across the ocean. I cuddled up to him, feeling content that wherever we were in the far-flung world we would always be together.

Afterwards, when we were alone in the privacy of our cabin, he was tender and loving. At first I was exceedingly nervous but I trusted John would know what to do. We drew the bedcurtains so the heavy drapes fell around us creating our private world. We slept cuddled up in the narrow bed, nightshirts tangled after an embrace of legs and arms joining us as man and wife. I lay awake long into the night listening to the strange sounds of the ship around me and the snores of my husband beside me. How I missed my late-night whispers with my sisters. My new life as a married woman was exceedingly different.

There was great excitement one morning when a ship appeared close enough to signal to us. It was only a merchant ship, the *Parthenope*, heading to London from Malaga. Other than that we saw only one other ship, a large sloop in the distance too far away to signal. John had orders to allow any Spaniards to pass unmolested, but he watched the sails until they disappeared over the horizon. Taking a Spanish ship as a prize would have meant great wealth for a Captain and his crew.

'When I was seventeen and serving on the *Weymouth* out in the West Indies we captured a Spanish galleon, the *St Joaquin*,' he told me. 'The Commander, that damned Spaniard Villanueva decided to confront the entire English squadron of seven warships in Jamaica. It was exciting to me as a young man even though there was no real fighting. Especially after Villanueva was killed with a well-judged musket shot.'

He wandered off to take bearings with his sextant and luckily we saw no more ships, Spanish or otherwise, and had no cause to fire muskets.

A month after we left the Solent we approached the island of Madeira and the ship anchored in Funchal Harbour. At once we were surrounded by a flotilla of small boats swarming around the *Tryall*.

I stood at the guardrail laughing at all the chaos. All the boatmen were shouting and waving, excited by the arrival of a British naval warship to whom they could sell their wares. The small boats crashed into each other as they jostled to get close and the boatmen held up all sorts of goods they wanted us to buy, including flagons of wine, barrels of water, ropes, cables and everything a ship could possibly want. I was offered a large fish still flapping, feathered chickens still squawking and a fine pair of calico trousers, which made me laugh.

'There's no way we can safely launch our boats in this melee,' John said. 'I will have to hire these local Portuguese boats if we are to get the *Tryall* watered and restocked.'

John relied on Durell to arrange this. They'd known each other as lieutenants on HMS *Launceston* in the West Indies.

'And add a few bottles of the famous Malmsey wine for the ship's company,' he shouted, much to the approval of the sailors standing within earshot.

The sailors would be pleased we were taking on fresh supplies. I'd heard them complaining about food and water rationing yet there always seemed to be plenty for us to eat and drink in the Captain's Dining Room.

'Tonight we'll dine well on fresh meat, my darling wife, and drink the local wine. And raise a toast for more wind to speed our crossing to the West Indies.'

John left me to attend to the supplies coming onboard and Jenny Bishop, the Master's wife, appeared at my side. She'd kept me company during the days while John was busy. She was a fearsome lady, tough as old boots. Her face was weathered and wrinkled by many years at sea. Her mouth turned downwards and she always looked down her large, hooked nose at me.

When I came on board at Galleon's Reach she'd told me in no uncertain terms, 'I'll clean yer cabin and wash yer petticoats but it's not my job to be yer Lady's Maid.'

I apologised that my maid would not come on the voyage across the ocean. Alice had told me that my maid threatened to run away rather than be brought with my trunk to the *Tryall*. I told Jenny I would get a maid as soon as I arrived in Jamaica. She raised her eyes to Heaven as she always did whenever I told her of my plans. When I expressed any disquiet about crossing the vast ocean, she shrugged.

'I've made numerous trips with Mr Bishop. He's an experienced Master so why should you be afraid? He's in charge of sailing the ship and he knows what he's doing, but I guess it is yer husband's first command.'

She told me over and again that Mr Bishop was long overdue promotion to Captain but Lieutenant Durell rather disparagingly whispered to me that Bishop was too old to get promoted. 'Anyway,' he said, 'he's an ordinary seaman who's risen through the ranks. He's not a gentleman. He'll never be a captain.' I didn't tell Jenny that.

One of the local boatmen, desperate to sell the haunches of meat he had strapped to his back, attempted to climb up the side of the ship. Lieutenant Durell fired a pistol shot into the air and the man fell back into his boat landing on the sides of pork. The smell of the raw, bloody meat crushed in the small boat suddenly made me retch. Nausea rushed through my body making me feel faint and I clutched Jenny's arm, fearing I would vomit over the side of the ship. I couldn't believe I felt seasick while we were anchored but the heat was oppressive in the confines of Funchal Harbour.

'What's up with you then?' She looked sideways at me suspiciously. 'Are you with child?'

I stared at her, hardly understanding what she was asking me.

'I haven't noticed any blood on your sheets or underclothes these last few months,' she said.

In all the upheaval of being at sea, I hadn't noticed that I'd missed my bleeds the last three months. Could the Good Lord have blessed me already with a child in my belly? I turned to her and smiled with sheer joy.

'Well, don't count yer blessings yet,' she retorted. 'There's plenty can go wrong. I'll tell yer husband to sleep in one of the officers' cabins. You don't want him disturbing you in the night. He might harm the baby.'

My momentary elation was tempered by her concerns. Every woman knew about the perils of childbirth but were there also risks during pregnancy?

When I told John about the baby he was so excited he raised a toast with the Malmsey wine as we sat down to dine. He announced to everyone around the table how delighted he was that we had started our family so soon. He was very attentive to me, fussing about me and waiting on me as if I was a queen. Jenny raised her eyes to Heaven but she couldn't spoil my joy.

Could my life be any better than it was just then? On our way to the West Indies, my loving husband by my side and a baby in my belly. My happiness was complete.

Once we had taken onboard water and fresh provisions we left Madeira and headed west, sailing towards the setting sun. The weather suddenly changed for the worse. Dark clouds and strong winds made crossing the Atlantic Ocean far more terrifying than when we had set off from England in calm weather. Huge grey storm clouds piled high as a mountain in the sky and the angry heavens sent down thunder and lightning and squalls of rain. The swell from the northwest mounted higher and higher. Great Atlantic rollers, their heads whipped off by the gale-force winds, spewed across the decks. The sailors heaved heavy wet sails and ropes, drenched to their skin, slipping and sliding on the rain-soaked decks. The ship was swept along by the great swell, racing away as if to escape an enemy force behind it.

John was busy on deck giving commands to the Master who stood strapped to the great wheel. He didn't have time for me now. His duties as Captain came first. I stayed in the cabin feeling nauseated, exhausted, neglected and rather sorry for myself. I tried not to be scared. After all, it had been my decision to come on this journey. It had all seemed so exciting a few days ago in Madeira.

I asked Georgie, my cabin boy, if he was afraid and he quickly answered that he trusted in the Captain.

'Surely you trust in the Good Lord more?' I said, horrified that the power of life or death was vested in my husband. 'Would you like to read the bible or pray with me when you are afraid?'

I had heard the sailors call out to Saint Nicholas to calm a storm or Saint Elmo to save them from a lightning strike so I knew they prayed for salvation in times of trouble.

'Perhaps,' he muttered, 'but I've noticed it's God's Providence who lives and who dies. The sailor next to you will be washed overboard or fall from the rigging and you wonder, why not me? It don't make no difference if you're saying your prayers or not.'

I was appalled that his God was so capricious but maybe he had faced more dangers than me in his young life. If he could trust his Captain, then so could I. John would never let any harm come to me. I fixed my resolve to be brave but nothing seemed to fix my sickness.

One night at the start of September a terrible storm fell upon us. A loud crash of thunder woke me. It was dark and I was all alone in the narrow bed as John had been told by Mrs Bishop to sleep elsewhere until the baby arrived. Hard rain battered on the roof of the cabin. The white foam from breaking waves hammered on the window of the cabin desperate to get in.

The ship rose precipitously to the crest of the wave and fell, crashing into the trough behind. Up and down the ship went, my stomach lurching with each rise and fall. On and on the waves came, enormous tumbling waves of froth that could swallow the ship whole. The *Tryall* was screaming in its efforts to survive, every wooden plank in the hull creaking, every piece of rope in the rigging whining, every timber in the masts groaning under the strain of the wind in the sails. I feared the ship would sink and we would surely perish. All souls aboard would be lost at sea.

'Please Lord,' I cried out, 'I am newlywed and I am with child. Don't forsake me now!'

Another clap of thunder and flash of lightning made me wonder if the Good Lord could hear me. At home when there was a storm at night, I would cuddle my sisters under the blankets. How I wished they were with me now to comfort me.

It was impossible to get comfortable in the small bed. I twisted and turned, this way and that, clutching my belly. I felt quite nauseated. Perhaps the food we took on board at Madeira hadn't been as fresh as I had thought. My guts were about to explode at any moment. I had to get up and make it to the privy heads on the opposite side of the cabin but I was terrified to leave my bed.

As I sat up, my head started spinning and I felt dizzy. The world had gone topsy-turvy as the cabin pitched violently from side to side. My heart was pounding very fast and I was shaking with fear that we would be shipwrecked at any moment. I was gasping for air, my nerves stretched to breaking point. Then I slumped over the side of the bed and vomited all over the floor.

I crawled out of bed and was halfway across the cabin when a huge swell tilted the ship sideways. I slid across the floor and hit the heavy wooden table leg, smack bang on my belly. The pain was excruciating but the cramps in my stomach demanded I continue to the heads. My bowels were opening and I was distressed to think of the mess I was going to cause if I didn't get to the privy.

I gathered my knees under me and crawled on all fours across the cabin. The ship was surging and rolling. Water was rushing in under the cabin door and the floor was soaking wet. I slipped and slid, falling and picking myself up, struggling on.

I didn't make it to the privy. My bowels opened and blood streamed out. Dark red blood was everywhere, soiling my nightgown, staining the rug and blackening the wooden floor. I tried to hold everything in but I knew in a heartbeat that I was losing my baby and I was helpless to stop it. Blood and gore were gushing out of my body. I looked down at the mess between my legs and my world went black.

It was some hours later that John found me, curled in a ball on the floor. He lifted my head gently and removed my stained chemise, before wrapping me in a woollen blanket and carrying me to the bed. Later still, I was aware of Richard Oakley, the ship's surgeon, sitting beside me encouraging me to drink a vile tonic.

I doubted the ship's surgeon had any experience with women's problems in general or miscarriage in particular. There were people on board who can repair anything on the ship but no one knew how to repair me.

I knew my baby wasn't inside me anymore. There was a cold, empty hollow where he had nestled a few hours ago. Tears streamed down my face. I didn't bother to wipe them away. Oakley was talking quietly to John, who was somewhere in the cabin, despite the storm raging outside. I wanted to shout out, go and save your ship, John, it's too late to save our baby, but I hadn't the strength to speak.

The next day I woke as if I'd been in a deep, dark hole for a long time. The wind had abated and the ship was creaking and rolling in its normal way, no longer fighting the elements as it had been all night. I still had pain in my belly and could feel blood seeping out between my legs.

Jenny sat on the sofa under the windows in my cabin. She was the last person I wanted to see at that moment. I shivered and drew the cover over me, even though the air in the cabin was hot and fetid.

'It's God's way,' she told me. 'It happens a lot. Not to me mind, but I know lots of women who lost their babies before they were born. We women must accept it. It's a lot better than having a child who dies afterwards. I've had four babies, all born alive and dead within a few months. Now that's real heartbreak. No, it's better you lost yer baby before it was born.'

I tried to block out her voice but she was bustling about the cabin, moving all John's possessions around.

'Oakley says you'll be weak for days yet,' she continued, unabated. 'You must stay in bed and rest as much as possible. Don't worry, I'll stay with you.'

'Where is John?' I asked her. 'Why doesn't he come to me?'

'You mustn't bother yer husband. After all, he is the Captain. He has his responsibilities. No, you must bear this on your own. Don't fret, I'm here to comfort you.'

I rolled over and curled up into a small ball trying to escape from her and the pain. It wasn't just the agonising cramps in my belly, it was the despair and misery in my heart.

Georgie brought me sweet tea and a small cake from Cook. 'We all hope you'll feel better soon, m'lady.'

I couldn't imagine ever feeling better but I smiled feebly and thanked him. I hoped he didn't know the truth about my malady. I didn't want everyone onboard to know my private shame.

I was overcome with a desperate desire to see John and seek his understanding and sympathy. I grabbed hold of Georgie's sleeve and pulled him closer. I whispered to him that I would like to see the Captain. He glanced over at Jenny, engrossed in her prayer book, and nodded furtively as he hurried out the door.

John came to see me later in the day and Jenny left us together, glad to have a break from her nursing duties.

'I hope you got some rest, my dearest.'

'Why didn't you come to comfort me? Why did you leave me alone?'

'Mrs Bishop told me not to bother you. She said it was for the best.'

My head sank into the pillow. 'I would rather be alone than have that woman sitting there gloating over my shame.'

John took my hand. Silent tears were running down his cheek. He wiped his face brusquely with his sleeve as if he was ashamed to be seen crying.

'There is no shame in what happened, Mary-Anne. I do not blame you at all for the loss of your pregnancy.'

'Was I to blame? Was it my fault?' I whispered. 'Did I do something wrong? I would never have done anything to harm my baby.'

'I know you wouldn't, my dearest. Oakley said it is not uncommon for the first pregnancy to be lost. He said it may not have been a baby at all, but something that would never form properly. He said it was a blessing that you survived and it was lost.'

Oakley was a ship's surgeon. What did he know about my baby? How could it be a blessing that he was lost?

'It was a baby, John. He was our son. He never got a chance to be born or to be named but we can't pretend he never lived.'

'Of course not, my dearest wife, you're right, but the most important thing now is that you are restored to health. That would be the greatest happiness in the world for me. As soon as you've recovered, we can try again for another child.'

I turned my head away from him. How I wished Mama was there to comfort me. Mama, who had borne four healthy children, would reassure me that our family was fertile and childbearing. Or would she tell me that I was to blame? That I had behaved so wickedly, marrying John in haste, running away to sea, defying my parents. That I wasn't Papa's good little girl any longer. That I didn't deserve happiness.

Three months ago I had been brimming over with excitement and joy at my wedded bliss. Now I felt wretched and pitiful.

HMS Tryall arrived at Port Royal, Jamaica in September 1727.

From the Captain's Log, HMS Tryall
25th September 1727
At Port Royal Harbour, Jamaica.
     "Fresh breeze with some rain. At ½ past 7 PM having Entered the Harbour of Port Royal I Saluted Capt. Edward St Lo, Commander-in-Chief of His Majesty's Ships at Jamaica (who has a broad pendant onboard the Superb) with nine Guns which he answered with same number. At 2 anchored in 8 fathoms water & moored ship. We found riding here His Majesty's Ships, (besides the Superb), the Bredah, Berwick & Lenox, the Rippon, Nottingham & Dunkirk, the Dragon, Tyger, Leopard & Portland, the Diamond & Greyhound, the Happy and Spence sloops. I Delivered the pacquet I was sent with from England to Capt. St Lo."

From the Captain's Log, HMS Tryall
1st October 1727
At Port Royal Harbour, Jamaica.
     "Moderate Breezes and fair weather. At 8 AM Every Captain in the Squadron in his Pinnace attended the Corpse of Admiral Hosier from Bredah to Happy sloop (which lies near the Cays) as did also a Commission Officer from each Ship in their Yawl, the boats rowing in two lines the Van's of which were on each Quarter of the Commodore. In the time of the procession each Ship of His Majesty's fired Twenty Guns by the half minute gaps, according to Seniority of the Captains."

4

Two weeks later, after another night of strong winds and heavy rain, the shout went out, 'Land Ahoy'. In the morning light, a sailor in the crow's nest had spotted an island on the horizon, with long, low clouds hanging over a dark shape. I came out on deck for the first time since I lost my baby and felt the heat of the fierce tropical sun on my face.

'That'll be the most northerly point of Grand Terre on Guadeloupe,' the Master shouted from the bridge. 'Ten miles due west.'

'Make all the sail we can,' John answered.

Someone cheered and I was so relieved that, with nothing to guide us except the sun and the stars, we had managed to cross the Atlantic Ocean and reach the West Indies. I dropped to my knees muttering a heartfelt thanks to the Good Lord, while the sailors shouted and danced around me on the deck. The crossing had taken nearly eight weeks and with delays in the Solent before we set sail, I had been on board the *Tryall* for over four months.

The ship swept past the islands of the West Indies, as we sailed north from Guadeloupe towards Jamaica. John pointed out to me the islands on a chart to mark our progress each day: Antigua, Monserrat, Nevis, St Christopher, Saba. The islands were covered in lush green jungle, with no sign of habitation. No fields, no towns, no church spires, just a dense Garden of Eden. The colours were vivid. Bright green trees, turquoise seas and white foam as the breaking surf tumbled onto the yellow, sandy shores. And an overpowering smell of rotting vegetation. Durell told me it was the mangrove swamps, home of the dreaded mosquitos.

Off the coast of Hispaniola one of the sailors pointed to the wreck of a ship off the starboard bow, the mast broken and the sails shredded. He shouted, 'Pirates,' but there were no other ships within sight so the crew went back to work.

That evening at dinner, I asked John what would happen if we met a pirate ship. He laughed and said not to worry, he knew how to deal with pirates.

40

'When I was Second Lieutenant on the *Launceston* we captured the *Vengeance* off Hispaniola back in April '22. It was the ship of a particularly blood-thirsty Spanish pirate called Matthew Luke. He sailed out of Puerto Rico and earlier that year he had plundered four English merchant ships and murdered everyone onboard.'

'I was there too,' Durell interrupted, 'as Third Lieutenant. Captain Bartholomew Candler was ordered to capture Luke.'

'Yes, we sailed to Hispaniola and lowered our colours, hoping to attract Luke's attention by masquerading as a merchant ship. Sure enough, the *Vengeance* appeared over the horizon, with a Spanish Jack flying. Candler instructed us to hide below the bulwarks and only attack when the *Vengeance* moved alongside.'

'And when we hailed her,' Durell said, 'that scoundrel Luke tried to claim he had a privateering commission from the Governor of Puerto Rico, one of the Spanish coast guards.'

'What Luke had done went far beyond seizing prize ships,' John said, as he took another sip of his wine. 'He was a cold-blooded murderer. Privateers don't murder the entire crew of captured ships.'

He looked into his wine, deep in thought, and I shivered at the thought of meeting any real, live pirates.

'Anyway, we joined Captain Candler's boarding party. There were only about twenty men on deck, a desperate cowardly bunch, and we had a good look around the ship. I found a paper wrap from a powder cartridge and recognised it as a page from the journal of the *Crean,* one of the vessels whose crew had been murdered. We seized the pirates without any resistance. In the hold we found the rest of the crew hiding, cowering in the dark like miserable rats. We arrested fifty-eight in all and brought them back to Jamaica with the *Vengeance* as a prize.'

'What happened to the pirates?' I asked.

'They were all tried and found to be guilty. One of them even confessed to killing twenty English men with his bare hands. Over forty pirates were hanged at Gallows Point that day and Captain Candler was hailed a hero.'

I reached out to take his hand across the dining table. My daring, courageous husband, who caught pirates by the shipload. He was strong and brave and honourable, a Captain of His Majesty's Navy.

A week later, John pointed out the eastern end of Jamaica and our island destination finally came into view. The high mountains were densely forested and the lowlands were cultivated fields. Windmills turned in the breeze and stone buildings were scattered on the hillside. The stench of burning sugar pervaded the wind. Some of the sailors muttered about the pleasures of women and rum that lay ahead in the fleshpots of Kingston Town but Durell reminded them of the cut-throat thieves, the dreaded mosquitoes and the tropical fevers that awaited them ashore.

As we approached Kingston we passed a sloop leaving the harbour that gave us news that the British Fleet was back from the blockade of Cartagena, bringing with them the body of Vice-Admiral Edward Hosier who had died six weeks ago. Rumour had it he died of a broken heart, having been under strict orders last year not to capture Porto Bello, which he could have easily achieved with the twenty ships under his command. Instead, he was forced to loiter off a mosquito-infested coast and thousands of his officers and men perished miserably of the fever they called the Yellow Jack. Hosier himself succumbed to the fever at the end of August. His body had been wrapped in a sheet and given a temporary burial place in the ballast of his flagship, HMS *Breda*, until it could be dispatched to England.

My blood ran cold. This was not at all the welcome I was expecting. I had assumed that Papa's great friend Vice-Admiral Hosier would be there to greet us when we arrived.

'What will happen to us now that Hosier has died?' I asked John. 'Where am I to live?'

'Don't worry, Mary-Anne. I'll sort it all out with St Lo. He's in charge now.'

The *Tryall* sailed through the off-shore islands into Kingston Harbour and John ordered a nine-gun salute to Captain Edward St Lo, the replacement Commander-in-Chief of His Majesty's Ships at Jamaica, who was on board his flagship, HMS *Superb*. The harbour was crowded with fifteen of His Majesty's Ships from Hosier's fleet that had come back to Jamaica to resupply and refit.

The air was humid and damp as if a cloud had sunk to envelope us in hot steam. Once the sailors lowered the heavy anchor and moored the ship, the oppressive heat made me feel drained and exhausted.

Perhaps it was the relief of having arrived. Perhaps it was the fatigue of everything being so different from what I had imagined.

John lowered the pinnace and was rowed over to the *Superb* with the packet of letters he'd brought from England. He returned with news of naval matters. It seemed Captain St Lo had more important matters to worry about than where I was going to live.

'St Lo has so much on his plate right now, it didn't seem the time to bother him,' John said. 'Don't worry, my dearest, you can stay on the *Tryall* for now until things settle down. The ships have returned from Cartagena in a very sorry state. It's going to be a challenge to repair them without stores and provisions from England. St Lo wants them to go back within the month.'

'What's so important about Cartagena?' I asked, as if St Lo's problems were of any interest to me.

'It's a port on the coast of Colombia. The Spanish galleons load up there with silver and emeralds. If a powerful force of British ships can block the port and prevent the galleons from leaving, we'll cut off the treasure going back to Spain. That will stop their warmongering against good old England, to be sure.'

Surely blocking some Spanish ships in harbour was not as important as finding somewhere for me to live.

John went ashore the next morning to start reconnoitring the naval facilities at Port Royal. Everything was in ruins after the terrible earthquake in 1692 and what buildings were still above sea level were damaged by a hurricane last November. He was looking for a suitable place for a careening wharf as the ships' wooden hulls needed to be painted with tar and brimstone every year to stop them from being eaten by a horrible shipworm that lived in the warm waters of the West Indies. Smaller ships could lie on their sides on a beach, but the larger navy warships needed a purpose-built careening wharf in the West Indies.

'If we don't build one in Kingston Harbour, the ships will have to go to Antigua or Barbados.'

'Shouldn't we be finding somewhere for me to live ashore?' I reminded him. 'You promised Papa I could stay with a respectable family in a grand plantation house.'

'Leave it a few days, dearest wife. You can stay onboard a bit longer. I have so much to do at present.'

The next day, in strong winds with thunder, lightning and rain, all the Squadron hoisted their colours half-mast and each ship fired twenty guns in a Funeral Ceremony for his late Majesty King George. The news had only just reached the fleet in John's packet.

'With all this going on, it's not a good day for us to go ashore to look for lodgings,' John said.

The next day wasn't a good day to go ashore either, as the whole Squadron had to hoist their colours and fire twenty guns each upon proclaiming the new King, George the Second.

So it went on. The following day, every captain and officer in the Squadron had to launch their small rowboat and row in two lines on each side of the corpse of Vice-Admiral Hosier as it was moved from his flagship HMS *Bredah* to the *Happy* sloop. More guns were fired, twenty by each ship, in order of seniority of the captains. Everyone was too busy hoisting flags and firing guns to worry about what was going to happen to me.

The *Happy* was preparing to leave for England with Hosier's body, so John got busy writing his report about a possible site for a new dockyard so it could be taken back to the Navy Board at the same time.

'There is a suitable place in Chocolate Hole, behind Fort Charles,' he told me as he sat at the huge table in our cabin on the *Tryall*, writing his report. 'It can be protected if attacked and the Government owns the land. I'll have to tell them everything will have to be made in England and shipped out for assembly here, all the wooden work like capstan pits, skids and storehouses. It'll be much cheaper and there's no way we can build anything here. They are still operating out of tents!'

I nodded my head in agreement as I assumed he wanted me to. I didn't like to remind him that he was supposed to be finding me somewhere to live.

Barely a week after we arrived, John received orders from Captain St Lo that the *Tryall* was to sail immediately to Havana to exchange the Spanish prisoners the Squadron brought back from Porto Bello.

'Why you? Why can't St Lo send one of his other ships to Cuba?'

'Mary-Anne, you're being unreasonable. You've seen the state of those ships. Anyway, I've been given orders and you can't argue with the Commander-in-Chief.'

No, I couldn't argue with orders. In his dreams, John had wanted a loving wife by his side, but in reality, there wasn't much room for me in his life as a Captain in His Majesty's Navy.

'So what will happen to me? Am I to go to Cuba with you?'

'Oh no. It may be dangerous. I think it would be best if you find somewhere to live in Kingston Town. Perhaps you could go and ask St Lo to find you naval lodgings in town.'

I hadn't set foot ashore yet and now, urgently, I had to go and ask the Commander-in-Chief for somewhere to live.

'You can't ask me to do that, John. I don't know how to ask St Lo for help. I thought you would sort it out with Admiral Hosier. This is not at all what I expected.'

I collapsed on the bed in floods of tears.

John pretended to study his chart of Cuba to avoid looking at me.

'Why ever did you bring me here, John, if you were going to leave on some expedition as soon as we arrived? Why did we ever get married?'

'Damn it, Mary-Anne. I didn't want to get married,' he said without looking up.

I gasped in horror. This was not what I had expected him to say.

'I wanted nothing more than to be the Captain of a warship in His Majesty's Navy. I owe everything to the Navy. I've learnt a profession, I've put aside some money, I've fought for my country and I am proud of what I have achieved. I never wanted a wife, the experience of my childhood was not conducive to that. In my twenties I watched my fellow officers marry perfectly nice girls, but I decided it was not for me. Until that night when I approached your father at the Naval Ball and I met you.'

I held my breath, waiting for some reassurance that our marriage was not a mistake, made in haste and now regretted.

He finally looked up at me with those big brown spaniel eyes. 'I was hoping for his support to get my first command, but while he was remembering our expedition to Vigo, you were smiling and laughing at his stories with such joy and gaiety that I fell hopelessly in love with you. I'd never met anyone as enchanting as you. I knew you would be my perfect wife so I asked you for every dance that night.'

I smiled at him, remembering that evening. 'Yes, Alice and Betty were very jealous. My feet were sore the next day but I was so happy you had favoured me.'

'Well, your father was true to his word and I got a Command of the *Tryall*, but without you by my side it was a hollow promotion. I love you, Mary-Anne, and I had to marry you and bring you with me. You must wait ashore for me while I fulfil my duties. I promise you I will think of you every day and come home to you as soon as I can.'

I got up from the bed and came over to put my hand on his shoulder. 'I know you will, John. And I will think of you every day, out there on the high seas fighting for King and Country and I will pray for your safe return to me.'

I kissed the locket with his miniature inside. I was resigned to my fate as his wife. He would send me ashore, all on my own, to Kingston Town while he sailed off to Cuba.

Later in the evening, Lieutenant Durell knocked on the cabin door. I told him John wasn't there. Surely he knew John was busy with the four Spanish prisoners who had arrived from the *Happy*, but it was me the Lieutenant had come to talk to.

'The Captain has explained to me that you need to find somewhere to live ashore and, with our new orders to sail to Cuba, time is short.'

I nodded. 'I'm not sure how to find a house in Kingston.'

'No, perhaps not. It is quite daunting to be in Jamaica for the first time. I remember when I arrived back in 1720. I was a young man, just twenty, and I'd never seen anything like it. People here are so greedy for wealth, so free with their pleasures.'

'What shall I do? Papa thought there might be a respectable family for me to stay with, but I know no one.'

'Would you allow me to make a suggestion?'

'Please do, Lieutenant Durell. Any suggestion you can make would be most welcome. I fear my husband is too busy with his duties to give it any thought to it at the moment.'

'I have a dear friend, Lady Caroline Sinclair. She has lived in Jamaica all her life and she inherited her father's sugar plantations when her brother died. Of course, that made her a most desirable heiress and she married Sir William Sinclair, some English aristocrat. He's in England a lot as he's a Member of Parliament so she's left on her own with two young children. I'm sure if I introduced you, she would be delighted if you stayed with her at Grosvenor Hall. It's a grand plantation house and you would be most comfortable there.'

'I couldn't impose on her. Why would she want me to stay with her?'

'I think, like you, she would enjoy some respectable female company. And the plantation owners like to extend hospitality to the British Navy. It serves their interests well to have us here, protecting their ships from pirates and foreign foes. Would you like me to send a letter this evening to ask her?'

'I would like that very much, Lieutenant Durell.'

At the thought of living in a grand plantation house, my spirits lifted for the first time since our arrival.

When John came to my cabin after dinner, I took his hand and drew him onto the bed. He was apologetic about the situation and reassured me everything would be alright. I realised nothing in Jamaica was quite what he had expected either and we clung onto each other, seeking reassurance that at least we had each other.

I told him of Durell's suggestion to solve the problem of where I was to live. He looked rather surprised at this development and I asked him how Durell knew Lady Sinclair.

'He met Caroline in October '21 when we arrived in Kingston on the *Launceston*. Caroline was a great beauty back then, the wife of Sir William Sinclair and their plantation was renowned as one of the most lavish. She was at every social event while her husband was away in London. He'd bought one of those Rotten Boroughs and was no doubt busy voting in the House of Commons to protect his sugar interest. In his absence, Caroline enjoyed the attentions of the young officers including Durell. He was a young lieutenant in Jamaica for the first time.'

I tried to imagine Lieutenant Durell as a young man and I remembered what he'd said about people being so free with their pleasures.

'When we captured the pirate, Matthew Luke, and returned to Jamaica as heroes in May '22, Caroline hosted a grand dinner in our honour. Durell didn't return to the ship that night and I assume they became lovers. I cannot condone his actions. Most men make do with a harlot in the back streets. I fear that Caroline encouraged his affections.

We went to sea again, sailing around Hispaniola looking for more pirate ships when a terrible hurricane hit Jamaica. Many ships were sunk. Over four hundred lives were lost and many buildings all over the island were severely damaged. When we came back to Kingston, Durell rushed off the ship and abandoned his post to go to Caroline. Her plantation had suffered a lot of damage. She was on her own with her young son. William Sinclair was in London and Durell stayed to help her.'

'What else could he do?' I pointed out. 'She had been abandoned by her husband and her plantation was devasted by a hurricane. He had to go to her rescue.'

He sighed as if it was not that straightforward and I understood his dilemma. He had to abandon his wife when he went away to sea. And he didn't want another man to come to my rescue.

'Well, anyway, it was a time of chaos,' he said. 'Captain Candler died of the fever and Captain Dent replaced him. No one knew what was going on. Durell stayed in Jamaica until William returned the following year and then he went home to wait for another commission. It was only last year he got a post as Lieutenant-at-Arms on the *Hampshire* in the Baltic. No Captain wants a deserter, but he's handy with a musket and broadsword. I met him in London earlier this year at the time I got my command of the *Tryall*. We exchanged memories of our time together on the *Launceston* and I was reminded that he's a useful man and an experienced officer, so I appointed him my Lieutenant.' He paused as if he was regretting that decision now. 'I'm not pleased to hear he's thinking of meeting Caroline Sinclair again. I hope on this visit to Jamaica, he remembers she's another man's wife.'

'You mustn't be angry with him, John. He only suggested it for my sake. He's helping me to find somewhere to live.'

'To my mind, there is nothing worse than taking another man's wife. If she were my wife, I would have challenged Durell to a duel.'

I was touched by his heroics so I didn't remind him that duels were illegal and Durell was handy with a musket and broadsword.

The next morning the *Happy* set sail for England with Vice-Admiral Hosier's corpse and John's report to the Navy Board about the careening wharf. Lieutenant Durell received a reply from Lady Caroline Sinclair saying that she would be delighted to meet me for lunch in Kingston that day.

John made recommendations for the new careening wharf within days of his arrival.

Letter to the Navy Board from Captain Gascoigne, HMS Tryall, Port Royal, Jamaica.
2nd October 1727

"The new careening wharf should be built in Chocolate Hole as it can be protected if attacked and the Government owns the land. He suggests with Mr Potter, that all the wooden work like capstan pits, houses, skids, store houses be made in England and shipped out for assembly there. It is much cheaper to build rather than relying on temporary measure under tents as at present."

Report on proceedings by John Potter, Principal Officer and Commissioner, Kingston, Jamaica.
9th October 1727

"Ready apprehension of the Place which indeed is so far reduced & altered from what it was some years since that it is not like itself having suffered so much by weather, many of the Principal Inhabitants have and are leaving the place and for some time have kept the Magazine of Stores on Kingston side. Capt Gascoigne whom I had the pleasure to talk with on that subject says it is so different from what it was he does not hold it a proper place for the stores, if a wharf be necessary which he was of opinion by what he has learned from conversation with the Hon. Surveyor in Portsmouth. as no proceedings thereon can be actually agreed for, I shall not forbear such necessary enquiries as may be forwarding thereunto of your Orders should come; and if the North part of the Town should be the place you believe is absolutely necessary to purchase that part of the ground as not belong to the King."

5

I had a sailor's rolling gait after so long at sea, which John found very comical. He had brought me ashore in the longboat to escort me to luncheon with Lady Caroline Sinclair. Before he set sail for Cuba with his Spanish prisoners, he was keen to visit John Potter, the Superintendent of the Jamaica Dockyard, who oversaw all the refurbishments and upgrade work to improve its docks, facilities and fortifications.

'Potter read my recommendation for the wharf at Chocolate Hole and yet he is still considering land on the south side of the Harbour. In my view it's entirely defenceless to enemy attack and all the buildings that weren't destroyed by the earthquake are in private ownership. That waterside is so reduced and altered from when I was here two years ago. Over half the houses are abandoned and running to decay. Everyone is moving to Kingston Town on the north side of the bay as soon as they can build or rent houses.'

I hated to see him thwarted in his plans. He was so enthusiastic about his ideas for a wharf at Chocolate Hole. I couldn't concentrate on what he was saying, I was so nervous about meeting Lady Sinclair. Would she take pity on me and invite me to stay at her plantation? I would have to cheer up and be brighter company than I had been since I lost my baby.

'My orders from the Admiralty Surveyor in Portsmouth were to assist Potter in building the careening wharf. Chocolate Hole is protected by Fort Charles and in my opinion, is the only suitable place. Potter will have to give up his ideas and accept my advice.'

Maybe, if he didn't, we'd be sent home sooner. I didn't want to get my hopes up. In the meantime, I needed to find a place to stay while John disappeared to Cuba with the Spanish prisoners-of-war.

John had ordered Lieutenant Durell to stay on the ship. He was hoping Durell wouldn't see Caroline and desert the ship again. He wanted his expertise with musket and broadsword when he sailed for Cuba.

It was the first time I'd come ashore to Kingston Town and I instantly hated the place. The stench was terrible. The acrid, sickly-sweet smell of the sugar fields and the sugar mills that covered most of Jamaica was overpowering and hung like a vapour over the town. Added to that, the stink of hordes of men blocking my passage along the quayside, Jack Tars, African slaves, Chinese coolies and rough and ready workmen. Some looked distinctly like pirates. The animal pens near the harbour where cattle were corralled before slaughter, the open-air markets displaying fetid meat and rotting fruits and the plagues of mosquitos all added to my discomfort. I covered my nose and mouth with my shawl to avoid breathing in the foul air.

There was a Guineaman ship on the quayside as we came ashore, unloading a cargo of slaves brought from West Africa to work on the sugar plantations. An auction was in progress and the slaves were quite wretched, standing naked on the quayside, ragged and downcast. Men, women and even children, some with metal collars around their necks, all with chains around their ankles, patiently waiting to be bought by the plantation owners who crowded around, rudely pushing and shoving each other, all shouting at the same time. They prodded the Africans with sticks, pinched the muscles in their arms and pulled their mouths open to inspect teeth.

John pulled me past hurriedly, but I couldn't help staring. I'd never seen such a horrific spectacle.

'Come away, Mary-Anne, this does not concern us,' he whispered. 'It's the way they do things here.' He was clearly as upset as me.

I lowered my gaze and took his arm to pass by, trying not to be concerned.

Lady Sinclair had invited me to her house in Kingston. It was in a genteel part of town where the houses were spacious with luxurious gardens providing shade from the midday sun. John escorted me to the front door but stopped short of coming in, saying his business with John Potter was most urgent. He assured me he would return at three o'clock to escort me back to the ship.

A footman opened the door and bowed low as I entered. Other footmen were waiting to attend on me, far more than I could possibly need. The hallway was quiet after the bustle outside, lavishly decorated with paintings from Europe, carpets from Persia and porcelain from China. Above me, a glass chandelier glowed with the light of a hundred candles even though the midday sun was high in the sky. The wealth and opulence were far greater than I had ever seen in any house in London. The contrast between this and my abode for the last five months in the cramped, damp, smelly cabin on the *Tryall* could not have been more extreme.

Caroline appeared from the parlour and welcomed me in a most friendly manner. John had told me she was a great beauty in her youth. Now six years after he first met her, she was still attractive, but her privileged life had made her plump and voluptuous. Tendrils escaped from her thick chestnut hair, carelessly piled up on her head and tied with a silk ribbon, and her ample bosoms spilt over the bodice of her gown, a beautiful floral silk of the latest fashion. It must have been shipped from London or Paris. She looked slightly dishevelled as if she had left her boudoir just moments ago.

She apologised that we must meet in her townhouse in Kingston rather than her plantation home at Grosvenor Hall.

'My husband, William, is busy all day so won't be able to join us for lunch, I'm afraid. He's in town to buy slaves down the quay. Perhaps you saw him there?' she asked and I looked down, desperate not to reveal my relief that one of those barbaric men at the quayside would not be lunching with us. I told her that I quite understood his absence.

'Lieutenant Durell isn't with you?' she asked, looking over my shoulder expecting to see him behind me. 'I thought he might have accompanied you through town?'

She spoke with a slow, lazy voice, relaxed and sultry as if nothing was to be rushed in this hot climate. Her sentences drifted slowly and ended with questions to which I had no answer. I was mesmerised by her full soft mouth and her dreamy green eyes. I explained that John had business in town with Mr Potter so Lieutenant Durell had been left in charge of the ship. Her face displayed no emotion but I sensed she was disappointed.

I told her all about our arrival in Jamaica. 'With Admiral Hosier having passed away, we have no other letter of introduction to Society.'

She laughed and said that Captain Gascoigne didn't need any letters of introduction, all the Naval Officers were welcome in Kingston. And she remembered John from his time in Jamaica as a young Lieutenant, which I was slightly uneasy about. I wondered if he too had fallen under her spell.

The valets served luncheon, large joints of meat and hams and all manner of bread and exotic fruits, far more than the two of us could eat.

I told her I had to find lodgings ashore as John must sail to Cuba in the following days but I couldn't imagine staying in the midst of this foreign city. I admitted that I had never lived on my own, without my Mama and three sisters around me. It all felt rather daunting and John's sudden departure to Cuba had unsettled me.

'I am often left alone at Grosvenor Hall, my plantation on the north side of the island. William stays in Kingston on business much of the time or goes to London for his duties as a Member of Parliament. So you must stay with me. I would enjoy your company. It's usually just me and my two children, Charles who's eight and Amy who's five. You don't mind children, do you?'

'On the contrary, I adore children. My sister, Annie, is the same age as your son, Charles.'

'It's decided then. Come and stay with me. I enjoy entertaining, dinners, luncheons and parties. My husband thinks they are useful to unite the white community. He sees them as necessary to maintain control on the island, but I see them as a chance to dance and enjoy myself.'

'I love dancing, too. That's how I met my husband.'

I told her all about the Naval Ball where John had first danced with me.

'I think I have loved him since our first dance together.'

She smiled at me as if she understood how such a thing could happen.

'Well, while your husband is away, we must make sure you have plenty of opportunities to dance while you are my guest.'

She described the house at Grosvenor Hall and it did sound wonderful, even more luxurious than this townhouse in Kingston. She told me of the balls and parties she had held there and I was swept up in her world of extravagance. Dancing was what I needed to raise my spirits. My only concern was that I didn't have sufficient ball gowns, but she assured me that she had plenty to spare and they could easily be altered to fit my slender frame.

I was so thankful for the kindness of this woman, my only friend in this unwelcoming place. As I finished my luncheon I thought life in

Jamaica might be quite pleasant after all, with a new friend to stay with, two young children to care for and an impressive plantation house to stay in.

Suddenly the door burst open and Lieutenant Durell rushed in. I was so surprised to see him that I dropped my knife on the floor and there was much confusion as several footmen rushed to my assistance.

Durell addressed me first, although I had my head under the table trying to retrieve my knife.

'Mrs Gascoigne, I beg your forbearance and ask that you do not tell your husband I am here. I have left the ship in the capable hands of the Master, Mr Bishop, and I will only stay a brief time.'

He turned to Caroline, 'I could not ignore your invitation, my love. I had to see you again. I have thought of you every day since our parting.'

It was such a romantic declaration that I expected her to rush into his arms, but she stayed seated and looked down at her plate. I could see she was blushing. He knelt beside her chair and gently raised her chin so she was looking at him.

'Tell me you have thought of me, even if for a second in the last four years.'

She leant forward and kissed him gently on the mouth. This made me blush at witnessing such a tender moment. The clock on the wall chimed three o'clock.

'John will be here any moment to collect me,' I said, loathe to interrupt the lovers. 'He must not find you here, Lieutenant Durell. You must leave and get back to the *Tryall* before he comes.'

If John found him there, I would not be allowed to stay with Caroline. And I had been totally seduced by this sultry, sensuous woman, her romantic entanglement with Durell and her exciting descriptions of the glamorous Grosvenor Hall.

'I will go now,' he said to Caroline. 'It was enough to see you before we sail. Perhaps we will have more time on my return in a month?'

'Yes,' is all she said, but so slowly that the word contained a thousand promises. Durell got to his feet and asked the nearest footman to direct him to the back entrance so he could leave without bumping into John.

Luckily, John was late and I managed to delay our departure by making arrangements with Caroline for my stay. On our way back to the *Tryall*, John was in a dark mood. Potter did not agree with his plans and had asked for further instructions from the Admiralty.

'I'm starting to suspect he's in league with Peter Beckford, who owns the land on the south side of the harbour. That Beckford is notorious as a greedy landholder. Some say he's the richest man in Jamaica but there are others who think he's a belligerent troublemaker.'

I let him talk about Beckford all the way back in the longboat, without listening to a word he said. My mind was distracted by the moment of passion I had just seen. Obviously, it was wrong of Durell to have seduced a married lady, and worse still for Caroline to have kissed him, but it was enchanting to bear witness to their brief encounter.

When we were alone together after dinner, John seemed to have recovered his humour so I told him all about my invitation to stay at Grosvenor Hall.

'Caroline was the most delightful company and it was wonderful to talk to a lady after all this time. She has lived on her plantation all her life, so she knows all about life in Jamaica. Her husband stays for much of the time in Kingston, leaving her alone. She is as excited by the prospect of some female company as I am and it will be wonderful to be with children again.'

'I've been giving it more thought, Mary-Anne and I don't think you should stay with Caroline Sinclair.'

I had not expected him to object.

'Why ever not, John? You promised Papa that I could stay at a grand plantation house. What objection could you have against Lady Caroline Sinclair?'

'What objections? Apart from her morality, you mean. I'm sure Durell was not her only lover. Who knows what assignations and seductions go on at Grosvenor Hall? I fear it is not a God-fearing household.'

For an awful moment, I thought he knew that Durell had abandoned his post that afternoon and gone to see Caroline.

'No,' he said, 'it would be better for you to take a house in Kingston and wait for me there. I will be back from Cuba within a month and I will be better able to visit you in town.'

I promised at the wedding altar to love, cherish and obey my husband and I had never argued with anyone, but I couldn't help it. I had to speak up.

'Please John, I want to live at Grosvenor Hall with my new friend and her two children. And I swear on my heart that I will never give you a moment of concern about my devotion to you.'

I held my breath, fearing he would be angry at me for speaking so forcibly.

'Well, I dare say some female company might suit you better than living alone in Kingston.'

I breathed out.

'And we haven't got any other alternative, have we?' I whispered.

He looked down at his charts of Cuba, carefully studying them while we discussed my future home.

'And you are due to sail in the next day or so,' I added.

He was silent as he acknowledged the truth of what I had said. He busied himself making marks on his chart.

'So, you agree that I should accept Caroline's offer of hospitality?'

He nodded his head without looking at me and continued studying his charts. I couldn't believe I had challenged my husband, but I did get my wish to live on a grand plantation.

'I'll visit you on my return but I'll probably stay with my ship most of the time.'

Of course. He was at home on his ship. He'd lived on a ship most of his life. He had no desire to live ashore. The best I could hope for was a visit on his return. Getting my wish left a bitter taste in my mouth.

The next morning John sent all the men's chests ashore to the storehouse in Kingston so there was more room on the *Tryall* for the Spanish prisoners and the extra provisions and water they needed for a voyage to Cuba and back.

'I doubt the Spanish Governor will offer to provision our ship in Havana,' he muttered.

More Spanish prisoners were to be sent aboard from other ships of the Squadron so John told me to prepare to disembark in the morning. I sent a message to Caroline.

The sailors loaded my trunk into the pinnace ready to go ashore. I had to say goodbye to my husband on the deck, surrounded by all the officers and sailors. John embraced me and gave me a quick kiss on the cheek. Now it had come to it, I didn't want to leave him. I stayed in his embrace for as long as I could. Eventually, he pushed me gently away, embarrassed in front of his crew.

'I won't be long, Mary-Anne, no more than a month and you will be safe at your grand plantation house.'

'And you'll be safe too, won't you?'

'Don't worry. I'll let Durell deal with the Spaniards,' he whispered. 'See how he handles himself in a fight.'

I wished he hadn't told me there would be a fight.

'When will you be leaving?'

'We sail at daybreak tomorrow.'

Caroline met me on the quayside in her fine carriage. We stopped on the hillside outside Kingston and I took one last look at the *Tryall* riding on anchor in the harbour. I sent up a silent prayer for John to return to me safely.

Then we turned and headed north, five hours' ride from Kingston across the Blue Mountains. As we approached Grosvenor Hall, Caroline stopped the carriage at the top of a hill and got out.

'The finest sight in Jamaica,' she said, 'and perhaps the whole of the world. It was once mine, you know, until it all passed to William on our marriage. Now I am the caretaker of my own home.'

In the distance, I could see the Great House, a handsome three-storey mansion with a veranda on each side to give shade at all hours of the day. The pale stone shone in the afternoon sun and its great size was a statement of the success and wealth of the Sinclairs. If only my friends back in Stratford, my parents and my sisters could see the grand house that would be my home in Jamaica! Everyone, even Papa, thought I was foolhardy to sail across the ocean with my newlywed husband. How envious they would be when I wrote and told them of my new life. I could feel the dark shadow of melancholy that had covered my heart since I lost my baby starting to lift. John would return from Cuba in a few weeks and we would try again for a baby.

We continued our journey through the fields of sugar cane, planted in rotation so there was a steady supply ready for cutting. In some fields, slaves were digging trenches, in others planting or tending young canes and in others the harvest was underway. It looked like very hard work, especially for the women and children under the hot tropical sun. The carriage slowed so that fallen palm leaves could be cleared from the road. The slaves in the nearest field stopped to watch us. Their weather-beaten faces showed nothing but empty blank stares.

I raised my hand to wave as I would to farmworkers in the fields near my village of Stratford.

Caroline slapped my hand down. 'Don't, Mary-Anne. They are slaves.'

An overseer approached with his whip ready. He was built like an ox, with huge fists and a terrifying pock-marked face. I turned away quickly. As John had told me, this was not my concern. It was how they did things in Jamaica.

Two weeks after we had arrived in Jamaica, HMS *Tryall* hoisted her topsails and made her way out of Kingston Harbour bound for Cuba. It was the first time John and I had been apart since we got married five months ago. I knew this was the reality of life for a naval wife and I would have to get used to it, however much my heart would ache until he returned.

On 9th October 1727 HMS Tryall was sent to Cuba to exchange prisoners of war. The ship was blown off course and the expedition took 2 months.

From the Captain's Log, HMS Tryall
26th October 1727
Off Campeachy Bank in the Gulf of Mexico

"Bad gales of wind, cloudy weather and a very Great Sea, At 2 PM the Mainsail being Split bent another. At 5 having run down into the Latitude of 23°00' and made no land, conclude we are drove to the Westward of the Island of Cuba, brought to with our head to the Westward. At 9 met with Soundings (40 fathoms water and clear ground) which Shoaled gradually to four and thirty in an hour, which depth and quality of the ground continued till 11 (as we stood to the N'ward with a press sail) when least we should stand into worse ground. & being near the Latitude of the dangerous Shoals off the Island Alacranes, anchored in 34 fathoms water & having a very great sea veer'd to a cable & half. At sun rising seeing neither Land nor Shoals confirmed it to us that we are on the Campeachy Bank. In endeavouring to weigh the anchor the Cable parted at the Clench. At 2 AM got under sail & stood away to the South East. By noon the water Shoaled gradually to two & 30 fathoms. Finding ourselves so far to the Westward, went to allowance of water a Quart a day Each Man."

From the Captain's Log, HMS Tryall
14th November 1727
At Havana in Cuba.

"Fresh gales & cloudy weather. Kept plying close to the mouth of the port till ½ past 4 PM when I saw 2 very large launches coming out with at least 120 men and officers in them. I stood into take them up: 56 of the men were English prisoners which I received and sent the 32 Spaniards ashore in the same boats, having towed them as near the mouth of the harbour as I could to safety. When the launches got ashore Mr Durell was allowed to come off to my Boat (he and every one of the Boat's crew having been kept in the boat under guard ever since he went ashore the second time). He brought me a very complimentary letter from the Governor but he excused giving me leave to water in any other of the ports on this coast as I desired having as he sent off what he thought might be sufficient for our return to Jamaica in one of his launches which was two tuns. Therefore being likely to get no other answer from him and the weather looking suspiciously to the N'ward at 9 I bore away and made all the sail I could to the W'ward."

6

T he great hall at Grosvenor Hall had been lavishly decorated with swathes of silks, bunches of exotic flowers and a grand display of peacock feathers. Caroline assured me it was no trouble to welcome back my husband and his brave lieutenant, John Durell, on their return from Cuba. They had been away for two months, despite John's assurance that the trip would take less than a month. I had missed him so much while he'd been away and I was hopeful that we would restore our marital intimacy that night in my large feather bed.

Caroline wanted to organise a dinner as she imagined it was done in the best houses in England, but the extravagant feasting and drinking that her grand wealth allowed were far in excess of anything back home.

While John had been away, exchanging his Spanish prisoners in Cuba, I had been kept busy at Grosvenor Hall. Caroline arranged dinners and dances several times a week and I was invited to social events at other grand houses. Ladies and gentlemen of note wanted to enjoy the hospitality on offer and make connections with the other prominent members of Society. I had a certain status as a Navy Captain's wife and everyone was grateful that my husband was keeping the Spaniards and pirates away.

The officers and young gentlemen were keen for a dancing partner but there were few single women on the island. Girls married young, at sixteen or seventeen, and attended the dinners with their wealthy planter husbands and their swollen pregnant bellies. As an unaccompanied young lady, I was very popular. Major Cartwright was my favourite dance partner and a regular visitor to Grosvenor Hall. He was a far more handsome, dashing officer than I ever won the attention of in English society. He could dance freely with me, knowing that as a married woman I would not misinterpret his intentions and start damaging rumours of *amour*.

'I usually invite half of Jamaica,' Caroline joked. 'You know, the sort of people William favours. Military and naval officers, influential members of the Assembly, powerful merchants and other wealthy planters. He thinks it will improve his fortune, but tonight will be a small dinner. Just twelve of us, so we can be together with friends and loved ones. I've invited Major Cartwright. I know he's fond of you. And while your husband leaves you alone for months on end, perhaps you also appreciate his company?'

She thought it was quite acceptable to have an admirer while her husband was away. I wanted to tell her that John didn't want to leave me alone for months on end. As a Naval Officer, he had no choice but to go when duty called, but she had walked off to rearrange some exotic blooms and the moment had passed.

I was seated between Major Cartwright and Mr Cuthbert, the Island Secretary, who was dripping with perspiration. He saw me watching the beads of sweat as they fell from his forehead and made a grand effort to divert me with talk of the unsettled weather, the burden of his official duties and other boring topics. He was all doom and gloom about the Maroons, the runaway slaves living up in the hills, preparing an uprising to kill women and children. He told me that the planters will achieve peace only through the brutal massacre of troublemakers.

Major Cartwright finally put a stop to his scaremongering by saying that the Army would deal with the renegade slaves so we could all rest easy in our beds. As we laughed with relief at the bravery of the Major and his men, the African slaves silently refilled everyone's glass with rum for a toast to the brave British Army.

John was watching me across the table, so I didn't laugh too gaily in case he thought I was impressed by the Major's bravado. As if to compete, he told us all about his trip to Cuba.

'The voyage started well enough and we made good progress to the western tip of Cuba,' he began. 'But as we rounded the Cape, the weather turned for the worse. All night the wind blew exceptionally hard. The deep swell heaped up and tossed the ship like a cork.'

Now, the Major was forgotten and everyone was listening to John. I wondered how many of the guests around the table had been at sea in a storm. They wouldn't look so thrilled if they had.

'By evening, having run south and seen no land, I had to conclude that we were driven far to the westward of Cuba. I feared we were near the dangerous Alacranes Shoals. Not a reef you'd want to meet on a wild, black night during a storm.'

Several of the ladies at the table looked faint, but the gentlemen urged him on with his tales of adventures on the high seas.

'At sun rising, we were so far off course that I ordered water to be rationed from a gallon to a quart a day for each man. The *Tryall* beat eastwards into wind with all the sail she could carry. Our progress was slow and it was another ten days before the lead finally struck ground on the Tortugas Bank north of Cuba.'

He paused to take a sip of rum and Durell was keen to carry on the story.

'We had been at sea almost five weeks but finally we anchored in the shadow of Morro Castle which guards the narrow entrance to Havana's harbour.'

'I've heard tales of that place,' Major Cartwright said. 'They say the fortress is built into the cliff face. They say it's impregnable, but I'd like to see British forces try.'

'We were close enough I could have taken a musket shot at one of the filthy Spanish guards,' Durell boasted.

John resumed his story. 'We were not there to kill Spaniards. I had other orders from St Lo.'

'Unless of course those orders did not go as planned,' Durell muttered under his breath.

'I sent Lieutenant Durell ashore with ten men and a flag of truce and a letter to the Governor to demand the English prisoners in exchange for the Spaniards we had brought. I wanted to do the trade and leave there as soon as we could.'

'They kept me waiting three hours before Captain Mandicti appeared, asking to meet the Captain with a message from the Governor,' Durell said.

'Mandicti was the Commander of the boats that patrol the harbour,' John explained, 'and luckily, between us, we spoke enough Spanish to understand the message. The Governor said that if the *Tryall* came into the harbour, our business could be concluded immediately and we could have all the refreshments and assistance the place could afford.'

One of the ladies remarked from behind her fan, 'Well at least you had a kind invitation from the Governor.'

John turned on her as if she was the stupidest fool at the table. 'It was clearly a trap, Madam. Once my ship was within the harbour walls, I would have been at their mercy. My orders were not to hand over the Spanish prisoners until we had the release of the English prisoners.'

The lady looked suitably chastised and I felt a glow of pride in my brave husband.

Durell nodded his head, 'Yes, the Captain sent me back with that old dog, Mandicti, to demand the English prisoners.'

'I told him I could not stay longer than the evening. If they were not sent out by then, I would carry the Spaniards back to Jamaica. Finally, late in the afternoon, two launches came out of the harbour bringing fifty-six English prisoners and two barrels of fresh water. We sent thirty-two Spaniards prisoners ashore in the same boats.'

'I had been held hostage at musket point until the Spanish prisoners got ashore,' Durell said rather dramatically, to gain the attention of the ladies. 'Only when they got ashore, was I allowed to go back to the *Tryall* with no further trouble.'

He grunted as if another chance for a fight had been missed but he told us the *Tryall* made swift progress westwards to Cape Antonio and then southeast, heading back to Jamaica.

'We stopped at the Isle of Pines,' John said, 'off the south coast of Cuba, being in great want of water, but there was no safe anchoring against that rocky shore. I was minded to abandon the plan and head straight for Jamaica.'

'The sailors were beginning to complain as they went about their work.'

'Who can blame them, Lieutenant,' John said. 'They had been on a water allowance of a quart a day for a month. The pilot knew of an anchorage on the north of the island which was worth a try although the shore looked wild and inhospitable. I sent the boats ashore and they found a watering place. We kept the boats going back and forward, night and day, constantly filling the ship with barrels of fresh water and wood for the stoves. After two days there was sufficient and I made the signal to call everyone back to the ship.'

'One of the wooders had strayed from the rest and did not return,' Durell told us.

'I sent one of the boats ashore again to make a great fire and told the men to fire a gun every hour to direct him back in case he was lost. By the next morning, there was no sight nor sound of the missing sailor and storm clouds were rising quickly to the northwards.'

'He was most likely eaten by an alligator,' Durell said, taking great delight in frightening us. 'Those fearsome creatures overrun the place. Their enormous jaws can easily get the better of a man.'

I shuddered at the thought of such a violent death. John assured me it wasn't my cabin boy, Georgie, although that skinny lad wouldn't have made much of a meal for an alligator.

Suddenly the threat of Maroons seemed insignificant, compared to the jeopardies John faced every day at sea.

After a few minutes, Caroline called to the fiddlers to strike up a merry tune to cheer us up. She turned to John on her right side and asked him what his plans were now he had returned a hero. I blocked out Mr Cuthbert's voice as he started to tell me yet again about the latest sugar quotas, so I could hear their conversation.

'Well, since we sailed for Cuba, Captain Hubbard and Captain Price have both died of the fever. So Commander St Lo has promoted me to Captain of the *Greyhound*, one of the ships in his Squadron. She's a 20-gun Sixth rate frigate,' he said proudly. 'I shall be off to join the blockade of Cartagena. If the Spanish treasure ships get home with all that silver, it will finance Spain's war against Great Britain for many years to come. Our task is to stop them from leaving.'

William nodded wisely. He understood why John must take a British warship and blockade a Spanish port on the coast of Colombia. Well, I didn't understand! This was totally different from a survey of the naval dockyards that John had said he was going to do in Jamaica.

Mr Cuthbert was in mid-flow about the poor quality of new buildings in Kingston when I turned to John.

'Is this true? Are you off to fight the Spaniards? On one of those sorry-looking warships we saw in the harbour when we arrived?'

He was embarrassed his wife had challenged him. Between gritted teeth, he said 'Mary-Anne, I am now the Captain of the *Greyhound*, part of the Squadron in the West Indies. It's a promotion for me and it's my duty as a naval officer.'

I could see the excitement in his eyes. St Lo had made him Captain of one of the warships in the British Squadron. He was going to sea again, fighting in the war against Spain with the rest of the fleet. It was what he wanted. I blamed St Lo. First, he sent John on a dangerous mission to Cuba, next he promoted him to Captain of the *Greyhound* and now he was sending him to Cartagena. Of course I was proud of John, but I feared dead men's shoes were an easy way to get a promotion in the Navy and St Lo was rather short of Captains for his ships at the moment.

'Don't worry, my dearest, we have to await the arrival of the new Commander-in-Chief to replace Hosier, which will be January at the earliest. And the *Greyhound* needs extensive repairs before she puts to sea again. She needs new planking on the hull, new masts, sails, cables, well, I fear everything will have to be repaired or replaced.'

As if that put my mind at rest. What could I say? I turned back to Mr Cuthbert in a sulk but he didn't seem to have noticed I hadn't been listening to him.

Caroline asked Lieutenant Durell about his plans, her voice displaying nervousness that he too would be sent off to Cartagena. Luckily for her, Durell was to stay with the *Tryall* and patrol the American coast to escort merchantmen supplying the new colonies. Captain George Berkeley had taken over command of the *Tryall* and the ship was off for a few weeks but would return regularly to Kingston. William seemed to approve of this protection for his sugar cargoes, but I caught the meaningful look exchanged by Caroline and Durell and knew that it would suit their affair very well.

Major Cartwright interrupted Mr Cuthbert and said to me, 'Well, Mary-Anne, it looks as if you'll be on your own for a while. If you need me to escort you to any social event, I am always at your service.'

John scowled at me, which seemed a bit unfair as I hadn't done anything wrong.

Once dinner was finished, Caroline insisted on dancing. Mr Cuthbert excused himself and gravitated towards the gaming table set up in the Smoking Room. William and John followed him along with several of the other guests. I was disappointed that John didn't want to partner me on the dance floor.

Durell gallantly asked me for a dance and Caroline partnered Major Cartwright. Suddenly the Major interrupted Durell and we swapped partners so that Durell could dance with Caroline. I had danced with the Major many times at Grosvenor Hall. He danced elegantly. Other dance partners leapt and twirled with reckless abandon and more than one had stepped on my toes. It could be very painful. That evening I felt awkward in case John was watching me so I tried not to skip too lightly or twirl my petticoats as if I was enjoying myself.

The Major complimented me on my dress. It was one of Caroline's cast-offs and the pale pink silk suited my black hair and the looser fit was more comfortable in the heat than my gowns with their stiff corsets and tight waists.

'Your husband told us quite a tale of heroics,' the Major whispered, leaning close to my ear as we passed in the centre of the dance floor. 'While I am stuck on the island, chasing runaway slaves.'

'Why, Major you sound almost jealous,' I answered as I pirouetted away to one side, proud that my husband was the hero of the evening. 'Perhaps you should have joined His Majesty's Navy instead of the Army.'

He laughed and we joined hands together in the centre. 'I would not like to be at sea for months on end. It must get lonely, stuck out on the high seas. If I were married, I would prefer to be at home with my wife.'

'You've never married, though, have you Major?'

'Well, if I'd met a girl as pretty as you, who knows, I might have been tempted.'

I blushed and he laughed at my discomfort. Luckily the music finished and I curtsied at the end of the dance. As Caroline decided which tune the fiddlers should play next, the Major took my arm and led me out onto the veranda where the air was cooler.

'Let us take some air outside, Mrs Gascoigne,' he said most politely.

It was a beautiful evening, the stars bright in a dark sky, the sugar canes swishing in the gentle breeze and the smell of exotic blooms in the garden. I felt quite giddy with the exhaustion of dancing and the effects of the rum I had drunk at dinner and I stumbled as if I might faint.

The Major caught me around the waist and spun me around so we were facing. I was suddenly on my guard, sensing danger and an unwelcome situation. I tried to step back, but he grabbed me roughly and pulled me closer to him.

'Please let me go,' I whispered, too quietly to have any effect.

'With your husband away to Cartagena, Mary-Anne, perhaps I'll have the opportunity to see more of you.'

66

His face was close to mine and then to my horror, he placed a kiss on my lips, as a sort of promise of what he had in mind once my husband had gone away to Cartagena.

Over his left shoulder, I saw John watching us from the Smoking Room.

No one moved for what seemed like an eternity. Then I pulled back sharply to extricate myself from the Major's grip and John rushed at the Major as if he would knock him over. He was shouting threats that he would kill him. I clutched at his arm to stop him from throwing a punch.

The commotion had attracted the attention of the other guests and Durell moved quickly to pull John away and firmly held his arm. The Major stood there, dusting down his jacket and grinning as if he had done nothing wrong.

'Come away, husband. It was nothing,' I pleaded. 'Just a terrible misunderstanding.'

Caroline was at my side. 'There is no need for a disturbance, Captain Gascoigne. The Major has drunk too much rum, but he's leaving now and we will continue our evening without further drama.'

She firmly placed her hand on the Major's arm and escorted him away. John was fighting off Durell's hold on him.

'Let me go,' he shouted. 'I should have challenged him to a duel.'

Durell, ever up for a fight, said quietly, 'Only pick the fights you will win, Captain.'

'I could have dealt with him,' John replied, but the conviction had left him and he turned on me. 'I am so disappointed in you, Mary-Anne. What will happen when I go to Cartagena, when I'm away fighting the Spanish?' he asked, spitting out his words in anger.

'Nothing will happen, John. This was not my fault. I will never give you cause to doubt me.'

Despite my tears, he turned and walked off into the moonlit garden. Durell and I were left standing on the veranda.

'And I thought I would be the one in trouble tonight,' he said in an attempt to lighten the mood.

'It must be difficult for you to see Caroline with her husband,' I replied, my mind distracted by John's anger.

'Yes, but I would rather see her again than stay away. It's hard to give up someone you love. Your husband once told me I should forget her and fall in love with someone more convenient. He told me that was the secret to happiness.'

Did John say that? Did John fall in love with me because I was convenient? Was that what he was looking for in a wife? Unmarried. Tick. A father-in-law who can get you a command. Tick. Dowry of two thousand five hundred pounds. Tick. I knew that was my dowry because Alice had listened at the keyhole when Papa was talking to the lawyer. Oh yes, I was very convenient.

Not so convenient now another man had paid me some attention. I should not have encouraged the Major as my dancing partner while John was away. I should have lived alone, in seclusion, waiting patiently for his return. I had behaved unwisely and now I was a disappointment to him.

He returned from his walk, his arms folded, unable to look me in the eye.

'As soon as I get back to Kingston I shall find you naval lodgings in town. Go to your bedroom, now. I shall calm myself for a few hours more at the card table.'

I wished he'd scream and shout at me so I could argue my defence. In the face of his calm ultimatum, there was nothing I could say. I had failed to live up to his expectations of the perfect wife.

I rushed upstairs to my beautiful bedroom, with fine linens on the feather bed and a bowl of scented flowers left by one of the many maids. I looked out over the lush garden to the shoreline and the moon on the sea beyond and started weeping uncontrollably. I had been so looking forward to John's kisses and passion again after his two-month absence. This was supposed to be our romantic reunion, a chance to spend the night together.

I knelt by the bed and said my prayers. 'Please Lord, do not send my husband off to fight the Spanish. I've been married for seven months already and I'm ready to try again for a baby. I so desperately want to have a child. It's what my husband expects of me but he isn't helping by going away to sea.'

Then I fell onto the bed without undressing and cried myself to sleep. I didn't dream of my husband. Instead, I was dancing in the arms of Major Cartwright, laughing and pirouetting and having fun.

When I woke early the next morning John had left Grosvenor Hall. There was no sign he had slept in my bed.

Before breakfast, I wrote a letter to Papa. I told him that Hosier was dead, that the new Commander-in-Chief, Edward St Lo, was sending John off to Cartagena and that Mr Potter didn't want a careening wharf at Chocolate Hole. I asked him to find some survey work for John so he didn't have to fight the Spanish. I begged him to get us out of Jamaica.

I handed the letter to Lieutenant Durell as he was leaving and asked him to give it to the next ship sailing for London. If I can't save John from the Spanish, surely Papa could.

In December 1727, John was given command of HMS Greyhound. After extensive repairs, the ship was ready to sail in March 1728.

From the Captain's Log, HMS Greyhound
18th March 1728
Anchored at the Grand Barru, off Cartagena, Colombia

"Fresh gales & hazy weather. At 3pm tacked in Playa Grande in 6 fathom of water (the Town of Cartagena E6S a mile & a half off & Point Canoa N3E) & brought to under the Topsails. We saw in the Harbour of Cartagena Sixteen Ships & two Sloops, viz, The southernmost Ship of 54 guns, rigged, Yards & Topmast down. Next a Ship of 64 guns with a Rear Admiral's flag hoisted. Then 3 Ships abreast, the westernmost has her Foremast out, the middle Ship rigged as the Rear Admiral's with Yards & Topmasts down & no Sails bent but their Spritsails. The innermost Ship Topmasts through the Caps, yards fore & aft in the Tops. The next two Ships abreast both their main masts out. Next Three Ships abreast, westernmost unrigged, Middle Ship rigged, the Innermost Topmasts through the Cap, unrigged. Then in the Northmost tier Six Ships together unrigged, some wanting Masts. Next the Town Two Sloops. At 3 having had a Satisfactory View of them, bore away for the Barru again. At ½ past 8 at night anchored at the Grand Barru in 8 fathom of water & this morning moored ship."

In May HMS Greyhound returned to Jamaica with news of Admiral Hopson's death but on 5th June 1728 John was ordered to return to Cartagena to inform the British Fleet of a Peace ith Spain.

From the Captain's Log, HMS Greyhound
13th June 1728
At noon Point Canoa NNE & the Town of Cartagena EbN

"Fresh gales & fair weather. Yesterday I saw two Spanish Ships of War bearing down for us with all the sail they could make and brought to and sent on board the Commanding Ship to enquire after our fleet. At ½ past 12 Mr Cusack returned & the account he brought was that a Spanish Ship of war of 50 guns (which was dispatched from Cadiz at the same time as the Solebay was sent from Gibraltar) was arrived at Cartagena two days ago with Duplicates of the same Orders, both from their Britanick and Catholick Majesties, which Orders having been communicated to Captain Grey by the Governor of Cartagena, he left this Coast yesterday morning with the whole Squadron & went for Jamaica. We made all the sail we could for Cartagena. I sent away the Pinnace with Mr Cusack to deliver the Dispatches I was discharged with to the Governor of Cartagena. At 11AM the Sea Breeze coming in, weighed and plyed up into Playa Grande."

7

In the cool of the early morning, before the midday heat became unbearable, I sat on the veranda of Grosvenor Hall looking out to sea, wondering where John was. The trade winds from the northwest blew across the vast ocean carving out huge rolling waves and I thought of the *Greyhound* out on the high seas. I worried about all the bad things that could happen to him, stormy weather, fierce Spanish sailors and the dreaded tropical fever. Now I knew why my mother was so anxious when Papa was away. She always said it was a burden that naval wives must bear with courage and duty.

It was late May and John had been away for five months. During the frequent storms at night, I imagined John standing on deck watching the same ominous dark skies as me, cowering his head as the thunder crashed and lightning flashed. I prayed that he had moored his ship in a protected bay where he would be safe.

That morning I was in a sad, reflective mood. The rain had stopped and fat drops of water dripped from the palm trees like tears and the exotic blooms in the garden smelled like wet, rotting vegetation. This tropical weather caused a sort of discontent and restlessness. The heat sapped me of energy. I tried to be grateful for all the comforts at Grosvenor Hall but my life felt empty.

I wished John hadn't left in anger back in December. The new Commander, Vice-Admiral Edward Hopson, had arrived in January and left a week later bound for Cartagena so there was no one to ask about lodgings for me in Kingston. John had sent me a brief note suggesting I stay with Caroline if that was my wish. Once he had sailed to Cartagena in February, I wasn't sure what I was supposed to do so I stayed there.

Caroline had invited me to a Grand Ball at the House of Records last night, but the extravagant feasting seemed rather decadent when John was risking his life in Cartagena to protect the islanders from the threat of the Spaniards. And anyway I didn't dance anymore and I hadn't seen Major Cartwright since that dreadful night. Caroline told me he was busy on military manoeuvres in the mountains, hunting down the runaway Maroons. I missed John so much and wished he was by my side, to accompany me to balls, to take my hand, to smile at me and dance with me as we did on the night we met.

Caroline attended many social events on the island while William Sinclair spent much of his time in Kingston. It suited her that he was an absentee husband. She spent her days flirting and gossiping, encouraging admirers and sharing secrets.

'My husband prefers his life in Kingston with his friends,' she said, 'showing off his wealth, doing business, wining and dining and gambling with rivals and officials.' She told me he was planning to return to England to sit in the Houses of Parliament to protect the lucrative sugar trade.

'I can't wait for him to leave and give me my freedom. He got his hands on my father's plantation and I have given him a son so he is satisfied with our union but there is no love between us.'

I knew her freedom means spending more time with Lieutenant Durell and I asked her if it was wise for him to visit her so often before her husband left.

'Do not judge me for wanting love and happiness in my life,' she replied harshly.

'Surely you must think of your reputation and that of your children.'

'Who cares about my reputation on this god-forsaken island? I hear that anyone in England with title or riches does not lead such a virtuous life as you would impose on me.'

It was one thing for men to have mistresses. Even our late King George lived openly with his German mistress, but for a wife to be accused of infidelity would mean disgrace. Surely that was too high a price to pay for passion.

Durell seemed to know when William Sinclair was staying in Kingston as he always visited when Caroline was alone. She rushed into his arms and I couldn't help feeling envious of her, while my husband was away fighting the Spanish. When he swung young Amy high in the air, it was obvious he was her father. The same red hair and freckled face. The result of their affair after the hurricane five years ago. I usually took young Charles out for a walk in the garden to leave the family together.

Suddenly there was a commotion at the front entrance and I turned to see John striding through the doorway as if my thinking of him had conjured him up before my eyes. I must have looked shocked to see him as he quickly allayed my fears.

'Mary-Anne, I am well and there is nothing wrong.'

I ran into his arms and held him tight to make sure he was not an illusion. His body felt strange to me, tired and thin, burnt by the sun.

He returned my embrace and kissed me sweetly. I prayed any misunderstanding between us had been forgotten. Footmen appeared to take his riding coat and bring us refreshments. John led me to the couch on the veranda where we sat side by side, holding hands tightly.

'I am delighted to see you, my dearest husband. I had no word that you had returned.'

'No, I apologise for that. My return to Jamaica was unexpected. Vice-Admiral Hopson died two weeks ago and I was ordered to intercept Captain St Lo on his way back to London. When I got to Hispaniola, they told me there had been no sign of any English ship these past ten weeks so I have returned for further orders.'

'Hopson has died! He only arrived in Jamaica in January. How is it possible that he died so quickly? Was he shot by the Spaniards?'

'No, he was struck down by the fever. It is far more deadly to our officers and sailors than any enemy fire. We haven't engaged the Spanish in a single battle this year but so many men have died from disease. Hopson fell ill one day and three days later he was dead. As the *Leopard* left Cartagena to set sail back to Jamaica with his body, we all fired twenty guns and every officer and seaman stood silently on the decks in the pouring rain, reminded that rank, privilege and wealth are no protection from this deadly fever.'

How would John ever escape this pestilence that stalked the West Indies and struck a man down in three days?

We ate our luncheon out on the veranda. I could hear Caroline and the children laughing in the house but we didn't join them. We treasured rare moments alone together.

'Are you now back in Jamaica?' I asked him. Surely with the Admiral dead, the fleet would return to await his replacement.

'I await orders from Captain St Lo. He's in charge again, but Mary-Anne, I think he will send the *Greyhound* back to Cartagena.'

My heart sank. 'Don't go back, John. I fear for your safety fighting the Spaniards.'

'I'm not fighting the Spaniards, dearest. The chance would be a fine thing. I would love to give chase to a Spanish treasure ship and claim the prize money.'

'Then what are you doing? You've been gone for five months. I've been so worried about you.'

'I told you, the *Greyhound* is part of the patrol outside the harbour of Cartagena which stops the Spanish galleons from taking their treasure back to Spain.'

'What, all this time you've been sailing up and down outside the harbour?' I tried to hide my disappointment at this rather mundane report of patrol duty which kept him away from me.

'It's my orders, Mary-Anne. And it's important to see what ships and sloops are in the harbour and what state of readiness to sail they're in.'

'More important than being here with your wife?' I asked him, sulkily.

'I have to obey my orders, Mary-Anne,' he said quietly. 'However much I want to be with you, my duties as a Captain in the British Navy have to come first.'

I knew he was right. The Navy could ask him to do anything, go anywhere and he would willingly risk his life to follow orders.

'I've also done some surveying work as well,' he said, looking more animated. 'The pilots didn't know the safe channels around the Salmadina Shoals so I took soundings with the lead line and fixes with the compass on landmarks ashore and found the clear passages running in from the sea. Hopson, may his soul rest in peace, was impressed by my survey and said he'd mention it in dispatches to the Admiralty. He said they might have a use for a captain with an eye for this sort of work. I don't know if he had a chance to do so before he passed away.'

'Can't you do survey work around Kingston?'

'You know I must go back to Cartagena if I'm ordered, Mary-Anne.'

'You will stay with me for one night, won't you?' I could hear the pleading in my voice. With all this talk of Hopson's death, I wanted to enjoy a night of John's kisses and embraces again. We'd been married for a year already and I was desperate to try again for a baby.

He hesitated as if he wasn't planning on staying but he changed his mind. 'Of course I'll stay. I'll have to leave early tomorrow. There are so many repairs that need to be done to the *Greyhound*. All the cables and the rigging must be replaced. I doubt I'll have time to fix the masts and sails as well.'

I bit my lip. It was not my place to tell him that the *Greyhound* was an old ship and not seaworthy. He knew that well enough.

After lunch, we strolled in the gardens. I took his arm and it reminded me of when we were courting in Stratford, only now the plants were exotic and the scents were strange. We watched Charles and Amy playing on a swing and I asked him about our children. Will they be boys or girls? What will we call them? What will they be like? What will they become?

John laughed at all my questions. 'Until I met you, I never thought I would marry or have children.'

'Why would you not want children?'

'My childhood was not spent with the loving family you had,' he said. 'My mother died giving birth to me and I was handed to a wet nurse who cared for me until I was four years old. By then my father had remarried and had another son, my half-brother James. My stepmother was a cold-hearted woman and showed no love to me. She persuaded my father to send me into the Navy when I was eleven. For the next seven years I lived at sea and the Navy became my family. I never heard from my father and by the time I returned to England to take my Lieutenant's examination at eighteen, he had passed away. My stepmother wanted nothing to do with me. She had no intention of sharing my father's meagre estate. I returned to sea as soon as I could and I haven't seen her since.'

A mother who died at childbirth, a neglectful father, a cruel stepmother, a half-brother he hardly knew and a lonely life spent at sea. It was so different from my happy childhood with my loving parents and three noisy sisters that I hardly knew how to comfort him.

'I changed my mind when I met you, Mary-Anne. You were so unlike my stepmother that I knew you would be the perfect wife and a wonderful mother to our huge brood of children, all of whom we will love and care for at home and never send away to sea.'

I couldn't wipe away all the unhappiness he had suffered before I met him but I could make sure our future was filled with love. I laughed out loud at the prospect of our large and happy family. John grabbed hold of my waist and swung me around. I fell into his arms and we sealed our love with a passionate kiss.

That night John was tender and loving. He caressed my skin, re-discovering my body after a long absence and kissed me passionately. I cried out in pain as he pressed himself into me but I held onto him tightly wanting to stop him from ever leaving me again. Afterwards he gathered me up in his arms, kissing the top of my head as I lay with my cheek upon his chest. At Grosvenor Hall we had the luxury of a large double bed and yet we lay closely embraced as we had learnt to do in the narrow bed on the *Tryall*. He told me how much he had missed me in Cartagena but not as much as when he went to Cuba.

'Your presence was everywhere on the *Tryall*, in the Dining Room, in our cabin, in our bed. It's easier to bear your absence when you are no part of the *Greyhound*,' he said softly. 'But whenever I see porpoises playing by the ship or the orange glow of a sunset or the stars twinkling in the night sky, I have to stop myself from calling out for you to come and see. And in the early morning light I remember your sweet face on the pillow and the softness of your hair.'

I could feel my heart breaking at the thought of him leaving the next morning.

At sunrise I watched from the porch as he rode away. He stopped at the gate and turned to wave to me. I didn't know when I would see him again so I waved until he was out of sight. The next day my monthly bleeds started and I mourned the child that might have been conceived on such a night of love.

One evening at the start of June, William Sinclair returned to Grosvenor Hall unexpectedly and told us that a ship had arrived in Kingston from Gibraltar with news of a Peace Agreement between Great Britain and Spain. William was delighted that his ships would be able to transport their cargoes of sugar cane, molasses and rum across the Atlantic without fear of attack from the Spanish. I fell to my knees and thanked the Good Lord. We were no longer at war with Spain. John would no longer have to patrol outside Cartagena, blocking the passage of the Spanish ships.

'I shall go first thing tomorrow to see Commander St Lo. It may be time for us to take a house in Kingston.'

'I wouldn't be in such a rush, Mrs Gascoigne. Your husband's ship, the *Greyhound*, sailed out of Kingston harbour this morning. I understand St Lo has sent him back to Cartagena to inform the British Squadron there of the Peace Agreement. I expect they will all come back eventually.'

St Lo had told him to go back to Cartagena so he had gone, but William was right, the British Fleet would come back to Jamaica now that we were no longer at war with Spain. As soon as John returned, I would move to a house in Kingston so he could visit me regularly from his ship while he finished his survey of the dockyards. I would be his perfect wife and a wonderful mother to our huge brood of children, just as he had said he wanted.

HMS Greyhound returned to Jamaica on 6ᵗʰ July 1728 and in August John was given command of HMS Alborough, charged with surveying the Carolina coast.

From the Captain's Log, HMS Alborough
29ᵗʰ August 1728
At Port Royal Harbour, Kingston, Jamaica.

    "This morning I Received a Commission from Edw. St Lo, Esq. Commander in Chief of His Majesty's Ships employed & to be employed at Jamaica to Command His Majesty's Ship the Alborough & came onboard her accordingly, but not having been able to go out of my Apartment since the 4ᵗʰ inst by coming aboard, the Fever, which I have laboured under by frequent relapses ever since the beginning of June returned upon me Violently."

Despite his illness, John set sail from Jamaica to Charles Town in October 1728.

From the Captain's Log, HMS Alborough
19ᵗʰ October 1728
At Port Royal Harbour, Kingston, Jamaica.

    "All the above observations taken out of the General Book, having been so extremely ill myself that I have not been able to keep any Account of Accidents. PM I Returned to the Ship in a very weak condition being afflicted with a complication of Distempers (the Jaundice, the Dropsie, the Scurvy & Gravel) the consequence of the very long fit of Sickness I have had. Unmoored with the Sea Breeze and at Daylight this morning got under Sail and Passing by the Plymouth saluted the Commodore with 15 guns. At ½ past 8 falling Calm anchored in the West channel in Ten Fathom water the Fort NE two miles off. The Ship's Company since my Command of her have been Victual'd with Fresh Meat once or twice a Week."

8

A month later a letter was delivered to me at Grosvenor Hall. John had returned from Cartagena and he asked me to come urgently to Kingston to meet him. I knew all was not well. Caroline helped me pack up my clothes and made her carriage available to me in great haste. All the way to Kingston I had to remind myself that at least John was home and he was alive, but I was not prepared for how ill he was. He could not rise from his bed, so afflicted was he with the tropical fever.

I had to go cap in hand to ask Commander St Lo if we could have Navy lodgings in Kingston. St Lo was preoccupied with all the ships in his Squadron which had returned from Cartagena so he didn't have time to see me. In the end, I took a longboat out to his flagship HMS *Lyon* so he had to give me an audience.

He was a short, stocky man in his mid-forties, well-built and weather-beaten, rather intimidating. He was made Captain at twenty-one and I knew John held him in great respect but I sensed that being Commander-in-Chief of the Jamaica station was the last thing he wanted. First Hosier and then Hopson had died, putting him back in charge again, the penalty for being so hale and hearty.

He was not helpful. 'You don't know the intolerable stress I've been under the past few weeks,' he told me.

'All I'm asking for is lodgings. John is very ill and he needs to be ashore where I can look after him.'

He got a ledger from a high shelf, opened it and shut it again quickly.

'Every house has been taken by the other officers. They returned from Cartagena over a month ago and everyone wants time ashore to recover. I'm sorry Mrs Gascoigne, but you're too late. I have nothing left to offer you.'

My blood boiled over in defence of John and I started shouting at St Lo.

'It's not John's fault he's a month late returning! You sent him back to Cartagena! The Spanish Governor had already told the British ships to leave! So by the time John got there, all your ships were safely back here!'

I couldn't believe I was shouting at the Commander-in-Chief and neither could he. I knew John was following orders, but I was so angry with St Lo for sending him back to Cartagena.

'Mrs Gascoigne, please calm down. His mission was vital to deliver letters to the Governor of Cartagena. And the South Sea Company's agent in Jamaica has been pestering me to get the Governor to restart the *assiento* slave trade so they can supply Africans to the Spanish colonies in South America.'

'As if I care about the slave traders,' I carried on shouting. 'And then he went to Porto Bello. That's where he got the fever. You know Porto Bello is where Vice-Admiral Hosier lost thousands of his men to the fever while he was blockading that very place.'

'He had to secure the release of any British prisoners held there.'

'Well, there weren't any there and if there ever were, they're all dead now.'

'So it seems,' he said, looking rather shaken at being spoken to in this manner. 'Captain Gascoigne is a good man, honourable and courageous. Let me see if I can find anything to offer you.'

He opened the ledger again and looked more carefully this time. After making me wait for an intolerable length of time, he scribbled an address on a slip of paper. He hesitated and picked up a pile of papers from his desk, which he handed to me with the address.

'Can you ask your husband to take a look at my survey of the harbour? And there's a draft of the harbour made by Nicholas Holst, a sworn surveyor and a most ingenious man. I would value Captain Gascoigne's opinion and hopefully his approval before I sent it back to the Navy Board.'

I couldn't believe he wanted John's views on his survey while he was laid low with fever, but I understood it was the price we must pay for him finding us a place to live.

He had allocated us rooms on the first floor of a large boarding house run by Mr and Mrs Clifford who lived on the ground floor. Mr Clifford was a retired corporal from the British Army, injured fighting the Spanish in Florida, who had invested his savings in a boarding house in Kingston. At this end of town the houses were run down and the streets were dangerous after dark. It was a far cry from the luxury of Grosvenor Hall.

The day we moved in the rain came down in a heavy downpour, turning the dirt road into a muddy river. Lieutenant Cusack helped me get John up the stairs and onto the bed. He was keen to retreat to his quarters on the *Greyhound*. Like everyone else, he wanted to stay well away from the fever. He offered to help me, but in his haste to unload our boxes from the cart, the trunk with the gowns that Caroline had given me as a leaving gift fell into the mud. I started crying before I had even crossed the threshold.

Our rooms were small, damp and smelled of dirt and mould. I collapsed into a chair, overcome by the thought of unpacking. I didn't want to be there. I wanted to go home. The summer heat was intolerable, damp and sultry like a vapour bath and the mosquitoes bit me relentlessly.

Mrs Clifford bustled in to sort me out. 'No one told me you were coming today,' she said, 'or I would have had the place ready for you.' She was a plump, middle-aged woman, neither black-skinned nor white.

'Mulatto,' John whispered when her back was turned as if it was something shameful, but Mrs Clifford seemed quite at ease in her brown skin.

'I believe Captain St Lo is rather busy at present,' I said, sniffing, angry with myself for defending St Lo. He couldn't even be bothered to tell her of our arrival.

'I'll send one of my girls to clean the place thoroughly, but I'm surprised you haven't got your own maid, a lady like yourself.'

I apologised for my failure to have a maid and explained that there were so many maids at Grosvenor Hall, I hadn't felt the need for one of my own since the day I arrived in Jamaica.

'Well, you can have Mercy to help you. You're going need some help, what with him not being able to get out of bed,' she said, glancing over at John lying helpless on the couch.

Pausing in the doorway, she turned to look back at me. 'We'll soon see what you're made of, m'lady.' Then she turned and shouted down the stairway for Mercy to get up there quickly.

She'd issued a challenge which made me feel rather pathetic, sitting there crying like a little girl. I was a married woman and it was up to me to care for John, in sickness and in health. I had waited so long for him to come home, I was not going to let him down now.

'Tell me how I can help,' I said, staggering to my feet. She handed me a linen apron to wear over my skirts and I took a deep breath. I'd never done housework before, but by the end of the day Mrs Clifford, Mercy and I had swept the apartment, unpacked the trunks and settled John in his bed. I momentarily wondered what my friends and family would think if they could see me. Would they be proud of me for rising to the challenge or shake their heads and say they knew it wouldn't end well?

I feared John had the dreaded fever the sailors call the Yellow Jack because his skin was tinged yellow, but he assured me he didn't. He'd seen many sailors die from the yellow fever so he knew the symptoms. Both Hosier and Hopson had died within a few days of falling ill. His illness had been lingering since June and he felt nauseous all the time with a persistent ache and a swelling in his abdomen. He had frequent relapses which affected him violently, making him sweat and shake.

The surgeon from the *Greyhound* came to see him, but he had no magic cure. His talents were more for butchery and he was skilled at chopping off arms and legs injured in battle. He gave John tonics to encourage his body to expel the sickness. It certainly resulted in a lot of vomit which necessitated Mercy having to launder his bedclothes and bedsheets daily so I hoped it truly was improving his health.

John was so frustrated and angry with his illness. He tried to get up, blaming me for keeping him from his duties but immediately collapsed back onto the bed. I had to reassure him that he would get better soon. He was restless all night and Mr Clifford set up a bed in the parlour for me so I could get some rest. It was not the marital reconciliation I had hoped for when my husband finally returned from fighting the Spanish.

One morning I went to wake him with another dose of his vile medicine and found him lying prostrate on the bed, the damp bedclothes tangled around his body as if he had fought with them in the night and lost the battle. He was so pale and gaunt that he could have been a corpse. He didn't look like the dashing naval hero I had married just last year. I was frozen to the spot. I didn't dare approach him or touch him. What if he was dead? I turned and rushed downstairs to get help from Mrs Clifford. If anyone knew what to do with a dead body, it was her.

She returned with me to the bedroom and felt for a pulse on his neck.

'He's weak, but still with us. He's so hot, he's burning up. It's probably that medicine the surgeon gives him. I'll fetch a jug of cool water and we can bathe him.'

Thank the Lord he was still alive. She returned with her husband who claimed to have some medical knowledge from his time in the Army.

'Well, if he's not dead, let me take a look at him.'

He inspected John's body as if it were a slab of meat on the butcher's counter and declared that he had an affliction of the bile known as jaundice.

'So it's not the Yellow Jack?' I asked him, terrified to hear the worst.

'No, it's not. Although yellow skin can be the deadly fever if it was, Captain Gascoigne would be dead by now,' he told me cheerfully. Which I suppose was some sort of comfort.

Mrs Clifford advised me to keep the bedroom well-ventilated to repel the malignant miasmas which hung around a sick body. She brought me bouquets of local herbs to scent the bedroom and told me to give the patient a drink of boiled water and lime juice every day.

'My father was at sea all his life and swore it's good for sailors,' she told me.

John needed me to care for him every day. I carefully shaved his chin in the mornings and washed off his feverish sweat in the evenings. As I bathed him I got to know his body well, the puckered scars from injuries at sea, his leathery forearms that had been in the tropical sun and his pale legs that had not. The rough patches, the tender spots and the ticklish parts. I explored the landscape of his male body as if I was discovering a foreign land while I rubbed soothing oils into his skin.

I sat beside him, reading to him or doing my needlework. Sometimes I took his hand and told him quietly about what we would do when he was better. He seemed to appreciate that I was there beside him, even if he didn't answer.

'I think Mrs Clifford's father might have been a pirate,' I told him one evening. 'She has all these funny treasures on display in her parlour, a shark's tooth, a bent gold coin and a huge curly seashell. My father never brought us such treasures home. I hope he was a good father to her and not away at sea all the time.'

I could have been talking about any naval father, not just a pirate, and I remembered how Papa was away for so much of my childhood. When he returned for a brief stay between commands, he spoilt us and indulged us. It was too early to say how good a father John would be.

He turned his head and opened one eye to look at me.

'I will try my best to be a good father,' he whispered as if he knew what I was thinking. 'I know you will be an excellent mother, Mary-Anne. You are everything I ever wanted in a wife.'

He fell asleep before I could ask him exactly what it was that he wanted in a wife. Was it a wife who patiently waited at home for him while he went off to do his duty on the High Seas? A wife who lovingly cared for him when he was sick? A wife who gave him plenty of children? A wife who was useful and capable and resilient? At that moment, I didn't feel I was any of those things.

Caroline came to visit me. She didn't want to stay long in this part of town where disease and pickpockets lurked in the shadows. She was shocked at the condition of my husband, the dashing Navy Captain. She was even more shocked at our bare rooms, without carpets, paintings, chandeliers or footmen and admonished me for not furnishing my home more comfortably. I had been so worried about John living or dying that I hadn't paid any attention to my home-making duties.

Her world of luxury could not save her from heartbreak. Her husband William had sailed for England, declaring that he had no intention of returning to his immoral, unfaithful whore of a wife and he had taken her son, Charles, with him to be schooled at Eton. He had declared to everyone in Society that she was not a fit mother and she would never see her son again.

Her lover, Lieutenant Durell was away, sailing onboard the *Tryall* on route to Philadelphia and she had to bear this tragic turn of events on her own. What words of comfort could I give her? She had made her choice and she had paid the ultimate price.

She told me William's public accusations had made Society shun her. Her friends no longer sent invitations or called on her at Grosvenor Hall. All those influential and powerful people who wanted to take advantage of William Sinclair's wealth and prestige had no need of Caroline now.

'You still have Amy,' I said, but it sounded hollow when she had lost her beloved son.

'He always knew she wasn't his child. The red hair rather gave it away. Or perhaps it was her gentle, loving nature.'

'And Durell will be back soon.'

'An illicit affair is one thing, but he can never be Master of Grosvenor Hall and he's even talking of returning to England to seek promotion. No one wants to stay in Jamaica forever. Except me. I will never leave,' she said defiantly.

After she'd left, I sat in the parlour as the light faded thinking of her. Caroline wanted freedom, but she got a prison. She didn't want to wait at home for her husband to return, patient and faithful, but there wasn't any alternative for married women. I caressed the locket around my neck, the likeness of John that he had given me on our Wedding Day. I couldn't bear the thought that he might leave me or worse still, take our son away so I could never see him again.

One morning at the end of August there was a loud banging on the front door. I poked my head out of the window as Mercy opened the door below. A young lad was standing there. He looked up at me.

'A letter for Capt'n Gasken.'

I came downstairs and exchanged the letter for a coin. It was from Captain St Lo, my least favourite person in Jamaica. I was tempted to tear it up, but I was a dutiful wife and the ship's boy was watching me, so I took it upstairs and placed it quietly next to John's bed for when he woke up.

An hour or so later John called me in from the parlour. He was holding the letter with a look of amazement on his face.

'St Lo says I am to assume command of the Alborough. The Navy Board wants me to make a survey,' and he read from the letter, "*of the Bahama Islands, Coast of Cuba, Gulf of Florida, Windward Passage, Charles Town Harbour and Port Royal Harbour in South Carolina.*" This is exactly what I wanted to do, Mary-Anne. I wonder if Admiral Hopson did send my survey of the Salmadina Shoals back to the Navy Board after all.'

I wondered if Papa got my letter and pulled strings at the Admiralty. I had asked him to get us out of Jamaica and find some survey work for John and he had answered my pleas.

'St Lo writes that the *Alborough* arrived at Kingston this morning and I am to assume command immediately. She's a Sixth-rate 20-gun, Mary-Anne, newly built. Captain Baker who brought her out will take over the *Greyhound* and I will need to find a new lieutenant as Lieutenant Pollock is to be transferred to the *Nottingham*. And I get the *Happy* sloop under my command to help me with the survey.'

I didn't know what to say. It sounded like an impossible task for someone who had laid in his sick bed for the past month.

John suddenly had the energy to clamber out of bed and find a chart. He pointed out to me the places mentioned in the letter, the Bahama Islands, Florida and South Carolina. It covered a huge area of ocean and he traced a line on the chart, touching all the islands with his finger as if he was marking out his kingdom.

'This is a fine promotion for me. We'll go and live in Charles Town in Carolina. It's one of the wealthiest and most fashionable cities in America. You'll be happy there, Mary-Anne. Happier than in Kingston, I think. We must make plans to leave immediately.'

John was used to getting orders and setting off immediately. Now St Lo said we had to leave Kingston and go to Charles Town, wherever that was. We clutched each other as if we had been rescued from drowning. I just hoped this was the salvation we needed.

Caroline had said no one wants to stay in Jamaica forever and it was true. I was pleased we were leaving. John would recover his health while he did his survey work and we would start our happy family in Charles Town.

Later that day we had another caller, Lieutenant James Gascoigne, John's half-brother. He had arrived in Kingston onboard HMS *Alborough*. He was shocked to discover how ill John was, but he hid it well. John was overjoyed to see his long-lost brother, his only living blood relative.

'You will need a good lieutenant, brother,' James announced, 'one who can assist you in the survey. It requires a lot of detailed measurement and not everyone is suited for such work, but I would be honoured to assist you.'

John was delighted and suddenly my place at John's side was usurped by this capable, young newcomer to our life. As someone who dearly loved her sisters, how could I complain that John was reunited with his brother?

Against my better advice, John was suddenly motivated to get up and dress in his Captain's blue frock coat with the gold-laced buttons and go down to the harbour with James to board the *Alborough* as ordered by Captain St Lo.

Two weeks later he returned to our lodgings as he was so ill.

'The fever came back most violently,' he told me. 'I've sent a message to St Lo. James had to write it as I'm too ill. St Lo's given me leave to return to the lodgings for a while.'

James visited John regularly with news from the *Alborough*. The ship's company were very sickly. The cook had died and a sailor sleeping on the gunwale had fallen overboard and drowned. The carpenter had been taken by HMS *Southampton* but had been replaced. The boatswain had been taken by HMS *Lark* but had been replaced. The men were complaining that the food was going off, especially the meat. There was always the hidden message in James' reports that the ship should set sail as soon as possible before anything else bad happened.

'At least wait for the hurricane season to be over,' I begged him and he seemed to accept this could be an excuse to delay our departure while he recuperated.

Finally, John couldn't resist James' hints anymore and in mid-October he declared that he felt somewhat better and ordered James to load the ship with final provisions and prepare to sail.

I had three days to pack our bags. I sent a letter to Caroline to tell her how excited I was to go to Charles Town. I was confident I would find happiness there.

When it was time to leave, I embraced Mrs Clifford and thanked Mr Clifford. I was quite sure that John would have died without their help. 'Captain Gascoigne is bound to get better in Charles Town,' I told them, 'and he won't be sent away to fight the Spanish so we'll finally have a chance to start our family.'

Mrs Clifford wished me well. She'd had to listen all summer long to my frustration of not being with child yet.

On the 19th of October 1728, we boarded HMS *Alborough*. John was in a weak condition, but I had a spring in my step and a light heart. Farewell to Jamaica! This was just the new start John and I needed.

Charles Town Harbour South Carolina, published 1739
Line engraving by Bishop Robert.
The New York Public Library

II

Charles Town, South Carolina

1728-1730

HMS Alborough arrived in Charles Town in November 1727, after mistaking the Edisto Inlet for Charles Town harbour, such was the lack of charts of this coastline at that time.

From the Captain's Log, HMS Alborough
24th November 1728
At anchor off Edistow Inlet on the Coast of South Carolina.

"Moderate Gales & hazy weather. The Guns I have fired giving little better report than Pistols, I desired Captain Douglas to stand as near in as he could with Safety and to make Signals for a Pilot, believing my guns could not be heard, for I saw one of them Loaded afresh with the whole allowance of Powder for Service. All the Guns we have fired for Signals in our Passage have blown a long time, some a full quarter of a minute & upon Examination had the Misfortune to find all the Powder aboard in the same condition. At 8 having less wind, fired another Gun, expecting (as the custom of this Port is, if it be Charles Town) to be answered by a Gun from Johnson's Fort & at 10 fired another, but received no answer. Wherefore at Break of Day I sent my Pinnace in. At noon she returned & brought us word this place is called St Helena Sound & Edistow Inlet & that Charles Town is 14 Leagues to the Northward. The appearance of that Land and this are so exactly alike that even the oldest Traders upon this coast are very frequently deceived, coming out of the sea without an Observation. The officer also brings word that there is no Dependence on getting a Pilot to come off at Port Royal (being but very few inhabitants there) or at any Place along this Coast except at Charles Town. The very Bad Condition we find our Powder in, puts us under an unavoidable necessity of going thither for a supply."

From the Captain's Log, HMS Alborough
29th November 1728
In Charles Town Harbour, South Carolina.

"Moderate gales & fair weather. At ½ past noon the wind coming to NNE, weigh'd and got in over the Bar & at ½ past 5 anchored in Ashley River & moored with the Stream Anchor. At 7 AM unmoor'd, at 8 weighed, at ½ past 10 anchored in Charles Town Harbour, about Midway between Johnson's Fort and the Town in 7 fathoms water & moored. We found here His Majesty's Ships the Garland & Solebay, the latter with her Foremast and Mizon-mast out."

9

The voyage from Jamaica was terrible, with gales and heavy rain every day. It wasn't just John who was ill; all the crew were sickly and several men died, including William Purser the surgeon's mate. He'd died before we'd even left Jamaica, whilst we were anchored in Blewfields Bay for ten days loading up with wood and water.

I had been aboard the *Alborough* for forty days and it was a blessed relief when finally a pilot came on board three days ago and we crossed the Bar into Charles Town Harbour. Ships must take onboard a skilled pilot to safely navigate the shallow maze of sandbars at the entrance to the harbour. Finally we were out of the huge swell of the ocean, the constant rolling and rocking in the waves.

I was looking forward to going ashore and I prayed the rain would hold off for a few hours so my petticoats wouldn't be ruined as I made my entry into Charles Town society. As the latest arrivals in Charles Town, John and I had been invited to dine with the Governor of South Carolina, the Honourable Arthur Middleton, Esquire, and his wife Sarah at their house in Charles Town.

As the pinnace was lowered, ready to take us ashore, I waited for John on deck taking in the view. Johnson's Fort, south of the town, was built on the banks of the Ashley River to act as the first defence of the harbour. White Point, named after the oyster shells the first settlers found there, marked the start of the town where the Ashley and Cooper Rivers diverged. Fortifications and cannons faced outwards to protect the town. From White Point the quayside stretched to the tall spire of St Philip's Church in the distance. It was impossible to believe a hurricane had struck the town a couple of months earlier and caused devastation to buildings, such was the good state of repair to the town.

Ships were loading and unloading at the docks and many more were anchored in the harbour, waiting for their turn at one of the wharves. I counted over fifty merchant ships. Rowboats scuttled between them, some with sails to take advantage of the breeze. The harbour was alive with activity, commerce and possibility. I was giddy with excitement and expectation and so pleased that we had finally arrived.

John was ready to go at last. He looked very fine, his wig freshly powdered with corn starch, curled at the ears and bound at the back in a pigtail. I straightened his blue frockcoat, arranged the frilled jabots on his shirt and gave him a smile of encouragement. He was still plagued with fever and headaches and I knew he would rather be quietly dining onboard, but this was an important occasion for us both.

He needed the support of Captain George Anson of HMS *Garland,* the Post Captain of Charles Town. 'Be nice to Captain Anson,' he told me. 'He'll be important to the success of my work here.'

'I promise to be agreeable to him,' I answered sweetly, thinking to myself, as long as he's nothing like St Lo.

Anson was in charge of supplying, refitting and maintaining the Navy ships in Charles Town, but as far I could see there are only two other Navy ships, the *Garland* and the *Solebay,* so he wouldn't be as busy as Commander St Lo.

John also needed the support of the Governor to get a new supply of gunpowder. Earlier that morning during a break in the rain, he had ordered all the gunpowder be taken ashore while the empty powder room was aired with a pot of fire.

'If I have to fire my cannons to give the signal for a pilot every time I want to cross the Bar into Charles Town harbour, I'll need to replace my gunpowder. It's all decayed and fallen to dust.'

And I needed friends for my new life. I was resolved that in Charles Town I would be a good wife for John. I would support him in his naval duties, set up our home and have our first baby. We had been married eighteen months and still had no children, although to be fair, John had either been away fighting the Spanish or so ill that we had been sleeping apart. Charles Town would be different, he only had some survey work to do.

Once John was comfortably seated in the pinnace, the sailors helped me down the chain ladder which was not easy with the hoops in my petticoats. James was to stay onboard in charge of the ship so I had my husband all to myself that afternoon. We were rowed across to Middle Bridge where ferry boats jostled for space on the quayside. Once we'd disembarked I suggested we take a carriage to arrive at the Governor's house in style, but John wanted to walk and explore our new home town. The rain had stopped for a while, so I agreed.

Fine buildings lined the harbourside, tall, short, squat, elegant houses, with straight streets between them and there were people everywhere I looked. Away from the bustle of the quayside, the streets were wide and straight, laid out in a grid pattern. Quite the opposite of the narrow, winding alleys and crowded, overhanging houses in London. In Charles Town each house was newly built and stood at least twenty paces from any other. We strolled along Broad Street which extended from the Cooper River to the Ashley River and divided the city into two parts. We passed Church Street and Meeting Street where some of the houses were splendid palaces with pillared porticoes. The folks back in England, who thought we had been sent to a backwater colony, would never believe the grandeur of the buildings. Most people we passed greeted us in English, but I heard other languages, which John told me were Dutch or German. There were many slaves on the streets running errands and a group of native Indians watched us pass by but didn't wave. It was very different from my hometown in Stratford in the County of Essex.

I was staring all around me, pointing out to John each grand house we passed and I was not concentrating on the uneven cobblestones. I'd forgotten how strange it was to walk on dry land after weeks at sea. As we approached the Governor's house on King Street, I stumbled and turned my ankle.

John pulled me upright. 'Take my arm so we can continue, Mary-Anne,' he said. 'We must go on.'

By the time we were shown into the hallway of the Governor's house, I was noticeably limping.

We were introduced to Arthur Middleton, a tall, stiff, elderly gentleman with a long serious face, a long grey wig and a long black jacket. A young woman, about my age, in a pink dress, stood at his side. Sarah Middleton, Arthur's wife, was his total opposite, small and pale, smiling and gracious, fidgeting with her fan and patting her powdered blonde hair.

A great fuss was made about my twisted ankle. Sarah summoned a chair so I could be carried by two footmen into the small parlour off the hallway while the men went through to the Reception Room.

'We can sit in here for a while until dinner is served,' Sarah said, taking a seat on the sofa. 'The men can talk about official business while we discuss more important issues, like how exciting it is to see a new face in Charles Town!'

I asked her who would be at the dinner.

'Well, we are the only ladies today, I'm afraid. You already know Captain Douglas from the *Happy*.'

'Oh yes, he sailed with us from Jamaica. The *Happy* sloop is under John's command for his survey work.'

'And then there's Captain Anson. He's been here for four years or so. Rather a cold fish, I'm afraid.'

'What exactly does he do here?' I wanted to know all about this man John had asked me to be nice to.

'Well, he's supposed to protect the coast against pirates and Spanish privateers, but he hasn't done much of that lately. I think the most exciting thing that's happened to him was when the *Garland* arrived in the summer, fresh from the dockyard in Deptford and Captain Morris promptly died of fever. Anson took over the ship before the poor captain was cold in his bed and sent his old ship home to be broken up for timbers.'

'Is he married?'

'Oh Lord no, he's been in the Navy far too long. He prefers drinking and gambling, not that that's stopped any man from marrying. Rumour has it that when he was younger, his advances were rejected by a promising young lady in London. Now he's reserved, a bit stand-offish, when it comes to women.'

I started to wonder if it would be that easy for me to charm him for John's sake.

'And Captain Warren of the *Solebay* is passing through. And my brother Ralph, well, no one will marry him.'

'Why ever not?' I asked, wondering if her brother had some hideous deformity.

'Oh, he caused a scandal last summer. Denied he was betrothed to young Lucy Smithson. There were a lot of tears and her father had to be paid off. It's ruined her reputation, of course, and that's rather put off all the other young ladies.'

'Was there some misunderstanding on her part?'

'Ralph claims he was shocked when he heard the news of their engagement. The thought of such an arrangement had never crossed his mind.'

She laughed as if that excused him, but I worried that the young lady must have suffered humiliation and embarrassment at the rejection.

'You and your husband make up the eight. A small gathering but easier to get acquainted, don't you think?'

'Perhaps, with my twisted ankle, a quieter introduction to Charles Town society will be better,' I said.

'Oh, do say you won't be disappointed. I am in sore need of a new friend to escape my husband's circle of boring government people. Why some of them even prefer a sermon to a dance! We will be friends, won't we, Mrs Gascoigne?'

Her hands kept moving, like butterflies, checking her lace necklace and her silk petticoats. I took her hands to stop their anxious flight and calm her.

'Of course we will and please call me Mary-Anne.'

She told me that she was the Governor's second wife. 'No one in Charles Town likes me. His first wife, Sarah Amory, died six years ago,' she whispered as if we might be overheard, but when I looked around, there was no one else in the room. 'She was well-liked and much respected around here and I fear everyone thinks I am such a frivolous replacement. Still, my father is a friend of Arthur's and it was all arranged when I was nineteen. What do they expect? I try so hard, but I fear I will never live up to Sarah Amory's grace and accomplishments.'

My heart went out to this young woman, married to a man more than thirty years her senior, living in the shadow of his former wife. Before I could reassure her that I would not find her lacking, the door suddenly burst open and a small child ran to Sarah and put his chubby arms around her knees.

'Thomas, what are you doing downstairs? Where is Abigail? She's supposed to be taking care of you.' The child grasped her more tightly and buried his head in her skirts. 'Mary-Anne, meet my son, Thomas. He's four years old and my pride and joy.'

A maid rushed in to take young Thomas away. Sarah apologised for the interruption, but I assured her that I loved children.

'Now we are settled in Charles Town for a few years, John and I are going to start our family.' Somehow telling her made it sound as if it was really going to happen.

'Oh, families!' she said, raising her eyebrows. 'I have inherited three step-children from Sarah Amory. William is eighteen, Henry eleven and Hester nine. They all hate me, of course, and tell me I will never replace their mother.'

Two footmen arrived to carry me on my chair through to the dining room. As I entered, a young man, standing apart from the other men, stepped forward and introduced himself as Sarah's younger brother, Ralph Wilkinson.

'Mrs Gascoigne, what a wonderfully dramatic entrance. You are a queen on her throne. Come and sit opposite me and I will pay you the homage you deserve. I have no doubt you will enliven this rather dull company.'

He took my hand and bowed low to kiss it gently. His fingers were long and slim, his nails clean and manicured. His long fair hair was unwigged and casually tied in a ponytail with a black silk ribbon. He carried off his ruffled shirt and elaborate silk waistcoat with a lazy insouciance as if he couldn't care less about his appearance despite the time and attention he had clearly spent to get it right. My sister Betty would, no doubt, have tutted loudly and called him a fop. I wanted to dislike him for being dishonourable to his would-be fiancée, but I liked him immediately. He seemed a fun, jovial sort of young man who smiled easily.

At dinner, I sat next to Captain Peter Warren of HMS *Solebay*, the ship that had brought news of the Peace to Kingston back in June. We discussed our memories of Jamaica. He was pleasant company, due to sail back to England in a few days once repairs to his ship were completed and he offered to take any letters I wished to send home. I thanked him and assured him I would write to my family that evening to let them know of our safe arrival.

On my other side was Captain George Anson. He was a similar age to John, some might call him handsome with his long straight nose, high forehead and dark eyes, but he was reserved and awkward in his conversation with me. His manners were polite but rather old-fashioned and, as Sarah had warned me, he was rather a cold fish. As I helped him to the numerous dishes of meat and poultry, fish and crayfish, beans and vegetables, pies and puddings, I asked him about his position as post-captain.

'My principal duty is to cruise along the coastline two or three times a year for the protection of the merchant ships coming in and out of Charles Town. Other than that, there's not a lot for me to do these days,' he admitted. 'Rather frustrating that the pirates have all been hung and the Spanish Fleet virtually eliminated in the war.'

'Yes, we all noticed the *Garland* is moored in harbour for most of the year,' Ralph muttered.

I was surprised at this rebuke, but Captain Anson ignored the comment and told me of his life in Charles Town. He was fond of music and dancing and even extolled the virtues of evenings at the gaming table. I sensed he was almost jealous that John had a useful survey mission to keep him occupied. He had been investing in land around Charles Town. Captain Warren had also speculated in land purchases in Carolina and the pair of them encouraged John to do the same. The gentlemen were excited by the prospect of the riches to be had from owning rice plantations.

I was not part of the men's conversation and turned my attention to Sarah and her brother seated opposite me. I asked them if they had any other siblings. Ralph told me they had an elder brother, the heir to the family fortune from plantations, which left him to live a life of leisure. I detected some frustration in the off-hand way he said this as if he was not sure that a life of leisure was what he wanted.

Ralph knew all the latest gossip about local dignitaries and their wives. He was most amusing and it made a refreshing change from talk of land acquisition or trade initiatives. The way he and Sarah talked excitedly at the same time reminded me of my sisters chatting at the dinner table.

At the head of the table the Governor, Arthur Middleton, sat next to John as his guest of honour and Captain William Douglas sat at the far end. Middleton talked to John with great enthusiasm about his plans to encourage the growth of the Colony. He was keen to strengthen the defences on the Southern Frontier and he encouraged John to start his surveys in Port Royal Harbour as soon as possible.

'You could not have arrived at a more opportune time, Captain Gascoigne. Port Royal is the frontier of our great colony, the buffer between us and the Spanish. We must bolster our defences to control the Indians to the south and discourage incursions into our territory. Last year the inhabitants of Granville County petitioned for a military force and we built an army garrison at Beaufort to protect the harbour, but we still need further reinforcements. Any coercive action we take against the Indians could bring about reprisals.'

'The coast of Carolina is in sore need of more accurate charts,' John told him. 'On our passage here, we steered into Edisto Inlet, mistaking it for the approach to Charles Town harbour. I sent my Lieutenant in the pinnace to fetch out a pilot. He was told that Charles Town was some fourteen leagues to the northward.'

Captain Warren nodded. 'A common mistake, resulting in some unfortunate shipwrecks. Even the oldest traders are frequently deceived upon this coast. And there's no chance of getting a pilot to come out at Port Royal, which makes crossing the Bar there quite treacherous.'

'Your survey will be a vital contribution to the Colony, Captain Gascoigne,' Middleton said encouragingly. 'We need to establish Port Royal as our second great harbour after Charles Town. Reliable charts will open up trade and settlement.'

To assist John's endeavours he agreed to supply the *Alborough* with ten barrels of gunpowder, as much as could be spared from the Magazine in town. 'And I'll order Colonel Beamour and Major Hazard of the Beaufort garrison at Port Royal to put two scout boats under your direction for as long as you need.'

John was delighted. 'Scout boats will be of great assistance in my survey of the Harbour.'

Not wanting to be left out, Captain Anson agreed to come to the *Alborough* the next morning to give an official condemnation of the gunpowder. The men were all excited about preparations for John's survey mission and the talk was all about getting supplies. Anson said he could arrange for the agent victualler at Charles Town to send provisions to the *Alborough* every two months.

'That would assist me greatly,' John said, 'and I will make plans to leave for Port Royal at the earliest dispatch.'

I could feel the ground sliding away beneath me. It was a repeat of our arrival in Jamaica all over again. John's only concern was to follow orders and start his surveys as soon as possible. He had no time to sort out a house for me to live in.

'Will you be leaving so soon, John?' I asked. 'Where will I live while you are away?'

Everyone turned to look at me as if I was a problem to be solved.

Sarah declared that I must stay with her at The Oaks, Arthur Middleton's plantation north of Charles Town, but I was hesitant after my experience in Jamaica. I wanted to get a home that John and I could share when he returned from his survey work.

To my surprise, it was Captain Anson who came to my rescue.

'I own several houses in the town which I rent out. There are always planters who want a place in town and merchants who visit on business.'

He turned to John. 'It would be my pleasure to assist your beautiful wife, Gascoigne. I would be happy to put one of my houses at your disposal. I have a single house at the south end of Church Street, the genteel end. It's too small for the planters and their large families but would suit a young lady on her own.'

'I would appreciate that, Anson,' John replied on my behalf. 'I fear I won't have the time or opportunity to arrange anything else. I need to ready my ship for departure.'

'Oh, it's no trouble,' he said. 'As Station Commander, it's my job to look after your wife while you're away. I would be delighted to offer her every assistance.'

I was a little nervous about the way he said that and when he reached out his hand to pat mine, I slipped my arm under the table so he couldn't touch me. I didn't want to be looked after by Anson, but I didn't want to upset John by refusing him. Still, a house in town would be pleasant for me and convenient for John when the *Alborough* returned from surveying Port Royal Harbour.

I caught Ralph's eye. He had been watching Anson closely as if he too sensed danger. He smiled at me and I was almost certain he winked.

'Don't worry about Mary-Anne,' Ralph said to Anson. 'She will not be left on her own. Sarah and I will sweep her up into our hectic whirl of social engagements in Charles Town, won't we dear sister?'

'Oh yes,' Sarah agreed. 'Now, you will need servants. Captain Gascoigne, you must go to the slave auction house and get Mary-Anne a cook, a maid and a houseboy at the very least.'

'I'm not sure I'll have time for that before I set sail,' John muttered. I knew he was reluctant to go to a slave auction after what we had seen in Kingston. 'Anson, does the house not come with servants? We may only be here a year or two, depending on how long my survey takes.'

'No,' Anson said, shaking his head. 'The planters and merchants bring their own households.'

'Dearest Sister, surely you have some slaves to spare?' Ralph asked. 'Can't you hire a couple out to Captain and Mrs Gascoigne?'

Sarah looked at him and I could see her thinking. 'Well now you mention it, there are a couple of servants I have no use for at present. A cook and a houseboy that used to work for Sarah Amory. They're not much use now and I have my own servants who are more useful. Arthur, could we not hire them to the Captain for a year or two?'

Arthur jumped at the opportunity to make money out of unwanted slaves. 'I am sure we can come to an arrangement,' he said.

'Oh, and take Bess. She can be your housemaid. I don't like her attitude. She's much too proud. Slaves should be meek and grateful, shouldn't they? We feed them and give them a place to live. Surely, it's not too much to expect them to be grateful, is it? I should be able to expect that, shouldn't I?' She looked around the table for agreement.

Ralph nearly choked on his wine. 'Oh yes dear sister, they should indeed be grateful. Especially that they work in your house and not out on your plantation, clearing the trees and digging ditches in the midday sun.'

The assembled company stared at him as if he had gone mad and said something quite ridiculous, but I remembered seeing the slaves working on Caroline's plantation in Jamaica and the brutal look of the overseer.

Sarah laughed to alleviate the tension. 'Well Peggy and Quame are too old for that and you'd be hard-pressed to get Bess to do any hard work.'

And so it was settled, John would hire these three slaves to help me in the house for a year or two at great expense, although from Sarah's description I was slightly nervous that they might not be worth it. Sarah and I retired from the dining room so the men could continue their drinking while we ladies enjoyed a hand of cards and discussed my new life in Charles Town.

On our way back to the ship, I couldn't help smiling. What an excellent result from the dinner. John had his new gunpowder and help with supplies. I had a house in town and friends to go out with in Society. Life in Charles Town would truly be everything I hoped for.

John departed on 23rd December 1728, to commence his survey of Port Royal Harbour, some 100 miles to the south.

From the Captain's Log, HMS Alborough
3rd January 1729
Port Royal Harbour, South Carolina.
    "Moderate gales & foggy weather with rain. At 3PM the fog cleared up and I went and measured the Marsh Island within Beaufort River and its distance from the shore on either side. The island itself is a morass so soft that will not bear the weight of a man. At daylight very thick fog and rain came on which continues till noon. From the accounts of the officers of the Garrison at Beaufort and the inhabitants about the settlement gave me that there is a good deal of reason to apprehend my boats may be attacked by the Indians and Spaniards of Saint Augustine who come frequently in long armed periaguas and cut off the inhabitants of these settlements hereabouts and what boats they could meet with as often as they have had fair opportunities. As I have had but one Lieutenant and the Master of the ship being a very infirm man, I gave Mr Ashby Utting, one of my midshipmen an order to act as Second Lieutenant till further order."

Records show that the winter of 1728/29 was particularly cold on the Eastern seaboard of America. The sailors also feared wild animals in the unexplored islands.

From the Captain's Log, HMS Alborough
10th January 1729
Anchored just within the Bar of Port Royal Harbour.
    "PM The weather being moderate I sounded with all the Boats & having found the Pitch of the Sand called Martin's Industry, laid a Buoy on it and another on the very SW point of the Shoal. In the night it blew very hard & continues to blow so hard till noon & there is so great a Sea that we cannot work in any Boats. The flags on Hilton Head, Scarborough Head and Phillips's Point are all flying, as we are obliged to leave them without any Body ashore to attend them, these Islands abounding with Tygers, Bears and other Beasts of Prey (in the winter season) as we perceive by great Numbers of fresh & old marks of their feet up on the sands all along the Shore."

10

T he day John left for Port Royal, on the southern frontier of South Carolina, I moved into Captain Anson's rental house on Church Street. It was small by Charles Town standards. Anson called it "*a single house*". It was built side-on to the street to make the most of the long narrow plot and catch the breeze blowing in from the harbour. The front door on the street didn't open into the hall as one might have expected, but onto a long porch or "*piazza*" as it was called in Charles Town, running along one side of the house. It was a shady space furnished with comfortable chairs and sofas. Halfway along the porch was the front door into the house. A side gate led down a narrow driveway in front of the porch to the yard at the back where there was a stable block and kitchen, with slave quarters built above.

Sarah visited me the day I moved in. She stepped through the front door and looked left to the reception room overlooking the street and right to the parlour at the rear. Up the central staircase was a formal drawing room at the front for entertaining away from the dust and noise of the street and there was a bedroom at the back. On the next floor, there were two smaller bedrooms, suitable for children.

'It's a very small house, Mary-Anne,' she exclaimed. 'You certainly won't be able to hold any grand dinners here. Anyway, look, I've brought your house slaves with me.'

Three Africans dutifully followed her into the house and Sarah led them straight through and out the back door to the yard.

'Peggy is a good enough cook and can run the kitchen quite adequately, but don't try to teach her anything new. She has resisted all my attempts to change her repertoire of dishes. And what suited Sarah Amory doesn't suit me at all.'

She looked at the cook accusingly as if she had made this point many times in the past and it had always gone unheeded. Peggy, a plump, elderly woman with a colourful scarf around her hair and her few possessions in a woven basket balanced on her head, didn't raise her eyes or acknowledge the rebuke. Only time would tell if her repertoire of dishes suited me.

'Quame can look after the yard and run errands for you.'

His ageing, skinny body and grey hair gave me no great expectations that he would run anywhere, but he looked willing enough.

'I tried to give him a proper name,' Sarah continued, 'but he only seems to answer to the name of Quame, which is what he went by in his own country.'

Bess, the housemaid, had been standing quietly, but she suddenly spoke up. 'Where he comes from, they name children after the day they were born. His name means born on Saturday. He don't want to change it,' she said as if that settled the matter.

Sarah looked shocked at being spoken to. Bess was roughly my age, tall and strong. The name of our Good Queen Bess suited her proud, regal bearing. Her hair was a mass of black curls and her face was long and thin, with huge dark eyes, that watched you warily as if she was waiting for the next slap or punch.

'Well, we'll see how you get on with that one,' Sarah said as she turned on her heels to return indoors. 'And that old lady watching us from next door looks pretty fierce.'

I ignored her comment about my kind neighbour, Mrs McAndrews.

Jean McAndrews had introduced herself as soon as I had arrived. She was a small, busy Scottish woman, earnest in her desire to help, which might appear rather overwhelming to some people. Of course, I was the ideal candidate for her attention as I needed all the help I could get.

She was married to the churchwarden at St Philip's Church. She and her husband had come to the new colony of Carolina over twenty years ago from Aberdeen, hoping to find a better life and more souls to convert to Christianity. So far, she admitted, her husband hadn't converted any of the native Indians and seemed resigned to caring for the congregation of townsfolk. Her two sons had grown up and returned to England so she devoted her time to charitable works through a Ladies' Society at the church which I promised I would join, just to please her.

Captain Anson arrived the next day to make sure I had settled in comfortably. I thanked him profusely and he assured me he was delighted to do me a favour. Remembering Caroline's disappointment in my home-making skills, I mentioned to him that the house was sparsely furnished.

'I usually rent it out to merchants and planters who want a bed in town for the night, not young ladies who want a comfortable home,' he said and he encouraged me to add whatever furnishings I wanted to make it more to my taste.

I got busy buying pretty, soft furnishings to make his house my home. It was surprising what turned up on the ships from England, glazed cotton fabrics for drapes and curtains, woven rugs from the Orient, tapestries, china tea sets, cushions, couches and down quilts. Sarah was pleased to donate some beautiful ornaments that once belonged to Sarah Amory. My favourite was a tall vase of blue Oriental porcelain, which I proudly displayed on a table in the hallway.

Despite being conveniently located in the centre of Charles Town, once I stepped through the door from the street, the porch was shady and quiet. The house was big enough for John to use the front room as his study and the bedrooms in the attic would be perfect for our children.

'Are you sure about this?' Ralph asked when he visited. Disappointment was written clearly on his face. 'It's hardly the grand house a Captain in His Majesty's Navy should aspire to.'

'It's perfect for me,' I told him. 'I like living in the town with people around and I can easily walk to Bay Street to catch the breeze and watch out for John's ship returning.'

One cold day in January, Sarah arranged a grand dinner at the Governor's house and invited a selection of politicians, planters and merchants who hoped to gain favour with the Governor. She begged me to come as her friend to keep her company. She took her role as the elderly Governor's wife seriously, but I found her efforts to win over the worthies of Charles Town rather pretentious. Still, she was a good friend to me and filled the lack of sisters in my life.

Ralph had offered to escort me, which was kind of him as I wouldn't have wanted to go on my own and Ralph was the perfect escort, funny, attentive and good-looking. That day his fair hair was loose, curling onto his shoulders. Under his thick overcoat, he was dressed in a frilly jabot at his neck and a frock coat cut away to reveal a fancy silk waistcoat. His cane was suspended by a loop from one of the waistcoat buttons leaving his gloved hands free to easily hold his snuff box or his handkerchief, making the cane more fashionable than useful.

'We'll look after each other,' he told me as I pulled on my warmest cape and bonnet and arranged my hair to curl prettily over my shoulder. 'I'll protect you from any unwelcome attention while you protect me from over-zealous young women.'

'What unwelcome attention will I attract?'

'Don't make me flatter you on your charming looks, Mary-Anne,' he teased and I blushed.

I knew his broken engagement to Lucy Smithson made him wary of young unmarried women assuming too much. The arrangement seemed to suit us both.

'Perhaps we could give the Governor's lunch a miss and go to one of the taverns,' he said. 'There's a theatre production at Shepheard's Tavern we could enjoy.'

'We must go. Sarah is expecting us to attend so she will have some friends to talk to.'

'I know, but old Middleton is such a bore. If he goes on and on about civil order and immigrants again, I shall have to get up and walk out, whether I've finished my lunch or not.'

'Aren't you interested in what's happening in Charles Town?'

'Only the gossip, Mary-Anne. Politics and business bore me.'

We laughed as we stroll arm-in-arm down the street. I imagined this was what it would have been like if I'd had a brother. I worried what would become of Ralph, with no prospects of inheriting and no career in the military, politics or business. Sarah told me that he had lost the chance of a career in a lawyer's office, but his father's allowance would not last forever.

Sarah was waiting for us and when we arrived she pushed us into the parlour off the hallway.

'Ralph, I must warn you that old man Smithson is here.'

I recognised the name of Lucy's father.

'He's come as a guest of Captain Anson,' she said. 'Apparently, they are business partners in some property deals. Please don't make a scene and embarrass me, will you, brother?'

'Why should I make a scene? It was his daughter who spread rumours about me and the old man was paid off handsomely for her mistake.'

'Well, stay out of his way and behave nicely, Ralph. For my sake. Smithson is an influential landowner and Arthur needs all the support he can get at the moment.'

'Is he still struggling to get his reforms through the Assembly?'

'Oh, you know how it is. All politicians have their own self-interest to guard. Everyone's arguing about how best to solve the problems and now the Assembly has stopped meeting.'

Ralph looked at me and raised his eyebrows. 'And you wonder why I don't follow politics. They would probably prefer it if some aristocratic lord from England turned up and told them what to do.'

'Don't say that Ralph,' Sarah said. 'There is talk of another Royal appointment being sent out to replace Arthur as Governor.'

'Disaster, dear sister. What will you do if you lose your position as the Governor's Wife?'

'I care nothing for my position. It's Arthur I worry about. All this dissension is making him unwell.'

We went through to the reception and accepted drinks of mint julep from the waiting footmen. I saw Captain Anson immediately as he was tall and imposing in his naval uniform. He was talking to a short, ugly man with a bulbous nose and a rotund stomach. If that was Mr Smithson, I hoped his daughter got her looks from her mother.

Captain Anson saw me and started to approach, but when he spotted Ralph at my side, he turned away and found someone else to talk to. Three ladies came over and introduced themselves, interested in finding out about the new arrival in town.

They cooed and simpered as they told me their latest news of babies and children. Mrs Ogilvie had had her fifth child, yet another daughter! Young Master Braithwaite was off to Eton school in the summer. Miss Fanshawe had got her first pony. They finally noticed I was not joining in and asked politely where my husband was this evening. I told them he was away surveying Port Royal Harbour. I didn't tell them that was the reason I hadn't got any children to boast about.

'Aren't you worried about him being on the Southern Frontier? The people there are constantly under threat from runaway slaves or worse, the Indians from St. Augustine,' said one.

'I heard they plan to murder all the white people and plunder their plantations,' her friend added.

'Oh yes, the Spanish give them rifles and encourage them,' she replied.

'Mrs Hayward's nephew is in the militia at Beaufort. He told her the local inhabitants are quite wretched with fear,' said the third.

They delighted in telling me all about the perils at Port Royal. Ralph seemed to sense I didn't need to hear their tales about the dangerous Southern Frontier and he took me off to the buffet table.

'Don't worry, Mary-Anne,' he said reassuringly. 'Your husband is the captain of a large British warship. No one will dare challenge him. He can always pull up his anchor and sail back to Charles Town. It's not like the locals who can't leave their plantations, although quite why they want to live in that backwater is beyond me.'

'But the Governor said he was keen to develop Port Royal as the second port of Carolina. He encouraged John to go and do the survey.'

'I suppose ports are important if you want to get goods to and from Philadelphia or Boston or across to Europe.'

He seemed to lose interest in discussing the development of Port Royal and excused himself to talk to his friends. I was left alone, trying not to worry about John.

I wondered if I should be nice to Captain Anson while I had the opportunity. He might go in his ship and check the *Alborough* was safe or even take a letter to John from me.

I put on my best smile and went over to him. He seemed delighted to see me and took my hand in his and asked, 'How are you settling into my house?'

'Very well,' I told him and I invited him to come round and see how I had furnished it. As he accepted my offer, he squeezed my hand before releasing it reluctantly.

A little flustered at the long hand holding, I swallowed hard and changed the subject by asking, 'Have you had any news of John?'

He told me that earlier that week John sent one of the scout boats to Charles Town by way of the inland waterway to get provisions for the boatmen. Colonel Beaumour, who was in charge of the Army garrison at Beaufort, had refused to victual them while they were working for the Navy.

'I sent them straight back again,' he said. 'I have no directions about victualling the men belonging to the scout boats. They are the Army's responsibility.'

Poor John, he always had such care for his men, but he couldn't take food from the sailor's allowance on the *Alborough*. It would upset him to see the boatmen so badly treated. He'd probably send the scout boats home and manage without them, rather than see them destitute. I felt Captain Anson could have helped him more.

'At least it means John is well,' was all I could think of to say.

'The boatmen said it was extremely cold. Some had frostbite in their fingers and feet.'

I was beginning to wish I hadn't asked him for news. I asked him if he had any plans to patrol the coastline to check all was well, but he said he was rather busy at the moment.

I turned away to hide my disappointment and seized the opportunity caused by the lull in conversation to go and talk to Sarah. She was fretting about her husband's position as he seemed to be losing the support of the Assembly.

I had nothing to say on local politics, but I reassured her that Arthur's governorship was safe. I couldn't imagine anyone who could uphold his authority with more restrained tact and firmness.

'I have no clear idea on how to be his wife, how to support him in his work or be a comfort to him.'

I started to tell her that I felt the same way about John, with his long absences at sea, when we were interrupted by shouting at the far side of the room. We pushed our way through the crowd of guests, who had all turned to see what was going on. Captain Anson was poking Ralph in the chest as he made various accusations.

'That young lady will never live down the disgrace, but it's hard to imagine why she should want to marry you. You are the worst sort of man, the sort I detest, the sort we don't want in the King's Navy.'

Ralph was as tall as Anson and looked him square in the face.

'If I am that sort of man, then you know I would never have suggested marriage. I was being pleasant to an unfortunate girl, neglected by her friends at that infernal ball and my attentions were misconstrued. She spun a proposal of marriage out of girlish daydreams, not from anything I said to her.' Ralph waved his hands as if spinning a web of the young lady's daydreams between his fingers.

Mr Smithson joined in the attack on Ralph.

'You are a disgrace to polite society. I'm surprised you show your face. You are only tolerated as the Governor's brother-in-law but that won't last. When Middleton's out of favour, you will have no such advantages.'

Sarah had heard enough and barged between the men.

'Gentlemen, I will not have my brother or any other guest treated in such a way. I must ask you, Mr Smithson, to take your leave. Perhaps you should go too, Captain Anson.'

As they shuffled off, I saw them exchanging handshakes and nods with other worthies and I feared for Ralph. Sarah had rescued him this time, but Smithson and Anson were influential people in Charles Town and not accustomed to being dismissed. Arthur would not be happy to lose their support in this precarious time while he clung on to power.

I watched Sarah take Ralph into the parlour and approached the open door in case I could give my friends any comfort. I could see Ralph sitting with his head in his hands, clearly upset by Sarah's remonstrations.

'Brother, you must find a wife if you want to stop these rumours and accusations.'

'How can I? I would need to find a wife who does not want children.'

'You will have to take a wife eventually. If only for appearance's sake. Think of your family's reputation, even if you care nothing for your own.'

I couldn't understand why Ralph would not want children. What woman would agree to such a condition in marriage? We were nothing in Society without children, as I was finding out. I felt quite distressed by all the commotion and slipped quietly out of the house unnoticed.

The following week, Captain Anson called round for tea and admired what I had done to his house. He was polite and didn't mention the unpleasantness with Ralph. Instead he told me, as he settled into my comfortable sofa in the parlour and drank tea from my beautiful china cups, that a sloop called the *Pearl* had arrived in Charles Town Harbour.

'The Master, Robert Bloodworth, spoke with Captain Gascoigne in Port Royal Harbour. The *Pearl* sailed from Jamaica last June bound for New York, under the convoy of HMS *Fox*. He left the convoy in the Gulf of Florida desiring to get sooner home and was taken the same day by a Spanish privateer out of Saint Augustine from where he has only just escaped. They were very ill-treated by the Spaniards.'

'Any news of John? Is he safe and well? Surely he's in no danger from the Spanish?'

Anson finished his tea slowly as if he wanted to delay telling me the news.

'Bloodworth said they were struggling in the bad weather. They've had thick fogs, hard rain and gales, much worse than we've had in Charles Town. The crew are scared to go ashore. They say the islands abound with tigers, bears and other beasts of prey.'

So, not just attacks by Indians and runaway slaves. Now I had to worry about Spanish pirates, frostbite and wild beasts as well. I cleared away the tea to get rid of Captain Anson before he told me any more news.

As he left, he touched my arm. 'I hope I have not alarmed you, Mrs Gascoigne. I would never do anything to upset you. If there is anything I can do to assist you in your husband's absence, please do not hesitate to ask me.'

I smiled sweetly and thanked him for his concern. I wanted to beg him again to sail down to Port Royal and check on the *Alborough*, but he had already told me he was too busy. Every night I prayed John was safe and well. I missed him so much and longed for him to come home soon.

For the next few weeks my time was taken up by Ralph, who had become a frequent visitor to my small house that he was so critical of at the start. Despite his earlier disdain, he seemed to enjoy sitting out on my porch, lazing for hours on end sipping rum and lime juice. Sarah berated him for causing a disturbance at her luncheon and upsetting influential guests. He was nervous to go out in Society after his abuse from Anson and Smithson and was convinced they were spreading bad rumours about him. Rather dramatically, he anticipated one of their henchmen would put a dagger into his ribs in an alley one dark night.

'You heard them, Mary-Anne. They threatened revenge. It's not my fault Lucy Smithson is so ugly that she'll never find another suitor. Yet they blame me for showing her some pity and dancing with her, just once mind, at Mrs Manigault's Ball. I am scared to talk to any unmarried lady now.'

He wasn't scared to talk to me and over the weeks, we became good friends. We couldn't help each other with our deepest concerns, my lack of children and his lack of employment, but he was easy company and our chat was light-hearted as we offered a friendly distraction from our worries.

Some days Ralph would walk with me to Bay Street to look in vain for the *Alborough*, but he didn't want to promenade for long. Without his usual whirl of social engagements, he was lethargic and tired. He no longer knew the latest gossip, he no longer preened his appearance, he no longer enjoyed his life in Charles Town and preferred to while away his time at my house.

My neighbour, Mrs McAndrews, popped in to check I was coping and pretended to be surprised to find Ralph still there, lazing on my couch, reading a book.

'Is your house the home for lost souls?' she asked.

Who was she talking about? Ralph or me?

John was determined to find a safe channel for ships to enter Port Royal Harbour, whether across the Bar or via Dawfoskee Creek to the west of Trench's Island (now called Hilton Head).

From the Captain's Log, HMS Alborough
10ᵗʰ February 1729
At anchor off Hilton Head in Port Royal Harbour, South Carolina.

    "PM We Row'd up the West side of Paris's island till we brought Skull Creek open. Sounded across to it & measured the Entrance of it & found it to be 158 fathom broad with 5 fathom in the Mid-Channel & to shoal gradually towards each Side, from thence Row'd over to the North End of Mackey's Island, which I Situated & found the Entrance to be 106 fathom broad & steep to. There has been a Fortification here to defend this passage, which runs down into Dawfoskee River by the West side of this island, as Skull Creek does on the East side of it. Therefore 'tis necessary to Enquire whether there is not a better Inlet for Vessels of Draught into this Harbour through these Creeks & whether if the Fort were Raised here again, this might not be a more Convenient Place for careening than the Look- out Creek. Having situated this point we sounded over in a Direct Line to Daw's Great Island, which has Deep water close to it. But by the time we got to Dolphin Head 'twas dark. At Break of Day it blew too hard for the Boats to work. At 10 proving more Moderate, put off with all the boats and sounded from the Ship toward Skull Island on the Shoal which runs from Daw's to find a Swatch I have heard of through it & the Exact Channel between it and the Islands."

The survey of Port Royal Harbour took six months, such was John's dedication. The constant exposure to bad weather made him very ill.

From the Captain's Log, HMS Alborough
21ˢᵗ April 1729
Just within the Bar of Port Royal Harbour, South Carolina.

    "PM Sounded the Inside of the South Channel & having found the two points which make the Entrance into it from the Sea & laid a Buoy on each of them, from thence Sounded in a direct line to the Ship. We were oblig'd to Steer NE notwithstanding the True line is N17W. The Flood sets so strong athwart the Channel so that, if there should be found a good Navigable Channel here, 'twill be Impossible to make use of it with Safety without Fixed Marks on the Land. Ever since my return to the Ship last night I have been so afflicted with a Violent Pain in my head, that I have not been able to go out of my Cabin and my Legs are swelled very much by sitting so continually in the Boat."

11

T he bitterly cold winter dragged on and I spent my time quietly at home, reading and embroidering. If I had no visitors or lunches to attend, the days stretched out into long, lonely evenings. How I missed my mother and sisters, the constant company and incessant chatter of my childhood. Before long I asked Bess if she would sit with me when she had finished her work. At first, she sat quietly in the corner, cleaning or mending. She was a quiet and reassuring presence and she gradually became my companion in the empty hours and days waiting for John to come home.

It wasn't long before we started chatting. I told her all about my life in Stratford and after much encouragement, she told me stories about her life before she came to Carolina. She had been a young woman of fifteen or sixteen when she was kidnapped from her village in Africa by men with muskets and made to walk for days in chains to the coast where she was shackled below decks on one of those dreadful Guineaman ships. She had been separated from her family on the long march and had never seen her parents or brothers and sisters again. From my own experience of crossing the Atlantic, it was unbelievable that she survived the conditions she described and many times during her stories I wondered if she was exaggerating to gain my pity. Surely if it was as bad as she said, the Admiralty in London would have done something about it. I vowed to write to Papa and ask him to look into it.

I often heard Peggy in the backyard, singing as she went about her tasks. I couldn't understand the strange words, but the slow, sad tunes reflected my own feelings of loneliness in a foreign land. When I asked Bess what the songs were, she told me they were lullabies. She said Peggy had lost her three children. I didn't like to ask how.

When I told Sarah about their stories of the ill-treatment, she said, 'You shouldn't talk to your slaves so much.'

'Why ever not? I used to talk to our cook and housemaids all the time at home in Stratford. And it's not all about torture and beatings, Quame tells me exciting tales about his home in Africa. He's seen lions, like Daniel in the lion's den.'

'Well, this is not Stratford and I don't suppose your houseboy was an African. Truthfully, Mary-Anne, it's best if you don't think about the slave ships. I don't. We need the Africans to clear the swamp forests and dig the ditches and plant the rice on our plantations. The local Indians are not as strong and hard-working and the Africans know all about rice production from their home country. But I'll admit, Arthur has told me those Guineaman Captains are the roughest sort of sailor.'

She resumed her reading of the magazine on her lap. It was the Ladies Diary, the Woman's Almanack, last year's edition which had been sent to her from London by a distant cousin. She was fascinated by the mathematical puzzles.

She proudly read from the cover, "*Containing many Delightful and Entertaining Particulars, Peculiarly Adapted for the Use and Diversion of the Fair-Sex. The magazine promises the women who read it that the cultivation of their minds will increase their attractiveness. Wit join'd to Beauty lead more Captive than the Conqu'ring Sword.*"

'Do you need wit to hold Arthur captive?' I asked.

'I am improving my mind,' she said, defensively. 'And it's not just mathematical questions. It gives all the usual calendar and astronomical observations.'

'For last year,' I pointed out.

She gave me a sideways look and continued, undeterred. 'And,' she lowered her voice to a whisper, 'it gives a calendar for marriage.'

'Oh, is there something I should know?'

'Well, it gives the dates when marriage is discouraged in the church calendar. It gives the exact dates you should not share your bed with your husband. Look here, it says "*Marriage goes out in Lent, on Sundays and on Fast Days.*"

'For last year,' I pointed out but still, no one had told me this.

'I'll let you have my copy of the magazine when I've completed the puzzles.'

I vowed to keep it handy. Sarah was indeed a good friend, in the absence of such advice from my mother. Thankfully John had been away during Lent in the two years since we married, so perhaps the Good Lord was not too displeased by my wifely behaviour. Still, with so many restrictions, my chances of falling pregnant were diminishing.

My household settled into a quiet routine. Quame kept busy sweeping the porch and feeding the chickens in the backyard, mending the rattling windows, running errands around town and carrying everything Peggy bought at the market. He declared that he would guard the women of the house while the Master was away so he slept every night on a makeshift bed near the gate, although I feared at his age he would not be much deterrent to any cut-throats who meant us harm.

Peggy's recipes seemed to suit my taste and palate, as they had pleased the former Mrs Middleton, and Bess needed no further instruction from me. She knew how to clean the house from top to bottom, scrub the floors, wash the linens, polish the silverware and serve at the table. She also looked after my clothes, helped me dress and arranged my hair, so I didn't have to worry about finding a Lady's maid. I spent much of my time in her company and we seemed to rub along quite amiably, although possibly because I didn't tell her what to do or how to do it. At home in Stratford, Mama and Betty had looked after the domestic arrangements and dealt with the servants, while I daydreamed of my wedding day. Not that that had done much good as it turned out.

At the start of February, Janet joined our household. A small, stocky Scottish lass, with a halo of frizzy red hair, she was under eighteen and over six months pregnant. She had arrived in Charles Town with her brother, Hamish, a year ago as an indentured servant in search of a better life than a small croft in the Scottish Highlands could offer. As one of eight children, there was not enough food to go around at home. Indentured servants had to work for seven years in exchange for their sea passage, board and lodgings and their freedom at the end, but everyone knew that their life was not an easy one and not many survived the indentured period.

Janet's master owned a rice plantation outside Charles Town. Her brother was employed to oversee the slaves working in the fields whilst Janet, unfortunately, caught the eye of the Master. Once she fell pregnant, the Lady of the House did not want her around and cast Janet out on the streets. Competition from unpaid slaves meant housework was hard to find for a poor white girl, especially one whose belly was starting to swell. Mrs McAndrews found her begging in the street.

'You've got a spare room so you can easily take her in,' Mrs McAndrews declared.

I couldn't argue with the force that was Mrs McAndrews.

Janet helped Peggy and Bess around in the house and despite her condition, even helped Quame in the yard. We all got on peaceably as the weeks rolled by and there was still no sign of the *Alborough* on my daily walks to Bay Street. I was beginning to wonder if John would ever return and find me in my small house on Church Street. Perhaps he had forgotten he had a wife, perhaps he had sailed back to England, perhaps he had been killed by Indians or Spanish pirates or wild animals. My thoughts became confused and fanciful.

As Janet's due date approached at the start of April, I bought a wooden cot and a fine lace shawl for the baby. I started sewing a patchwork bed quilt from rags like the ones the Dutch women sold in the market. Janet slept in one of the attic bedrooms, not the slaves' quarters in the yard, so I could be near when the baby was born.

One night I heard a baby's cry and I rushed up to Janet's room. It turned out Bess knew all about delivering babies. I was sorry they hadn't woken me so I could be there for the birth, but when I saw all the blood and mess on the bedsheets, I felt faint and collapsed into a chair.

The baby was a tiny mite, but I didn't fear for him, hearing his loud cry and seeing him hungrily nuzzling at Janet's breast. His head was covered in the softest red down.

'A true Scot,' Janet announced, 'I'll call him Douglas, after my father.' From what she'd told me, I doubted her father would care much about his grandson, just another hungry mouth to feed.

We were all besotted by the newest member of our household and life outside the house was forgotten. It was as if we had drunk from a chalice of magic potion that had caused us to be spellbound. We couldn't do anything else, talk of anything else or think of anything else.

I didn't want to leave the house or have any other distractions. I didn't want to miss a moment, even though Baby Douglas didn't do much except sleep and feed at Janet's breast. When he smiled at me or held my finger in his tiny fist, my spirit lifted to Heaven.

Peggy rocked him to sleep, cuddled against her large breasts while she sang her soft lullabies. Bess was more practical and showed Janet how to feed him, wash him and wrap him in swaddling. I watched and learnt, eager for my turn. Even Quame scared the barking dogs away from the house when the baby was sleeping and more than once,

I'd caught him standing guard over his crib, batting away the flies and mosquitos.

Four weeks after Baby Douglas arrived, Janet had a visit from her brother, Hamish. They sat out in the yard for an hour, deep in conversation. That evening she asked me what would become of her and the baby when the Master returned.

'We'll all live here together,' I told her. As soon as I said it, I knew that John would not be happy with such an arrangement. People would think his forbearance in allowing a servant and her baby to live in his house indicated his guilty part in it. I wondered if she was thinking the same.

It was not yet dawn the following morning when I heard Janet moving around in her room. I wondered if she'd like me to take Baby Douglas into my bed for an hour or two so she could start on her chores, but when I entered her room, she'd dressed in her thin cape and wrapped the baby in his lace shawl.

'I never meant to wake you, Mistress. I must leave. Hamish will take me and the baby. We'll head west and find a place to settle. You mustn't tell anyone, please, Mistress.'

'You can't take the baby. It'll be dangerous. You'll be attacked by Indians and eaten by wild animals. Please don't take Douglas.'

'I have to go now.'

She started to leave and I couldn't help it, I reached out and tried to grab the baby from her. We wrestled with the tiny bundle between us, each holding onto the baby we loved, refusing to let go.

'Please leave the baby with me,' I begged. 'I promise I'll look after him and love him as if he were my own.'

'Let go! You cannot have my baby. He's all I have. I will not give him up.'

'I'll pay you. Name your price. You need the money.'

She shoved me away roughly and I fell to my knees. She clasped the baby close to her chest and pushed past me out of the door. When she turned at the top of the stairs, her look was one of pity. I collapsed in a heap on the floor, weeping. How would I survive without my daily cuddles, the sweet smell of his skin and his pudgy fingers clawing at my breast?

After a while, I calmed myself and looked around the room. She had left none of her few belongings so I knew they were not coming back. Still, I sent Quame out to search for them, but he returned at nightfall empty-handed. He had found no trace of mother or baby.

When Ralph visited the following day, I sent him out to search for them. He knew everything that went on in Charles Town and sure enough, he returned a few hours later with news.

'A group of Scotch settlers, some twenty or thirty, left Charles Town under cover of darkness early yesterday morning, trekking west in search of land. There's a hue and cry out for the indentured servants and Hamish's name was mentioned. Maybe they'll find them and bring them back. But I doubt it, by now they could be anywhere.'

I was distraught. 'Janet can't walk anywhere with a small baby.'

'They had a couple of wagons for the women, Mary-Anne. Don't fret.'

'How will they live in the wilderness? She'll starve to death until the first harvest. She won't be able to care for the baby. How could she want such a life?'

'What other life is there for her? She'll live with her brother and raise her child. If she's lucky, one of the settlers will take her as his wife. And if not, well...' His voice trailed off and I tried to imagine what her life would be if she didn't marry. She would end up as an unpaid servant in her brother's house. 'You do know she couldn't stay here, don't you?'

'She could have left the baby. I would have cared for him as if he were my own.'

'Why would you care for someone else's baby?' he asked horrified. 'Your husband would get an unwelcome surprise on his return to find you'd had a baby in his absence.'

How could I explain to Ralph that I would welcome any baby into my heart? I'd been married for two years and had begun to despair of ever having a baby of my own. Douglas could have stayed and I would have raised him as my own. I was sure John would have understood. He wanted a family too.

As well as my prayers for John, I prayed every night for Baby Douglas. When I closed my eyes at night, I saw that tiny, red-haired baby, lying in the mud outside some ramshackle shack wrapped in his fine lace shawl.

Mrs McAndrews tried to console me by telling me I helped Janet when she needed me, but I must let her go now. Her faith was strong and she trusted the Lord to take care of them. She encouraged me to

120

join her Ladies' Society at the church and help other women, but how could I help anyone else when the loss of that baby, so fleetingly in my home and in my arms, had left such a huge hole in my heart?

'I don't provide a home for lost souls,' I told her. 'I am a lost soul myself.' She smiled but didn't disagree.

Ralph went to Philadelphia to escape the summer in Charles Town, or perhaps to avoid his enemies seeking revenge. I went out with Sarah to lunches, dances and even some of the plays that were being performed in the taverns, but it was not the same after Baby Douglas left. I watched everyone else dining and dancing, laughing and chatting as if through a cloudy lens on one of John's telescopes. Women's small talk mainly centred around babies and children. I felt distant from them and all alone.

At the start of May, Captain Anson told me that the victualling agent in Charles Town had sent another two months of provisions to the *Alborough* in Port Royal Harbour. At my request, he finally agreed to cruise south on his ship, the *Garland*. He returned a week later to report that he had anchored off the South channel, seen the *Alborough* safely moored in Port Royal Harbour and sailed away at daylight the following morning. He said the sea was too rough for him to cross the Bar so he didn't speak to John or deliver my letter, but I was grateful for his report that John's ship was safe.

By the middle of May, John had been away for five months and I'd almost forgotten what he looked like. I lay awake at night alone in my bed, trying to remember the warmth of his smile, the passionate feel of his embrace, the strong smell of his body and the salty taste of his kisses. My senses were numb, like my empty womb.

HMS Alborough returned to Charles Town in May 1729 where John immediately set to work on his survey report.

From the Captain's Log, HMS Alborough
25th May 1729
At Charles Town in South Carolina
      "Little wind & hazy weather, inclinable to calm. At 2 PM anchored in Cooper River abreast of Charles Town in 6 fathom water and sat down immediately to finish my Original draught of Port Royal Harbour in Order to make a fair Draught from it for my Lords of the Admiralty. We found riding here His Majesty's Ships Garland & Dursley Galley and 53 Merchant Vessels. My Company are very sickly, lying so long at Port Royal without Refreshments, several of whom I have sent ashore to Quarters, some immediately upon my arrival."

The hurricane season, from July to October, restricted sailing in the summer months.

From the Captain's Log, HMS Alborough
29th July 1729
At Charles Town in South Carolina
      "The cloudy uncertain weather we have had for some time past, has given every Body here both afloat and ashore, such apprehensions of a hurricane (which have usually happen'd about this Season) that the Station'd Ships are Stripped & the merchant Ships have all left the Town & are gone up the Rivers for their better security and all inhabitants of the Town are Securing their Windows & Doors, to bear the Fury of it. Wherefore we began to Unrig also. There happened a very Severe hurricane last Year on the 1st of August, by which all the wall of the Town was beaten down and many Ships lost."

12

One morning at the end of May, Quame came rushing in with the news I had long been waiting for.

'The *Alborough* has arrived! She came over the Bar this morning and anchored in Cooper River this afternoon just abreast of the town,' he told me. 'The Master is home,' he shouted to Peggy and Bess.

He was excited. They all were. They hadn't met Captain John Gascoigne, the Master of the House. He had been away for five months.

I was resting on the chaise longue on the porch. A malaise had come over me ever since Baby Douglas disappeared. The last month had passed in a daze and I had no strength to do anything or go anywhere. Quame brought my bonnet and expected me to get up and go with him to the harbour.

The wharves along Bay Street were bustling with ships loading rice, indigo, lumber, leather and deerskins bound for England and unloading all the furniture, wine, books, tea, stockings, silks, shoes, hats, everything the colony needed. It was so busy I felt quite overwhelmed, but at least there were no Guineamen ships on the dock that day. In the summer heat, they had started unloading at the Pest House on Sullivan's Island in case the Africans brought the dreaded fever with them.

There were so many ships riding on anchor in the harbour that Quame had to point out the *Alborough,* even though I was the Captain's wife. The small jetty for ferries was busy, but Quame pushed through the crowds and secured a boat to take me out to the *Alborough.*

The boatman pointed out the pirate ship that Captain Forrester recently captured as a prize.

'I thought all the pirates had been caught and hung,' I said, alarmed that pirates still terrorized Charles Town.

'They're Spanish, that'll do,' he said. 'Captain Forrester killed five of 'em and wounded twenty more before the scoundrels surrendered. They'll be sailing to Jamaica within the week.'

'Good riddance,' I said. 'We don't want any pirate ships here in Charles Town.'

I found John in the Officers' Dining room. The table was covered with books, ledgers, rolled-up charts, navigational equipment and all manner of strange instruments. He looked up and seemed surprised to see me standing there in front of him. He staggered to his feet to greet me.

'Ah, Mary-Anne, I was going to send word I was home, but first I wanted to make a few changes to this draft of Port Royal Harbour while they're still fresh in my mind.'

I was shocked by how thin he looked, worn out and exhausted. His eyes had sunk into hollows in his gaunt face. I went over and put my arms around his thin body. Then I took the pen out of his hand and laid it on the desk.

'You're not well, John. You must come ashore with me. You can bring all your drafts and books, but you need to rest. Let me look after you for a few days.'

'I fear you're right, my dearest wife. I have been very ill of late. All the crew are sickly. I'm going to send some men ashore to quarters today.'

'James can take care of all that as your Lieutenant. You must take care of yourself now, John.'

To my surprise, he didn't put up any objection. He was resigned to the sense of what I was saying. I helped him gather up his books and charts and paraphernalia into a chest which a couple of sailors loaded into the ferryboat with us.

Quame was waiting excitedly on the quayside. He took John's arm and helped him into a carriage that would take us the short distance to the house on Church Street. I hoped he wasn't disappointed that his Master was this frail and sickly man.

As Ralph had foreseen, John didn't like the house at all.

'You can have the room at the front of the house as your study,' I suggested.

'It's dark and airless and the view is into the street. I can see the neighbours walking right in front of the window and the noise of carts and dogs and children will distract me from working.'

He was used to a constant breeze, a view as far as the horizon and a safe distance from other ships.

I suggested he use my parlour at the back overlooking the yard.

'I think all the frills on the curtains and the cushions on the sofa make it more of a lady's parlour, Mary-Anne. Besides, I don't want the slaves to think I'm spying on them in their quarters.'

Nothing about my house pleased him, but in the end he had to settle on the front room as his study. I fetched his books and charts and journals and he seemed comforted by having his work to do.

That night he slept in the chair in his study. He said he didn't want to disturb me. I lay in my bed in the dark, sensing his presence in the house, listening for his step on the stair, craving a kiss or caress. I had checked The Ladies Diary and this was a date when marriage came in, so I was disappointed.

By the next morning, he was already feeling guilty about being absent from the *Alborough,* even though it was moored safely in Charles Town Harbour and his brother James was in charge. He had been at sea for most of his life and found it hard to be stuck indoors in such a small house.

'Captain Douglas is taking the *Happy* to the careening wharf at Hobcaw Creek today. Anson and Forrester sent word that they're going up there to inspect the hull. I think I'm feeling well enough this morning to go with them.'

I was doubtful he could manage the trip unaided and I offered to accompany him.

'No, Mary-Anne, I must show that I am able to do my duties without the help of my wife.'

He returned in the evening, exhausted. 'Captain Douglas was taken so ill during the inspection that he was obliged to come back to Charles Town this afternoon.'

'You should have come back earlier with him, John. I told you it would be too much for you.'

He shrugged as if he refused to admit it and retired to his bed.

A letter arrived from Captain Douglas a few days later. Without a supply of hemp cables, he wrote, the *Happy* sloop could not anchor or perform the service expected from her and there were no cables to be had in this country. John threw the letter aside in dismay. He declared that he could not continue with the orders he had been given without a second ship to assist. He ordered Captain Douglas to proceed with the utmost despatch to Jamaica and apply to the Commander-in-Chief for such cables as he needed and then return immediately.

'I do hope St Lo can help,' I said to pacify him.

'Oh, didn't you hear? St Lo died of the yellow fever back in April. It's a shame as he'd just been made Vice-Admiral the month before. Captain William Smith of the *Faversham* is in charge now.'

The news of St Lo's death shocked me. I had never liked the man but he had always looked so strong and healthy. I couldn't believe he too had been struck down by the tropical fever. I recalled Georgie, the cabin boy on the *Tryall*, telling me it was God's Providence who lived and who died. I thanked the Good Lord we had escaped from Jamaica and I prayed that John never had to return, whether he needed more cables or not.

He spent the first weeks of June making his report and preparing his plan of Port Royal Harbour. 'The British Navy will need this if Port Royal is to be the second harbour in South Carolina after Charles Town,' he said proudly.

One morning I took him a glass of Madeira wine to revive his spirits and asked him how it was possible to survey the whole harbour.

'It's as well I did, as the existing plans are woefully inaccurate. The first thing I had to do was find a convenient watering hole. Not just for the crew's use, but to keep all our water barrels filled up. If the *Alborough* and the *Happy* sit as deep in the sea as possible, when we touch ground in the uncharted shallows, we can jettison the water to rise up and float off.'

He pointed to his chart. 'I started marking the North Channel across the Bar with buoys so I'd knew where it would be safe to cross coming in from the sea. There are no pilots to be had in Port Royal and the few ships that attempt to cross the Bar take their lives in their hands without proper channel markings. But the weather was so bad that some days we couldn't see the buoys in the fog or they had broken from their anchors in the gales in the night and were lost. I went out with the men in the small rowboats most days, unless it was raining too hard or the wind was too strong. I can't tell you the number of times we had to struggle back to the ship against the tide and the wind. It was so cold the rain froze as ice on the deck but, by the end of January, I'd completed the survey of the North Channel. It was too dangerous to continue in the violent weather, so I left the South Channel until later and went up into the shelter of the harbour near Beaufort town. The

126

Happy broke her anchor cable during a storm in February so had to come back to Charles Town for two weeks to get a replacement.'

'I never knew the *Happy* came back to Charles Town!' I interrupted. 'You could have sent me a letter, John.'

'I didn't want to worry you with the terrible weather we were suffering.'

'It would have been enough to know you were safe.'

'Well, I had to carry on and do the survey around Pariss Island without the help of Captain Douglas. We were so unlucky with the weather, day after day of heavy rain and strong winds. My crew became dispirited, but I had to make the most of any break in the weather, launching the small boats so we could explore the shoreline, lay buoys, take soundings and fix flags ashore for sightings. Some days I made the men start at daybreak, other days continue until midnight. I had to keep encouraging them so I could complete the survey properly. It was exhausting, Mary-Anne. I wouldn't have known how to tell you in a letter how badly I fared without giving you concern.'

My dutiful husband. The Admiralty had ordered him to survey Port Royal Harbour so he did so, come rain or storm.

'During March I surveyed the whole of the Port Royal River and Beaufort River and in April I surveyed around Trench's Island. By then the ship's company was sickly. And I had such terrible headaches that I had to remain in the dark of my cabin and my legs swelled up from sitting so long every day in a small rowboat in the pouring rain. But I still had to survey the South Channel before I was satisfied I had done everything I possibly could.'

'What are all these little numbers on your drawing? There are hundreds of them, all over the place.'

'Each one records a sounding we made,' he explained and I was staggered by the level of detail.

No wonder he had made himself ill sitting in a small boat day after day recording all these measurements with a lead line.

In the middle of June, John packed up all his work and delivered a box to James Omer, Master of the *Truelove of London* with instructions to take his draft and written description of Port Royal Harbour to the Honourable Josiah Burchett, Secretary of the Admiralty of Great Britain in London. As was the Navy way, he sent a duplicate with John Jordan, Master of the *Charming Sally* which sailed two weeks later.

It continued to be excessively hot all summer, with torrential rain most days, often accompanied by dramatic thunder and lightning out in the harbour. John returned to his ship whenever he felt strong enough and I spent my days on the shady porch, fanning myself lazily. The street outside our house was often flooded and the mosquitos were a plague. Everyone lived in expectation of a hurricane, which were common on this coast in the summer, and took precautions as best they can. Mrs McAndrews was forever reminding Quame to secure the windows with shutters against the gales that shook the house and tore down trees.

John went up to Hobcaw Creek to supervise the work being done on the *Alborough* in the careening wharf. If the weather looked ominous, he ordered James, as his Lieutenant, to get the topmasts down and lay extra anchors, but his health did not permit him to stay long onboard so he returned to my small house in Church Street where I was his nursemaid.

Some evenings Captain Anson visited us for supper. They were the only two Naval Captains stationed in Charles Town over the summer so it was inevitable they would forge a friendship of sorts.

Anson, despite his polite reserve, was pleasant company and we played cards for small stakes. It was part of the folklore of the town that four years ago Anson had won a plot of land north of Charles Town from the Customs Collector, Mr Thomas Gadsden, in a single hand of cards, but with John's Navy pay, the stakes were a lot smaller.

I came to appreciate Anson's visits, especially with the dearth of any other company during the summer. Many of the colonial elite had sailed to England to enjoy the Summer Season at Bath and the Autumn Season in London. Ralph was in Philadelphia and Sarah stayed at The Oaks, the Middleton plantation outside town to avoid the summer heat and the dreaded fever. She told me tensions were running high at the Governor's house as political infighting was rife in the Assembly.

By the end of August, John was bored with being at home with me and returned to his ship to begin a survey within Charles Town harbour. It gave him something to occupy his time until the *Happy* sloop returned from Jamaica with new anchor cables.

One afternoon, while John was away, Captain Anson visited me. He seemed ill at ease, wandering around the parlour inspecting all my ornaments, looking out of the window and staring at the pictures on the walls instead of sitting down. He suddenly turned round and complimented me on the silk ribbon in my hair, my choice of furnishings and the way I prepared the tea. It was most peculiar, but I excused his rather odd ways. He asked politely where John was and what he was doing and I got the impression he was envious of John having his survey work to keep him occupied.

When John returned home some days later, he told me I shouldn't entertain Captain Anson on my own, but I explained to him that I was often on my own, while he was busy with his surveys, so I couldn't turn away all callers. He looked at me through guarded eyes but said nothing more on the subject. I didn't admit to him that I quite enjoyed Anson's attention. Especially when my husband gave more thought and consideration to the *Alborough* than he did to me.

In early September the *Happy* returned from Jamaica and John made plans to leave in October once the threat of hurricanes was over. By the end of the month, he had rigged the *Alborough*, completed the victualling, got his gunpowder onboard and impressed able men to replace the great number of sickly ones who remained ashore. He'd asked Governor Middleton to order the scout boats at Beaufort to assist him again.

'I intend to continue my survey by sounding south of Trench's Island between Tybee and Callibogy Point,' he told me.

The night before he returned to his ship, he came to my bed. I tried to embrace him, but his body was a stranger to me, all sharp angles, sore places, rough skin and bone. His husbandly duty was done quickly without any of the affection and care that made the early days of our marriage so loving.

The next day, with John in command, the *Alborough* ran down the Cooper River in a north-easterly wind and crossed the Bar. That evening, I went up to the attic bedroom and rocked the empty cradle, humming the lullabies I used to sing to Baby Douglas. I prayed that after last night I might have a baby inside me, but in my heart I knew I didn't.

On his next visit, Captain Anson sat out on the porch with me while we drank mint juleps.

'I hope you don't mind me visiting you at home, Mrs Gascoigne. With your husband away, you must get lonely,' he said, studiously looking into his drink to avoid my eye.

I confessed to him that I did get lonely when John was away for months on end, but I told him I was happy living in my house in the heart of Charles Town.

'My house,' he reminded me and we both laughed, embarrassed by my mistake. 'Perhaps we can come to an arrangement that suits us both. You could stay here as long as you like and I could visit you, now and again. I am not at ease with other ladies in this town and I don't want to encourage any unmarried ladies as it's uncertain how much longer I'll be in Charles Town.'

I remembered Sarah telling me that a young lady in London had rejected his advances and I momentarily felt sorry for him. No doubt he wished to avoid such humiliation a second time. It was easier for him to visit me, the married wife of his subordinate.

'I understand, Captain Anson,' I said.

'Please, call me George,' he replied, which made me wonder what arrangement we had come to.

HMS Alborough sailed in October 1729 bound for Port Royal, but was unable to cross the Bar so proceeded southwards along the coast of Florida to Providence in the Bahamas.

From the Captain's Log, HMS Alborough
17th October 1729
Off the Bar at Port Royal.

"*Moderate gales & fair weather. At 4PM when we came off the Bar of Port Royal, found too great a Sea to send the Boats up to Beaufort for the Two Scout Boats, which are Ordered to Attend me in Surveying the Sound between Trench's Island & that of Tybee. The wind & weather being fair, I propose to continue sounding off the Coast within the View of the Land, all the way if possible down to Cape Florida. At 6 Anchored off Trench's Island in 7 fathom water. At Daylight weigh'd & drove 'till 8AM then made sail to the Southward.*"

John met the Governor of the Bahamas and did a much-needed survey of Providence harbour.

From the Captain's Log, HMS Alborough
9th November 1729
In Providence Harbour, Bahamas.

"*Moderate gales & fair weather. At 1 PM His Excellency Woodes Roger Governor of the Bahama Islands who resides here coming aboard to dine with me, I saluted him with 19 guns. This day observed the rising, setting and flowing of the tides in order to survey this Harbour and the adjacent islands.*"

13

I did a twirl in my new dress. The pattern of red flowers on blue silk showed off my pale skin and dark hair very prettily. Although the neckline was low, my breasts were modestly covered with a lace fichu. The hoops were bell-shaped, not too wide to interfere with my dance steps.

I had treated myself to a new gown as tonight was the highlight of the social calendar in Charles Town, the Governor's Christmas Ball hosted by Arthur and Sarah Middleton at The Oaks Plantation. It was mid-December and everyone in Charles Town society would be there. Everyone except John of course, as he was somewhere in Port Royal harbour, setting buoys and taking his soundings. I hadn't heard from him for the past two months.

I took another sip of wine to calm my excitement about an evening of gaiety and dancing. It seemed a long time since I had enjoyed myself.

Ralph returned from Philadelphia in October with a plan to marry an old, wealthy widow. He had attended his friend's wedding in the summer and told me, 'The dowager appreciates his youthful good looks, while he appreciates her vast fortune. She's too old to want more children, so it's the perfect arrangement.'

Tonight he was the escort of Lady Gaysborough, an elderly widow from New York who was visiting her daughter in Charles Town. So when George asked if he could escort me to the Governor's Ball, I accepted his kind invitation. After all, I couldn't turn up at a Ball on my own. Surely John couldn't expect me to live in Charles Town in seclusion, not going to the Governor's Ball, not seeing my friends, not being part of Society.

Ralph expressed disquiet about George's intentions, but I told him that John had asked me to be nice to him. It was important to the success of his surveys.

'What about the success of his marriage?' he muttered under his breath.

I didn't respond. I knew I could trust George. He told me it was his duty, as Commander of the Station, to look after the only Navy wife in Charles Town while her husband was away at sea. He was nervous about escorting any other woman who might spark rumours of his affections. Hopefully, John appreciated that I was doing what he asked of me, to keep George happy.

George arrived on time and complimented my new dress. He seemed slightly anxious about being my escort so I offered him a glass of John's favourite Malmsey wine to put him at ease.

We didn't stay at my house long as Quame had already hailed a carriage to take us to The Oaks. It was not like Quame to be rude, but he did seem offhand with George, almost pushing him out of the door into the waiting carriage.

The long driveway up to the house was beautifully lit with torches, but I couldn't tell Sarah it was not a patch on Caroline's plantation house in Jamaica. The Middleton wealth did not compare to the riches of the Sinclairs. John had told me the Jamaican Sugar Barons were ten times as rich as anyone in England.

George helped me alight from the carriage. He was flustered about whether he should take my hand so I took his arm to show him we were friends. I did find it slightly confusing walking into the reception on the arm of the wrong Naval Captain. Especially as this one was fighting fit and didn't walk with a limp.

Sarah and I exchanged compliments on our dresses. Her fair complexion suited the pale ivory silk, but the wide hoops in her skirt made it quite difficult for her to move elegantly through the doorways without turning sideways and all the bows attached to her petticoat were quite overpowering. I felt pleased with my own choice of gown. She raised an eyebrow at my choice of escort but welcomed us most politely.

George got me a drink of rum and excused himself to speak to his friends and I nodded to Ralph, standing on one side, tending to an old lady seated by his side. He came over to talk to me.

'Let me mark your card now for several dances, Mary-Anne. Lady Gaysborough's knees prevent her from standing, let alone dancing. I am beginning to think my plan of marriage is a high price to pay for riches.'

I had to laugh even though I felt some sympathy for Ralph. He would not inherit from his father so he had to find some means of supporting himself once his father's allowance died. Many times he had expressed envy at John's naval career, but it was hard to imagine Ralph accepting the discipline of the Navy. I told him in jest that the only seafaring career open to him would be as a gentleman pirate.

Dancing with Ralph was easy. He knew all the dances and he was delicate and precise with his feet, which was more than could be said for some of the men on the dance floor. Sarah interrupted us as she too needed Ralph as a dance partner. The Governor was too busy talking politics for the frivolities of dancing.

I was abandoned and wandered over to a dark corner where I hoped to find an empty chair. I felt quite exhausted after all my exertions on the dance floor. Unfortunately, all the chairs were taken so I stood by a pillar watching the dancers in the centre of the room. A passing footman handed me yet another glass of rum.

I was not aware of George standing close behind me until he leant forward and ran his fingers along the back of my arm. It was unexpected and I didn't know whether to move out of reach or ignore the intimate gesture.

He spoke softly into my ear. 'How are you enjoying the ball, Mary-Anne? I've been waiting for a chance to ask you for a dance, but it seems you are in demand. Which is no surprise as you look very beautiful tonight.'

His mouth was close to my cheek and I could smell the rum on his breath. I turned around quickly, but he was not looking at me. He was focussing his gaze on the dancers pirouetting gracefully in the middle of the room. Perhaps I had misheard the compliment.

He held out his hand and led me onto the dance floor. It was a simple minuet, controlled and graceful, but George stumbled a couple of times, which was unlike him, as he was usually a good dancer. I began to wonder if he had drunk rather too much. I worried that he might trip so when he moved closer, I offered him my hand to steady him. He took it gratefully, grasping it so tightly it hurt. He didn't speak to me, he didn't look at me, he just clung to my hand as if he would never let go.

I used the change of direction to extricate myself and I twirled away from him but, feeling he had been abandoned, he lurched forward clumsily to grab me. His fingers caught the lace trim on my bodice and the fabric came away with it, leaving my breasts exposed. The sound of the fabric ripping was loud and alarming. I stood in the middle of the dance floor, immobilized by the shock of what had happened.

There was a gasp from the other dancers and everyone turned to stare at me. The music stopped and the musicians lowered their instruments. George was looking back and forth at my breasts and then at the lace in his hand as if he had no idea how it got there.

Ralph pushed his way forward out of the crowd. He took off his jacket and put it around my shoulders to cover me and restore my modesty. He stood beside me, facing George.

'Well, what's going on here? The fine upstanding Captain ripping ladies' gowns on the dance floor.'

'Ralph, please, it was an accident,' I whispered, fearing how this might play out between the two adversaries.

George was swaying slightly, his eyes trying to focus on Ralph, then me, then the lace in his hand. I realised he had indeed drunk a great deal this evening. He couldn't think of a suitable riposte to Ralph, who now had the upper hand. He poked George in the chest and slowly repeated the accusations George had levelled at him earlier in the year.

'You are a disgrace, Captain Anson. I'm surprised you show your face in polite society.'

George had no response. He handed me the lace trim and hung his head in shame.

'It was an accident, Ralph, leave him alone,' I said quietly.

Ralph looked at me as if I had betrayed him by taking George's side.

Sarah was at my side and pulled me away, making light of the incident to her guests. 'Come with me Mary-Anne, dear, and I'll get my maid to fix your lace in no time.'

As soon as we were out of the reception room, she turned on me angrily.

'What are you doing? People are talking about you and Captain Anson. Why did you come with him, of all people?'

'Why shouldn't I? He's John's superior officer. It's his job to look after me.' I saw the suspicious look in her eye and added, 'There is nothing between us.'

'Well, your reputation is at stake this evening, Mary-Anne. As your friend, I am telling you to leave now before rumours start. I'll order a carriage for you.'

She enjoyed throwing guests out if they cast any disgrace over her social functions. She had her own reputation to uphold. I didn't want to go home and have the evening end in such ignominy.

'Please don't make me leave. I've done nothing wrong. I can fix my gown.' I started fumbling with the lace trim, but it was obvious the bodice was ruined.

'I have my position as Governor's wife to think of and I can't have you embarrass me,' she said as she turned to go. One of her footmen handed me my cape and bonnet in exchange for Ralph's jacket and escorted me to the door, so I had no choice but to head out into the warm night. The sky was midnight blue with a million stars shining down. Was John seeing the same sky? I wished he was with me, then none of this unpleasantness would have happened and we could have enjoyed a pleasant sociable evening with our friends.

The footman whistled for a carriage and as I waited, George came out to find me.

'How can you ever forgive me, Mary-Anne? I have behaved so ungallantly.'

'It wasn't your fault, George. Please think on it no more.'

He sat down heavily on the entrance step, as if he was carrying a heavy burden, and dropped his head into his hands. I feared he was crying, but when he raised his head, his face was flushed but his eyes were dry.

'The least I can do is see you safely home,' he said, getting up as if he has a new purpose.

I didn't want him to take me home. I was upset by how the evening ended and I wanted to be alone to nurse my disappointment, but I didn't want to hurt his feelings. He was embarrassed by what had happened on the dance floor. Before I could say anything, he handed me into the waiting carriage and climbed in to sit beside me. He sat, eyes closed, and I hoped he'd gone to sleep.

The carriage clattered and lurched over all the cobbles and potholes in the road. Every jolt made me feel sick. I had not eaten from the buffet table between dances, which might have settled my stomach. I could taste the stale rum in the back of my throat. I sat perfectly still, praying I didn't vomit all over the carriage.

I stared out of the window and all I could see was my poor reflection, downcast and sad. What a wretched end to the evening.

Tears started trickling down my face as I thought how the evening hadn't been as much fun as I'd hoped. I must have sighed rather too loudly because George turned to look at me.

'Oh no, I have upset you, Mary-Anne. I would never want to cause you any offence. Please forgive me if I have behaved boorishly.'

'It's not you George. I feel rather sad recently. I am so lonely with John away. I thought I would enjoy myself this evening but I miss him terribly.'

He put an arm around my shoulders to comfort me. 'You are such a good wife to John,' he said.

The damp, salty tang of his jacket smelled like John's and I nestled into his chest feeling very sleepy and sorry for myself.

He gently kissed the top of my head and it was kind and tender. It felt so long since anyone had embraced me.

'We are the same, Mary-Anne. I too feel sad and lonely, especially in Society, when others have their wives to accompany them. I sometimes feel I have no one in the world who cares for me.'

'Oh George, I care for you. I am so grateful that you invited me to the dance this evening. Really I am.'

We sat quietly for the rest of the journey. It was relaxing to be nestled against his chest. He smelled strong and manly, just like a naval officer should. Without looking up at his face, I could almost make-believe it was John sitting beside me.

I must have dozed off as the next thing I knew, he was placing me gently on the couch in my parlour at home. He must have lifted me from the carriage and carried me into the house in his arms. It gave him a shock when I sat up abruptly.

'Forgive me, Mary-Anne, I didn't want to wake you. You looked so peaceful sleeping.'

I could feel my cheeks burning that he saw me in such an intimate moment. I stood up quickly, to regain my dignity. Too quickly, as my knees gave way and I fell forwards. Ever the gentleman, George instinctively responded by catching me in his arms.

We looked into each other's eyes for a moment that lasts an eternity. Then he leant down and pressed his lips gently against mine.

I was shocked, but I couldn't say it was unexpected. It was obvious that his amorous feelings for me had been simmering all summer. My moment of hesitation encouraged him to tighten his embrace. He buried his face in my hair, deeply breathing in my scent.

'Mary-Anne I cannot deny my feelings for you. I have loved you since the moment we met. I wish with all my heart and soul that you were my wife.'

He started kissing my hair, then moved down to my cheek, my neck, my breast. I was suddenly terror-struck. This should not be happening. I struggled frantically, desperate to extricate myself from his embrace, but he was big and strong and I was small and weak and he was holding me so tightly.

He pushed me back onto the couch and fell on top of me. He knocked the breath out of me and all I could do was whimper, 'Don't do this George. I beg you, don't do this.'

He was groaning with desire and kissed me hard on the lips to stop me from talking. His breath stank of rum and lust. With one hand he roughly grabbed my breast and with the other hand, he pulled up my petticoats. His knee suddenly pushed my legs apart with a violent urgency.

'I must have you for myself, Mary-Anne. You cannot deny me.'

I cried out in terror, 'George! Don't do this.'

He didn't heed me. He was fumbling with his breeches. His passion could not be controlled.

I shouted hysterically. 'Stop! Help! Someone help me.' There was no one in the house to hear me, let alone save me. I squirmed and struggled under him, but he was too heavy to push off. I hadn't the strength to fight him. I closed my eyes tightly, scared and tearful. I had no idea how to escape from this nightmare.

Suddenly there was a loud crash and George fell away to one side. Quame was standing behind him with the remains of Sarah's blue Oriental vase in his hands. I pushed the limp body off me and got up, adjusting my clothing for decency.

'He's not a good man, Mistress. He should not be doing that to the Master's wife.'

I put my cheek near George's face and felt his faint breath on my skin. Thank the Lord. Not dead, just knocked out. For a slave to attack a naval officer was surely a hanging offence. To kill him was definitely much worse.

'Help me lift him onto that chair, Quame. He can sleep it off until morning.'

'We should leave him out on the porch. Then when he wakes, he can creep away like the dog he is.'

I hadn't realised how much he disliked George, but it was a good idea so we dragged his body outside and placed him on the sofa.

'Quame, you must leave right now and sleep next door in Mrs McAndrews' yard. Do not return until Captain Anson has left.'

He hesitated as if he didn't want to leave me with the inert form of Captain Anson. I assured him that he could do me no harm in his current state.

'Go quickly, Quame. I'll bolt the door and be safe in my room. Tell no one what has happened.'

I grabbed his hand and shook it vigorously. My whole body was shaking with nerves.

'Thank you, Quame. You have saved me from a fate worse than death itself.'

He nodded by way of acknowledgement, went out the gate into the street and disappeared into next door's yard.

In the morning when I awoke, George had gone. Bess cleared up the broken shards of the smashed vase and tutted about how clumsy Quame was. I told her it was not Quame's fault, but mine.

I had a heavy head and desperately wanted to forget the details of last night., but I could think of nothing else. Did he mean to harm me or was it a few kisses that got overzealous? Was I to blame? Did I encourage him with my kindness? Did I give him hope that I had affections for him?

John had been upset when Major Cartwright kissed me at Grosvenor House. How would he react if he heard George had attacked me? Would he challenge him to a duel? I remembered Durell's advice to pick the fights you will win and I feared that John, crippled by swollen legs and weak with fever, would be no match for Captain Anson.

No, John must never know what happened. Surely George would never say anything, his reputation depended on it. I would swear Quame to silence, his life depended on it. And I would never tell a soul, my marriage depended on it.

By the end of January, John had completed his survey of Providence Harbour and returned to Charles Town on 9th February 1730 to work on his drafts.

From the Captain's Log, HMS Alborough
22nd January 1730
In Providence Harbour, Bahamas.
    "Little wind and fair weather. This day finished the Survey of the Harbour of Providence and of the Islands adjacent, a Plan of the Fortification & have drawn a Prospect of it & the Town. But to mention the particulars of every Trip I made in the Boats on this Service would only have been bringing the Racks and Spits upon the Table with the Meat, & after all that can be said it would neither have been satisfactory or intelligible without a Sketch of the Place, which I shall therefore add when I have Leisure, together with a General Description of the Port & shall let it suffice in the meantime (instead of the particulars, which may be referr'd to in the Book kept for that purpose) to say that whenever the weather has allow'd the Boats a Possibility of passing, I have not lost one moment in the Performance of this Service."

His survey of Providence Harbour was sent to the British Admiralty three months later.

From the Captain's Log, HMS Alborough
2nd May 1730
At Charles Town in South Carolina
    "Fresh gales & hazy weather. This morning I delivered the following Fair Draughts, Viz the Survey of Providence Harbour & of the Adjacent Islands, a Plan of the Fortification and a Prospect of it, & the Town of Nassau to Captain Thomas Arnold of HMS Fox in a Box directed to the Honourable Josiah Burchett, Esquire Secretary of the Admiralty of Great Britain & took a Receipt for them. These Draughts & the Duplicates (to be left here when I sail next) have taken up the whole time my State of Health would allow me to Sit to it since my arrival in this Harbour."

14

When John returned to Charles Town in February, he told me he'd spent the last five months surveying Providence Harbour in the Bahama Islands. He had brought me a beautiful curly conch shell as a gift, just like Mrs Clifford's, and I displayed it proudly on the hall table in place of the blue Oriental vase.

'I thought you were surveying Port Royal Harbour again,' I said, surprised.

'We were blown off course by the gales from the north. We couldn't get across the Bar at Port Royal and ended up down the coast of Florida. The only way back was to sail eastwards. When we sighted The Hole in the Rock, one of the small islands of the Bahamas, I decided to go to Providence for supplies. A survey of the Bahamas was on my original orders. I had been asked by the Admiralty to visit the Governor, Woodes Rogers.'

'The Admiralty! Why would the Admiralty want you to visit the Governor?'

'I had orders to check on him. Since he was reappointed, he's been trying to build up the defences against pirates. He's imposed a local tax to pay for it and the local landowners have complained to the Government. So they tasked me with finding out what was going on.'

'What, spy on him? That doesn't sound like you, John.'

'Well, keep an eye on him anyway. I surveyed the harbour while I was there. It's long overdue,' he said, almost to himself. 'The approach is dangerously exposed to the sea and storms. My pilot had no idea of the depths on the Bar. Many ships are lost anchoring outside the harbour waiting for the high tide.'

I had to smile. My husband was so open and guileless that he would make a hopeless spy, but he would have been quite happy doing a survey of the harbour.

John told me he'd been giving a lot of thought to where we would live. He didn't want to stay any longer in Captain Anson's small townhouse and a land agent had told him about a property for sale on Hog Island, on the other side of Cooper River facing Charles Town.

'The house is built on a high bluff,' he told me. 'It's said to command an entire prospect of the harbour, stretching from the ocean to the town.' He spread his arms expansively as if the view was the most important thing for any house. 'It would be a real home for us, Mary-Anne, not like this small house in the backstreets of town. Space for us to settle, space for you to have a baby. You'd like that, wouldn't you?'

I thought of the cradle in the attic bedroom. Space wasn't the problem. There was space for a baby anywhere.

'I'm told it's a delightful wilderness with shady walks and arbours, cool in the hottest summer. I'll be able to get all the rest and recuperation I need there. It will take you less than an hour to get across to Charles Town by ferry.'

An hour to get to Charles Town by ferry! Still, I didn't go out in Charles Town society anymore. I didn't want to bump into George Anson. I hid away at home, ashamed that what happened was my fault. Had I encouraged him with my favours?

I couldn't face Sarah and Ralph in case they saw the guilt in my eyes, so I turned down their invitations to lunches, dances and plays. They were confused and hurt by my rejections, as they both needed me to be their friend at that moment. Ralph was still worried about a violent attack from his adversaries and Sarah was busy fending off rumours that a new Royal Governor had been appointed by the King. I couldn't help them. I didn't know how to deal with my own dishonour. So what did it matter if I was an hour from Charles Town by ferry?

'I'll easily be able to visit from the *Alborough* when she's in harbour,' John continued, unaware of my inner turmoil. 'Even if she's anchored in Rebellion Road or upriver at the careening wharf at Hobcaw Creek. I may be here for a while as the *Happy* has been summoned back to Jamaica. I'll have to wait for her to return before I can do any more survey work, but I can't stay in this small house.'

No, we couldn't stay there, that was for sure. I could no longer go into the parlour. I couldn't go near the couch and I avoided looking at the empty table by the door where the large blue Oriental vase once stood. I wanted to move out of Captain Anson's small house. The sooner, the better.

John was delighted when I agreed to go with him immediately to see the house on Hog Island.

'I thought you might need more persuasion,' he said, smiling broadly at me.

We took a ferry from Middle Bridge and the boatman rowed us across the Cooper River. It was a fine day, the river was calm and the journey was pleasant, sitting in the small boat next to John. I clung to his arm to reassure myself that, after all that has happened, he was still my dearest husband. He was excited and pointed to the *Alborough*, swinging on her anchors off Johnson's Fort. I avoided looking when he pointed to the *Garland* in case I saw Captain Anson standing on the deck.

John gave me a tour of the seventeen acres that made up the higher ground on Hog Island. On the west the High Bluff cliffs looked over the Cooper River towards Charles Town, on the south was Sullivan's Creek, on the east an open bay in front of Mount Pleasant Town and on the north a small salt marsh creek. We were surrounded by water. It was almost like being on a ship. John loved the place instantly.

'On the deeds it's called Hog Island, but I don't like that name. I have in mind to change the name to Mount Edgecombe, after the grand house on the cliff overlooking Plymouth Sound. Every time I sailed past that house, I vowed I would one day own a house of my own.'

It sounded rather pretentious for this small estate, hardly a grand English house. I thought it might confuse the ferrymen, but I wanted him to be happy so I nodded my head. He could call it whatever he liked.

He showed me the jetty where ferry boats docked. 'We'll get a small rowboat, Mary-Anne, always available for you to get across to the town.' He showed me the creek, where the water had been sucked away by the low tide. 'At high tide, the fish jump right out of the water. They'll be plenty for us and fishermen can take the extra across to market in town.' He showed me the orchards of oranges, peaches, nectarines and plums. 'Over there would be a perfect place to plant a vineyard and we will make our own wine.' And he showed me the cliff at High Bluff where the small trees were bent crooked by the wind. 'Look at that view of the harbour, Mary-Anne. Isn't it the finest sight in the world!'

I was nervous to go too near the edge of the cliff. It was wild and exposed to the elements, but I had to agree it was a fine view. The clouds scudded across the open sky and seabirds wheeled over the wave crests, disappearing into the water in search of fish. The wind on my face was cooling, a respite from the humid heat, and if I stood there long enough the memory of Captain Anson might be blown away.

'Look,' John said, grabbing my arm, 'you can see all the ships anchored everywhere, in Rebellion Roads, in Sullivan Cove, in the Cooper River, on the town jetties.' He pointed out the *Alborough* and told me I could watch for his return from this vantage point. I laughed at his enthusiasm and promised him I would come here every day to watch for his ship.

'Colonel Parris has owned Hog Island since 1708, but I don't think he ever lived here,' John told me. 'He owned several houses in Charles Town, including a mansion on Bay Street. This was built as a summer retreat for his wife. He's an old man now and lives on his plantation on Parris Island in Port Royal Harbour. I met him and his wife Mary last year when I was surveying the harbour.'

It was a good substantial house, with brick chimneys at each end and glazed windows and shutters to keep out the wind. A shady porch ran the whole length of the house. The rooms were tall and spacious and stood empty, with no evidence of the previous owner, devoid of any family history. It was the most isolated, desolate and lonely house I had ever seen and it suited my reclusive mood very well. I could hide away and John would never know my shame. I took his hand and told him it was just the home we had been looking for.

John settled with the land agent and on the 4th of March 1730, *"the property at Hog Island was conveyed to Captain John Gascoigne of His Majesty's Ship the Alborough"*. The next day the *Alborough* went to the careening wharf at Hobcaw Creek with John's brother in charge and we moved into the house on Hog Island.

Our days were spent settling into our new home. Captain Anson let me take all my fineries away, saying that the planters who stayed at his house had no use for them. It was the least he could do, in the circumstances. So I filled the house with all my furniture and furnishings. John asked after the blue Oriental vase which once stood by the front door. I innocently shrugged my shoulders and told him I liked the conch shell he gave me better.

He stopped me from putting any frilly drapes or fancy cushions in his study, which he filled with books and charts. We arranged our new home as we wanted it, like any married couple. It was large enough for me to have my own bed chamber. We hired a couple more slaves. Sissy, the scullery maid, would help Peggy in the kitchen and two young men, Cuffee and Mungo, would help Quame tend the orchards and gardens.

'They're strong enough to row you across to Charles Town whenever you want,' John assured me.

I wanted to fill our new home with love and children, but the Ladies Diary reminded me that during Lent *"Marriage goes out"*, so I slept in my own bed chamber, craving John's embrace to erase the memory of George Anson's hands on my body, his lips on my mouth. My beloved husband was still suffering from fever and swollen legs so seemed relieved that I did not demand his company at night. We would have to wait until Easter.

In April, John went to his ship to receive a new pinnace rowboat and various supplies which had arrived from England. He was angry that the supplies didn't include the precious theodolite he'd requested. His previous one had broken during the storm off the Florida coast when his pistol fell off the shelf and smashed it. It was vital for his surveying work, but the Admiralty had not sent him a replacement. Almost in passing, he told me George Anson had come to dine with him onboard the *Alborough* while the supplies were being loaded. My heart stopped and I held my breath.

'He's leaving Charles Town next month. Heading back to England.'

'Leaving?' My voice was trembling.

'Yes, apparently he asked for a transfer at the end of last year. Seems he wants to leave Charles Town. Well, he's been here six years already so it's no surprise. He admitted that his service in Carolina has been in no way brilliant. He needs to prove himself with more action if he's ever going to get promoted.'

'I have often sensed that he envied you having your survey work to do.'

'Yes, in fact, he said as much to me. It made my work seem more worthwhile. We'll miss his company at dinner and cards, won't we? He was a good friend to us, wasn't he? He seemed to like you, anyway.'

I nodded vaguely as if I had no further interest in talking about George Anson. I should bear some guilt that he had to leave Charles Town, but inside my heart was bursting with joy. George Anson leaving

Charles Town was the best thing that could happen and I could feel a heavy weight lift from my heart. To celebrate, I invited my dear friends, Sarah and Ralph, to our new residence on Hog Island. Governor Middleton was engaged on official business so we were saved from a lecture on politics. John invited his brother to join us.

Sarah immediately loved Hog Island. 'What a perfect escape, away from the heat and disease of Charles Town.'

Ralph stepped warily from the boat as if getting his satin shoes wet would be a calamity. 'I could not live here,' he exclaimed as we made our way into the house, 'and have to travel in a small boat every time I want to go to a dinner. What happens at night or in bad weather?'

'Well, I haven't gone to many dinners lately. John and I keep to ourselves,' I replied, clasping John's arm in a show of solidarity.

'We like it here,' John said. 'Peace and quiet, well away from the maddening social whirl.'

Ralph looked at him quizzically to see if he was joking.

James suddenly said, 'I guess your life is just one maddening social whirl, Mr Wilkinson.'

It seemed unnecessary, even rude, but Ralph calmly replied, 'Who can say that it is worse than any other gentleman's life, Lieutenant Gascoigne?'

Over dinner, James seemed determined to tell stories about his adventures on the *Alborough* as if to prove his life was no worse than Ralph's.

'When we left in October, we were hit by bad storms that threw us down the coast of Florida. The men caught a shark and as they were hauling it aboard, John Stanover, the Boatswain, got too close and the shark bit his foot off.'

He paused to make sure he had everyone's attention.

'But his shoe buckle got lodged in the shark's jaw so old Stanover disentangled his foot and the shark swallowed the shoe. When the men cut the shark open, they retrieved the shoe from the belly and presented it to Stanover with much formality for him to wear again. It was covered in gore, but he put it on and strutted around the deck, much to the hilarity of the crew.'

He and John laughed at the memory, but stories about sharks biting a man's shoe off did not amuse the rest of us. It was a very different world from the maddening social whirl of Charles Town.

'So, did you meet the infamous Governor in Nassau?' Ralph asked John.

Sarah wanted to know why he was infamous.

'Providence used to be a notorious pirate hideout in the old days,' Ralph told us. 'No one could find it, a tiny island somewhere in the middle of the ocean. Woodes Rogers was Governor ten years ago and he was successful at getting rid of the pirates. The cost bankrupted him and when he returned to England he was thrown into debtors' prison. To restore his finances he sold his stories to that book, *"Robberies & Murders of the Most Notorious Pyrates."* You must have read it.'

John nodded. 'I remember it. It was so popular at the time that Rogers became a national hero and the King has reappointed him Governor again.'

'Now he's back, what's he up to?' Ralph asked, taking a casual drink of wine and looking at John carefully over the rim of the glass.

I glanced at John to warn him. Did Ralph know John's now a spy? Surely John wouldn't reveal any secret information. Not to the worst gossip in Charles Town.

'Well, I found him most amenable but I hardly met him. I was busy surveying the harbour. It took much longer than I expected.' John leant over and took my hand, smiling at me with those spaniel eyes. 'But whenever the weather allowed the boats to be out, I lost not a moment in completing the survey so I could return to my darling wife as soon as possible.'

I blushed in front of my guests. Sometimes he reminded me why I loved him and he had managed to divert the conversation away from Woodes Roger.

'Talking of Governors,' Ralph said, 'you've heard that Middleton's out and Robert Johnson has been appointed the new Royal Governor. Well, not new, as he was the Governor some ten years ago, but he was kicked out by the Assembly. Now he's coming back and Sarah's cross that she will lose her social prominence.'

'No I'm not,' Sarah said petulantly. 'I'm relieved that Arthur can relinquish his post. All this worry has made him quite unwell. You won't be invited to any more dances at the Governor's Residence, dear brother!'

'Why do we need someone from England to be Governor?' I asked. 'I thought Arthur was doing a good job.'

'Well, I heard that the Lords Proprietors want to sell the colony to the British Government and apparently Johnson is the man to negotiate the deal,' Ralph said. 'He's got great plans to encourage settlers in Carolina with his township system to counter the threat from the Spanish in Florida, the French in Louisiana and the Natives in the west. They think we are under constant apprehension of invasion.'

'And are we?' I asked, looking around, although it was hard to imagine Charles Town being invaded, with the cannons at the Battery at White Point protecting the harbour and the local inhabitants parading in their finery along Bay Street.

'Well, I expect we'll be invaded by thousands of immigrant settlers, but I don't suppose anyone's worried about them.'

We all laughed in amusement and Ralph told us all about his recent visit to Philadelphia

'It's the most enlightened, tolerant and cultured place in America,' he declared. 'It has schools, libraries and a theatre, something Charles Town sorely lacks. I have made the acquaintance of an impressive gentleman, Mr Benjamin Franklin. He's busy with his civic works in Philadelphia, but last year he started publishing a newspaper, *The Pennsylvania Gazette,* which is very popular and he has asked me to contribute an article about Charles Town. This might be the fourth largest city in the colonies but it boasts the wealthiest residents by far and I am nervous about how to tell colonists in the north how we live in Carolina.'

'Why are you nervous?' Sarah asked. 'We have a good life, don't we?'

'Well for a start, they don't have plantations worked by African slaves as we do. I'm not sure folk in the North appreciate the necessity of slavery here in the South.'

We all fell silent. I knew Sarah had definite views on the necessity for slaves to work on Arthur's rice plantation. To her, they were cheap plentiful labour, capable of doing all the back-breaking, but we were all in no doubt that their brutal treatment was nothing to be proud of.

'Maybe I'll write about the imminent arrival of the new Governor, instead.'

'Don't keep going on about it,' his sister said crossly.

After lunch, Ralph and Sarah were taken back to Charles Town by ferry boat and James returned to the *Alborough* in the new pinnace. John and I relaxed on the porch in the late afternoon sun, happy in our new home.

Two weeks later, at the start of May, John had completed the drafts of his survey of Providence Harbour and the adjacent islands and a plan of the fortification and the town of Nassau. He delivered the papers to Captain Arnold of HMS *Fox* in a box directed to Josiah Burchett at the Admiralty. Since his return in February, it had taken up all his time, or at least the days he was well enough to sit for long at his desk.

'I do wonder what happens to the reports I send back to the Admiralty in London,' he told me. 'I sometimes wonder if they are ever read. They're probably stored away and not looked at again.'

'Surely Papa knows that accurate charts are important. I'm sure he gives your reports the attention they deserve.'

He looked at me and smiled. 'Of course, Mary-Anne, but I guess there are more important charts to make at the moment than one of Providence Harbour, but who knows, one day it may be needed.'

'If there's another war with the Spanish, they'll need accurate charts of all the harbours in the Americas.'

'You're right and in the meantime, all I can do is fulfil my orders.'

On the morning of the 20th of May, John and I walked up to the High Bluff to watch Captain George Anson sail down the Cooper River in HMS *Garland* bound for London. He was saluted by all the forts as he passed by. It was quite a rousing and emotional send-off and I was caught up in the euphoria. I waved my bonnet wildly, even though I knew there was no way he could see me. John watched me, surprised at my enthusiasm in saying farewell to our friend.

'I hope he finds what he is looking for in England,' I told him.

Anson's replacement Captain Matthew Norris arrived in June aboard HMS *Lowestoft*. He was made welcome by Governor Middleton, but the next time I saw Sarah, she told me she was not impressed.

'I never thought I'd miss your old friend Captain Anson. Young Norris is so political, always arguing against any idea of American freedom. Says people should not have any unrealistic ideas about independence from the King, that sort of thing!'

'It's only to be expected when this new Royal Governor is turning up soon.'

'As if independence will ever happen! It's ridiculous. He shouldn't argue about it so much.'

'Well, Norris is a young man,' I told her. 'Only twenty-five. I'm sure he'll settle into Carolina life soon.'

'Yes, I hope all this trouble-making talk about independence will soon be forgotten. I'm hoping for a more peaceful life once Arthur hands over to the new Governor.'

The *Happy* returned from Jamaica, under the command of Captain James Lloyd. Now that he had finished his report of Providence, John decided to fill his days until the Hurricane Season was over finishing his survey of Charles Town Bar, the shifting sandbanks and shoals which caused such a hazard to ships entering and leaving harbour.

We embraced before he stepped into the pinnace to return to the *Alborough*. He promised not to be gone for long. I stood on the dock and waved until he was out of sight. I might be blessed with a loving husband and a comfortable home, but all I really wanted was a baby and, despite our best efforts, there seemed to be no prospect of that.

**Unable to head southwards during the Hurricane Season, John surveyed
the treacherous Bar at the entrance to Charles Town Harbour. He had to
abandon this within the month due to ill health.**

From the Captain's Log, HMS Alborough
23rd July 1730
In Charles Town Harbour.

"*Little wind & fair weather. At 10 at night returned to the Ship with all the
Boats & brought all the Buoys and Flags with me, finding myself unable to
continue this Service for the Present, for that the Swelling in my Legs which came
upon me after the Long illness I had in Jamaica (& which was much increased &
confirmed by the frequent long sittings I was obliged to undergo in the Survey of
Port Royal, Providence & this Harbour) returned upon me in a much greater
Degree than I have ever hitherto had it, insomuch that I have not been able to get
a Shoe on since I came aboard.*"

A violent storm struck Charles Town in late August 1730.

From the Captain's Log, HMS Alborough
27th August 1730
In Charles Town Harbour.

"*Hard gales and Very Dark hazy weather with Small Rain. PM Several
Merchant Ships which Lay against the Town, not liking the Dismal appearance of
the weather, ran up the Rivers for better security. It Blew so hard that the house I
was Lodged in (tho' the Walls were of Brick two foot thick & well Bound with
Strong Timber) shook with Several Violent Gusts of Wind during the time of the
hurricane so much that the Shocks were like those of a Ship Striking against the
ground. This Ship Struck her Mizon-topmast & got down the Cross Jack & Mizon
topsail Yard. It blew a very hard gale of wind all night & the violence increased
till 11 AM when by good Providence the wind Shifted to the SE. Otherwise the Sea
had in all Probability very much Damaged the Front of the Town if it had not
beat it all Down, for tho' at that time it was low Tide, the wind having Blown
Violently in the NE Quarter, the Sea was so Great that it ran up to some of the
Front Houses. It Continued to Blow most Violently till noon when it was observed
that the Longboat is drove from her Moorings & that all the Merchant Ships that
lay against the Town were Drove ashore except two who have lost their Masts.*"

15

As soon as John left to finish his survey of the Bar in Charles Town harbour, the weather took a turn for the worse. Violent thunderstorms and heavy rains day after day. At night I lay in bed listening to the wind banging on the shuttered windows and the rain beating on the roof. I got Quame to barricade the doors and windows at night so the storm couldn't get into the house. It rained every day which seemed to suit the mosquitos that thrived in the floods and continued to plague me with bites.

I worried about John at sea in the gales, but he was within the harbour. He would know what to do. He'd bring the *Alborough* inside the Bar for better protection if he needed to. He'd take down the sails and lay the masts along the deck.

Out on Hog Island, we were in the path of the wild winds which hurtled in from the sea, trying to sweep up the house and take it along as it roared onwards up the river. The waves in the Cooper River crashed against the High Bluff, all but knocking it down.

A week or so after he had left, John returned home. It was late afternoon and I rushed down to the dock to greet the pinnace as it approached, but when I saw him being carried ashore by two sailors, I cried out in alarm. Henry Curry, the ship's surgeon and Robert Leith, the surgeon's mate, were at his side and his leg was grossly swollen and wrapped loosely in cloth.

'Don't fret Mary-Anne,' he said, in a futile attempt to allay my fears. 'A large tumour has arisen on the bottom of my left foot. This morning Mr Curry decided that my foot must be cut open and the tumour removed. He thought it best if I move ashore for the operation.'

The sailors carried John into the parlour and placed him on the sofa with his left foot propped up on a footstool. I feared I would faint at the sight of the operation, so I retired in distress to my bedroom. Luckily Bess had the presence of mind to lay old cloths over the floor and fetch bowls of water before John's foot was sliced open and the tumour cut out. I had to block my ears to shut out his screams of pain and I collapsed in a faint on my bed.

The next morning I woke to find that John has slept on the sofa in the parlour, which had been made into a makeshift bed. The surgeon had slept in the chair, keeping a vigil all night at John's side.

'I have removed the tumour, Mrs Gascoigne,' he told me, rather brusquely, 'but I must return to the ship. I shall visit regularly, but Captain Gascoigne will not be able to move from his bed or set his foot upon the ground for at least a month.'

The surgeon and his mate departed with the two sailors and I was left to nurse my husband back to health. I remembered my lessons from Kingston and made sure the room was well aired with fresh herbs to clear the sickness miasma. I showed Sissy how to make the drink of lime juice recommended by Mrs Clifford while Bess and I tended his dressings, ran all his errands and waited on him at all times.

One afternoon as I sat next to his bed in the parlour, I had an overwhelming urge to be embraced, to be reminded that this invalid, lying helpless on his bed, was still my husband and I was his wife, not just his nursemaid. I climbed onto the narrow bed to lie next to him, fitting into the curve of his body. He embraced me tightly to hold me close.

'I was so worried about you, John. I had terrible nightmares of the *Alborough* being shipwrecked.'

'I wanted to survey the East Channel despite the bad weather,' he told me, 'but I couldn't risk going outside the Bar. Then one night the swelling in my legs was far worse than it ever had been, so I had to return to the ship in the night as I was unable to continue.'

'You do too much, John. You still haven't fully recovered from the illness you had in Jamaica and it's been made worse by sitting in a small boat all these months.'

'You're right, with the surveys of Port Royal and Providence and then this Harbour, I have made myself very ill. This time it seems much worse. A livid spot appeared on the bottom of my foot a few days before the tumour appeared.'

'Promise me you will be well again soon.'

'Yes, I will be. I'm sure of it. The surgeon says he's cut out the tumour so I have to wait for the incision to heal.'

'At least you are at home with me now.'

We lay like two spoons in the drawer for a few hours, content to be together, but there was not much opportunity for me to rest. It was hard work to look after John, to clean and bandage his foot every day, to wash him while he lay abed, to change his bedlinen, to fetch his food and drinks, to keep him amused when he was awake and to be quiet when he was asleep. He was not my husband anymore, my handsome naval officer, so manly and strong, so dashing and brave. He was an invalid, angry and impatient and frustrated by being laid low. At night I fell exhausted into my bed, feeling helpless to aid his recovery.

Over the next few days, there was no wind but the dark clouds hung ominously low, blocking out the sun. The temperatures rose, higher and higher until there was no respite even in the shade.

One day at the end of August the clouds turned black and Quame came running into the house.

'Everyone is preparing for a hurricane. All the ships that lay at the wharves have hauled off to anchor in the stream or gone upriver into the swamps. We must barricade the windows and take refuge upstairs. The creek behind the house is rising fast in the flood.'

Every summer the inhabitants of Charles Town lived in dread of hurricanes. The storm in 1722 had damaged St. Philip's Church, repairs to which were still unfinished and in August 1724, a storm caused widespread damage to crops and ruined several of the wooden wharves in the port. In August 1728 a storm had struck Charles Town just before we arrived. I asked Quame what it had been like.

'During that summer the weather was uncommonly hot,' he said, 'much worse even than this year. A dreadful hurricane came upon us and the heavy rains overflowed the town and the fields. I was at the Governor's house and we took refuge on the upper story to escape the floods.'

He told me that the following day the streets of Charles Town were covered with the wrecks of boats, broken barrel staves and furniture swept from wharves and houses. Twenty-three ships had been driven ashore, most of which were badly damaged or dashed to pieces. The *Fox* and the *Garland*, the two warships stationed there, were the only ships that rode out the storm.

'Many lives were lost that day, both white men and Africans,' he said as he hung his head, upset by the memory.

Cuffee and Mungo were busy boarding up all the windows and tying down the furniture on the porch, before taking refuge in their quarters. I hastily bid Peggy and Bess and young Sissy to come with me as Quame helped John hobble up to an attic room. We sat huddled together away from the windows in the centre of the room, listening to the violent gusts of wind trying to rip the roof away, if not the whole house. I sat next to John, holding his hand tightly, taking comfort from his quiet demeanour. He'd seen hurricanes before and survived, but I had a great fear in my heart that we would all surely perish.

Every nerve of my body tensed with each new gust of wind, each new clatter of rain against the shutters. Debris hit the roof. 'Broken branches,' Quame declared and I dreaded that a whole tree would come crashing down onto the house at any moment.

The wind blew so hard that several violent gusts caused the whole house to shake, even though the walls were built of solid brick and timber. After one extremely violent tremble, Sissy cried out in terror and John, who had been so calm and quiet all this time, raised his eyes to the roof, as if he expected it to have been blown away. He whispered to me, 'That felt like the shock of a ship striking against the ground,' and I knew he was worried about the *Alborough*, anchored out in the harbour.

We stayed up in the attic, trying to sleep but failing due to the noise of the wind and fear of imminent disaster. The slaves clung to each other, muttering chants in their own tongue and I prayed with all my might for the Lord to save us. The noise of the wind was deafening. Just when I thought that it couldn't get worse, the wind picked up even more.

Around midnight the storm was so ferocious there was no respite for my nerves, and then I heard panicking voices shouting outside. It sounded like Cuffee and Mungo were out in the storm. John was dozing fitfully, but he would be no help with his bandaged foot. Bess looked up as she had heard them too.

She and I crept downstairs and grabbed our bonnets and capes as if they could protect us from the elements. I gingerly opened the back door and, from the shouts coming from the dock, I realised that Cuffee and Mungo were trying to secure the rowboat.

As I stepped outside I was nearly blown off my feet so I grabbed Bess' arm. She was taller and stronger than me, my anchor. She flinched momentarily. It was the first time I had touched her, but I tightened my grasp and she leaned into me, trying to protect me. We held onto the side of the house, the window shutters and the porch railings as we made our way around the house,

I could see Cuffee and Mungo at the dock. They had managed to drag the rowboat ashore but were having difficulties moving it away from the water's edge. We ran towards them, weaving and swaying in the wind, our heads bowed against the driving rain.

Together we dragged the boat into the mangroves that grew on the swampy shore and Cuffee secured it by ropes to a couple of trees.

'That boat is our only access to the town,' he shouted to be heard. 'We couldn't lose it.'

A gust of wind suddenly swept up a wave of seawater which drenched us all and I realised how fool-hardy this had been.

'A boat could be replaced, Cuffee, but you can't. Let's get back to shelter quickly.'

We all crouched down and the men put their arms over Bess and me to shield us as we ran back to the house. We fell exhausted into the hallway. I was amazed we had all survived.

However, in the morning, my prayers were answered and the Good Lord mercifully came to our rescue. By noon the wind had dropped and the rain had stopped. The storm had passed and the flood waters had drained away. Cuffee and Mungo started sweeping away the debris that littered the gardens and repairing the damage to the outbuildings that had taken a battering. James, who had been on board the *Alborough* during the storm, sent John a message that the ship was safe, although the longboat had been driven from her moorings and smashed all to pieces.

Quame heard from passing boatmen that the storm had done a lot of damage in Charles Town. Dozens of ships were damaged in the harbour and many were driven ashore into the streets of the town. Roofs had blown off several dwelling houses, leaving their occupants without shelter from the wind and rain, and some buildings had been flattened, including the Baptists' wooden meeting house. Thousands of barrels of rice stacked up on the harbourfront had been lost. There were stories of a ship with German Palatines aboard which had been driven into the marsh near James Island and the passengers tossed from side to side. About twenty of them had lost their lives.

Quame reported that it was generally agreed that the damage could have been worse if the worst of the storm had arrived at high tide. Nevertheless, everyone had their own story of loss and damage. Sarah told me that their valuable rice crop, like so many other plantations near Charles Town, had been decimated by the storm. I thought life in Stratford was uneventful, but I would have given anything to be back with my family in the safety of a pleasant English summer. At least out there on Hog Island we had escaped with our lives.

By the middle of September, John's foot still hadn't healed, but he'd had enough of lying on a makeshift bed in the parlour. James had been visiting him regularly with updates and one morning John told me, 'I've sent the *Alborough* up to the careening dock at Hobcaw Creek to be cleaned.'

Had he forgotten already the terror of the hurricane that struck only weeks earlier?

'Don't go, John. At least wait until the Hurricane Season is over. You can't move out of the room or set your foot on the ground.'

'That's why I've ordered James, as my Lieutenant, to take the ship to Hobcaw Creek. To give me time to recover.'

I didn't want him to go back to sea. Some days I prayed he would never leave. It was hard work to look after him, but at least I knew he was safe with me on Hog Island.

He took my hand gently and said, 'You know I must return to duties, Mary-Anne. I have to finish the survey of Port Royal Harbour. I have to obey my orders from the Admiralty.'

There was nothing I could do or say to change the mind of my dutiful husband. Illness, injury, storms, hurricanes, Spaniards, pirates. Was there nothing that would stop him from obeying his orders from the Admiralty and staying home with his wife?

The *Alborough* came down from Hobcaw Creek at the start of October and moored against the Town Quay in Charles Town to get water on board and complete the provisioning. Two days later, four sailors arrived in the pinnace and carried John back to his ship as he still couldn't walk.

This summer had been exhausting, what with surviving a hurricane and nursing John's crippled foot. As I stood on the High Bluff and watched the *Alborough* sail across the Bar and out of Charles Town Harbour, I had never felt so lost and lonely in my whole life. The gales continued for the rest of October.

Despite not being able to walk, John set off in October to complete his survey of Port Royal.

From the Captain's Log, HMS Alborough
8th October 1730
Off the South end of Coffin-land
   "Moderate gales and fair weather. At 6 this morning the Ship was Unmoor'd. At 9 I was carried down to the Boat (not being able as yet to Walk) & went aboard. At 10 Weigh'd & at Noon Anchor'd in Rebellion Road in 7 fathom water."

Bad weather caused him to abandon this voyage and return to Charles Town 3 weeks later.

From the Captain's Log, HMS Alborough
26th October 1730
Off the South end of Coffin-land
   "Moderate gales and cloudy weather. PM The Foresail being Split in a Squall, bent another. The latter part little wind; when being Drove by the Gulph Stream (in the time of the Bad weather) within Fifty Leagues of Charles Town, being separated from the Happy & Dark Nights coming on, before we can possibly get back into the Gulph again, made sail for Carolina."

16

One morning in November, as I sat alone in the parlour, trying to focus on my needlework, the door burst open and Quame rushed in without knocking. 'Another letter has arrived, Mistress!'

Only yesterday John had sent me a letter. The *Alborough* never made it to Port Royal Harbour because of the severe gales and high seas and he was back in Charles Town. His ship was anchored in Rebellion Road, while he continued his survey of the Bar that he had abandoned in July when the tumour had appeared on his foot. He had written to tell me that sitting so constantly in the small boat for the past ten days taking his soundings had brought on the swelling of his legs again, to almost as great a degree as he was afflicted with at Port Royal.

I had sent a reply that he was to return home as soon as he could so I could care for him. Another letter made me fear the worst, but as I took the letter, I instantly recognised the handwriting as that of my sister, Alice.

I was surprised, as she didn't write to me often. Letters from home were from Mama or Betty, with details of daily life in Stratford, mainly concerning who had been born, married or died in the village. Mama made her disappointment clear that there had been no more marriages or births in our family but thankfully no deaths either. She had to rely on other families in the village for any news.

I ripped the seal to open it, interested in what Alice had to tell me.

Stratford, Co. Essex
20th August 1730

My dearest sister,
I hope these few lines will find you in a good state of health as we are at present thanks be to God for it. I have the most exciting news to tell you. Papa has arranged for me to travel to Charles Town as the Lady's Companion to the new Governor's Wife.

It all happened because in April the Schoolmaster, Mr Gilbert Bottomley, called upon us to see if Papa had any eligible daughters that he could marry. Mama made us all dress up prettily and sit nicely in a row on the sofa so that when our gentleman visitor was shown into the parlour, there we were, like three peas in a pod. Annie, of course, is only ten years old so she was discounted at his first glance. Which left Betty and me. Now you know I don't like to speak badly of my sister but in the two years you have been away she has not much improved in her countenance and she already looks matronly even though she's only twenty-three. She is as bossy as ever and kept interrupting Mr Bottomley to ask him questions about the position he was offering. We all know she would be perfect as a schoolmaster's wife. She would organise him and everyone else in the school, teachers, servants and pupils, which is exactly what the unfortunate man needs in a wife.

But his eye settled on me, even though I was trying to look as small and quiet and unassuming as I could so he wouldn't notice me. It was my own fault, pretending to be a docile little mouse. Who could have imagined he would find that desirable in a wife? Never fear, I told Papa later that day, I will never marry Mr Gilbert Bottomley and if he made me, I would run away. Can you imagine me as a schoolmaster's wife? Papa said I was unlikely to find a husband among Stratford's eligible bachelors and I heartily agreed.

Anyway, through an old friend in the Admiralty, Papa heard that Mr Robert Johnson has been appointed Governor of South Carolina. For the second time. He is returning to Charles Town to take up office by the end of the year. No doubt you know all about the political situation much better than I do, but Papa says that Mr Johnson resigned as Governor six years ago and has spent all his time in London seeking another royal appointment. Did you know that when he was Governor of Carolina last time, back in 1718, he captured and hung the notorious Gentleman Pirate, Stede Bonnet, off the coast of Carolina? It's so exciting.

His elderly wife Margaret, who suffers from ill health, was looking for a Lady's Companion to accompany her on the long sea voyage and keep her company in Charles Town so Papa suggested me for the position. I have a feeling he thinks his life will be easier if I go and live in Carolina. And you are there too, so it will be a happy reunion for us after these two years past.

As an Admiral's daughter I am, of course, most suitable for the position. Mr Burchett at the Admiralty recommended me so I went for tea with Mrs Roberts a fortnight ago and I must have impressed her as I have been offered the position. I don't think it will be too much work, as Mrs Roberts has her lady's maid to take care of her. She is travelling with her youngest child, a daughter, also called Margaret, so I will call her Meg. My role will be to entertain her and keep Meg amused. Meg is only seven and, as I am used to looking after Annie, I am perfect for the role. I will even be paid my own private allowance. Imagine it, I'm a lady of means at twenty-two.

I have already packed my travel chest and eagerly await our departure. Do you remember how envious I was of you when you were leaving on the Tryall three years ago? Well, now it's my turn for adventure. Mr Johnson plans to leave before the end of October and while we wait, I have asked Papa to arrange for this letter to be sent to you as soon as possible on one of his Navy ships so that you can have everything made ready for my arrival.

I look forward to seeing you soon. It will be just like the old days. What fun we will have.

Your loving sister,
Alice.

I had to read the letter several times before I could believe that Alice would shortly be arriving in Charles Town with the new Governor. Sarah would have to relinquish her social position as the Governor's Wife to Mrs Margaret Johnson, although from the sound of Alice's letter she was elderly and ill, so would pale in comparison.

I wasn't sure it would be just like the old days. It seemed such a long time ago that she and I had rushed to the church in secret so I could elope with John. These days, John was no longer the dashing naval officer I had run off to marry. He could hardly walk without a stick and I feared he would always limp on his bad foot. Alice wouldn't be sympathetic to his fever attacks or his swollen legs. I couldn't bear the thought that she would find fault with my husband. He was the most conscientious, dutiful and honourable man in the whole world and whatever his physical ailments I loved him dearly.

Still, in truth, he was away at sea a great deal and it would be wonderful to have Alice with me again, my sister, my best friend, my childhood companion and my trusted confidante.

I leant back in my chair, my needlework forgotten. The storm clouds were clearing and I knew my life was going to be happier once Alice arrived.

Detail of a 1780 map drawn by a British engineer of the Charleston defences
There is an island of high land in the marsh near the Eastern edge of Charleston Harbour
designated Hog Island.
Boston Public Library Digital Map Collection

III

Charles Town, South Carolina

1730-1732

Even within the protection of Charles Town Harbour, a single anchor could prove insufficient in a strong wind.

From the Captain's Log, HMS Alborough
11th December 1730
At Charles Town Harbour.

"Fresh gales & Cloudy weather, the latter part Rain. At 8PM Mr Maurice Harvey, the Pilot of a Brigantine arriv'd here from Poole yesterday, had gone onboard the Triton Pink of Bristol arrived from Barbados, Thomas Gale Master. He reports that having no Charge there, he went to Sleep, that waking about Midnight & hearing it blow very Fresh, he call'd out for Some-body to come to him, the Ship being at Single Anchor & bid the Man that answer'd him, to see if the Ship did not require more Cable. But by the time the Man got upon Deck, they felt a Stroke against the Ship and they immediately found 'twas the Ship striking against the Ground & that She was in the Breakers, which She bore very few Shocks of before she went all to pieces & John Hog the Pilot of her & several of the Men were Drowned. The Master and the rest of the Company got ashore on parts of the Wreck. Mr Harvey & the Master & Mate of the Brigantine, saved themselves in the Boat. She was lost against Coffing's Land (commonly call'd Coffin-land) so near five Leagues from where she had laid."

Governor Johnson arrived in Charles Town on 15th December 1730.

From the Captain's Log, HMS Alborough
15th December 1730
At Charles Town Harbour.

"Little wind and much Rain. PM Robert Johnson Esq. Governor Captain General & Commander in Chief in & over this his Majesty's Province, arriving here in His Majesty's Ship the Fox, which is at Anchor without the Bar, as is also the Lowestoffe. His Excellency was first Saluted by them & at his Landing by all the Forts & Merchant Ships in the harbour & by this Ship with 15 guns."

17

A large crowd on the quayside jostled for their first sight of the new Governor, Mr Robert Johnson. HMS *Fox* anchored in the harbour yesterday afternoon, with all its colours flying. It seemed the whole town wanted to welcome him, men and women, dignitaries and servants, white and black, old and young. I even saw a couple of Indian chiefs in their flamboyant feather headdresses. Soldiers were trying to keep order, but everyone was shoulder to shoulder, pushing and shoving, struggling to get a better view. Despite the threat of rain, there was a carnival atmosphere, with people dressed in their finest, flags flying and street hawkers selling flowers, chestnuts, sweet cakes and all manner of geegaws. A military band drummed loudly and friends shouted greetings to each other.

'It won't be possible to get through and meet Alice,' I said to John at my side.

I was so excited to see my beloved sister again after three years away from home, but we had arrived too late, the crowds were already five or six deep.

John grabbed my arm and somehow we managed to make our way through the tightly packed mass until we were nearer the front. Perhaps they respected his naval captain's uniform, perhaps they took pity on him, limping with his cane.

There was a flotilla of rowboats hovering around the *Fox* and when the Governor appeared on deck and climbed into a waiting pinnace all the forts and ships in the harbour fired their guns to welcome him. John had left instructions for James onboard the *Alborough* to fire fifteen guns to salute the new Governor, Captain-General and Commander-in-Chief of his Majesty's providence of Carolina. The noise was deafening.

As Johnson stepped ashore at Middle Quay, the crowd surged forward and erupted with jubilant cheers and shouts, throwing hats and bonnets in the air. I wasn't sure Arthur Middleton ever got such an enthusiastic reception. Sarah had told me her husband had relinquished power peacefully, although in the face of such rapturous public approval, it was hard to see that he could have done anything else.

I saw Alice as she came ashore with the Johnson family, but I was still too far back in the crowd to catch her attention. She was dressed in a fine travelling cape of scarlet velvet and a matching hat with tall black feathers.

She was smiling and waving at the crowd as if they had come to greet her and I hesitated to rush forward. She seemed at ease with her new family, smiling and talking to the Governor as if they were old friends. I couldn't say she was giving much assistance to his elderly wife as she struggled to climb out of the longboat or much attention to the young daughter, who appeared very shy. Instead, she stood proudly beside Johnson and all eyes were on her.

John muttered in my ear, 'Not so much a Lady's Companion as the Governor's Companion, I think.'

I punched him playfully on his arm to reproach him, but he was only saying what everyone must have been thinking.

It was impossible to catch her attention and speak to her on the quayside so John suggested we go to the Governor's House and be there to greet the family as they arrived. There was to be a grand Welcome Reception to which all the local dignitaries were invited; Arthur Middleton and all the members of the Assembly, Captain Norris, John and all the other naval captains, all the local officials and anyone who felt they were important enough in Charles Town to be there.

The crowds parted as the Johnson family made their way up the street to the Governor's House. Mr Johnson was shaking hands, exchanging words and giving thanks to his supporters as he passed well-wishers. His wife shuffled behind him, unnoticed next to Alice. I hardly recognised my little sister. She was a confident young lady of twenty-three, radiant with excitement, proud of the attention and confident of her attraction.

She saw me in the crowd and waved. 'Mary-Anne,' she shouted. 'Come over here!'

The folk in front of me stepped aside so we could greet each other. We had been apart for three years and seven months and I was overjoyed to embrace her to me at last. I would have held her for a long time, but she quickly pulled back and regained her composure, as if everyone was watching her, which of course they were.

She took my arm in hers and dragged me along in the procession. She gave no thought to John who couldn't push through the crowds or keep up. I glanced back at him helplessly, but he waved and shouted, 'See you at the reception.'

We walked arm in arm, giggling at the attention we were getting. She acted as my little sister until we arrived at the Governor's House. She suddenly let go of my arm, straightened her skirts, rearranged her curls and stood up straighter. Everyone had come early to be sure of a place, but there were far too many people to fit into the house and people spilt out into the street and garden.

'I am so pleased to see you, dearest sister,' she said. 'We may not get the chance to talk privately at the reception. Do call on me tomorrow morning and I will give you all the news from home. Don't have too much expectation, as it is all very dull.'

This was not what I expected from my reunion with Alice. As the eldest sister, I thought I would be welcoming her to Charles Town, not kept at a distance and given an invitation to visit her tomorrow. I managed to stammer, 'Of course, if that suits you, but our family is well?'

'Oh yes, they are all perfectly well. Come at eleven tomorrow and we'll talk then.'

'Won't you visit me at Hog Island?'

'Oh no! It will be more convenient for you to visit me in town, don't you think?'

With that, she turned and walked away to join the Roberts family as they entered their new home.

She was right, of course, I didn't get a chance to talk to her alone at the reception. All the ladies of Charles Town wanted to talk to her. They wanted to know if her gown was the latest fashion in England - it was. They wanted to know how she fared on her sea voyage - very comfortably. They wanted to know what the most popular dance in England was - the gavotte. And so on and so on. Alice was the latest arrival from England and must tell us what is new and must be copied in the Colonies. She held court among the ladies and enchanted everyone.

John was bemused by Alice's popularity. 'I can't understand her attraction,' he told me. 'She is not the prettiest girl here. And she talks too loudly.'

I didn't tell him that Alice might not be the prettiest girl there, but she sparkled like the brightest candle and everyone wanted to be in her glow. Yes, she talked loudly and laughed without reserve, as if she was enjoying herself. She smiled and looked directly at people without embarrassment as if she was interested in them. Even Ralph wanted to be introduced. I was surprised to see him there, but he claimed, as a gentleman, he was eligible for an invitation and Sarah needed his moral support.

'Who could have guessed my sister's place at the centre of Society would be so instantly usurped,' he whispered to me. 'She didn't think old Mrs Johnson would be too much of her challenge to her popularity, but she hadn't anticipated your sister.'

Neither had I, but I bit my lip, confused by my jealousy of Alice's immediate popularity and adoration by Charles Town society.

When I introduced him to Alice, he appeared tongue-tied and did not impress her with his wit and charm as he had me. She looked him up and down, from his blonde ponytail to his satin slippers, and rather rudely asked him what he did in Charles Town. Ralph has battled with that question all his life and had no answer. He made a joke about being the font of all gossip in Charles Town which caused her to stare at him. Was this a new trait of my sister or had I never noticed it before? She stared quite intently at people when they were talking to her, as if she was trying to see behind their face and inside their mind.

'Well, hopefully you will be kind enough to let me know what the gossip is about me,' she said, smiling fetchingly as she moved away to speak to some other dignitary, who wanted to know what the latest play was showing in London theatres - The Beggar's Opera.

Ralph was transfixed and couldn't speak or move. I nudged his arm to bring him back to me.

'What a creature!' he whispered under his breath. 'So fearless and brave. Your sister is unlike any woman I ever have met before.'

So even Ralph, my best friend, my charming escort and delightful dance partner, had fallen under her spell. Suddenly I wanted to leave the reception immediately and hear no more talk about the fabulous Alice Mighells. My only hope was that she would not have the time or inclination to befriend Ralph.

John was tired of standing around and happy to leave. His legs were swollen and his foot hurt. We made our hasty farewells and, as we were rowed home to Hog Island, the commotion of the celebrations in town faded. I took deep breaths to calm my anxious heart.

John sat quietly, exhausted, and didn't ask my opinion of the day's events, which was just as well because I was confused and hurt. I told myself that it was a busy, public event and it was not surprising I could hardly exchange a word with my sister in private.

'I'll return to my ship this afternoon,' he said. 'That old ketch, the *Cruizer*, arrived here two weeks ago to assist me as a second ship and now all this fuss with the new Governor arriving, my crew may need the reassurance of their Captain onboard. It was only last week that the *Triton Pink of Bristol* was wrecked on Coffin Land. The pilot and several of the men drowned. At least the Master and the rest of the company got ashore on parts of the wreck.'

I was disappointed that John wanted to go to his ship rather than stay at home with me. I knew he was happiest when he was on board his ship, but I wondered, not for the first time, how I had come to have such a lonely life. I always thought marriage would give me a family of my own, to replace my parents and sisters.

Thinking of sisters, I told John I had been invited to visit Alice tomorrow and he narrowed his eyes.

'I do hope her presence here in Charles Town will be a credit to your family.'

'A credit to our family,' I corrected him. 'She is your sister too, now we are married.'

'Hmm,' he said as if he never agreed to that at the altar. 'Her behaviour may be all the fashion in London society, but it is frowned upon here among more church-going folk.'

He turned away to watch his beloved *Alborough* swinging on her anchors.

The next morning I dressed carefully, painfully aware that my clothes were rather drab and old-fashioned. I decided on my best blue silk gown, the one I got married in so many years ago. It was rather faded now and the fabric had rotted under the armpits where I sweated in the damp summer heat, but it was still the most flattering to my looks. I was much thinner than when I left England and the fabric hung off me like a sack. Bess arranged my hair and I got cross with her for not having any knowledge of the latest styles in England and I instantly regretted my scolding.

The wind was fresh and the boat bounced along in the waves as Cuffee rowed me across the river to the town quay. I clutched at my bonnet and gave up all hope that my hair would look presentable by the time I arrived. The doorman at the Governor's House showed me into the small parlour where I had met Sarah two years ago after I twisted my ankle on arriving for dinner. My clumsy entrance into Charles Town society seemed a world away from Alice's triumphant arrival. I was expecting to look after Alice when she arrived in Charles Town. Papa would expect nothing less from me but, as I waited in the parlour, it was hard to imagine my little sister needing my assistance.

She didn't keep me waiting long and I was delighted that she had brought letters from home. She instructed me to read them later when I got home.

'There's nothing interesting to read,' she said.

'But tell me, is everyone well?'

'Oh yes. Mr Bottomley, the schoolmaster, didn't want to marry Betty, so she's still without a suitor. That's made her even more unbearable than she was. Annie is still a child and Papa still goes to work every day, despite Mama nagging him to stay home. I think he only goes to escape her nagging. Is it any wonder I had to leave home? Imagine spending one's whole life in Stratford.'

She laughed as she recounted their sad lives and I didn't recognise the family that I had been so homesick for.

'You know it's true. Anyway, tell me all about your life in Charles Town. How exciting that now I am here to share it with you.'

I told her about our home at Hog Island, but I didn't mention the empty bedrooms in the attic. I told her how much I enjoyed married life, but I didn't mention how ill John had been lately. I told her about John's important survey work, but I didn't mention how lonely I was when he was away. I made it sound as if my married life was full of harmony and happiness.

She interrupted me as she wasn't interested in harmony and happiness.

'I'm so pleased to see you Mary-Anne. You won't believe how dull Mrs Roberts is. I have to read to her, even though she's dozed off most of the time. She's terribly ill, of course so won't live for long. And Meg is such a pest, always demanding her father's attention. I don't think I'll ever have children,' she announced. 'I confess I'm surprised you haven't had a baby yet. I thought you wanted lots of children.'

I could feel my cheeks burning with shame. 'No, not yet but I'm sure the Good Lord will bless us very soon.'

'Well, perhaps it's for the best. Perfectly healthy women die in childbirth, you know. Do you remember Kate Thomas who lived down the road from us in Stratford? Well, she died giving birth to her second child and she was only your age.'

Every woman was terrified at the prospect of childbirth, the pain, the agony and the uncertainty of life or death. We had heard Mama's screams as her body was torn in half bringing our sister Annie into the world. So many women died in childbirth but many more survive and bear four, five, six children.

'We have no choice, Alice. Whatever the risk, it's the duty of married women to have children,' I told her. I knew only too well that without children, married women had no value in Society.

'Well, who knows I may remain a spinster.'

I despaired of her. A woman who was unmarried had even less value.

She suddenly dropped her voice to a conspiratorial whisper. 'Unless of course a certain governor finds himself in need of a second wife.'

'Alice! You mustn't say that. What will people think?'

Alice didn't care what other people thought. She started telling me how marvellous Robert Johnson was.

'On our voyage across the Atlantic, he shared with me all his plans for the growth of the colony. His Township Plan is so exciting. He wants to establish eleven townships in the interior, all of them on rivers. This will encourage lots of Europeans to come to South Carolina. Oh, he has such a wonderful vision for the future.'

I listened to her, appalled. John's remark that she was more of a companion for the Governor than for his wife rang true. I could see them on the ship, after his ailing, elderly wife had retired to bed, talking late into the night about his plans for the colony. Alice would be a much better helpmate for Robert Johnson than his sickly wife.

Suddenly she got up and came to sit close to me on the sofa.

'There is something I need to ask you,' she whispered. 'When John sends his reports back to Josiah Burchett at the Admiralty in

London, do you think there would be an opportunity for you to slip in a letter from me without his knowing?'

'Why would you need to send a letter without him knowing?'

'He might question why I am sending letters to Mr Burchett.'

I was taken aback by this unexpected turn in our conversation. 'Why are you sending letters to Mr Burchett? He's the Secretary of the Admiralty, isn't he?'

'If I tell you, Mary-Anne, this has to be a secret between us. Why do you think the Admiralty recommended me to be Mrs Johnson's companion? Mr Burchett is paying me to spy on the Governor.'

'Oh Alice, what have you got yourself into?'

'Don't look at me like that, sister. The allowance that Mrs Johnson pays me doesn't go far. I've had to buy new outfits to come to Charles Town, so the extra money from the Admiralty comes in very handy. But I wish I hadn't agreed to it now. I don't want to spy on Robert. I need to make something up and send a letter to Mr Burchett or he'll stop paying me.'

'What if Mr Johnson finds out?'

'I don't think Robert would ever suspect me. He trusts me and he tells me everything. In fact, I could be an excellent spy if I wanted to be, but the problem is, I don't want to. I like Robert too much.'

'Does Papa know what you're up to? Perhaps he can get you out of this situation?'

'What do you think! Papa recommended me to Mr Burchett. They are good friends and arranged this between them. You must help me, Mary-Anne. You are the only person I can trust.'

I was shocked. I couldn't believe Papa would encourage Alice in this way. He must have known it would lead her into trouble.

'Oh, I don't know, Alice. I wouldn't want to keep anything secret from John. And I don't think he will be pleased when he hears you are spying on the Governor.'

'You mustn't tell John! We have to keep it between us. I have to know I can trust you.' She took my chin in her hand and turned my face so I was looking directly at her. 'Can I trust you, Mary-Anne? Will you help me?'

Her large eyes were the darkest blue, almost black, so innocent, so hypnotic. They penetrated right into me as if she could read my innermost thoughts.

I hesitated a moment too long.

She turned away. 'Oh, forget I ever mentioned it. I thought you were my friend. You're obviously not the sister I thought you were.'

She got up, impatient for me to leave if I wouldn't help her in her nefarious activities.

I didn't want to leave without making peace with my sister. I wanted to be her friend, but I didn't want to get involved in her schemes and I didn't want to keep secrets from John. Before I had a chance to apologise or explain, she'd called the doorman who handed me my cape and bonnet and ushered me out of the front door.

My thoughts were tumbling around in my head and I started walking in the wrong direction, away from the harbour. Before long I was standing outside St Philip's Church. I attended Mass there on Sundays when the church was busy and crowded, but this morning it was deserted. The cool air in the quiet stone church was calming and sunlight streamed through the tall windows. I found an empty pew at the back and got down on my knees. I prayed as hard as I could that my family in England were well, that Betty would find a husband soon, that John would be safe at sea and that Alice wouldn't do anything foolish. Most of all I prayed that I would have a baby very soon.

The sun must have gone behind a cloud as a shadow passed over me. I had a sudden dread that the Lord was punishing me in some way and I could feel a cold stone sitting in my womb where a baby should be growing. I rushed out of the church in tears and collapsed on the grass in the warm sunshine, swearing to be a better wife to John and a better sister to Alice. I would do whatever it took for the Lord to bless me with a child.

HMS Alborough returned from the careening wharf at Hobcaw Creek at the end of March and took provisions onboard. The Governor came onboard to dine.

From the Captain's Log, HMS Alborough
26ᵗʰ March 1731
In Cooper River in South Carolina

"*Little wind & fair weather, the latter part Squally weather with Rain. Receiv'd Rum & Beer to compleat our Victualing for four Months. At Noon his Excellency Robert Johnson Esq Governor of this Province, the Lieutenant Governor, coming aboard to Dine with me, I saluted him at his coming into the Ship with 17 Guns. In the Evening I saluted the Governor at his going from the Ship with 19 Guns. The two Sloops Saluted him also at his coming & going.*"

John departed on 3ʳᵈ April 1731, bound for the Bahamas. With only four pilots in Charles Town, all taken by the Naval Ships that day, two merchant sloops ran great risks attempting to cross the Bar.

From the Captain's Log, HMS Alborough
3ʳᵈ April 1731
Off Charles Town Bar

"*Fresh gales & fair weather. At 6 this morning having made the signal unmoor'd. At ½ past 9 weighed & at 11 crossed the Bar in 17 feet water. When we got into 6 fathom water, we were Obliged to Anchor, the Tide of the Ebb being made strong to the Northward & the wind Southerly, that we could not hold our own, for the Boat to get aboard and take the Pilots out. The Lowestoffe anchored also for the same reason with this Ship and the two Sloops. Two Merchant Sloops attempted to follow us out from the Harbour, on board one of which was Governor Rogers of the Bahamas, the other was bound also to Providence & St Christopher's which latter ran ashore on the North Breaker Head and was lost, but the People saved themselves in their Boat & the Governor's Sloop narrowly escaping, ran up the Harbour again. They had neither of them Pilots aboard, the number of Pilots for this Port being limited to Four by the Laws of the Province, who are now one on board each Man of War, so that if there had been a Fleet of Merchant Ships to have come out at the same time with us, there would have been no Pilot for any of them & they might all have been lost by that means, for this Bar is a very Difficult place for People not perfectly acquainted with it.*"

18

Alice's spying activities were not mentioned again for several months. She had decided not to talk to me about whatever she was up to and I didn't want to ask, especially in front of John. He was displeased with all the gossip about the "*Governor's wife's companion*", which he told me was said with a wink and nod in most salons in town. If I asked her to think of her reputation, she laughed and told me more about Mr Johnson's exciting plans for the expansion of the colony.

It didn't help my marriage though. John thought that as the elder sister, I should be responsible for her behaviour. His displeasure was clear and he preferred to spend time onboard the *Alborough* than take tea with my sister and me. The Admiralty had given him a second sloop in addition to the *Happy* to help with his surveys, but the *Cruizer* didn't seem seaworthy and Captain Billopp was so old and infirm that John had appointed his son, Thomas, to act as captain in his place.

John had orders to back go to Providence. He wanted to survey the Abaco Islands because the Bahamas were of great strategic importance in our hostility with the Spanish, lying to the east of Florida and north of Cuba. I reminded him that we were not at war with Spain, but these last few weeks he had been too busy up at Hobcaw Creek getting repairs done to his ships to listen to my views.

At the start of April, the *Alborough,* together with the support sloops, the *Happy* and the *Cruizer,* sailed out of Charles Town Harbour, heading back to the Bahamas in convoy with the Governor of the Bahamas, Woodes Rogers.

Before he sailed, John had told me that Governor Robert Johnson had come onboard the *Alborough* to dine with him.

'Is he as interested in your surveys as Middleton was?' I'd asked him.

'Actually, he was more interested in your sister.'

'Alice? Why was he talking to you about her?'

'He asked me if I thought she was trustworthy.'

My blood ran cold. No one who knew Alice could ever describe her as trustworthy.

'What a strange question,' I said. 'What did you tell him?'

'I told him Alice was many things, spirited, independent and headstrong, but trustworthiness was probably not one of her attributes.'

'Oh John, that was a very disloyal thing to say about your sister-in-law.'

He tutted as if he wasn't prepared to lie, especially for his troublesome sister-in-law.

So, while John was away, I had to warn Alice that Johnson suspected her of spying. If I could get her to stop, I could solve two problems at once. Alice could distance herself from the Governor and stop the rumours and John would be pleased with me when he returned.

Cuffee rowed me in the boat across to Middle Bridge and I called on Alice at the Governor's Residence. To avoid us being overheard, I invited her to walk with me along Bay Street. She liked to be seen promenading and she got her cloak and bonnet.

As soon as we were clear of the house, I told her about the Governor's dinner with John and his question about her trustworthiness.

She looked thoughtful. 'What a shame, I was enjoying myself. I never reported any real secrets, but I enjoyed writing entertaining letters to Mr Burchett. I don't want him to stop my payments.'

'Promise me you'll stop, Alice. It could be dangerous if Mr Johnson discovers what you're up to. There must be laws in Carolina about spying on the Governor. You might be sent to jail.'

'Oh, don't fuss so. There are government spies in every important household, don't you know? The Government pays well for secrets. Robert's valet is definitely spying on him, but perhaps you're right. Last week young Meg discovered me listening at Robert's study door while he was meeting some of the councillors. She's such a sneaky child and she told her father what I was doing. Luckily he has no time for her and I denied everything she said. That's probably what instigated his questions to John.'

She looked thoughtful but wouldn't hear any more from me on the subject so we passed the rest of our walk commenting on the gowns of the other ladies we meet. Behind their backs, we judged the quality of lace on their gowns, the amount of alum on their faces and the width of the hoops in their skirts. It felt good to be exchanging trivial conversations with my sister and she even deigned to walk arm-in-arm with me. In the spirit of newfound camaraderie, she invited me to a Ball at the Governor's house on Saturday. Without John to escort me, I was reluctant to go out in Society, but I agreed in order to keep an eye on her.

At the Ball, Alice was escorted by the Governor himself. Excuses were made that his wife had taken to her bed with sickness. Alice was wearing a beautiful dress, with flowing pleats down the back in the French style. It looked so relaxed compared to the gowns other ladies were wearing. The red silk, embroidered with a vibrant floral pattern, suited her pale complexion and black hair, which cascaded in curls onto her bare shoulders. Every woman who had powdered their hair white and donned a pale pastel, stiff-bodied mantua gown looked pale and insipid next to her rich colours. The extra payments from Josiah Burchett at the Admiralty were obviously well spent at her dressmaker.

She stood beside the Governor, captivating all the dignitaries who surrounded him. She smiled coyly at Mr Johnson, touching his arm lightly. I was relieved John wasn't there to see her wanton behaviour.

She had no time to talk to me so I was delighted to see Sarah and Ralph chatting in a corner. Ralph had become besotted with Alice since I had introduced her. He told me he adored her wilful spirit and defiance of convention.

'She is so unlike any of the insipid, silly young ladies that fill most of the drawing rooms of Charles Town.'

Sarah hated her because Ralph was acting like a lovesick teenager and because no one sought Sarah's favour anymore, now that Arthur Middleton was just another councillor. Like everyone, she couldn't help talking about my sister, complaining that everything Alice wore would be discussed for days on end. I smiled when she told me that Alice started wearing a band of lace around her neck, telling everyone it was the latest fashion from Paris. I told her it was because Alice had no jewellery to wear.

'Well, it doesn't matter now. All the ladies who matter in Carolina society have taken off their jewels and now wear lace around their necks.'

She seemed to blame me for introducing Alice into Charles Town society as if I had done this deliberately to spite her.

'It's not enough humiliation that Johnson has usurped my poor Arthur as Governor. Your sister has usurped my position in Society. Well, I hope you are happy,' she said, flouncing off in a huff.

Ralph, embarrassed by his sister's accusations, kindly invited me to dance. I used to enjoy dancing, but this evening my heart was not in it. I thanked him after one dance and retired to the shadows. I watched everyone enjoying themselves and felt tearful that I was all alone, a married woman without a husband.

I sought out Alice and made an excuse about leaving to get back to Hog Island before it got too late. It was raining heavily and I had foolishly let Cuffee go back earlier in the evening. Asking him to wait for me in the rain while I enjoyed an evening of dancing seemed thoughtless and I could always hire a ferryman.

She dragged me into the small parlour off the reception hallway.

'I need you to take a letter for me.'

I pulled away from her.

'No, Alice don't ask me. John's away, there's nothing I can do to help you.'

'Hush Mary-Anne, be quiet and listen carefully. There is a brigantine on the quayside, the *Charming Mary*. She's sailing for London at dawn tomorrow and the Master, Daniel Bell, has agreed to take a letter for me.'

'I thought you promised me you would stop all his nonsense.'

'I am going to stop, but I have to send one last letter to explain the situation and I can't leave here tonight without attracting suspicion. You must see that.'

I turned away and looked into the hallway to check no one was passing by, listening to us.

'Don't ask me to do this,' I whimpered.

'Even if you won't help your own sister, think about your duty to the Admiralty. Your father and your husband have devoted their lives to serving the nation and when I ask you to do this simple thing, you fail me.'

She thrust the letter into my hand and pushed my hand inside my cape.

'I am trusting you to do this one thing for me, Mary-Anne. You will do it, won't you?' She looked at me long and hard, waiting for me to agree.

If I had said no, she would have said again that I wasn't her friend. I was a fool for desperately wanting her favour. I stood there with my hand on the letter inside my cape, unable to resist her.

'Oh, and don't worry,' she said as she turned to leave, 'it's in secret cypher so, if it gets into the wrong hands, no one will be able to read it.'

As if that made me feel any better.

The ferry dock was at Middle Bridge. Even on a rainy evening, it was busy and well-lit by torches, a public place. Soldiers needed to get across to the fort, passengers needed to get out to merchant sloops anchored in the bay and farmers needed to get across to Sullivan Island. I would have been quite safe waiting for a ferry to take me home to Hog Island.

The docks where the trading vessels sat quietly, waiting for morning to load and unload their cargoes, stretched away into the darkness. I regretted sending Cuffee home, he could have come with me. I gathered my cape closer around me and asked the nearest ferryman where I might find the *Charming Mary.* He pointed to the darkness on my left.

'Down at the far end, Crockatt's Bridge. But mind your step, m'lady, you have no business down there at this time of night. It ain't safe for the likes of you.'

He didn't need to tell me. Every bone in my body was shaking. I wanted to run back to the ferry, throw the letter into the water and tell Alice I did as she asked me, but I was more afraid of facing her again. She would know instantly I was lying.

I tried not to look about at the dark shadows, where mad dogs or drunk men might be lurking. I walked purposefully down the quayside, checking the name of each vessel I passed.

A group of six or seven men stood around a fire in a brazier. I thought of asking them for more directions, but they were busy distributing money from a bag and would not appreciate any interruption to their villainous activities. I hoped the lure of gold coins would allow me to pass by unnoticed. Unfortunately, one of the men saw me and left his comrades to stand in front of me, blocking my way.

'What have we here? A whore in a fancy dress.'

His face was misshapen into a terrible grimace. I could smell his evil breath, see his rotten teeth, anticipate the danger I was looking at. He meant me harm.

I was too scared to make a move for fear I would faint with terror, but I looked into his grotesque face and was emboldened. I would not be molested on this stinking wet quayside. I had too much to lose, my marriage, my reputation, my life.

His friends had started jeering and cheering him on. I cast my eyes around looking for an escape route. I should turn and run, but I was rooted to the ground. Among the rubbish discarded on the quayside I spotted the broken handle of a wooden oar. Without thinking I bobbed down, feigning a curtsey, and grabbed the wooden weapon. As I rose, I swung it hard into the side of his arm.

He swore loudly in anger and pain and then I found my voice, a terrifying scream.

Suddenly the man stepped back and held both hands up in submission.

'I meant no harm,' he mumbled and turned to flee. His friends had melted away into the darkness.

I brandished my weapon wildly in front of me, hollering and shouting after him, drunk with my success.

Then I sensed a presence standing behind me and turned around, my wooden oar raised in defence. The man in front of me was an imposing figure, sturdy and broad-shouldered, wrapped in a thick black cloak, his black hat obscuring his face. Three men stood behind him. Big, tough men carrying muskets. No wonder my attacker had run off when he saw them. I didn't know if they were there to help me or threaten me, but I knew my broken wooden oar was no defence against them.

'Dangerous to walk down here at this time of night,' the man said to me. 'You would do better to seek business in the taverns in town. Although possibly not armed with such a weapon.'

He slowly reached out and took the weapon from me. As he leaned forward, I noticed he was grinning and finding the situation most amusing. I felt quite crest-fallen after my heroics a moment ago. He was watching me closely, waiting for me to explain myself.

'I am not a whore,' I said quietly. I'd never said that word before. I was scared to tell him who I was. What business would the wife of Captain John Gascoigne of His Majesty's Ship *Alborough* have down at the docks late at night, all on her own?

As I lowered my eyes in modesty, I spotted the letter that Alice wanted me to deliver, lying on the wet ground out of my reach. It must have dropped from my cape when I grabbed the oar. The man followed my gaze and picked it up.

'What's this? A letter addressed to the Admiralty Office in London. I was not expecting that.'

He teased me by offering the letter and then withdrawing it out of my reach. He was smiling at my discomfort.

'Please let me have that letter. I need to deliver it to Master Bell of the *Charming Mary*. He is expecting to receive it before he sails at dawn tomorrow.'

After a short hesitation, while he assessed the situation, he reached out to shake my hand most politely.

'Allow me to introduce myself. Mr Thomas Gadsden, Collector of His Majesty's Customs in Charles Town, at your service. I often patrol here with my men at night to catch smugglers and foreigners, anyone who chooses to carry on their clandestine activities under cover of darkness.'

He looked at me as if I might be one of those operating under cover of darkness. I straightened my petticoats as best I could to look respectable. I hesitated to introduce myself. I couldn't involve John in this mess. Without thinking I blurted out, 'And I am Miss Alice Mighells. I want to give this letter to Master Bell and then return home.'

'The *Charming Mary* is moored down at Crockatt's Bridge. Perhaps you will allow me and my men to escort you.'

We walked in silence past five or six ships, which lay in darkness, the sailors either asleep below decks or somewhere in the back streets of Charles Town, spending their pay on rum, ale and real whores. When we came alongside the *Charming Mary*, Gadsden banged his fist against the side of the ship and shouted, 'Master Daniel Bell, you have a visitor.'

I was pleased Mr Gadsden was there. He knew the ship and the Master. I would never have been able to shout loud enough to wake Master Bell. My whole mission was dangerous and fanciful and I will never forgive Alice for getting me into this. After an eternity, a man appeared at the gunwale.

'I am Daniel Bell, the Master of this ship. Who wants to speak to me at this time of night?'

'I have Miss Alice Mighells with a letter she wants you to take to the Admiralty Office in London. She says you are expecting her?'

He furtively nodded his head. I understood from his guilty look that he had been paid to deliver Alice's letter and didn't appreciate the Collector of Customs being involved.

Gadsden handed over the letter and Bell grabbed it quickly and disappeared below, like a rabbit down his hole.

As we turned away, Gadsden asked where he should take me now. I couldn't think of anywhere better than my old house on Church Street. It was quite comforting walking beside Mr Gadsden, with his henchmen following behind.

'Please don't tell anyone,' I said. I had never met this man before, but I had to trust him. 'No one can know about that letter. It's a matter of national security,' I added rather grandly.

He laughed and said nothing more. We walked in companionable silence, bound together by our secret of national security.

I bade him farewell at the corner of Church Street with an assurance that I would be fine from there and would go straight home. He and his men turned and disappeared into the night. I waited for the count of twenty and then ran down to the ferry dock and got a boatman to take me across to Hog Island and the safety of home. I was shaking all the way and was overjoyed to see Cuffee waiting on the dock to help me ashore.

I rushed up to my room and collapsed on the bed, gasping for breath. How differently the evening might have ended if Mr Gadsden hadn't come along at that moment and saved me. I would never forgive Alice for putting me in such danger. Imagine if John knew what she had asked of me and what had nearly happened. He would never forgive her, or me.

One thing was certain, I must never meet Mr Gadsden again. He must never know my true identity or meet the real Alice Mighells.

Bad weather and damage to the ships caused John to abandon his survey of the Bahamas and return to Charles Town in May 1731.

From the Captain's Log, HMS Alborough
19ᵗʰ April 1731
At noon the South End of Abaco W27°N40°

"Hard Squalls of wind & rain. At 1PM had a Violent Tornado with wind all round the Compass. At 4 saw the Hole in the Rock, bearing WSW 2 Leagues off. Got down the Topgallant Yards, the Squalls succeeding one & other with great Violence, every two or three hours, in one of which put abroad a light in the Main top & another on the Poop & sailed away before it under the Foresail. At noon being within 2 Leagues of the Shore of Ilathera, my Pilot (George Dorset) not knowing the Land, I made the Signal for the Happy, whose Pilot (one Flavell) affirms it to be the North part of Abaco, but we are certain 'tis Ilathera but for want of an Observation are at a Loss to know how far to the Southward or Northward the part we see is. The Cruizer lost company in the night."

From the Captain's Log, HMS Alborough
16ᵗʰ May 1731
Anchored In Rebellion Road

"Surveyed the edge of the white water of the Bahama Bank but the wind blew directly off the bank so that the ships cold not follow the boats. We kept our wind with all the sail we could make in order to view the whole range of the North Cays of the Abaco and from thence to stretch over to Providence for the Cruizer Sloop and having visited the adjacent islands thereabouts, but at 5 this morning Captain Lloyd of the Happy wrote me notice that on Friday night last his small Bower cable parted but he was obliged to leave the anchor and part of the cable behind, but he has now out two anchors aboard & does not think it safe (least another such accident should happen) to go among the islands where we have met with abundance of foul ground, till he is supplied with another anchor for the better security of the sloop . Therefore at 7 bore away for Carolina this ship having also broken the anchor off Hind's Bluff."

19

John returned to Charles Town in late May. He had only been away six weeks and he was not in the best of humour. Although he had done some surveying in the Islands of the Bahamas, the old *Cruizer* had such problems with her rotten sails that she couldn't keep up. When the Captain sent word that the windlass was also damaged so he couldn't anchor at night, John ordered him to go to the nearest place to get wood to make a new one and to join him at Providence. Then the *Happy* lost her anchors on a reef so John decided to abort his mission and return home to get repairs done.

I hoped there would be peace as Alice wasn't in Charles Town at the moment. She had accompanied Governor Johnson and his wife on a visit to New York. Life would be easier if John and Alice weren't in the same town.

'What on earth can you do with your sister, Mary-Anne? Can't you find a suitable husband for her? That would put an end to the rumours.'

He seemed to think that, as her eldest sister, I should find a solution to the problem that was Alice. He was exhausted, getting new sails for the *Cruizer* and new anchors for the *Happy*. He didn't want the extra stress of what to do with Alice. I couldn't tell him that Alice had set her cap on marrying the Governor as soon as he was widowed.

To avoid talking to me about it, he spent most of his time onboard the *Alborough* so we had no time together as a married couple. It seemed that any plans I had to get pregnant again would have to wait until his ships were repaired and Alice was married off.

But who would marry her, with such a reputation? Papa would expect me to find her a naval captain, but Captain Norris of the *Lowestoffe*, the Senior Naval Captain in Charles Town, would have nothing to do with her, nor Captain Lloyd of the *Happy* and Captain Billop of the *Cruizer* was an old, infirm man.

One afternoon at the end of May, as the sun was starting to fall in the sky to the west over Charles Town, I was relaxing on the porch at Hog Island with my dear friends, Sarah and Ralph.

The air was heavy with the fragrance of spring blossoms after the rain and we were lazily drinking mint juleps. Ralph told us the latest gossip in town, who had just arrived from England, who was eligible for marriage, who was having an affair. We started talking about Mrs Manigault's upcoming Summer Ball, the pinnacle of the Charles Town social calendar and the source of Ralph's discomfort three years ago. Sarah asked Ralph, rather facetiously, if he planned to escort Alice to the Ball and started teasing him about his infatuation with my sister. It was true that they had become good friends recently, but Sarah warned him that Alice was only toying with him to divert attention from rumours of her affair with the Governor. He laughed and said he wasn't jealous of Robert Johnson.

The solution to the problem that was Alice suddenly came to me. I asked Ralph if he would marry Alice.

Sarah sat up suddenly and agreed that it was an excellent idea.

'You are hopelessly devoted to the young lady,' she said. 'And you and she would make the perfect couple. What with your beauty and her charm, you'd be quite the Society Couple.'

He looked at us aghast, but Sarah could see the benefits and carried on. 'You would be back in favour with Charles Town society and I would once again be invited to all the best events in town.'

He turned to face me and said most earnestly, 'I love your sister dearly, Mary-Anne, but only as a friend. You must know I am not the marrying kind.'

His sister would not let him escape so easily. 'We all know that you will have to take a wife eventually. For appearance's sake, for our family's reputation and for my position in Society. You could escort her to Mrs Manigault's Summer Ball and propose to her there.'

He slumped forward with his head between his hands. 'You know I can never marry, Sarah. It would be unfair on any young lady as I would never want children,' he said as if that excludes him from marriage.

'Then you two would be well suited,' I told him.

Alice had made it clear that childbirth was a pain too great to bear. I thought about how easily Janet gave birth and wanted to argue with her. When I started to tell her that the risk was worth it for the joy of holding a newborn baby in your arms, she looked at me as if to say, what would you know about it? And obviously, I didn't know anything about it.

Ralph would not be persuaded or cajoled or bullied into proposing marriage to Alice. I even told him of the dowry she would bring, in order to bribe him.

'I will get down on my knees and offer her my lifelong devotion, but I will not offer her my hand in marriage,' he declared. 'It would ruin a beautiful friendship.'

My plans to find Alice a husband were thwarted and Ralph left Charles Town a week later to stay with his friend in Philadelphia for the summer. Sarah and I knew he had gone to escape any schemes we might have had for his upcoming marriage.

John's problems with his ships continued. At the start of June, he sailed again for Providence, but as soon as he left Charles Town he found the bowsprit on the *Alborough* was rotten. Back he came, got a new bowsprit fitted, left again ten days later but had to return after three days.

'As we headed out towards the Bar I heard a crack as loud as a pistol at the head of the mainmast,' he told me. 'We anchored in Rebellion Road and I discovered that the mast, and the cheeks that hold it upright, were also rotten.'

Lucky for me though, as John was now stuck in Charles Town. The *Alborough* couldn't go anywhere without a new mast. He could be my escort to Mrs Manigault's Summer Ball at the end of June. Mr Peter Manigault was reputed to be the wealthiest man in Charles Town, if not the whole of the American colonies, and the Ball promised to be a very grand affair.

The Governor's entourage returned from New York in the middle of June and to avoid any worsening of the rumours, I invited Alice to come to the Summer Ball with John and me. I was surprised when she accepted my invitation, but her demeanour had changed since the trip to New York

'I have been so stupid, Mary-Anne,' she confessed to me in a moment of sisterly confidence. 'I asked Robert what would become of me when Mrs Johnson passed away. She was so ill in New York; it is surely only a matter of months. He said I could stay on in the household, perhaps as Meg's governess. A governess! It is quite clear, my dear sister, that he has no intention of marrying me.'

'Did he give you expectations?' I asked, well aware that young women can sometimes misunderstand the attentions of men.

'No, not exactly. He never said anything, but I thought he was being a gentleman. Now I realise he never loved me. Oh, I know what people say about me, but it's not true. I am not his mistress. I was holding out for the higher prize, but it has all been in vain. I so wanted to be a Governor's wife.'

'Perhaps it is for the best, Alice,' was all I could say. 'You couldn't marry Mr Roberts just because he was a Governor. You must marry someone who loves you.'

'Oh it's fine for you to talk. You have a loving husband. Anyone can see you are beloved.'

I touched my locket with John's miniature to reassure myself I had a loving husband. I didn't always feel beloved, not when John put his naval duties above me, but I bit my lip.

'Anyway, I'll never find another suitor with my reputation, so now I am ruined.'

'Who knows, perhaps we can find a suitable husband for you at the Ball,' I said hopefully, but she was right. With her reputation who would court her now?

Mrs Manigault's grand mansion was as impressive as any of her husband's plantation houses, a large three-storied double house, fronting Meeting House Street. On the evening of the Ball, the house and gardens were lit with torches and a thousand candles. Ralph often joked that the rich folk in Charles Town were as near as the Colonies got to royalty.

The Great Hall, with its tall ceilings and elaborate chandeliers, had a grand stairway, leading up to a landing that commanded an impressive view over the rooftops to the Cooper River. As we entered, the doorman solemnly announced us as 'Captain and Mrs John Gascoigne of His Majesty's Navy and Miss Alice Mighells.'

I knew Alice turned heads, but I was pleased to see that next to her, I also got a few admiring glances. We looked very similar. It was clear we were sisters.

John wandered off to talk to Captain Norris, the Post Captain who had replaced George Anson last year. Alice and I made our way up the staircase to the landing where small tables had been set out. From this vantage point we could see the guests standing below. I noticed

Governor Robert Johnson by the buffet, talking loudly to the Councillors gathered around him. His wife was a silent shadow next to him. Alice saw them and took a deep breath, standing taller, head held high, composing herself for the evening on her own.

John joined us for supper but, when the dancing resumed, Alice made her excuses and wandered off into the gaming rooms to join a table where Faro was being dealt.

John muttered under his breath about the perils of gambling, but she'd wandered off without taking heed.

'It's only Faro, John,' I said to pacify him. 'Everyone is playing it these days, especially ladies. Where's the harm in a bit of fun?'

'There are many stories of fortunes changing hands over the gaming table. I do hope her virtue will not be put at risk if she finds herself beholden to a male creditor,' he replied.

To distract him from worrying about Alice's virtue, I asked him if we could dance the minuet, but he made his excuses, saying his foot still hurt him. It was almost a year since his operation but when would we ever dance together again?

We stood and watched the dancers. Friends came and talked to us and, with my husband beside me, I was greeted as a respectable married woman. One lady, who didn't know me well, asked after our children and I had the embarrassment of explaining we didn't have any yet. John went quiet and I felt his disappointment that, after four years of marriage, we were still childless.

After an awkward silence and in an attempt to change the conversation, one of the ladies pointed out that Mr Thomas Gadsden had just walked into the Ballroom. All eyes turned to look. He looked a great deal more refined than when I last saw him on the dockside, out to scare smugglers and thieves. He cut a dashing figure in his fancy silk waistcoat, despite being at least forty years old.

'Such a shame about the second Mrs Gadsden dying last year,' one of the gossips whispered.

'Still, I don't suppose it'll be long before he finds another wife. They say he's very rich.'

'Well, for my liking he would have to curb his fascination for the gaming tables.'

As they sniggered among themselves, John and I politely extricated ourselves from the group.

'Do you know that gentleman?' I asked him when they were out of hearing.

'Yes, he's the Collector of Customs and despite what they say, he's a respectable gentleman. Whenever I've dealt with him over the supplies from the Admiralty, he seems most professional. I've seen his warnings posted at the docks that smugglers who carry on clandestine and illegal trade with Spaniards and other foreigners must obey the law or risk prosecution. I have a lot of respect for the man. Oh look, there he is now!'

To my horror, he gave Gadsden a friendly wave. Gadsden looked over and I saw the flash of recognition in his eyes as he noticed me standing beside John. He hesitated for a second and then he walked slowly towards us.

I wanted to collapse on the floor in a faint, run screaming from the room or slap the nearest lady across her cheek. Anything to cause a diversion, to stop him from approaching. I prayed that he had forgotten our midnight meeting last month. My mind raced as to how I could explain, both to him and John, that the lady he had rescued on the docks was not Miss Alice Mighells.

He was upon us and greeted John in a most cordial way. He turned to me with a charming smile.

'Miss Mighells, I am delighted to make your acquaintance again.'

So, he hadn't forgotten our meeting! John looked confused. 'Mary-Anne is no longer Miss Mighells, Gadsden. Allow me to introduce my wife, Mrs Mary-Anne Gascoigne.'

'My mistake. Please excuse my error,' he said, bowing humbly. He was grinning as if he knew my secret all along.

'Miss Alice Mighells is her sister. They do look quite alike, I'll admit. That's her over there,' John said pointing to Alice.

At that moment, Alice threw back her head and laughed loudly, as if she knew we were looking at her. Despite her troubles, she was so full of joyfulness and gaiety, so irresistible and exciting.

After staring at her for longer than was polite, Gadsden said to me, 'Perhaps you will do me the honour of introducing me to that Miss Alice Mighells.'

I felt instinctively that I should keep this man from meeting my sister. Was he a suitable gentleman? Who were his family? What would Papa think of him? He was the Collector of Customs who wandered the docks at night looking for criminals, but I had to seize this opportunity to get him away from John.

'Of course, I would be delighted,' I said, feigning brightness, as I took his arm and pulled him away.

'Mr Gadsden,' I whispered as soon as we were out of John's hearing. 'I am grateful for your assistance at the docks. I believe you saved my life, but please don't say anything to my husband about my errand for my sister. And please don't mention my misadventures to Alice. I promise I'll speak to her and it won't happen again.'

He was trying not to laugh and I realised he was finding my discomfort amusing. He was quite attractive in a devilish way and I surreptitiously removed my hand from his arm in case I gave him the wrong impression of my gratitude.

'I have seen your sister in the company of the Governor,' he said. 'Perhaps I should speak to her, warn her about the dangers of secret letters delivered to the docks at midnight.'

'Well, she may listen to you more than she takes heed of me. She doesn't realise the dangers involved.'

'Let's hope she is working for the right side. The patriots could do with brave informants at this time.'

'She doesn't work for the patriots! My sister is the daughter of Vice-Admiral James Mighells. She is acting in the interests of His Majesty's Government.'

He laughed. 'Then I definitely need to have words with her.'

Now I knew he was teasing me and I wasn't sure how to keep our conversation on a respectable level.

'Mr Gadsden, please be serious. She might be in danger. It's not a game she's playing.'

'Not a game, no, but if it were, I cannot imagine more delightful pawns.'

I wanted to admonish him for the mischievous way he said that, but we had reached the table where Alice was playing cards. I touched her shoulder to interrupt her game and introduced her to Mr Thomas Gadsden.

She turned and looked him up and down slowly. Time seemed to stop, waiting for her response. Then finally, and very slowly, she lifted her hand to arrange the curls of her hair coquettishly on her bare shoulder. A clearer gesture of interest could not have been given.

Gadsden bowed low, without taking his eyes off her bare shoulder. I blushed at the intimacy of his stare. Alice held out her hand and he grasped it. She laughed and, unusually for my sister who always stared so directly at people, she lowered her eyes as he placed a kiss on her hand.

'Mr Gadsden,' she said, 'your notoriety precedes you. The story of how you lost a landholding to Captain Anson in a single hand of cards some five years ago has worked its way into the city's folklore, but I am winning at cards tonight so will not be needing your advice.'

I looked from one to another, bewildered that they were talking about my former admirer, George Anson. Still, perhaps with his dubious reputation as a gambler, Gadsden could hardly comment on her reputation as the Governor's paramour.

'A small acreage north of Charles Town, I assure you Miss Mighells, although as the city grows perhaps it may be more of a loss in a few years.'

'I trust you have other landholdings that you take better care of.'

'Have no fear, my dear lady. My fortune remains intact.'

'I am pleased to hear it, sir.'

They were smiling at each other as if sharing a private joke, holding eye contact longer than was respectable. An understanding had been reached, a bargain struck, a pact agreed upon.

He gently took the playing cards out of her other hand, laid them discarded on the gaming table and asked if she would honour him with a dance.

He seemed to pull her to her feet or did Alice rise up from her chair into his arms? Who could blame her? He was bold and handsome and most attractively gallant. A chivalrous man who could rescue you from any danger. A dashing hero who could resurrect your reputation.

As I watched them walk towards the dance floor, I was left standing alone by the Faro table, forgotten by Thomas Gadsden and my sister. Everyone turned to watch them pass. They moved closer together and when he placed his hand on her lower back, just above her bustle, to guide her through the crowd, I knew in an instant what the future held.

I had an overwhelming memory of when John first asked me to dance at the Naval Ball. It seemed so long ago when I was a giddy young girl, so naïve and optimistic about my future. When I thought life would turn out just as I imagined, a big wedding, a devoted husband and lots of children. I sat down heavily on the chair Alice had vacated at the card table and realised I had been dealt a different hand of cards.

During the summer of 1731, HMS Alborough was in Charles Town for repairs, including a new main mast.

From the Captain's Log, HMS Alborough
10th July 1731
Anchored In Rebellion Road

"Little wind & hazy weather. The hottest weather that ever was known here in the General opinion of the Inhabitants. This morning a Tree for a Mainmast & White Oak for a pair of cheeks to it, were brought down the River & hauled up to be made. A Tumour arose in my Right hand that I cannot Draw and 'tis with Difficulty I write, so that most of the following remarks are taken out of the General Log Book & such as I caused my Clerk to make, till I could use a pen again."

From the Captain's Log, HMS Alborough
11th August 1731
At Charles Town in South Carolina

"Moderate Gales & cloudy weather, the latter part little wind. Judging it now to be the proper time for the Carpenter to go about fitting the Cheeks and making the new Mainmast so as to be ready to Careen & go to Sea as soon as the Hurricane Season is over (having allow'd all the time since they were brought down for their Drying & Shrinking), I gave Orders to the Master Carpenter accordingly, but he informs me that the Cheeks are so very Green, that they would not be fit to be worked in a Considerable time, whereupon I desired Captain Norris would order them to be View'd & that the Officers appointed on this Survey might give me their opinions under their hands, in what time they may be fit to be brought on to the Mast, & desired also a Survey on all the Standing and Running rigging of this Ship."

20

L ate one afternoon in September, Alice and I were sitting on the shady porch at Hog Island, idly doing our needlework but mostly fanning ourselves to stay cool. We were waiting for Gadsden to visit. The heat stopped us from stirring from the pillowed sofas. The summer was the hottest ever known in Charles Town, although people said that last year as well. It didn't help tempers on Hog Island and we irritated each other, scratching away at vexations as well as the infernal mosquito bites.

Alice lived with me at Hog Island now. Once Thomas Gadsden started courting her, she left the employ of Mrs Margaret Johnson and moved into our house. Of course, having her with me was everything I had desired, but it did make my marriage with John fraught with arguments. He didn't like the noise she made, stomping up and down the stairs, banging doors, singing loudly, shouting at the servants, practising her rifle shooting.

I knew I should accompany Alice on her walks around the gardens with Gadsden, but I also found the rifle practice too noisy. When he invited her to dinners and dances in Charles Town, John said I must go as a chaperone. It was only to be expected in genteel society. Ralph sometimes escorted me. He had become best friends with Alice and Gadsden. They enjoyed drinking and gambling and gossiping and I was soon forgotten, sitting alone in the corner.

I avoided the other women who boasted loudly about their precious offspring, as if the ability to walk and talk was a miraculous achievement of their child alone. What could I contribute to a conversation about sons and daughters?

The clouds were getting darker and thicker and Quame told us we should go inside while he and Cuffee barricaded the windows.

'All the merchant ships have run up the river for better security, so they must be expecting a hurricane,' he told us.

'Not another hurricane,' I sighed. 'Perhaps we'll wait until it starts raining before going inside.'

Alice was on edge waiting for Gadsden and I told her he was busy in his role as Collector of Customs. She huffed as if nothing should stand in his way of calling on her, not even hurricanes. We watched Quame and Cuffee put up the shutters, but we did not rush inside where the afternoon heat was stifling.

'I can't understand how you can sit around here all day long, with nothing to do,' Alice said. 'John is busy repairing his ships, he never visits you. You wait here patiently. Well, I shan't be left to fade away in an isolated, windswept house.'

She flung her needlework to one side, frustrated that Gadsden hadn't appeared yet to whisk her away. We carried on sitting on the porch with nothing to do except wait.

'Do you think I should marry him if he asks me?'

She didn't want my advice so I stayed quiet. Sweat was running into my eyes and I found it hard to concentrate on my stitches.

'Do you think he's respectable enough? After all, I am an Admiral's daughter. Some people say he's an ideal catch,' she told me as if she sensed my doubts about his suitability. 'He's very rich, he owns several plantations and a house in town. He's well-respected in Society and he's extremely fond of me. I think he would make an excellent husband, don't you?'

She'd said this a thousand times before. He was all those things, but was he of sufficient social standing to satisfy Papa? He would get her dowry if she married, so would Papa want a say on the arrangement? Although he must know that Alice, of all his daughters, would marry whomever she wished, whether that was for monetary, social or romantic reasons.

'The only problem is his son, but I'm sure there's a way around that.'

His son Christopher was seven years old and known as "*Kittie*". His mother had died four years ago and Gadsden had remarried a lady from England, but she had only survived two years, dying of the fever last summer.

'I feel sorry for poor Kittie,' I said. 'He's already lost his mother and stepmother in his short life.'

'Well, I don't like him. He's a particularly precocious, demanding child. I shall find an excuse to send him away. A boarding school in England, perhaps?'

I suspected she found him competition for Gadsden's attention.

'Mr Gadsden's first three children died in infancy,' I told her. 'No wonder he dotes on his only child. He won't want to lose him.'

'Well, I'll give him another son and he can dote on him instead. We'll have a child as soon as we're married. I don't want to wait.'

Time seemed to stop. Dust motes hung motionless in the moist damp air. I silently willed her not to speak further. She laid back on the cushions lazily, so sure that her life would work out as she planned. I stared at my needlework. My humiliation brought tears to my eyes, but I pretended it was sweat I was wiping away. My heart was heavier than I had ever imagined possible. All my life I had been the eldest sister. I was the first to get married. I should be the first to have a child. I didn't want to wait either! She seemed to sense my silence and sat up suddenly.

'Oh Mary-Anne, have I upset you? I didn't mean to say you don't want a child. I mean, it can't help that John is so preoccupied with his ship,' she helpfully pointed out. 'Or that he is a cripple. And now this terrible impairment with his hand. He never seems to have any time to spend with you. It's no wonder you haven't had got with child yet, but I'm sure it will happen soon.'

She was so unfair to John. It was true he still walked with a cane, but in the last two months my dear husband had suffered such a series of misfortunes, it was no wonder he hadn't had any time for me.

At the start of July, a tree was finally brought down the river to be made into the main mast for his ship. He wanted the Carpenter to fit it so he could go to sea as soon as the hurricane season was over, but the Carpenter said it would be many weeks before it was seasoned enough to be used, so he must be patient.

Then he got a large tumour in his right hand so that he could hardly hold his pen and couldn't write his reports or draw his charts. Two weeks later, the pinnace on the *Alborough* fell from a great height while it was being hoisted onboard and smashed into pieces against the guns on the ship's side. Until it was replaced, it was difficult for him to come and go from his ship anchored in the harbour.

Then at the start of August the Master of the *Lovely Anne* carrying stores sent from Deptford for the *Alborough*, arrived with what little was saved of his ship, which was wrecked on the coast of North Carolina in June. All that was saved were three coils of cordage and twelve barge oars. John sent a letter to the Navy Board immediately to tell them of the loss of the stores sent for the use of his ship, but it would be many months before replacements arrived.

'I had to get my clerk to write the letter,' he told me. 'I can't even write my name, such is the torture with this damned tumour in my hand.'

I asked him to rest awhile at Hog Island, but he told me it was impossible to rest in the house. He could not find any peace with my sister living there. I was no comfort to him. Most days I retired to my bedroom, where I could lie on my bed motionless, dressed only in my chemise, and melt into the damp heat, fanning myself half-heartedly to disturb the mosquitos.

Alice was right, I did sit around all day with nothing to do. But how would I ever get pregnant again unless John shared my bed? Every time I asked him to stay the night with me, he had an excuse for why he needed to stay onboard the *Alborough*. His hand was painful so he needed to be near the ship's Surgeon. He couldn't hold a pen so he needed his brother to write up his reports. He needed to supervise repairs or supplies or the careening of the ships at Hobcaw Creek. The summer heat was so unbearable in the house without the sea breeze on his ship. Alice was too loud and excitable so he could not concentrate on drawing his charts. He didn't say that I was one extra worry he could do without. His needy, barren wife. As I lay alone at night, I worried that he regretted marrying me in such haste. Perhaps he no longer loved me, which was why he invented so many excuses to avoid our marriage bed.

By the start of October, the hurricane season was over and John was desperate to get back to sea, but his ship was still without a main mast. The Carpenter claimed the wood was still not yet sufficiently seasoned.

His right hand, which had been lame ever since the tumour in July still proved troublesome, and at the end of September a splinter flaked off from a bone in the middle finger and appeared through the skin. The surgeon removed it, but it was so painful that John could not suffer anyone or anything to touch his hand.

Despite all that, he decided it was the right time for surveying D'Awfoskee Sound in Port Royal Harbour.

'Rather than lose the time until the *Alborough* is ready,' he told me, excited by the prospect of getting back to his surveys, 'I think it best for His Majesty's service to send the two sloops under my command round to Port Royal Harbour by sea. I will travel with my crew in the two remaining pinnaces from the *Alborough* by the Inland Passage and meet them there.'

With his good hand, he pointed to a very ill-drawn chart. 'A proper survey of the passage is needed and I'll also be able to see if any of the inlets we pass are worthy of an actual survey.'

I peered closely at the chart which showed a rough waterway heading south from the Ashley River in Charles Town.

'Once we arrive, I'll have the two pinnaces to do the survey work and I can stay aboard the *Happy* with Captain Lloyd. I can carry on with my orders without the *Alborough*,' he announced proudly.

The trip had to be delayed a few days after another piece of the bone started appearing through the skin of his right hand. John was in so much pain and three days later it was taken out by the Surgeon, who declared that the tumour John had in the summer must be pushing out broken bones. This piece was much larger than the splinter taken out before and I started to worry that all the bones in his hand would be expelled one by one.

The next day, John claimed his hand felt somewhat easier and he set off down Wapo Creek with a flood tide in the two pinnaces, one of ten oars, the other of eight, armed and victualled for the three-day trip along the rivers and creeks that had been joined by roughly dug channels to make a route for canoes to pass between Charles Town and Beaufort.

However treacherous the journey, however painful his hand, however inconvenient the survey, he was happier doing the Navy's bidding than staying at home with me. Alice was right, I couldn't sit around on Hog Island waiting for something that might never happen. I was going to have to pray a lot harder!

With no mast, HMS Alborough was out of action, so in October John went down the Inland Passage to meet his two support ships in Port Royal Harbour and complete his survey.

From the Captain's Log, HMS Alborough
9th October 1731
Going to Port Royal in the Boats by way of Inland Passage

"Little wind and Fairweather. At 8 this morning I put off with the two Pinnaces of this ship (one of 10 oars the other of eight) completely armed and victualled for the passage to meet the sloops at Port Royal by the inland passage having given orders to my Lieutenant to cause all possible dispatch to be made in completing the mainmast and then without loss of time to clean and grave the ship at Hobcaw, to fit her in all respects for the sea and give me notice at Dawforske by special Messenger in the Canoa of the time the ship will be ready to come out of the Creek that I may return to carry her about as soon as possible. At 9:30 entered Wapo Creek with the tide of flood. At 10:30 passage through Wapo bridge having rowed some little way against the flood from Stono and immediately entered Stono River which we are rowing up at noon."

He returned to Charles Town in November and spent the winter working on his plans of Dawforskee Sound.

From the Captain's Log, HMS Alborough
18th February 1732
At Charles Town in South Carolina

"Fresh gales & Cloudy weather. This morning I delivered a box directed to the Honourable Josiah Burchett Esq. Secretary of the Admiralty of Great Britain, containing a plan of the River & Sound of Dawforskee in this province & also a draught of the Islands Biminis on the East side of the Gulph of Florida to Mr William Bell, Master of the ship American, which fell down to Rebellion Road bound to Great Britain, who has promised to deliver upon his arrival there & a letter directed on His Majesty's Service in same manner."

21

After John left in October, the weather improved and I paid a visit to St Philip's Church in town, thinking that once-a-week worship on a Sunday might not be enough for the Good Lord to look favourably on my marriage. Mr McAndrews was the churchwarden, so I was not surprised to see his wife, Jean, my neighbour from Church Street, busily rearranging flowers at the end of each pew, ruthlessly discarding any fading or dead blooms into a basket she carried on her arm.

'Hello, Mary-Anne,' she said. 'I hope you're well. It must have been so cool living out on Hog Island this summer. I would love to feel the sea breeze on my face, but I fear Mr McAndrews would not like to be so exposed to the weather. We would feel rather isolated there, unable to do our work at the church.'

'My sister Alice is living with me now,' I told her, 'but she is busy with her beau, Mr Thomas Gadsden. My husband has just left to continue his surveys in Port Royal Harbour. To be honest, I too feel rather isolated out at Hog Island.'

'Why don't you join my Ladies' Society?' she suggested. 'We meet every Wednesday morning at the Church and it would give you the opportunity to meet some gentlewomen.'

So I started going along to her Ladies' Society, a group of ten women, most of whom I had seen at church on Sundays. They were the wives of storekeepers, craftsmen, merchants and traders, a different class from the gossips I met at Society Events.

Although it was nice to meet for a chat, the purpose of the group was to visit poor mothers and there were plenty of women in Charles Town who needed our help. Many were left destitute with a new baby when men sailed home to England, never to return. The unforgiving summer heat and incessant tropical diseases caused so many problems for mothers and babies, most of them tragic.

'I don't do much except hold their hands,' one of the ladies told me.

'I make pomanders from oranges and cloves and leave them in the houses to counteract the foul odours,' said another.

One afternoon, Jean invited me to accompany her on a visit to a woman who had suffered a miscarriage.

As we made our way to the streets at the far end of town, I told her I would like to be of more use than making pomanders, but I might not be the best person, having lost a pregnancy myself.

'I know these terrible things happen,' she said, 'and it's hard for us to understand why, but we must put our faith in the Lord. Still, I think your counsel may help these women, having been through the same pain and grief. Sometimes they need to know that they are not suffering alone in this world.'

I wondered if counselling this unhappy woman would help me or if it would remind me of the sorrow.

Soon we were standing outside a ramshackle house in the backstreets of Charles Town. It was dark inside and I could hardly make out the small room with a table and two chairs, an open fireplace with a pot hanging over and a tumbledown staircase leading up to the upper room.

A woman was sitting on one of the chairs, her face hidden in a shawl. She sat with her arms across her chest, hugging herself tightly, making a protective shield to ward off a despair that I recognised immediately

We spent the next hour telling her how much we cared about her but I knew that was little consolation. To my surprise, she found more comfort in the prayer I suggested for the tiny soul that was lost before he had a chance to live.

Jean offered more practical help. She was very keen on washing to fend off all sorts of infections and she sent me out to fetch water from the trough in the street. She boiled some up over the fire with a few herbs from her pocket and made the poor woman sip the foul-smelling drink.

On our way home I asked Jean, 'Could you show me how to be useful? A neighbour in Kingston helped me when I was nursing John's fever. She recommended fresh air and lime juice. It helped with the fevers, but I fear it won't be much use for miscarriages.'

'Of course I will,' she said. 'I would be very pleased to have you help me. Although all I can do is restore confidence that the next child will surely live.' She stopped in her tracks, turned and looked hard at me. Without saying anything, I realised she was trying to restore my confidence at the same time.

Over the next few weeks, we visited several women who had given birth and I got to cradle newborn babies in my arms. Bess sometimes came with me on visits and she was more useful in a practical way, sweeping the floor, washing clothes and bedding, that sort of thing. Jean insisted on washing everything in hot water and soap, our hands, our aprons, the baby, the mother, the cradle and the swaddling clothes. She had a religious fervour as if Death itself lurked in any trace of dirt or blood or gore. Our hands were red raw by the time we left.

Sarah was horrified that I was visiting the poor and needy in the back streets of Charles Town.

'You must think of yourself, Mary-Anne, and not risk your health visiting the less fortunate.'

It was different for her. She had a family of her own. She didn't have to visit strangers to be with children.

By the time John returned in November, the *Alborough* had her new mast. I was afraid he would immediately head off again, but the season was too far advanced to attempt anything either in the Gulf of Florida or the Bahamas.

After another piece of bone was taken out of the middle finger of his right hand by the surgeon, he resigned himself to staying in Charles Town over the winter. He stayed onboard his ship so he could work undisturbed on his surveys with the help of his brother. His trip via the Inland Passage had gone well and he was making a detailed report of his survey of the D'Awfoskee Sound, the passage into Port Royal Harbour to the west of Trench's Island which avoided crossing the notorious sandbar.

At least my weekly visits with Mrs McAndrews had given me a new sense of purpose. I enjoyed visiting new mothers after their babies had been born. Cradling the tiny, undernourished, impoverished mites brought back memories of Janet's baby, Douglas. How was it so easy for some women to fall pregnant, even if they didn't want to, while I remained barren and empty? My heart started aching for my own child.

Alice got her proposal from Thomas Gadsden in January and a large wedding was planned for the summer. Everyone was delighted. John was relieved that his sister-in-law was now respectable and rumours concerning the Governor were a thing of the past. I was tempted to write to Papa and tell him Gadsden was not a suitable husband if only to defer the inevitability of her having a child first, but in the end I gave him my blessing. He was obviously devoted to her.

I needed to get John into my bed if we were to have a child before she was wed in the summer, but on the nights he did stay at Hog Island, he seemed to have an excuse not to sleep next to me. He was busy working on his survey so he'd sleep in the study, his hand was too painful so he couldn't bear to be touched or he was too exhausted by the trials of getting his ships repaired so he wouldn't sleep well.

I pleaded with him to sleep in my bed, but even when he did, he cuddled up to me and stroked my hair, telling me how much he loved me. A cuddle would not make a baby and I was too afraid to ask for more. He turned away in frustration at the trials he faced in his life. I didn't want to become one more.

I confided in Sarah and she understood my plight. Her elderly husband also suffered from a lack of enthusiasm for his young wife in bed. She whispered that the Apothecary sold an elixir that guaranteed satisfaction for disappointed wives.

'It has helped my husband become a loving bedfellow on a number of occasions,' she confided in a whispered giggle

The Apothecary's shop was down a narrow alley off Church Street. The interior of the shop was small and dark, the shelves and cabinets crowded with jars and pots labelled with strange ornate lettering. Weighing scales and exotic curiosities sat on the large counter. Herbs hung in great bunches from the ceiling, giving off an overpowering aroma that made me feel drowsy. The apothecary stood behind the large counter. He was a small man with a narrow, pinched face and a large, hooked nose.

'Good morning Mrs Gascoigne, have you come for more remedies for your husband's ailments?'

He had on previous occasions given me salves and potions for John, but I didn't want him to know about this particular ailment, so I said, 'Oh no, a good friend asked me to collect some of your Gentleman's Elixir. It's not for me, it's for her. I'm running an errand for a friend.'

He looked at me through narrowed eyes. I hadn't noticed his resemblance to a rat before but his mouth had quite an unpleasant smirk.

'Ah, my famous Gentleman's Elixir, so popular with the married gentlewomen in Charles Town. I make it myself from the very finest ingredients from Persia.'

He took a small phial off a shelf behind him and placed it on the counter between us.

In a hushed voice he told me, 'Add a few drops in your husband's wine at dinner and it will fortify his nerves, raise his animal spirits and allow him to prolong his embrace to provide you with all the pleasure you desire.'

He knew my deepest secrets. I blushed scarlet and felt quite faint in this strange world of unfamiliar smells and potions. I tipped the coins from my purse onto the counter and he took all my money. It must be an elixir from Heaven to cost that much, but if it worked, it was worth every penny. I grabbed the phial, stumbled out of the shop and collapsed onto the bench outside. I dropped my head in my hands. What was I thinking? I couldn't do this.

After a few minutes, I regained my composure, took a deep breath and stood up straight. Of course I could do this. I could do anything to have a baby.

I took a detour back to the ferry dock, avoiding St Philip's Church. I didn't want the Good Lord to see that I had given up on prayer and succumbed to black magic potions. I took the phial back to Hog Island and hid it in my chest, until such time as I could drug my husband.

One February afternoon such a chance arose when I had an unexpected visit from John. He'd delivered his plans of D'Awfoskee Sound to the *American*, anchored in Rebellion Road and due to sail for England. Now his survey was completed, he was making his ships ready to leave. He wanted to survey the Windward Passage from Carolina to Jamaica. He told me he would be gone for several months.

This was my moment and I knew I must seize it. I ran upstairs to get the phial and hide it in my pocket. I noticed a copy of the latest Ladies Diary in the chest and quickly turned it over. I didn't want its advice on when I could have marital relations with my husband. I would take any chance I had these days.

As I descended the stairs slowly and serenely, I said in a most charming voice, 'Stay with me, my dearest husband, just for tonight. We can celebrate the despatch of your survey. You've worked so hard on it since your return in November.'

He was putting on his jacket. 'I told the Officers I'd dine onboard with them tonight. They'll be waiting for me.' He turned to leave, but I was desperate. I would accept no excuses. His survey was done, so he couldn't claim he was too busy. His ship was ready to sail, so he couldn't argue that he must do repairs. His hand was slowly healing, so he couldn't say he was in too much pain. Alice was with Gadsden, so we would be alone tonight.

I grabbed his arm so he could not escape. 'I am sure they will manage without you for one night.'

He looked at me, surprised that I had challenged him, but I slipped my hand into the crook of his arm and guided him lovingly up the path to the cliff at High Bluff.

'Tonight, my darling husband, let us dine together on the clifftop.'

Cuffee and Mungo followed us with a small dining table and two chairs. Quame set up a canopy in case of rain, but for once the evening was cloudless. The three of them had to run up and down from the house with plates and glasses, candles and cutlery, food and wine, but it was worth it to dine outside with a view of Charles Town Harbour. John had once said it was his favourite view in the whole world so that night I hoped it would put him at ease.

I sat him at the table and made sure he was relaxed, his hand comfortable and his feet rested. I pulled up my chair so I could lean in closer to him. I'd watched Alice flirt and I tried some of her tricks to draw his attention to my mouth, my neck and my low-cut bodice. I smiled coyly, looking up at him adoringly. I fiddled with my hair, pulling a loose curl over my bare shoulder. I played with the locket he had given me which hung around my neck. I arranged the lace at my breast prettily. I was acting like a different woman and John was staring at me as if I had gone quite mad. Well, that night I had.

When Cuffee and Mungo retreated to the house and Quame's back was turned, I deliberately dropped my napkin to the floor. While John gallantly stooped to retrieve it from under the table, I sneaked the small bottle of elixir out of my pocket and poured a couple of drops into his wine.

He handed me my napkin, picked up his glass and, as he put it to his lips, we held eye contact for what seemed an eternity. I was trembling with fear that my subterfuge would be discovered, but I recognised those big brown eyes, wanting my approval, eager to please. His look was not one of challenge and reprimand, it was a look of adoration. Once he loved me enough to marry me impulsively and bring me across the Atlantic to be with him. Surely his recent lack of interest in me was due to his worries about his ship and not my tragic failure to bear his children.

'Your hair looks very nice tonight, Mary-Anne,' he said, reaching over to rearrange the curl I had coquettishly placed on my shoulder.

I caught his hand and grasped it tightly. It was still swollen and tender. He winced in pain and I loosened my grip, apologetically.

'I only want to please you, John,' I said in an alluring, simpering voice. My intentions could not be mistaken. My cheeks were burning with my own audacity and brazenness.

He didn't take his hand away and we sat, smiling at each other while I gently traced my finger along the scars on his hand. He had suffered so much ill health over the last few years, my darling, dutiful husband.

After we'd finished eating and John had drunk every last drop of his wine, I asked him to sit with me on a blanket near the edge of the cliff. We watched the ships anchored in the Harbour and John pointed out the *Alborough* swinging on its anchors. It seemed to give him comfort that she was within sight. The stars twinkled in the dark night sky. Thunder rumbled in the distance. A warm wind blew down the river from the north.

'The breeze is just right to cross the Bar,' he said, almost to himself. His thoughts were already on leaving.

I snuggled closer, against his rough jacket, with its familiar smell of salt spray. We gazed across the river at the lights of Charles Town, the flickering lamps on the dockside where ferrymen were calling for work and the torches of those that had found a passenger to row across the river. We were apart from all the bustle in the town. There on the clifftop it was John and me, husband and wife, that no man can put asunder. We had each other and that must be good enough for what I had in mind tonight.

I wanted him to kiss me, but I couldn't demurely wait forever. So I pulled him towards me and kissed him passionately on his mouth. He was surprised by my forwardness but responded ardently to my kisses and I could taste the wine on his lips. Please Lord, make that potion work its magic tonight.

My attempts at seduction succeeded. That night on the cliff at High Bluff, with a view of Charles Town across the river and all the ships anchored in the Harbour, we embraced like long-lost lovers and rekindled our intimate desires.

He gathered me up in his embrace and we fell to the ground, arms and legs entwined. With fumbling, nervous fingers I undid the buttons on his breeches. He moaned softly and I could feel he was aroused. I lifted my petticoats, spread my legs and pulled him down on top of me. I held him tight until I could feel his seed inside me, giving life to a baby.

In May HMS Alborough returned to Providence, but without the support of the Cruizer which had returned to Jamaica or the Happy which was still in the repair yard, his survey work in the Bahamas was limited and he returned to Charles Town in June for the summer.

From the Captain's Log, HMS Alborough
25th May 1732
In Providence Harbour, Bahamas
*   "Moderate gales & fair weather. His Excellency Woodes Rogers Esq. Governor of this colony, desired me to spare him some provisions, the Garrison being very much in want which I promised to do when I left the place. At 4 in the morning unmoored the Ship. At 6 the Governor's boat came aboard & took off provisions I supplied him with for His Majesty's Garrison here, viz. 8 barrels of Flour containing 1280 pounds. 12 barrels of Beef containing 621 four-pound pieces and 3 barrels of Pork containing 300 two-pound pieces. At 9 carried out a Borrowed Anchor & Cable to the E'ward of the best Bower to hang the ship by the Stern with which to bring her to sail, then (having steadied the Ship between two good hawsers) weighed the best Bower anchor & at noon slipp'd the Borrowed Cable & the two hawsers, set the sails at once & got out having 3 fathom water on the Shoalest part of the Bar. We left an old condemned buoy rope & wooden buoy to the Borrowed anchor, having no opportunity of sending for them without a Risque of leaving the Boats behind."*

Charles Town was not a pleasant place to be in the summer, with hot muggy weather and outbreaks of disease, especially yellow fever spread by mosquitos.

From the Captain's Log, HMS Alborough
6th August 1732
At Charles Town in South Carolina
*   "Little wind, thick hazy weather & Excessively hot. The Malignancy of the Distemper which rages like a pestilence rather increases than abates."*

22

J oy of joys! I was with child. I had missed five of my monthly bleeds so I calculated the baby would be born in November and I rejoiced daily in the discomfort, the sickness, the heartburn, the headaches and the stomach cramps. This was what it felt like to finally become a mother.

I stayed at home, trying not to worry about John, about Alice, about the summer heat and the pestilence which raged in town. The summer plague had started as early as May and was worse than ever. The physicians didn't know how to treat the fever which was so sudden and of such a fatal nature.

I had to come to Charles Town as it was the 25th of July 1732, Alice's Wedding Day. The invitations had been sent out, the banns read and the wedding was scheduled for noon. Luckily John had returned early from Providence so would be able to attend. Everyone in Charles Town society was invited, but many of the grandees had returned to England for the Summer Season. It was a surprise the wedding was in July with the heat and the fever making Charles Town unbearable. Governor Johnson's wife was dying and sadly, would not last the month, and I wondered if Gadsden wanted to secure his bride before she changed her mind and pursued her dream of becoming the Governor's next wife.

Ever since that evening when I introduced Gadsden to my sister, he had pursued her with a passion. He was still diligent in the performance of his duties as Custom Collector and yet he seemed to have time to court Alice.

'At least he's not in the Navy,' Alice said. 'I couldn't bear him to be away at sea for so long. How you must miss your husband when he's away. No, I was never going to take after you and Mama in the choice of my husband.'

She boasted about his wealth as if to justify her choice of husband. Gadsden owned large tracts of land and Alice was excited by his ambitious plans for the future. The key to prosperity in Carolina was the acquisition of land. Anyone could rise in Society if they were wealthy enough from plantations.

I helped Jean McAndrews arrange the flowers in St Philip's Church before the ceremony. She told me she remembered when Gadsden's son, Christopher, was christened at the church eight years ago.

I told her of Alice's plan to send the boy to school in England as soon as she was married. 'She says it will be good for him to be educated in England. He can stay with Gadsden's relatives in Bristol and attend a boarding school.'

'Oh, the poor mite, so young to be sent away. He's used to being the apple of his father's eye. It'll be unsettling for him to go to England, just when he gets another mother.'

I didn't tell her that Alice had no interest in being his mother and didn't want Kittie around, especially when she had sons of her own. Hopefully, the young lad would find a more loving home among Gadsden's relatives in England.

'Still, it won't be long before you have a christening here in St Philip's,' she said taking my arm as we left the church. 'But you must look after yourself now, Mary-Anne. Take it easy for a while. Don't come to Charles Town to help other mothers, especially in this heat.'

I promised her that after the wedding, I would return to Hog Island, safely away from any harm.

She made me promise that I would send word to her when the baby was due in November so she could be with me for the birth. I was happy that she would help me, in the absence of Mama, who was far away across the ocean.

Poor Mama! I knew from her letters to me that she was upset about not attending Alice's wedding. Two daughters married and she hadn't attended either wedding. I hoped she'd be pleased when her first grandchild was christened, even though she wouldn't be at that service either.

We didn't have much time before the service was due to start so Jean and I hurried back to her house to change. Alice was there and she'd had a beautiful gown made for the occasion. The cream silk brocade was richly embroidered in gold thread and patterned with flowers in vivid reds and greens, but the heavy fabric would be unbearable to wear in the heat of a Charles Town summer. I was wearing one of Caroline's old cast-offs which was much lighter and looser. I instinctively rubbed my slight bump lovingly.

Bess was now getting quite adept at styling my hair and Alice insisted she did hers as well. I had started pinning my hair up and wearing a lace cap, but Alice preferred to leave her dark locks loose to flow in curls over her shoulders. For the wedding she wanted Bess to fluff up her hair with grey corn starch to make it stand up high on her head and decorate it with ribbons and feathers. I hoped she'd get her own lady's maid once she was married. She couldn't have Bess, my dearest companion.

As Papa was not in Charles Town to give Alice away, John had been delegated to escort Alice down the aisle. I was her Maid of Honour, as she was mine, but in truth, Alice's wedding was nothing like mine. No sneaking out of the house at dawn to a ceremony hastily arranged by licence the day before and witnessed by a few strangers. Today the church bells were ringing loudly, the pews were full and the flowers Jean and I had arranged looked beautiful.

I looked around the church as I followed Alice and John down the aisle to where Gadsden was waiting. Young Kittie was at his side, with a rather unattractive scowl on his face.

I was surprised by how many well-wishers were still in Charles Town. I saw the Governor, Robert Johnson, sitting in one of the pews on my left with his young daughter Meg, a thin, sickly girl, ten or eleven years old. Perhaps it was for the best that Alice was marrying Gadsden and not Robert Johnson. Alice might be able to send Kittie to England, but surely she could not have got rid of young Meg.

There were a good number of ship owners, planters and merchants with their wives and children, as well as many civic dignitaries. Gadsden's role as Customs Collector brought him into contact with both politics and commerce and it was in all their interests to stay on his right side to make trade work smoothly and Charles Town prosper.

Sarah and her husband Arthur sat to my right, surrounded by their four children. Sarah had made peace with her stepchildren. Middleton's eldest son, William was now twenty-two and worked as a respectable lawyer in Charles Town. Henry was fifteen and Hester thirteen, while her own son Thomas was eight. They were quite the happy family these days, especially since Arthur gave up his governorship and concentrated on his rice plantation. He'd doubled his land holdings in the last two years and with restrictions on rice exports lifted, he was doing very well for himself. I hadn't seen as much of Sarah since I moved to Hog Island, especially after Alice arrived, but she gave me a surreptitious wave and I gave her my best smile. Now that Alice was getting married and leaving Hog Island, I vowed to resume my friendship with Sarah. I used to be envious of her children, but with a baby inside me, I knew I would soon be elevated to the ranks of motherhood.

I saw Captain George Anson in the congregation and nearly tripped over in surprise. I looked away quickly, not wanting to catch his eye. I knew he had returned to Charles Town the previous week, but I was not prepared for our first encounter. John had told me he spent last year doing duty in the Channel but received no promotion so he had jumped at the chance to return on HMS *Squirrel* as Station Commander of South Carolina again. He replaced Captain Norris who had sailed home on the *Lowestoffe* earlier this year. I was disappointed that John did not get the position as he would have been based in Charles Town, instead of sailing off to Port Royal or the Bahamas or who knows where.

I idly wondered what might have happened if Anson had been there when Alice arrived but no, she was better off with Gadsden and she always protested that she never wanted a naval officer and it would not have been easy to welcome him into our family.

Ralph was sitting on the opposite side of the church. He had delayed his annual trip to Philadelphia until after the ceremony.

I had once asked John why Anson was so hostile to Ralph and he had replied in a rather offhand way, 'Men like Ralph aren't popular in the Navy,' as if that explained everything. 'But I don't expect your friend has any intention of joining the Navy, does he?'

No, I couldn't imagine Ralph in the Navy. He was the opposite of John who was so diligent and conscientious and dutiful, who obeyed his orders from the Admiralty even if his life was in danger and his ship in total disrepair.

'But you do like him don't you, John?'

'Well, I would rather he escorts my wife around town in my absence than any other man.'

After the vows were said and the marriage recorded in the register, Gadsden was now my brother-in-law. John and I were among the select few who were invited to a nearby tavern for the Wedding

Luncheon after the service. There was much gaiety, food, drink and toasting and Gadsden made a fine speech that invoked my sympathy about his two previous wives.

James was seated beside me. He whispered to me that his first wife was rumoured to be the daughter of an Irish indentured servant. Contrary to his intentions, it made me like Gadsden more as I thought of Janet's son, Douglas, the son of an indentured servant, who would be a boy of three by then and would one day grow up to become a husband and father.

After declaring his fatherly love for young Kittie, Gadsden went on to announce that he was looking forward to creating a new dynasty of sons with his new young bride.

Alice, who was once so adamant that she didn't want children, looked up at him adoringly. Gadsden had a son and heir in young Kittie, but Alice was excited that her sons would be a new dynasty.

It was the duty of every wife to have children and I knew that whatever the risks, it would be worth it to hold my newborn in my arms.

After the meal, gaming tables were set up and the fiddlers struck up a tune for dancing. John professed that he was too tired to stay for the festivities and I was keen to return to the safety and seclusion of Hog Island.

As we were saying our goodbyes, Captain Anson approached. I had forgotten how dashing he looked in his naval uniform, tall and smartly attired. John looked slightly dishevelled by comparison, smaller and rounder, his shirt untucked, his wig askew, his damaged right hand stuffed in his coat pocket.

As he drew near, John whispered, 'You speak to him, Mary-Anne, and welcome our old friend back. I am still undecided on how to answer the letter he brought from Mr Burchett telling me the Admiralty have no other sloop to assist with my survey work.'

He rushed off to talk to his brother, leaving me standing on my own. I straightened my skirts and was quite pleased that my gown draped very prettily over my hoops. I tucked a stray curl of hair under my lace cap and hoped I was not blushing.

'Good day to you, Mrs Gascoigne,' George said, politely, taking my hand and bowing low over it. I notice he didn't risk a kiss as might be considered courteous among old friends. 'I trust you are keeping well.'

I told him I was with child, five months gone.

He looked away as if shocked by my blunt admission. Perhaps I should have started with more introductory pleasantries after two and a half years.

After an awkward silence, he said, 'You are indeed the perfect wife Mary-Anne. Captain Gascoigne is a lucky man. I wish you and your family all the very best.'

With that, he turned and slowly walked away, his head held high. I knew then that his unwanted advances after the Governor's Christmas Ball would never be spoken of again and I felt a sadness inside me. I had thought I would be scared or angry if I ever met him again, but instead I felt pity for him, for his clumsy protestations of unrequited love. As I watched him corner John with a congratulatory handshake, I prayed he would find a perfect wife of his own soon, but we all knew it was not an easy task for a naval officer who was away at sea most of his life.

When we arrived back at Hog Island, John sat beside me on the sofa on the porch as we watched the sun sink in the west over Charles Town.

'Did you enjoy yourself today, Mary-Anne? It was a much grander affair than our wedding, wasn't it?'

'Our wedding day may not have been as grand, but I was happy to be marrying you.'

'What did Anson have to say for himself? Did he mention that I am not to have a sloop to replace the *Cruizer* now she's gone back to Jamaica? Did you tell him that the *Happy* has been in the repair yard since March?'

'No, he didn't mention ships, John. I told him about the baby and he wished us all the best.'

'Of course, my dearest. Forgive my worries over naval matters. Let us enjoy this moment.'

He gently rested his good hand on my belly and I wondered if he could feel the baby moving.

'I knew there was nothing wrong with you,' he said. 'I knew this would happen in good time. When you have a child, you won't be so lonely without me, you'll have a baby to fill your days.'

'But I will miss Alice,' I told him. 'I got used to her being with me at Hog Island. It's a shame she couldn't stay until the baby is born to help me.'

'It's a lot more peaceful without her,' he laughed, 'and I don't think your sister would be much help at the birth of our child. Anyway, I am certain the Lord will bless us with a fine healthy son.'

I prayed with all my heart that my baby would be the son John wanted. At least he would be born before Alice had her first child, the start of her new dynasty with Gadsden. My baby would be the first Mighells boy. Papa and Mama would be so proud of me and I would be the perfect wife for John.

I sat peacefully beside my dear husband on the porch as the sun sank to the horizon. A beautiful sunset to end a very happy, joyous day. My sister was married, my husband was by my side and my baby was safe in my belly. At last, all my dreams were coming true.

In October 1732, John was preoccupied with the relaunch of his support sloop, the Happy, at the time of his son's birth.

From the Captain's Log, HMS Alborough
9th October 1732
At Charles Town in South Carolina
"Little wind & fair weather. This morning the Happy was Endeavour'd to be launched but the water fell before she could be got off, her works have been so much retarded by the great Sickness & mortality that has raged here, that she could not possibly be completed far enough to launch till this time. Otherwise according to the Opinion of all the Master Carpenters who were appointed to make an Estimate, she would have been ready by the latter end of the Hurricane Season. And as there has not been a Shipwright or Caulker to be had either than from the King's Ships here or in the Province Except what were at work on the Happy, the caulking and fitting this Ship for the Carine could not be begun before this day at noon."

From the Captain's Log, HMS Alborough
12th October 1732
At Charles Town in South Carolina
"Little wind & fair weather. At 1pm fired 19 guns being the Anniversary of the King's Coronation. AM the knotting round the Quarters and the Barricades being entirely unserviceable made new."

23

T he morning of the 12th of October 1732 dawned fresh and clear over Hog Island. The worst of the stifling summer heat had abated and the hurricane season was over. After Alice's wedding, I stayed away from the city. My unborn baby and I were safe in the isolation of Hog Island. My pregnancy was now in the eighth month and Jean McAndrews assured me that miscarriages usually occur in the first three months. So I was determined to avoid any excitement, upset or disease. I didn't want anything to go wrong with my pregnancy.

John had left earlier that day to prepare the *Alborough* for the marking of the Anniversary of the King's Coronation. At one o'clock that afternoon all naval ships would fire nineteen guns. He also wanted to ready his ship for the careening dock at Hobcaw. Finally, after spending most of the year in the repair yard, the *Happy* had been launched yesterday on the high tide so John was preparing to leave on his next survey mission after the baby was born.

We still had a month to go before the baby was due and I sat alone on the porch to watch white clouds scudding across a bright blue sky. I felt so happy and contented and couldn't help rubbing my belly and talking to the child inside. I told him how much John and I were looking forward to meeting him and that we would love him dearly all his days. I assured him I would finish the embroidery on the christening robe I had brought from England five years ago so it would be ready for his baptism. I told him that his cradle, bought for Janet's baby, was ready for him in the nursery, lined with calico and the colourful patchwork quilt that I had finally finished. I had ordered four yards of fine linen for swaddling bands to have his trousseau ready for his arrival.

Peggy was spoiling me with treats from her kitchen and Bess ran around all day taking care of me. Even Quame wouldn't let me lift or carry anything and insisted on helping me, despite his age and infirmity. We were all excited to meet the new child growing inside me.

My happy reveries were disturbed by Quame who approached with a letter.

'The ferrymen brought a letter for you, Mistress. They're waiting at the dock for your answer.'

I recognised Alice's handwriting and opened it with interest.

She was in a very nervous state, terrified that she might be pregnant. She was nauseous and dizzy, she was tearful and couldn't sleep, she needed my reassurance and support. She begged me to visit her that morning at Gadsden's townhouse in Bay Street.

I didn't want to go across the river to Charles Town. I didn't want to leave Hog Island, my safe place, near the nursery and far away from the diseases in the town.

But Alice wrote that she needed me. She had paid the ferrymen to take me across the Cooper River to Charles Town and the weather was fair and the breeze light. I didn't have an excuse to ignore her cries for help. Perhaps today would be a good day to visit her and then I could tell her I couldn't come again in the next few months. She would have to visit me during my confinement.

Quame was horrified at my decision. 'You can't go on that small ferry boat across to Charles Town, Mistress. Not in your condition.'

'You don't understand, Quame. My sister needs to see me and I need to put a stop to her nonsense. She must understand that having a baby is a wife's calling. Why else would Mr Gadsden have married her?'

I didn't expect him to answer that question, but he looked at me fearfully. 'Well, if you insist on going, I will travel with you and keep you safe.'

He looked too old and frail to keep me safe, but it would be sensible to have some company on the trip and Quame was an easy travelling companion, cheerful, helpful and kind. He would be able to arrange a carriage from the quayside to Gadsden's house so I didn't have to walk far and it would be nice to show off my wonderful swollen belly to Alice. I couldn't help laughing aloud. I was a proud mother already, what would I be like once I had a babe in my arms to show everyone?

As I took my cape from the peg by the door, I snatched one of John's old tricorn hats from the dresser and plopped it on Quame's curly grey hair. Without a wig underneath, the hat was far too big for him and it flopped over his eyes. He pushed it back out of his eyes and looked up at me. I could tell he was very proud to wear it.

'You will be the captain of the ship today,' I said to him, playfully saluting him. It seemed a fun, spontaneous thing to do on our excursion to Charles Town after all this time. Quame was nervous about crossing the river and I wanted to put him at ease. Usually it was Cuffee who rowed me across in my own boat, but Alice had sent a ferry boat with two oarsmen.

Quame gallantly helped me climb clumsily into the front of the ferry boat, where I sat on a seat facing forwards. My belly was swollen and it was hard to believe I had another month to go before I was due to give birth. From my seat in the bow I could see Charles Town across the river and I felt quite excited at the thought of visiting Alice again. The river was calm, the sky cloudless. It was a bright sunny day and all was well with the world. A perfect day to visit my sister in Charles Town.

Quame took his place at the back of the boat. His hat kept flopping down over his face and he was constantly pushing it back so he could see out from under it. I knew he wouldn't take it off though.

The ferrymen pushed off from the dock and their oars pulled us out into the river with every powerful stroke. The tide was on the ebb that morning and the oarsmen muttered to each other about where to cross the river to use the current so that we ended up at Middle Quay. They would have to avoid the merchant ships taking advantage of the strong current to leave the quayside and make their way under full sail out across the Bar.

A large merchantman, fully laden with cargo bound for England, bore down on our small boat very fast, unable to change her course without adjusting her full sails. I cried out in alarm, fearing she would strike us and cause our boat to sink. The younger ferryman pulled hard on his oar on one side to swing the bow around and the huge ship passed precariously close to us. Our little boat was tossed to one side in the waves of her wake and nearly tipped over. I hid my face in my cape, terrified we would capsize.

Quame shouted. I looked around to see what had happened. His hat had gone overboard. I watched, helpless, as he stood up in the back of the boat and reached out to grab the hat floating on the water. It was out of his reach. He stretched too far and tumbled out of the boat, which tipped violently to the opposite side so he was lost from my sight.

As the boat righted itself, the ferrymen fumbled as they dropped their oars. One man reached his hand over the side of the boat and managed to catch Quame's hand, but his wet fingers slipped slowly out of his grasp. He was already too far away to grab him again.

'Save me, Mistress,' he called out to me in a panic, but what could I do? I reached my hand out, pathetically.

The older ferryman extended his oar out towards Quame.

'Grab the oar!' he shouted, but the oar was slippery and wet and Quame was flailing his arms about. He couldn't grab hold of it. The current was so strong he had drifted away from the boat. The ferryman pulled his oar back in, shoved it back in the rowlocks and pulled hard to turn the boat around.

I watched Quame's head go under the water, then bob back up, then go under again. His wet jacket and heavy boots were pulling him under. I didn't want to watch him drown, but I couldn't look away and abandon my beloved friend.

At that moment, there was a thunderous explosion as the guns were fired from all the ships in the harbour and all the forts on the headland to celebrate the Anniversary of the King's Coronation. Over and over again, nineteen times. The noise was deafening and I dropped into a crouch with my hands over my ears waiting for it to be over. Once the cannons finished and the smoke and spray cleared, I looked up, but Quame was nowhere to be seen. I screamed his name into the wind, twisting and turning in my seat to scan the water. He had been swept away in the current and disappeared under the waves.

I shouted at the ferrymen, 'Row down the river, we must find him.'

They looked at each other dubiously, reluctant to turn the boat into the tide. 'We won't get back to the quay if we go down river, m'lady,' said the older man. 'We haven't the strength to battle against the tide.'

'We can't leave him to drown,' I whimpered, but I knew it was hopeless. They wouldn't change their minds. All the fight went out of me and I collapsed backwards into the boat, faint with the terrible realisation that Quame wouldn't be rescued.

The ferrymen rowed as fast as they could to Middle Bridge. The boat was secured to the dock, but I hadn't the strength to crawl ashore. Someone reached down, grabbed me under the arms and dragged me onto the stone quayside, where I lay, weeping, oblivious to the passers-by gathering around to stare at me.

The ferryman shouted to a docker to report the drowning to the harbour master. I heard someone in the crowd mutter, 'What's happened?' and he was answered, 'It's just an African man who's drowned.'

Just the kindest, bravest, dearest African man I had ever known. My faithful friend, who looked after me every day, who cared for me during hurricanes, sickness and other disasters, who rescued me from Captain Anson. I hadn't the energy to speak, let alone argue.

Someone else in the crowd said, 'No doubt the alligators will make a good breakfast of him,' and people laughed.

Nothing around me felt real anymore. I couldn't move. I couldn't speak. I suddenly felt very cold and started shaking uncontrollably. I couldn't bear the thought of such a ghastly end for Quame. I'd had many terrible nightmares of John drowning. It was the worst death I could imagine, without a priest or loved ones at your bedside, claimed by the sea into a watery grave that no one could visit. Now it had happened to Quame. He was always afraid of the river. I shouldn't have brought him with me, it was all my fault. I should never have left Hog Island. I should never have given him that stupid hat. I should never have answered Alice's call. Then I vomited all over the dockside.

Someone recognised me as the sister of the Customs Collector's wife. 'Fetch Thomas Gadsden! He'll know what to do,' he shouted.

The Custom House was on the quayside and within minutes Gadsden was kneeling beside me.

'Try to get up, Mary Anne. I'll launch a boat to search for your man. Come away now, there's nothing more you can do here.'

I tried to sit up, but there was a severe pain in my belly.

'Something's wrong.' I grabbed his sleeve fiercely. 'It's coming. The baby's coming.'

'Are you sure?'

'I don't know. I felt him moving.'

'Let me help you to get up.'

I didn't want to move, but I couldn't stay there and give birth to my child on the quayside, covered in vomit and tears, in front of a crowd of spectators.

'What can I do to help you?' he asked.

'Perhaps you could get me to Mrs McAndrew's house in Church Street?' I whispered. 'She'll know what to do.'

He picked me up gently in his arms and carried me to a horse and cart, waiting patiently for a load. He lay me carefully in the straw and talked to his men about launching a boat to search for a drowned slave. I could hear them muttering their protests and I wondered if anyone cared about Quame.

Gadsden jumped on the cart beside me and cradled me in his lap. As the driver whipped the horse into motion, he shouted to one of his men, 'Send word to Captain Gascoigne on the *Alborough* and to my wife at Bay Street.'

The journey from the dockside to Jean's house in Church Street only took a few minutes, but every cobble, every lurch of the cart made my belly contort with agony.

Word travelled fast and Jean was waiting for me outside her house. I tried to tell her about Quame, but she knew everything and told me to hush and stay calm. She directed Gadsden to carry me up to her bedroom and then shooed him out of the house.

'If you want to be helpful, wait outside for Captain Gascoigne.'

She put her ear on my belly and listened as if the baby was telling her what was happening. Then she sat on the bed, took my hand and said softly, 'Mary-Anne, I think the shock you have just suffered may cause the baby to come early.'

'No, it's much too early. There's a month yet to go. He won't be ready!'

'He's going to come, ready or not, my dear and there's nothing we can do to stop him.'

The midwife was sent for, but she was busy and hadn't arrived before my contractions started. Jean sat me on the birthing chair in the corner of her room. It hadn't been used for thirty years, but it was good to have chair arms to grip as each contraction passed like a wave of unbearable pain across my belly. Watery fluid started leaking from my body and I could feel the baby pressing downwards, trying to come out.

I hadn't expected the terrible pain of childbirth. I wasn't sure I was strong enough to bear it. I wanted to stop and lie down, abandon the whole thing. It was too early. The baby wasn't ready. I wasn't ready.

Jean told me to push and to breathe and to push and to breathe, again and again, for what seemed like an eternity. My body was being

223

ripped apart by this baby who wouldn't wait a moment longer, who was desperate to get out into the world.

'I see the head appearing. One final push Mary-Anne. Come on, don't give up now!'

One more push and the tiny baby slithered out of me into her hands.

'It's a boy, the Lord be praised.'

'Give him to me, give me my son!' I shouted angrily as if she was trying to take him away from me.

He was so small, covered in blood and bodily mess, but he was my son. The first Mighells boy, so greatly wanted, so long-awaited. The miracle of a baby boy in my arms filled me with wonder and love. I looked into his eyes and held him to my breast. He didn't scream and grab as Douglas had to Janet.

'Hello, my sweetest boy,' I said trying to coax him to my nipple. 'I have been waiting a long time to greet you.'

I looked up and saw the look on Jean's face.

'What's the matter? What's wrong? He's perfect, isn't he? Why is he so still and quiet? Is there something wrong with his breathing? Why doesn't he cry?'

The room went quiet. She held my stare without blinking and I knew something was most definitely wrong. He was too small, too quiet. I knew in a heartbeat that he would not live for long and I died inside at that moment.

Jean cut the birth cord and took the baby to the basin to wash him and wrap him in an old gown that had once belonged to her son. A son that lived and grew up and left home and married and had his own children.

She gently washed me and put me to bed, covered by a blanket. She laid the baby back in my arms, but I turned away from her in shame. I wanted to be in a private world with my son. My perfect tiny boy, with dark hair, huge melancholy eyes and long fingers. He wouldn't grow up like other boys, but for now, he was there with me.

Sometime later, John rushed in, smelling of gunpowder. He sat on the bed and put his arms around me and the baby. I knew he'd spoken to Jean and she would have explained everything. Tears ran down his face, but he didn't say anything and I was grateful to him for that. What was there to say?

Our private moment was interrupted by Alice, who burst into the room, shrieking and wailing loudly.

'Are you alright Mary-Anne? Tell me you are alright. I couldn't bear the thought of losing you. How is the baby? Tell me he's alright. Mrs McAndrews says we must christen him immediately.'

She was right. He must be christened that afternoon.

'I want to call him Mighells,' I whispered to John without taking my eyes off the baby.

Mr McAndrews was on hand to do a private baptism service there in the bedroom. Alice and Jean acted as godmothers, Gadsden as godfather. It was not how it was supposed to happen. I was going to embroider the christening robe ready for the first Mighells boy. After my confinement, John and I would stand as proud parents in St Phillips Church and celebrate the baptism of our first son in front of family and friends. Instead, it was the least joyful occasion I could imagine. Alice sobbed quietly, comforted by Gadsden. John was stoic and silent. I held Mighells up, praying that the holy water Mr McAndrews painted in a cross on his forehead would revive him but it didn't.

He closed his eyes and sank into himself as if he'd seen enough of the world and had no interest in staying longer. I sang lullabies to him while his life slowly seeped out of him and he ceased to breathe. I kissed his cold cheek and silently asked Quame to look after him and take his hand so they could enter Heaven together.

The day that had started so brightly had descended into darkness. I lay in Jean's bed with Mighells beside me, watching the shadows darken the room until the dawn crept up the walls. I didn't sleep. I wouldn't leave my baby all alone.

The next morning, John returned so we could take the baby to church for a final blessing. I had to be carried in a sedan chair as I was too weak in body and spirit to walk the short distance to St Philip's Church. I cut a lock of his dark hair, black like mine, which I would wear in my locket necklace every day of my life.

Mr McAndrews wrote in the Register of Baptisms:

"Mighells, the Son of Capt. John Gascoigne, Commander of His Majesties Ship the Alborough by his wife Mary Anne Eldest daughter of the Honourable James Mighells Esq: Comptroller of His Majesty's Navy, was born 12th October 1732 and Dyed the said day in the afternoon, being first christened."

Such a short life, summed up in a few words.

I knelt in prayer and asked the Good Lord to take care of my baby, Mighells, and my friend, Quame. Mr McAndrews said something about accepting the will of God, but deep in my heart, I was struggling to understand why God let these innocent souls die. I only knew that I felt utterly lost. I needed to grieve. I needed to go into a dark room, shut out the world and break into a million pieces of loss, regret and failure.

After his son's death, John kept busy with HMS Alborough in the careening wharf in Hobcaw Creek.

From the Captain's Log, HMS Alborough
24th October 1732
Hove down at Careening Wharf in Hobcaw Creek.

"Light wind & fair weather. PM got the remains of the Ballast & provisions & all the Officers Stores (Except an Iron Stanchion which dropt overboard & was lost) & by 7 were ready to heave down. At Break of Day began to heave & at ½ past 7 the Keel was out. At 9 righted with 4 foot 5 inches water in the hold having clean'd & grav'd the Larboard side without any Accident Except that in trying down the Rough Turpentine, one of the Kettles caught fire and one barrel of it was burnt before the fire could be put out."

At the end of November, he spent a week surveying the Charles Town Bar at North Edistow.

From the Captain's Log, HMS Alborough
28th November 1732
At Charles Town in South Carolina

"Little wind & fair weather. At 1 PM anchor'd against Charles Town in 7 fath water, unbent the sails & strip'd the Ship to preserve the Rigging. A Merchant Ship sailed hence whose salute of 5 guns was answer'd with three. At 9 moored ship. At midnight a Sloop from Barbados in great distress for want of provisions since he came on the coast by the long continuance of the foggy weather, came in here without Anchors, Cables or provisions. The Master, several Passengers & most of the Crew being Starved to death & the Survivors of them scarce able to stand alone. This morning I ordered a Survey of the Eight Oared boat by the Master Carpenters of the Shoreham, Happy Sloop & this Ship who find 12 of her floor timbers. 28 futtocks in the stern, the keel Stern Port & Transom all broke, the bottom very much decayed & that she is entirely unserviceable past repair."

24

I lay in Jean's bed for two days, unable to believe what had happened. I had Mighells in the bed next to me, wrapped up in the old gown that Jean had used for her sons. While I was sleeping, she laid him in the cradle beside my bed and when I woke up, I panicked that someone had stolen him from me.

John told me not to blame myself, so I added guilt to the list of feelings that overcame me, anguish, sadness, numbness and emptiness. My breasts were tender and full of milk and sometimes, when my baby was lying close to me, I heard him crying to be fed. I picked him up expecting him to be a normal, living baby, but he was cold and still and silent. I could hear them whispering in the corner. They thought I had gone mad.

'We must bury him today, Mary-Anne,' John said, as gently as he could.

I turned my head away. The finality was too hard to accept. I was not ready to bury him yet. I wanted to hold him for longer.

'The undertaker has delivered a small coffin and I want to know where you think we should bury him. There is a place in the graveyard at St Phillip's Church. We could take him there this afternoon.'

I couldn't leave him in a cold and lonely graveyard on his own.

'Can't we take him home with us?'

'What, to Hog Island? Bury him there?'

'Somewhere close to me. So I can watch over him.'

'Well, I suppose High Bluff would be a fine place to be laid to rest. The open skies, the sea breeze, the view of Charles Town.'

'And it is where he was conceived,' I reminded him.

So it was agreed that we would take Mighells back to Hog Island that afternoon. Friends and family assembled to make a sad funeral procession down to the ferry dock. Mr McAndrews led the way, holding his prayer book. He would conduct the burial service. John followed him, carrying the tiny wooden coffin. I needed the support of Jean on one side, Alice on the other, to stagger down the road behind him. Thomas Gadsden, Captain James Lloyd from the *Happy* and Captain

George Anson followed us. A big, rough, dirty man trailed silently at the back. Jean told me he was the gravedigger.

My heart was breaking with every step I took. I didn't want to reach the docks. I didn't want to get in the boat. I didn't want to bury my son. The docks were crowded and noisy, but people stepped aside to watch our pitiful procession. Some of the sailors doffed their hats, although that might be due to the three Naval Captains in uniform looking very sombre.

As we approached Middle Quay, I suddenly remembered the last time I was there, at that exact spot, three days ago. Quame had drowned and I had collapsed in the throes of premature labour. It seemed a lifetime ago. His body had still not been found. He had no coffin, no funeral procession, no final resting place.

John stepped into the rowboat and set the tiny coffin at the back of the boat. He held out his hand to help me down the steps, but I lurched back. That was where Quame had sat. What if there was another accident? What if Mighells' coffin went overboard, slipping below the waves out of my reach?

I couldn't get in the boat, I just couldn't. I sank to the ground, slithering out of the grasp of Alice and Jean.

The boatmen looked at each other, concerned. They didn't want John to get out of the boat, leaving them with the coffin, but they could hardly force me to get in the boat. I had collapsed in a heap on the dockside like a sack of rice. No one knew what to do with me.

It was George Anson who spoke up. 'Mrs Gascoigne is welcome to rest at my house in Church Street. It's empty at the moment and next door to Mrs McAndrews, so she can look after her. She can stay as long as she wants.'

No one had a better idea. Alice clung to Gadsden, who announced that they would go with John to get the burial done. Captain Lloyd said he'd go too. They got into the boat followed by Mr McAndrews and the silent gravedigger.

George swept me up in his arms. Jean was at my side, trotting to keep up with George's long strides as we retraced our steps back to Church Street.

Jean was talking all the while to me. 'Don't worry, my dear. Mr McAndrews will sort it out. He'll help your husband. It has to be done today. Your sister and her husband are with him. It will be a very nice service. Everything will be alright. It's best for the baby. He has to be buried today.'

Her words washed over me. I wasn't listening to her. I was numb to everything around me. John had taken my baby away. I would never see him again.

George laid me on the bed in my old house and then excused himself. He was visibly upset by what was happening and glad to leave the house.

Jean put a cover over me and took a seat by the window. 'I'll stay with you till they get back,' she said

They didn't come back before Jean had given me a draught of her herbal tea. I sank into a heavy, dreamless, hopeless sleep which I hoped I would never wake from. It was finished. It was over.

Of course, it was not over. When I woke the next morning, the sun had come up again and life went on.

Bess and Peggy arrived to look after me, with Cuffee who'd become the houseboy now Quame had gone. They had very long faces. They were mourning the sudden loss of a member of their own family. Quame had no grave they could visit to say goodbye and pay their last respects. They had been looking forward to the new baby and now he'd gone before they'd had a chance to meet him.

Bess was angry she wasn't there with me, but I reassured her that there was nothing she or anyone could have done. He wasn't ready for this world. It was exhausting trying to cheer them up so I shut myself away in my room.

I didn't want to go out and I didn't want to see people. I had a dread of any visit by an old acquaintance. I couldn't face the thought of seeing other mothers with their babies. If I opened the window, I could hear babies crying and children playing in the street. Mostly I stayed in bed, unable to fight my way out of this fog of heart-wrenching grief.

Alice insisted on visiting me every day. She wanted to make sure I was recovering.

'You're looking better today, sister,' she said brightly every time she came into my bedroom, which we both knew was a lie.

She was desperate for my forgiveness. If she hadn't summoned me to her side and I hadn't made that boat trip, Quame wouldn't have drowned and Mighells wouldn't have been born prematurely. So no, I couldn't forgive her. She wasn't even pregnant.

230

Sarah visited in the afternoons. She was very worried about me. The dark shadows under my eyes showed that I hadn't been sleeping. I couldn't tell her that I stayed awake at night as long as possible to avoid the nightmares of Quame rising up from below the water and seizing my baby from my arms. I couldn't hold on to Mighells, no matter how hard I tried and I had to watch him disappear into the watery darkness.

She wanted to cheer me up and encouraged me to get out of bed, wash my face and brush my hair. She meant well but day-to-day life had become a burden. I had no interest in my appearance and couldn't concentrate on even the smallest task. I did the bare minimum to simply survive.

I sighed with relief when she gave up and left. I pulled the covers over my head. I preferred to be left on my own so I could cry. Everyone was losing patience with me. They wanted me to get better as if I was ill. As if I could take some medicine to mend my broken heart.

John didn't stay long on his visits. He was too busy and he made his excuses to leave after a short time and hurried off. The *Alborough* had been hauled out at Hobcaw Creek. The sides had to be cleaned and graved, tarred and blackened. He didn't know how to deal with my grief and I was grateful to him for not trying. He didn't know the words to comfort me. When I looked at him, I could see the disappointment and confusion on his face. I had done what he asked of me. I had given him a son and it had all come to nothing. When masts or rigging or cables on his ship were found to be unserviceable, he got replacements, but he couldn't replace my baby.

I could hear him talking to Jean outside my door. They discussed how I could be made to swallow the disgusting medicine the doctor had given me, how I could be made to get up, how I could be cured.

After John had gone back to his ship, Jean sat on the edge of the bed and rocked me in her arms. I sobbed so long and so hard that eventually I collapsed, exhausted, onto my pillow. She prayed I would find rest so I closed my eyes and feigned sleep. I didn't want to let her down. She never said cheer up.

One evening, as she left to return home to prepare Mr McAndrews' supper, she said to me, 'Captain Gascoigne says there'll be a storm tonight. Strong gales and heavy rain. There's likely to be thunder and lightning.'

When I showed total disinterest in the weather, she added, 'Don't worry, I'll speak to Cuffee about it. He'll make sure your windows are closed and the shutters tightly fixed. You stay there, safe and warm in your bed.'

Once she'd left, all I could hear were her words. Strong gales and heavy rain. Thunder and lightning. I would stay snug in my bed. I imagined I was holding Mighells in my arms, keeping him safe and warm, just as any mother would do.

I wasn't though, was I? I was not doing what a mother would do. John had left him alone on High Bluff on Hog Island. The winds swept in across the clifftop, bending the trees crooked and eroding the rocks to dust. My baby was out there all alone.

John was busy checking the anchor chains, worrying about his ship. I was hiding under the blanket in my bedroom, worrying about myself. No one was worrying about Mighells.

I got up and went to the window. I could see dark clouds low on the horizon to the north. I could see torrents of rain falling in dark curtains below them. The storm would get to Mighells within the hour.

I crept down the stairs without making a sound to alert the servants. I grabbed my purse on the way out of the door and wrapped a cape around my nightgown. I made my way to the quayside. It had started to rain heavily. Too late, I realised I should have worn shoes, but I couldn't go back now. The ferrymen had packed up and were sheltering in taverns in the town. No one wanted to be out on the water in the coming storm.

A man was lurking in the shadows. I hadn't seen him before. He wasn't a regular ferryman. His tattered, dirty clothes suggested he'd do anything for money, so I approached him. He looked at me through guarded, slitted eyes.

Yes, he knew Hog Island. No, he wouldn't row me across there for the regular fare, not tonight. He hesitated and looked me up and down. I must have looked like a lunatic, my hair wild, my feet bare and my cape clasped over my nightgown. He looked around to make sure no one heard him.

'I'll do it if you pay me extra.'

I offered him everything in my purse and it seemed to be enough because he dragged his bedraggled boat out from under the bridge, round to the steps and helped me climb onboard. I sat in the bow facing Hog Island, straining my eyes until I could see the cliff through the rain where High Bluff dropped into the water.

He dropped me at the dock, but he wouldn't wait. I hadn't paid him enough for a return trip. He wasn't going to cross the river back to Charles Town tonight. He cast off and rowed to the nearest safe inlet on the east side of Cooper River.

Hog Island was deathly quiet. Only Mungo remained to take care of the house, but there was no sight nor sound of him. I stood on the dock in the driving rain, confused by what I was doing there. And then I remembered Mighells. I wasn't even sure where John had buried him, but I made my way through the gardens, across the orchards and out onto the cliff.

I saw a simple wooden cross in the grass. I had to stoop to walk against the wind and found it was easier to make progress on my hands and knees. My cape was drenched, my nightgown was drenched, my hair was drenched. Everything about me was dripping with rain, but this was not the time to think selfishly about myself. I had come to tend to Mighells.

John had painted on the cross *"Beloved Mighells. Now with the angels."* It was so simple and sad that it broke my heart and I collapsed on the mound of earth sobbing, curled up as if my body could shield the ground where he lay from the storm. I wanted to dig up his body and cuddle him to my breast, but my fingernails made feeble impressions in the soil. No doubt the sturdy gravedigger would have buried him deep in the earth, well out of reach.

I hoped he could feel my presence, on the ground above him, sheltering him from the storm. I sang gentle lullabies to reassure him that I would always love him and always take care of him. The wind had picked up and it was very cold out on the exposed clifftop. In a perverse way, I relished each clap of thunder, each streak of lightning. They wanted to scare me away, make me run into the house and abandon my post, but I wouldn't go. Let them do their worst. I would not leave Mighells alone on a night as wild as this.

The swirling wind conjured up images of wraiths dancing in the air. Quame was there, hopping from one foot to another, waving his arms above his head to gain my attention. Men and women, hundreds and thousands of them, all colours, all races, all ages, appeared fleetingly in the mist, reaching out to me as they swirled past in the wind. I searched for Mighells, but there were so many babies, I couldn't find him. It was exhausting trying to look for him so I gave up. I was so cold and tired. I'd find him in the morning. I'd stay and sleep for a while.

Did I sleep or did I lose consciousness? I'd never know. I heard voices shouting my name. Over and over. Louder and louder. I opened one eye and saw the sun dawning on the horizon over to the east. The rain had stopped, the wind had dropped and the storm had passed.

I couldn't move, my body was stiff with cold. I lay there, waiting for the voices to find me. I could hear them approaching, still shouting my name, hoping for a response. I couldn't speak, my throat had dried up.

Then John was kneeling beside me, cradling my head in his lap.

'Mary-Anne, my dearest, thank the Lord I've found you. We have been searching Charles Town all night.'

I could see Thomas Gadsden standing beside him. There were more men behind them. I guessed they were Gadsden's henchmen who had helped in the search.

'Gadsden, for God's sake, carry her to the house,' John shouted, frustrated that his crippled foot and maimed hand made it impossible for him to lift me off the wet ground.

My body was lifeless and gave no resistance as Gadsden swept me up in his arms and carried me down the hill to the house. He felt strong and warm and comforting after a night spent on the clifftop with the wraiths. John led the way to our bedroom and I shut my eyes tightly so I didn't see into the empty nursery as we passed.

Once I was laid on the bed, John found Mungo asleep in his quarters and sent him back to Charles Town with Gadsden and his men to fetch Jean and the servants to look after me.

I was still wearing my sodden nightgown and I shivered violently. John fetched a dry chemise from the chest and helped me change. He wrapped my cold feet in woollen socks and put gloves on my shaking hands. He rubbed my wet hair with a cloth and delicately dried my face. He made me drink a small brandy which felt like fire going down my throat.

All the while he was talking, telling me about a hue and cry calling the townspeople out in the middle of the night to search for me. Everyone was hoping no foul play was involved and I would be found alive and well. None of the ferrymen said they had brought me across the river so it was only as a last chance at dawn, just as he was starting to lose hope, that he came to Hog Island to look for me.

It hurt my throat to speak, but I whispered, 'You knew I'd be worried about Mighells,'

'I was worried about the living, Mary-Anne, not the dead.'

He wrapped a blanket around my shoulders to warm me up and sat on the bed next to me.

'I am grieving for our son, too, Mary-Anne, but you can't bring him back. He's in Heaven now. You must let him go.'

I didn't want to let Mighells go.

I pulled away from him and beat his chest with my fists. 'Why can't you do something? Why can't you bring him back?'

He put his arms around me to draw me in tight so I couldn't move my arms to strike him again. I looked up at him for comfort, but tears were streaming down his face and I knew he had none to give me.

'Mary-Anne, I don't know what I can say that will make it better, but I can tell you how much I love you. I've loved you from the very first moment I saw you. I knew I wanted to marry you and live the rest of my life with you. I haven't been the best husband, have I? Leaving you on your own while I am away at sea. I assumed you'd be used to that, what with your father in the Navy. I thought you'd know how to cope without me. Wherever I went and whatever I did, I was always thinking of you, your smile, your laugh and your sweet kindness. You cared for me when I was ill with the fever and you looked after me when I couldn't walk. You have been the best wife a man could ever hope for. I love you so much, Mary-Anne. I haven't told you that often enough, have I? When you went missing last night, I thought I'd lost you and I realised my life is nothing without you. I don't want to ever lose you again. My most beloved wife.'

He stopped talking and leaned down to kiss my cheek, my nose and my mouth, over and over. His face was wet with tears and so was mine. I didn't have the strength to tell him how much I loved him back, so I fell into his embrace and prayed that I could survive this ordeal, knowing that I was his beloved wife.

'But what use am I if I can't give you a son?'

235

'Don't speak like that, Mary-Anne. Right now, you are all I care about. You are all I want in my life. We can discuss another child later.'

'I don't want to discuss another child, I want Mighells. Another child could never replace him.'

A View of Charles-Town, South Carolina',
engraved by Samuel Smith, after Thomas Leitch
published in London 1776
Art Museums of Colonial Williamsburg

IV

Charles Town, South Carolina

1732-1734

After extensive repairs, HMS Alborough set off in March 1733 to chart the Caribbean islands between Florida and Cuba, returning at the end of May.

From the Captain's Log, HMS Alborough
29th May 1733
Anchored at Charles Town. South Carolina.

"Little wind & thick hazy weather. PM HMS Squirrel anchored here from Cruising. The weather being so excessively hot that several of the Boats crews are taken sick in passing on the Common Services of the Ships. Defer going to St Helena Sound till the heats are somewhat abated & have begun to make rough draughts from my observations on the West India Voyage we are just now return'd from."

The summer of 1733 was excessively hot.

From the Captain's Log, HMS Alborough
12th September 1733
At Charles Town

"Little wind & fairy weather. This day is appointed for a General Fast and Humiliation throughout this Province on account of the Excessive heat & draught, by which most part of the Crop of grain is entirely burnt up & the small remainder likely also to be destroy'd."

25

T he grief that filled me up from my head to my toes was like the tide that filled up the creek at the back of Hog Island until it overflowed the banks. I feared the ebb tide, when it would flow out again, would never come. So it was a surprise to me early one April morning, as I stood by the open window, I noticed the glorious rosy glow of the sunrise across the horizon and smelled the salty sea breeze coming into my bedroom.

I asked Bess to fill the bathtub and I lay in the water while she rubbed my skin, trying to slough off one more layer of sadness. I could hear Cuffee singing as he swept the porch. A low rhythmic chant, melodic and mournful.

'What is he singing, Bess?'

'Mistress, those songs remind him of his village back home. They are lullabies to comfort children. Maybe your baby hears him singing too?'

I liked the thought that Mighells could hear Cuffee's lullabies. We could all be near Mighells, take him flowers and sing him lullabies.

After breakfast, I strolled through the garden to visit the graves. It had been six months since the day Mighells died and Quame drowned. Quame's body had never been found, but I had asked John to fix a cross for him on the High Bluff next to Mighells.

'His spirit will know where to come to find some rest,' I told John, remembering those restless wraiths in the storm.

'And you must rely on Quame to look after our baby and not spend the night out on the cliff ever again.'

John had gone back to sea. After Mighells died, he stayed in Charles Town to be near me, but by March he'd had enough of being shore-bound or perhaps my grief was too hard to live with.

Before he left, he completed the purchase of a plot of ninety-one acres of land to the north of Charles Town opposite Hobcaw Creek on Captain Anson's recommendation.

'It borders on Anson's Bowling Green plantation, the one he won from Gadsden in 1727. It's uncultivated at the moment. Anson uses his land for horse races but, if you like, we could build a house on our land. They say indigo is the thing to grow now or we can grow rice or keep cattle. A grand plantation house might suit you well, Mary-Anne.'

Had he done this for me? A grand house of my own. Sarah had a grand house outside Charles Town. Alice had one. I could have one. It would mean leaving Mighells on Hog Island all alone so it was out of the question.

The *Alborough* sailed out of Charles Town Harbour at the end of March, heading south to the island of Hispaniola. 'This season I want to situate and draw the appearance of the most remarkable points and places on my way to the south side of Hispaniola,' John had announced before he left and I wondered if he had chosen an island as far away as he possibly could.

I sat on the clifftop next to the graves, looking out to sea wondering where John was and what he was doing. He'd once said that wherever he was, he was thinking of me. Which wouldn't be very interesting as I sit around at home, lost in my thoughts of Mighells. I would never know his first step, his first word or his favourite game. I would never watch him grow into a boy and then a man. I would never see him again. No wonder I spent my days crying.

Sarah came to my rescue. A week after John left, she invited me to tea and for the first time since Mighells' death, I ventured across to Charles Town to visit her at her townhouse. She had thoughtfully ensured that her children were out of the house and we passed a most enjoyable morning together, like old friends. She prattled on about the latest gossip and, to my surprise, I found myself smiling and taking an interest in who was doing what. Our girlish laughter was a sound I'd forgotten. We managed to avoid talking about Mighells and it was a blessed relief to have an hour or two when he was not uppermost in my thoughts.

On another visit, Ralph was there and amused us with his stories. I was so pleased he'd returned from Philadelphia.

'When I got a letter from Alice telling me you were dying, I thought she was being dramatic. When I got another letter from Sarah telling me the same, I knew it was serious! I had to rush back and save you, Mary-Anne.' He laughed as if it was inconceivable Ralph Wilkinson could save anyone.

He'd started writing articles for Thomas Whitmarsh's newspaper, *The South Carolina Gazette,* which began publication in Charles Town in January last year. Whitmarsh had worked for Mr Benjamin Franklin, the man Ralph had so admired in Philadelphia and who owned *The Pennsylvania Gazette.* Ralph, who knew everything that was going on in Society, contributed news on engagements and marriages and rumours of affairs.

'I always try and say something nice about the bride-to-be. "*A young lady of distinguishable merit and a good fortune*" is one of my favourites if I can't comment favourably on her appearance.'

We laughed at his tongue-in-cheek compliments and I was delighted for my friend. He had found some employment that made him feel useful. So far, his articles had been about the gossip of Charles Town society, but he told me that Gadsden was encouraging him to write about the growing interest in political independence from the British crown. Many of the settlers were now of European origin who came to escape religious persecution and some people had even started calling themselves American. To them, it was strange to think this colony was part of Britain.

One day Sarah and I took a stroll along Bay Street to visit the dressmaker's shop. Sarah pretended the visit was for her to order a new dress, but I recognised the encouragement she was giving me to look at the fabrics newly arrived from London and I was grateful to her for it. On the way, we met Jean McAndrews who asked after my health. Once we had exchanged pleasantries, I apologised that I had not returned to the weekly meetings of her Ladies' Society.

'Mary-Anne, you must give yourself time to heal,' she said clutching at my hand. 'You have suffered the greatest of earthly miseries. I would understand if you wanted to avoid the pain and anguish of other mothers.'

I was tearful at the emotion in her words, but I started promising to resume my visits soon. Sarah interrupted me and made our excuses, telling Jean we were in a rush to get to the dressmaker, but she would give some money to the church when she was next passing.

'Don't you worry about those poor mothers,' Sarah said as soon as we were out of Jean's hearing. 'You must think of your own recovery. Time might be a great healer, but your husband won't wait for ever. He will expect intimacy before too long.'

How could I tell her that I feared this was not John's expectation? When he was not away at sea, he stayed on his beloved ship, writing up his surveys or overseeing repairs. When he came home, he no longer had any interest in intimacy with me.

We walked on in silence, but I had lost any enthusiasm to get a new dress. What was the point?

John was away for six weeks, returning to Charles Town at the end of May. He proudly showed me on the chart the places he had visited, but when James visited, he had a different report about the trip

'The ship's company fell sickly,' he told me. 'The Master, the Boatswain, the Gunner and thirty-five petty officers and foremast men couldn't do anything due to their sickness. Even the Surgeon was so ill that he had to keep to his cabin.'

The *Alborough* returned as the excessive heat of the summer began. So many of the crew were sick that John had to defer any plans he had to survey St Helena Sound.

The summer was as hot as anyone could remember and there was another outbreak of the fever. Poor Mr Whitmarsh, the printer of *The South Carolina Gazette*, died of the fever in August and the last issue of the newspaper appeared in September 1733. Ralph was so distraught at losing the one job he enjoyed that he wrote immediately to Mr Franklin to send another of his printers to replace Whitmarsh.

'The newspaper is so popular,' he told me, 'there's not a single house in Charles Town where you wouldn't find a copy. I can't let it be abandoned.'

One evening late in September, John and I ate a quiet supper together in our spacious dining room, which could seat a dozen guests. The sultry heat made us both feel lethargic. John stared out of the window. I thought he was dispirited by the bad weather, the disrepair of his ship and the lack of interest in his surveys from the Admiralty, but it appeared he had other matters on his mind as he suddenly leant forward to talk to me.

'I'll return to my ship tomorrow, Mary-Anne. I must make progress on the report of my recent voyage to Hispaniola.'

I wondered if his concern for his reports was now an excuse for his lack of desire for me. I needed to know the truth about our marriage so I asked him if he would spend his last night in my bed.

'I don't want to disturb you, my dearest. You must recover your strength. I have given the matter a great deal of thought and I have decided that we will not try for a child again. It's too dangerous for you. My own mother died giving birth to me and I don't want to risk losing you again. That night I searched Charles Town for you was the worst night of my life. I can't live without you and I would rather have you in my life, my darling wife, than any child. I am quite decided in this so we will talk no more on the matter.'

He got up suddenly and walked out of the dining room. His study door closed behind him to shut me out. Just like that, he'd decided our marriage would be childless. Just like that, he'd killed all my hopes and dreams. I sat in silent shock, trying to comprehend what he'd said.

The next morning, I visited Mighells' grave and talked it over with the mound of earth that was my son.

'John's right, childbirth is too dangerous. His own mother died in childbirth. You died, I nearly died. Poor John, he might have lost us both. He's only thinking of me. He says he loves me so much he doesn't want to lose me.'

So really, he was only thinking of himself, a small voice answered in my head. What do you want?

'I'm so confused. I'm not sure I can go through this again. I don't want to die.'

But you didn't die in childbirth, the voice persisted.

'No, but the sadness inside me nearly killed me.'

But that grief will lessen in time.

'It was a terrible day,' I told him. 'I was so grateful that Jean McAndrews was there with me. Imagine if I'd had to go through it on my own. I expect there are so many mothers who are alone and frightened. What about the poor mothers I used to visit before I was pregnant? I used to enjoy helping Jean McAndrews at her Ladies Society. Of course, if I can't hold you in my arms, Mighells, I wouldn't want to be near other people's babies.'

As soon as I said that I knew it was a lie. Even if I couldn't have children, I couldn't bear the thought of never holding a babe in my arms again.

'Would you mind terribly if I did start visiting other mothers, my darling boy? Who knows, maybe if I talk about you, it might help other mothers cope with their grief. It might even help me. I'll go and see Jean next week and see if she thinks I'd be useful. After all I've been through, I know a lot more than I did before.'

A few days later Ralph visited me and I told him of my plan. He seemed sceptical of the idea that I was in any fit state to help the poor women of Charles Town.

'Do you know what you're asking of yourself, Mary-Anne? I would have thought you needed more time to grieve.'

How could I tell him that it was the only way I could think of to get over the grief that was consuming me?

By the start of October, I was ready to go across to Charles Town to attend the weekly meeting of the Ladies' Society.

Jean McAndrews was delighted to see me, but it was not an auspicious start. The talk at the meeting was about a poor woman who had died of childbed fever. Jean told us it was a difficult birth, the poor mother was undernourished, just skin and bone, and the baby refused to move down from her belly. She sent one of the skinny lads, standing in shock at his mother's bedside, to run and fetch the physician. When the doctor arrived an hour later, he was covered in blood.

'He announced that he'd rushed there from dissecting the corpse of a woman who died in childbirth, as if we should be grateful for his attendance,' she told the meeting. She had been horrified at his appearance and begged him to wash his hands before assisting with the delivery.

'He said to me, in a most pompous manner, Madam, I am a gentleman. I do not need to wash my hands and I don't need you to tell me what to do. Then he reached up inside the poor woman, pulled out the dead baby and took it away wrapped in a cloth to dispose of.'

We gasped in shock at the heartless action of the physician. How glad I was that at least I held my baby, if only for the shortest time.

Three days later the skinny lad appeared at Jean's door asking for help. His mother had developed severe abdominal pains and fever.

'I knew exactly what it was,' she told us. 'I've seen mothers die of childbed fever before. The only treatment is bleeding to get rid of the bad blood. By the time I arrived the poor woman was dying and extracting even a thimble of blood would have killed her quicker. I marched around to confront that physician. I am convinced that his dirty hands played a part in it, but he made excuses about the disgraceful conditions of the hovel she lived in, as if it was her fault and she got what she deserved. I confess that I shouted at him. I hope the Good Lord will forgive my outburst of anger.'

We reassured her that the Good Lord was forgiving and it made Jean even more evangelical about the importance of washing.

She asked me if I was resilient enough to help her with her visits.

'But it would only be worse for them if we don't help,' I said. 'And you'll need help with all that washing.'

My first visit with Jean was to a woman who had been delivered of a healthy baby boy. What a joy to hold a babe in my arms again. He grinned up at me and clenched his tiny fists. He was a feisty survivor alright, and much to my disappointment wanted to be returned to his mother's breast to feed.

As I watched him greedily sucking, my heart cried out, that could have been me. My body bent double, convulsed in the heartbreak of never having my babe suckling at my breast. How could I ever come to terms with what John had decided? How could I live in a childless marriage?

Due to sickness, John struggled to complete the draft of his surveys of the West Indies. In October 1733 he set off to survey St Helena Sound, but returned two days later unable to find any suitable passage for shipping.

From the Captain's Log, HMS Alborough
17th October 1733
At Charles Town

"Moderate gales and cloudy weather. As I have been so much disordered in my health that I have not been able (notwithstanding an assiduous Application) to compleat the Rough Draught I am making from my Observations taken in the West Indies on the Summer voyage which I was in hopes to have done in time to have made use of this Month's Moon to finish my draught of the Gulph of Florida. It being now five days past the full moon, I propose to view St Helena Sound that I may determine whether to go about the Survey of that place or endeavour to compleat the Description of the Gulph as soon as I have done the draughts above mentioned."

Strong winds and fog prevented HMS *Alborough* crossing the Bar during November so the ship stayed in harbour for the winter.

From the Captain's Log, HMS Alborough
15th December 1733
Anchored at Charles Town, South Carolina.

"Little wind & cloudy weather the latter part fresh gales. At 8 this morning a fire broke out onboard the Abigail & Anne (Mr Thomas Henning Master) one of the Merchant ships at Mr Wragg's Wharf which raged with so much fury that notwithstanding all the Assistance of Men, Buckets, Anchors, Warps & all other necessarys on the occasion immediately sent from the Men at War, the after part of her burnt down to the water's edge. By the timely assistance the fire, that had three times got hold of the Rainbow, a Guineaman, which lay next to her was put out by the gallant Behaviour of the Officers and Seamen (it being generally known there was a considerable quantity of Gunpowder on board her) by which means not only that ship & her cargo but in all probability all the Ships and Vessels at the next wharfe (several of them being aground) just to leeward of her & as the wind was, all the South part of the Town were saved from Burning, several of these Vessels as well as the Wharfes being loaded with pitch tar and turpentine. We lost by this accident two leather buckets."

26

J ohn remained in Charles Town for the winter. Repairs to the *Happy* sloop were not finished until October, delayed by the great sickness. John himself was so sick that it had taken him since May to complete the rough draft of his trip to Hispaniola. He wanted to return to the coast of Florida, but a dramatic change in the weather meant that fog and severe gales delayed his departure. The easterly winds had been so continuous since September that no ship could leave Charles Town across the Bar. Ten merchant ships lay wind-bound in the harbour. And now the violent northerly winds were expected, from which there was no shelter in the Gulf of Florida. By November he had to admit defeat, both by the weather and his sickness, and return to Hog Island to rest.

One morning in December, as I strolled up to High Bluff to put flowers on the graves, my attention was caught by a fiery glow from one of the wharves across the river in Charles Town. A ship was on fire!

I rushed back to the house, but John was already on his way to the dock where the pinnace from the *Alborough* had come alongside.

'Captain Gascoigne, Sir,' the sailor shouted, 'Come immediately. A fire has broken out onboard the *Abigail & Anne* at Mr Wragg's Wharf. Captain Anson's given orders that all the Men at War must help. She lies next to a Guineaman with gunpowder on board her. If she catches alight, the ships at the next wharf will certainly burn and the fire will spread to the town.'

John hurriedly got into the pinnace as fast as he could. Everyone knew that fires were a constant threat to a town built of mostly wooden buildings and it hadn't rained in weeks, leaving the houses particularly dry. All it needed was a strong wind off the harbour and the fire would be indiscriminately blown into the town.

At least the Guineaman had unloaded her cargo of slaves. Ralph had told me earlier in the week that Joseph Wragg had held another auction at his office on the west side of Bay Street, opposite his wharf. The demand for Africans to work on plantations was insatiable as more and more of the swamps and marshes were put under rice cultivation.

A few hours later, I saw a boat approaching and I rushed to the dock, expecting John to return, my brave, heroic husband, back from fighting fires and saving Charles Town from burning., but it was Alice sitting in the back of the boat.

She looked like a duchess in her red velvet jacket with her hands resting on her belly. I knew in an instant what her news was. I had been dreading this day ever since she met Gadsden at Mrs Manigault's Summer Ball in June '31. So no, I wasn't surprised but nothing prepared me for the gut-wrenching agony of realising she was pregnant.

'Hello, Alice, I wasn't expecting you,' I said as calmly as I could in the circumstances. 'John has had to rush over to Charles Town. I thought the boat was him returning.'

'Yes, I saw the chaos going on at the docks. Some slave ship is on fire. I had a terrible job finding a ferryman.'

Our friendship had been strained these past few months and we hadn't seen much of each other lately. I couldn't forget it was her fault that Quame drowned and Mighells was born too early. I heard she was a great success in Society as the respectable wife of the Customs Collector, but her world of glamorous dinners and lively gambling parties, political intrigues and social gossip seemed a long way from my quiet life on Hog Island.

She climbed awkwardly out of the boat. We strolled up to the house and I asked Bess to serve us mint juleps on the porch.

Perversely, I didn't mention her condition but asked her how she was finding married life. 'At least, now you're married, you're not doing any more dangerous spying,' I said.

'Oh no, I wouldn't spy for the British Government anymore. My husband is furious at their attempts to tax us here in South Carolina to pay for their stupid wars in Europe.'

Ralph had told me he'd seen Gadsden talking at meetings in town. 'Quite the firebrand,' he'd said, 'talking about no taxation without representation in Parliament. It's revolutionary talk, saying we shouldn't pay taxes to Britain and we should fight for our freedom.'

Alice didn't want to talk about wars in Europe and she got straight to the matter at hand.

'Mary-Anne, I am with child, due in April. Look how fat I am and there are still four months to go.'

'You look well enough, Alice.'

She was glowing with health so no one need be concerned for her well-being.

'But Thomas wants more sons, so here we are.' She looked down at her belly, which seemed to be growing larger as we watched. 'Of course, he'll be a good father, and that's what matters in deciding to have a child.'

Is that all that mattered? John would have been a good father to our children. I bit my lip. We would never know. John had decided it was too dangerous for me to bear another child. I couldn't argue with Alice, not when she was with child and I was barren.

'I confess I am very nervous about the birth. You will be there for me, won't you, Mary-Anne?'

I smiled and nodded vaguely. I wasn't sure yet how I was going to cope when my little sister gave birth to a healthy baby son.

She didn't press me for an answer and, perhaps to make amends for her bluntness, she said, 'Why don't you come for lunch one day soon? Or stay with me at the plantation? You should get out and about for a few days, get a change of air. It would do you good. You can't sit around all day moping. Do say you'll come.'

'I'm needed here to take care of John.'

She rolled her eyes in exasperation. She couldn't understand how I had settled for a life as the childless nursemaid to a sick husband. I wasn't sure I understood it either. He was the invalid, not me, but it was my life he sought to protect by not wanting a child. Ever since he'd declared we would not risk another childbirth in case I died, he had been distant. He no longer embraced me or kissed me. I sometimes wondered if he visited the rougher part of Charles Town to satisfy his desires, but I suspected his illness laid him so low that he had no such desires.

'I'm not sure I'll be a very good mother,' Alice continued. 'I was never very good with Meg or Kittie. I don't really like children.'

'I'm sure it will be different when it's your own child, Alice,' I said coldly, clearing up the glasses to make it obvious I wanted her to leave. I did not want to discuss with her the unfairness that she, of all people, was having a child and not me. I loved children.

As she got up to leave, she feigned that she'd just remembered something, but it was obvious this was the real reason for her social call.

'I wanted to ask you, dearest sister, if you could give me the lace christening gown that I packed for you when you left England? I want my baby to wear it when he's christened. If it's a boy, I shall name him James after Papa.'

She couldn't help smiling with joy at her blessed life. A husband who never went away to sea, who was never ill, who had put a baby son in her belly, the start of the dynasty he so desperately wanted.

I went upstairs to the nursery to fetch the christening robe. How could I not? Mighells never wore it. I had packed it away carefully with sweet herbs from the garden. I shook them out, letting the scented leaves fall like snow onto the empty crib.

Before I went downstairs, I knelt beside the empty cradle, clasped my hands in prayer and begged the Good Lord to send Alice a daughter. That would upset her plans for a new dynasty. It was a selfish, mean thing to do but the chances were high. After all, Mama had four daughters and no sons. Maybe daughters ran in our family.

John returned late in the evening, exhausted but relieved that the fire had been contained and had not spread to the other ships or docks. His hands were battered and bruised from hauling buckets, his clothes smelled of burning timbers and ash.

We sat out on the porch in the warm evening and I rubbed his hands gently with healing oils. He told me quietly and calmly that he had written to the Admiralty requesting a recall of the *Alborough* back to England.

'Service in the Tropics has taken its toll on the ship,' he said. 'She is in need of a complete refit and repair, more work that can be done at Hobcaw Creek. She will need to be repaired at Deptford Docks.'

It had taken its toll on him as well. I wondered if he could ever be repaired.

'You would like to go home, I think, Mary-Anne.'

'Yes, but will you get another command, John? I mean you are not in the best of health.'

'I shall ask for leave for a short time to recuperate and complete my surveys. We'll take a house in Stratford, near to your parents and sisters.'

'When will we leave?' I asked, desperate to know if it would be before or after Alice had her baby in April.

251

'We must await orders, Mary Anne. You know how long we waited at Portsmouth all those years ago.'

'We will have to take Mighells with us. I won't leave him here,' I told him.

He nodded his head slowly. 'We could take his coffin home to England for a proper burial.'

'A proper burial at home in Stratford. I would like that very much.'

He gently stroked my hair and I felt a comfort having him there with me. I would like to go home, after seven years away, and I would like a house in Stratford, near to my family, but it wouldn't be the triumphant homecoming I had imagined. I would be returning with an invalid husband, an empty womb and a little coffin in need of a proper burial.

In March 1734 John received orders to return HMS Alborough to England for a complete refit. The refit would take 2 years and cost £7,222 (worth about £1.3 million in 2022), almost as much as she cost to build in 1728.

From the Captain's Log, HMS Alborough
27th March 1734
Anchored at Charles Town, South Carolina.

    "Strong gales and hazy weather. PM a new red Ensign was made out of Bunting had from Town & a sloop pass'd by us up the River from Georgia. At 6 this morning got up Topgallant Yard, unmoored and hove short. At 9 arrived the ship Hopewell, James Moffant Master, of and from London who brings me orders from the Rt. Honourable the Lords Commissioners of the Admiralty of Great Britain for repairing home with this ship & to leave the Happy under the command of the Captain of the Squirrel attending on this province till further orders. I gave Captain Lloyd orders accordingly and at 10 weighed and ran up to Charles Town to take in the stores which are ashore and do what is necessary to be done in regard to my draughts before I leave the place. Upon my weighing, several of the Merchants ships saluted & were answered together with 11 guns. At 11 anchored against the Storehouse in Charles Town in 7 fathom water. And a great number of Yarns in each of the Bower Cables breaking when we unmoor'd & weighed in Rebellion Road, they were surveyed & condemned unserviceable."

Quame's death was based on the drowning of a sailor from HMS Alborough, Martin Dunn.

The Pennsylvania Gazette March 1734
    "Charleston, March 2. On the 23rd last in the morning, one Martin Dunn, belonging to his Majesty's Ship the Alborough, happened to be with Benjamin Story in his Periauger* in the Northern Branch of Store's River, and striking an Alligator, fell over board and down to the Ground immediately. No doubt but the Alligator made a good breakfast on him."
*a Periauger is a shallow draft sailing vessel.

27

S ince the start of the year, John had been waiting for orders recalling HMS *Alborough* to England.

'Knowing the Admiralty, the official orders could take several months,' he told me. 'I should have time to fit in one last trip to the Florida Gulf to complete that survey. It's been on my mind that I couldn't do a thorough job last year when we were so afflicted by sickness and northerly gales.'

If he was planning another trip, he must have thought it would be several months before we leave. Still, by the first week of February he was sufficiently confident of our imminent departure to place an advertisement in *The South Carolina Gazette* to dispose of our home:

"To be let or sold: An Island opposite to Charles Town commonly Called Hogg-Island being a very commodious Situation for a carining wharf and for a Ferry. The Creeks round it affording perfect security for Boats and Periaguas in the most stormy Weather, as the Main-Creeks doth for Ships of the greatest Draught, and they abound with such a continual plenty of Fish that the Town may be constantly serv'd from thence. On the Island is a new Dwelling House &c. built on the high Bluff, which commands an entire prospect of the Harbour, from the Bar to the Town. A delightful Wilderness with shady Walks and Arbours, cool in the hottest Seasons. A piece of Garden-ground where all the best kinds of Fruit and Kitchen Greens are produced, and planted with Orange, Apple, Peach, Nectarine and Plum trees capable of being made a very good Vineyard and of other great Improvements, and subject to the Quit-Rent of an Ear of Indian Corn. Enquire of Capt. Gascoigne in Charles Town."

Ralph showed me the advertisement. I recognised John's words. It was as he had described our home to me four long years ago. It appeared in the first edition of the newspaper published by Mr Lewis Timothy, the new proprietor. Much to Ralph's delight, Mr Franklin did send another of his employees to revive the newspaper.

Ralph looked at me, waiting for my reaction. 'Are you really leaving, Mary-Anne? When will you go?'

What could I say? It seemed so unreal that we would ever leave.

'Knowing the Admiralty, it could take several months for orders to arrive,' I told him, quoting John.

One morning at the end of March, those orders did arrive. The *Alborough* and the *Happy* were anchored in Rebellion Road ready to depart to the Florida Gulf. Last-minute repairs had been done. The provisions, water and gunpowder were onboard. Spare sails and replacement tarpaulin were stowed below. The pilot was standing by the wheel. All John needed was a fair wind to get across the Bar, but for the past week the wind had been either too calm or too strong, from the east or from the south, all of which prevented safe passage out of Charles Town Harbour. Eight outbound merchant ships waited with him.

With a southerly wind, the *Hopewell,* arrived from London, came in across the Bar and anchored in the harbour. Without delay the Master, James Moffant, lowered his pinnace and was rowed across to the *Alborough*. He had a letter for Captain John Gascoigne from the Right Honourable Lords Commissioners of the Admiralty of Great Britain with orders to return home in HMS *Alborough* and to leave the *Happy* under the command of Captain Anson until further orders.

John returned immediately to Charles Town and moored the *Alborough* against the storehouse to prepare for the Atlantic voyage. His advertisement had procured a purchaser so he proceeded that same afternoon to the attorney's office to "*convey to James Searles, Esquire, of Charles Town, Victualler, the seventeen acres heretofore known by the name of Hog Island and since by the name of Mount Edgecombe.*"

Five days later, the *Londonderry*, James Kilpatrick Master, one of the merchant ships John had left anchored in Rebellion Road, tried to get out of the harbour with a contrary wind and was wrecked on the Bar. Everyone on board was lost in the disaster. The tragic news reminded me of the perils I must face on the voyage home.

The next day, John had an unexpected visitor. The Honourable James Oglethorpe, Trustee for establishing the Colony of Georgia, came on board the *Alborough* to arrange his passage to England with his retinue, together with a delegation of nine Indian Chiefs who were to meet the British Government.

It would be a month or so before the ship was ready to make a voyage across the Atlantic. Outstanding repairs had to be expedited, the hull scrubbed and tarred, extra water got onboard and worn sails converted to extra hammocks for the passengers.

I didn't ask John if his ship would be ready before or after Alice had her baby. Everyone expected me to help Alice when her time came. Jean said I would be able to give her reassurance and support.

'It's unlikely I will be able to help,' I told her. 'I've heard Mr Gadsden wants a doctor to be present.'

'Yes, I imagine after he lost his first three children, he's nervous. Even more reason for you to be there with her.'

John assumed I would go and stay with Alice close to the time of her confinement.

'Why must I help her? What did she do to help Mighells?'

Sarah thought I must be excited to welcome a baby into our family.

'My mother came to help when William was born. It was comforting to have family present and you are all the family she has in Charles Town.'

Even Ralph told me I must help my sister.

'You were always on her side,' I shouted.

'I didn't know there were sides for sisters,' he replied. 'I would never be on a different side to Sarah. So many things can go wrong with childbirth, I thought you'd want to help.'

They didn't need to remind me how perilous childbirth could be. I heard them all and yet I was paralysed with jealousy, humiliation and the fear of what could go wrong. So I didn't do anything. I didn't visit her. I didn't go to stay with her. I kept busy packing up and preparing for our departure. Two weeks passed and I started to wonder if she'd had her baby and not told me. What could I do? The doctor would be there. He would know what to do. How would I cope if something did go wrong?

On the morning of the 13th of April, a note was delivered to Hog Island. It was short and to the point. *Please come to me. I need you. Alice.*

These past weeks I had wondered what I would do if she asked me to come. Now the moment had come, I didn't hesitate. I had to be with her, I wanted to be with her.

John was away supervising supplies for the voyage so I went without him. Bess came with me. She was always more practical than me and would definitely be more useful.

I told Cuffee to row faster and we ended up quite flustered by the time we got to Middle Bridge and clambered ashore. He summoned a carriage for us as we had to travel to the Gadsden Plantation, some ten miles out of town. I was afraid we would be too late and I told the driver to make the horses gallop faster.

'It's a matter of life or death,' I told him.

When we got to Gadsden's house, the baby hadn't been born and the doctor hadn't arrived. Alice was in bed, shouting orders at everyone. I knew she was nervous so I let her poor servants go with Bess to prepare hot water to wash everything, as Jean always did. I asked Gadsden to wait outside and keep watch for the doctor. He seemed relieved to have a role.

Alice grabbed hold of my sleeve and dragged me close so she could whisper in my ear. 'The baby has been doing acrobatics inside me. He's twisting and turning. What is he playing at? Make him stop. I don't want to do this, Mary-Anne.'

'You have to do it, Alice. You will be fine. You are strong and healthy. Everything will be fine. I'm here now and I will help you. I won't leave your side, I promise.'

At least I could explain to her what would happen as she had no experience of childbirth and had no idea of what was involved, but when I told her, it distressed her even more and she shrieked as the first contraction made her belly cramp.

'There will be plenty more of those,' I told her. 'You must breathe through them, like this.'

We huffed and puffed together. The contractions started coming more frequently. I called Bess to sit next to me by the bed as I found her presence very reassuring.

'No sign of the doctor yet?' I asked her.

'No, Mistress. I think we may have to do this ourselves.'

She didn't sound that alarmed at the prospect, but Alice started wailing.

'I asked Thomas to fetch the doctor. I want a doctor. I can't do this with just you two to help me!'

'Don't pay her any attention to her, Bess, it's her nerves talking. She will be glad she's got us in a minute.'

Bess grinned, 'I'll tell you when she really has to start pushing, Mistress.'

Alice was hysterical and I had to shout at her to make myself heard.

'Come on, Alice, we can do this together.'

I moved closer so our faces were almost touching. We locked eyes. She took deep breaths in when I did. She exhaled when I did.

'I don't want to do this, Mary-Anne. I can't stand the pain. I'm going to get ripped in half. I'm going to die.'

She took my hand and crushed it in her fist.

'Promise me that you'll take care of the baby when I die. Take it and love it as if it were your own. Promise me, now.'

'I promise Alice,' I said to stop her fretting. 'But you are not going to die. I am here to help you.'

'I can see the head appearing,' Bess said. 'Tell her to push more.'

The baby's head appeared at the entrance to the birth canal but appeared to be stuck.

'Push harder, Alice. One final time. The baby is coming out.'

But the head didn't move.

'The cord may be round his neck,' Bess whispered to me. 'I've seen this before. My Ma, she used to help with babies born. You have to slip it off.' She did a quick flick with her hand to show me how.

My heart stopped and I thought I might faint. I couldn't do that. Alice had heard her.

'Do it, Mary-Anne, do what she says,' she shouted.

'You have to do it quick before the baby strangle himself,' Bess whispered.

'Get him out of me,' Alice shouted, even louder.

I felt gently around the sides of the baby's head and Bess was right, the cord was around his neck, but it was too tight to pull it over the head. His chin jutted out too far.

I held my breath.

Maybe I could push the cord back over his shoulders. I moved it gently and opened a loop wide enough for the baby to slither out into Bess' waiting hands.

'It's a boy,' she said as she held him up.

The three of us stared at the little miracle in silence. Even Alice was speechless.

At that moment, the doctor came rushing through the door with Gadsden. He was annoyed that we had delivered the baby without waiting for him and he demanded his fee anyway.

Bess and I faded away to the corner, knowing our rightful place in the room. I took Bess' bloody hand and whispered to her, 'We did it, Bess. We did it!'

She reached for the hot water in the ewer to wash our hands. In our rush of relief and joy and pride, we enthusiastically scrubbed our hands until they were raw.

'Mrs McAndrews, she would want us to wash everything now,' she said.

'I know and as soon as the doctor leaves, we will.'

The doctor cut the cord and checked that everything was satisfactory. I prayed he wouldn't find fault with what we did. He seemed satisfied and left the room, giving me an angry look to reprimand me for interfering.

Gadsden sat on the bed and gazed proudly at his son, lying on top of Alice.

'I want to call him James,' she said. 'After my father. His second grandson.'

I couldn't believe she'd just honoured my Mighells as the first grandson. Tears streamed down my face. Gadsden held out his hand to me and drew me back to the bedside.

'And how do you like your nephew, Mary-Anne? Alice tells me I have a lot to thank you for,' he said.

'We both do,' Alice said. 'You saved my baby. He would have died without you.'

I was embarrassed by their praise.

I suggested Gadsden left the bedroom while we women cleaned up. Bess organised the servants to bring jugs and jugs of warm water to bathe the mother and baby. We changed the bedsheets and helped Alice remove her soiled, sweaty, bloody chemise and slip on a pristine, clean, white one. The baby was washed and wrapped in swaddling and I took the opportunity to hold Baby James for a moment.

He smiled up at me as if to say, thank you for saving my life.

'You're most welcome,' I whispered. I loved this baby already with all my heart.

I reluctantly handed him back to Alice.

'I could never have done this without you,' she said.

'You did fine, my darling, brave sister.'

'If I can do this, then so can you, Mary-Anne. You were always the brave sister, the best of us all.'

At that moment, I knew in my deepest soul that my desire for a child had not gone away. I would never forget Mighells. From the moment I woke up to the moment I fell asleep, I could not forget him. Another child would never take his place but could be his brother or sister. I would have to change John's decision. We had to try again for a child.

HMS Alborough left Charles Town in May 1734, arriving at Deptford on 5 July. Mr Oglethorpe and his retinue with nine Chiefs of the Indian nations of Georgia were on board for passage to England.

From the Captain's Log, HMS Alborough
6ᵗʰ May 1734
Anchored in Rebellion Road
    "Moderate gales & fair weather the latter part fresh gales. At ½ past 8 weighed (wind at NE) & at 10 anchored in Rebellion Road in 7 fathom water the wind coming about to ENE that we could not get any farther. At passing by the Lower fort of Charles Town called Granville's Bastion, the Governor was pleas'd to do me the Honour of a Salute of Fifteen guns which I answered with the Same Number. Mr Oglethorpe and his Retinue with nine Chiefs of the Indian nations in the neighbourhood of the colony of Georgia came aboard."

The passage was extremely cold and the ship met an iceberg.

From the Captain's Log, HMS Alborough
25ᵗʰ May 1734
Latitude 45° 8', Longitude 35°58'.
    "Moderate gales & thick foggy weather. At midnight the Tiller Rope broke. At 4 AM the weather became Extremely cold. At ½ past 5 saw an Island bearing NE about 4 miles off but had no ground with 170 fathom of line and the Appearance of it altering every minute, we soon found it to be an Island of Ice floating in the Sea. I drew three Several Views of it as it turned about, very different one from the other in half an hour's time the ship lying by. At noon fresh gales & very dark hazy weather."

28

A sailor in the crow's nest shouted out in alarm, 'An island sighted to the northeast!'

How could there be an island in the middle of the Atlantic Ocean? A sailor quickly threw out the line to take soundings but found no ground. After eighteen days at sea, we should have been a long way from any land. It had been a tough voyage, but the *Alborough* had been making swift progress eastwards, sailing into the morning sun, through gales and driving rain, through thick fog and high battering seas, through freezing temperatures and bitterly cold winds.

I hadn't been on board a ship for six years and I'd forgotten the stench of a hundred men living below decks, the sound of a huge wooden ship creaking and groaning in her rigging and the constant pitching and rolling as she fought the wind and waves. After the isolation of Hog Island, the crowds of men, the loud noises and the constant activity were overwhelming.

John called me to come out of my cabin so I grabbed my thickest cloak. I stood next to him on the deck and he wrapped an arm around me to keep me warm. He was fascinated by the island apparition and watched it constantly through his glass. He hadn't been this animated since we left Charles Town.

'It alters its appearance every minute,' he said. 'I believe it to be an island of ice floating in the sea.'

He ordered the ship to lay by while he drew three views of the island of ice as it turned about in half an hour. The weather was so cold that I was afraid the ship itself would freeze over and become another floating island of ice.

Standing on the deck, a short distance from me was the only other woman on board, Senauki, the wife of the chief of the Yamacraw Indians. Our illustrious passenger, James Oglethorpe, returning to London to report to the Georgia Trustees, was accompanied by a Yamacraw chief, Tomochichi, his wife and grandnephew, a handsome boy of fifteen, plus a delegation of Indians and the interpreter, John Musgrove.

The Indians were seeking assurances that their people would receive education and fair trade from the British in Georgia. Tomochichi was an old man but had the upright and proud bearing of someone much younger.

John saw me staring at Senauki. She was an ugly old crone with only one good eye, swollen cheeks and two or three teeth protruding from her mouth.

'She doesn't speak a word of English, I'm afraid. It's a shame John Musgrove's wife Mary isn't here,' John said. 'She's the best interpreter. She's the daughter of an English trader and a Creek Indian mother, so speaks their language. Mind you, the boy, Toahowi, reads very well and comprehends a great deal of English.'

'Why is she accompanying the men to England?'

'Tomochichi includes her in everything. In their culture, the presence of a woman represents the peaceful nature of the meeting.'

Suddenly I saw her in a new light, not as an old woman, but as a calming influence on her husband and the other Indians. She had her role to play and she stood proudly at her husband's side.

'Can you ask Mr Musgrove if she would like some warmer clothing? I have some old gowns I could give her and the lad is poorly dressed to cope with the freezing temperatures. There might be some clothes that a young midshipman has outgrown.'

The Master found a complete naval outfit for Toahowi and he looked fine in his blue frockcoat, white shirt and breeches, socks and shoes. And my old pink petticoat and lace-up jacket, with a few adjustments, fitted Senauki well enough.

'She says she'll wear it to meet the King of England,' Musgrove told me and I was flattered. I learned from him that she and the chief had no children so they had adopted her grandnephew Toahowi as their heir.

'The boy's father was taken by the Spaniards and burnt because he would not be a Christian,' he told me.

'Then it's no surprise that Tomochichi is keen for his Indian people to attend church and become Christians,' I muttered under my breath.

Musgrove also lowered his voice, although Senauki could not hear us. 'Mind you it's a wonder he hasn't taken a second wife, someone young enough to give him a son.'

I caught my breath. Was that what men thought? Was that what John thought? If I had died that night on the clifftop, he could have taken a second wife, someone who could give him a son.

'But he can't have a second wife while his wife lives,' I stammered. 'Not if they want to be Christians.'

He rolled his eyes as if he didn't believe they were Christians.

However old and ugly she was, Tomochichi stood close to her, and she was a source of comfort to him. By adopting their grandnephew, they had found a solution to their childlessness. Later, when I was back in the confines of my cabin, I couldn't help but imagine a scenario where John and I, unable to have a child of our own, adopt my nephew, James, but of course, that would mean Alice had died so I quickly dismissed it.

How I missed Alice! My heart had broken when I held her close to say our farewells before we departed. She had come to the dock with Gadsden and Baby James. I begged her to come home with me. but the baby was too young and it was too soon after her confinement. Gadsden was not a young man, but he seemed rejuvenated by his young bride and new son. How I wished John has such joy in his life to lift his spirits.

All my friends came to say goodbye. I wanted to stay with her to help Alice with the baby, with my friends Sarah and Ralph to gossip about life in Charles Town and with Jean to help her with her visits to the poor and needy. But John didn't want to stay. The Admiralty had given him orders to return, so we must obey. I had said my goodbyes and promised to write regularly. There was nothing more I could do. We were finally going home to England. Ralph waved wildly as our rowboat left the dock to take us out to the *Alborough*. He promised to write regularly, but I knew in my heart that I would never see him again.

Mighells' tiny coffin was safely stowed below decks and I had brought his wooden cross from High Bluff. I had asked Cuffee to climb over the edge of the cliff to place Quame's cross where the new owner would never find it but Quame's spirit will see it as he roamed the Cooper River. At the last minute, Bess had refused to come with me. She wouldn't go on a ship again. The terrible memories of the Guineaman that had brought her to Charles Town still gave her nightmares. Sarah didn't want her back, but Alice had been delighted to take her to help with the new baby and Peggy went with her to the Gadsden plantation house. Sissy, Cuffee and Mungo had been bought by the new owner of Hog Island.

Jean had held my hands tightly as she said her goodbyes and reassured me that time was a healer and that I should pray to the Good Lord to send me another child soon. 'You will make a wonderful mother one day, Mary-Anne.'

When would that day come? After holding Alice's baby, I knew I wanted a child, whatever the risks, but John was quite determined in his decision that we would not try again in case it was I who died next time and not the infant. He was my husband and, at the altar on our Wedding Day, I had vowed to love, honour and obey him.

He was struggling with his duties as Captain while he battled his own demons of ill health. Luckily James got on well with Mr Oglethorpe so John did not need to entertain him. I did not share his Captain's Cabin but stayed in a small cabin nearby, wrapped up in blankets against the biting cold. My heart was slowly icing over and I feared we would all freeze to death. Somehow it seemed a fitting end to my sad life. My marriage was an empty shell now that my dreams of children had been stripped away.

On the 17th of June 1734 HMS *Alborough* anchored at Spithead, off Portsmouth, among ten other ships of the fleet. John was delighted that the six-week passage across the Atlantic had been brisk and uneventful.

'I wanted to get home as soon as possible,' he told me.

I was surprised he had wanted to rush home. He hadn't finished writing up his surveys of the Florida coastline and he didn't think the Admiralty valued his surveys of Port Royal. HMS *Alborough*, his ship for the last six years, would be sent for repairs at the Deptford Dockyard. What hope had he to get a new command with his poor state of health?

At noon Mr Oglethorpe, his retinue and all the Indians disembarked to a salute of thirteen guns. John asked me if I want to disembark with them and travel to Stratford by coach, but I was afraid to go home without him so I told him I'd stay onboard until we reached Deptford. He looked at me quizzically. Even I couldn't believe I was choosing to stay on board rather than go ashore.

'I'll send my parents a letter to let them know we've arrived safely,' I told him casually, but I never wrote that letter. I didn't know what to say to them.

I knew I should be excited about going home. I'd see Papa and Mama again, Betty and Annie, but every time I imagined walking in the front door of the family home in Stratford, I saw their looks of disappointment as I helped John limp over the threshold with his walking stick, no babe in my arms or child at my side. I was returning after seven years of marriage, the barren wife of an invalid husband. This was not the life I had imagined, not the homecoming I had foreseen.

Three weeks later the sailors heaved in the mooring chain against the dock at Deptford. John was immediately handed orders to sort out the pay books for the crew and return his mathematical instruments to the storekeeper at Deptford. His Command of HMS *Alborough* was over without any ceremony or recognition of his duties.

We disembarked, collected our trunks and Mighells' coffin and travelled home by stagecoach to Stratford.

We alighted in the town square. John looked grand in his naval uniform and I had on my best travel cloak. We turned heads, but no one recognised us. John arranged for our trunks to be delivered and we walked arm-in-arm down the lane to my family's home. It was so cool and quiet in the Essex countryside. Leaves rustled in the wind, birds sang in the hedgerow and a farmer on horseback trotted down the lane. We met two maids returning from the orchards, arms laden with cherries. The bucolic country scene seemed unreal after seven years away.

The housemaid was sweeping our front step and dropped the broom in a panic as she recognised me. She ran inside shouting, 'Miss Mary-Anne is returned at last, with her fancy naval officer.'

Betty and Annie came running out of the house and smothered me in hugs. They were shy in front of John, but he shook their hands warmly and everyone laughed with happiness at our return.

Mama appeared at the door, dressed in black widow's weeds, and my laughter stopped abruptly.

'Where's Papa?' I asked, but from her dress and demeanour, I already knew the answer.

'So, you're home at last, Mary-Anne. Didn't you get my letter? I wrote to you at the end of March.'

'Your letter had not arrived by the time we left Charles Town in early May,' John said on my behalf as I found I couldn't speak.

266

'Then you won't have heard your father has passed away. We buried him in Lowestoft some three months ago.'

My knees gave way and I would have fallen if John hadn't caught me as I collapsed. He helped me into the parlour and settled me on the sofa. Betty told us at great length, pausing when my wailing got too loud, that Papa had been working as Comptroller at the Admiralty right up to the week before he died. He felt under the weather, exhausted and tired, so he returned to Stratford where he retired to his bed, never to rise again.

'There wasn't anything wrong with him and he didn't complain to me about anything,' Mama said as if she was to blame for not saving him. 'I think it was old age catching up on him. He was nearly sixty-nine. He shouldn't have been working. I kept telling him to stop. It was too much work for an old man to control all the payments and examine everyone's accounts, the Officers, the Treasurer, the Victuallers, the Storekeepers. The Admiralty should have let him retire years ago.'

Betty patted her arm as if she had heard her complaints a thousand times before. 'We know, Mama, but he didn't want to retire, despite your best advice. Still, he died peacefully in his bed, which is more than a lot of Navy Admirals do, and he had a nice burial service in St Margaret's Church, didn't he? Well-attended and very respectful. And the Admiralty paid for a nice memorial monument for him. You must go and see it, Mary-Anne.'

'And the priest wrote a kind eulogy in the parish record,' Annie added. 'Be sure to read that as well.'

Betty went to the bureau. 'The priest made a fair copy of it for us to bring home.'

She handed me a sheet of paper on which was written, "*In his public capacity, no one had more at heart than the true honour and interest of his king and country. As a sea official he was beloved by all under his command. He was brave and valiant nor was his judgement and conduct less than his courage. In his last office he was constant and unwearied in application; no one durst tempt him to alienate his trust. To his family he was careful indulgent and tender; to his relations useful and generous; to his friends kind sincere and hearty; and to all the world a man of the strictest honour, justice and honesty.*"

It was such a wonderful tribute to my darling Papa that I could hardly breathe between my uncontrollable sobs. I regained my composure long enough to reassure Mama that I would go and pay my respects as soon as I could.

'The last time I saw him was when he came to the *Tryall* to fetch me home,' I told them. 'Do you remember it, John? He said he'd see me soon. I always thought I'd see him again. I never thought he'd die before I came home. I would never have gone if I'd known that.'

'Well, you did go, Mary-Anne,' Mama said crossly. 'He told you not to but you went. You weren't here when he died and that's the end of it.'

Her admonishments started me crying again. Mama clearly had never forgiven me for going and Papa may not have done so either. Was this the curse on my marriage, the reason I could not have children?

'Anyway,' Betty said, keen to change the subject, 'tell us about Alice. She hardly ever writes. Does she have any children yet?'

News of Papa's death and Baby James' birth must have crossed on the high seas. At least Alice had given the family a reason to be cheerful.

Stratford Le Bow, Co. Essex
Published 1809

V

Stratford, Essex, England

1735-1741

**Wall tablet in St Margaret's Church, Lowestoft, Suffolk
commemorating Vice-Admiral James Mighells**

To the Memory of
JAMES MIGHELLS Esq.
Late Vice Admiral and Comptroller of the Royal Navy.
Whose Publick and Private Character
Justly deserves Remembrance
If Courage and Conduct in a Commissioner
Fidelity and Diligence in a Commissioner
Sincerity in a Friend
Usefulness in a Relation
Love and Affection in a Husband
Love and Indulgence in a Parent
And the Strictest Justice and Honesty to all Men
Deserves To Be Remembered.

29

I t was a harsh winter and the snow was thick on the ground. Christmas had passed in a sombre mood. I needed something to look forward to in the dark February days so I invited my family round to celebrate my birthday. Although I wasn't sure there was much cause for celebration. At thirty I was now past my best, still childless and fading into an old maid.

John and I had taken a small house in the village of Stratford. It was all we could afford with John on sick leave and half-pay since we returned to England last summer. It was big enough for the two of us and a couple of servants. These days we lived simply and quietly.

The fire was burning bright in the hearth and my family were assembled around the dining table. John, as the only man at the celebrations, had been put in charge of the Punch Bowl and it smelled delicious, steaming wine infused with roasted apples, sugar and spices. Betty took charge of giving everyone a cup, even though she was a guest in my home. Luckily, it wouldn't be long before she was mistress of her own house. She was betrothed to Mr Ezekiel Hall, a wealthy merchant in the City of London and their marriage was set for April.

She would be leaving us to live in London. She didn't want to spend her life looking after Mama. She wanted her own household and a brood of children. With her wide hips and large breasts, she was built for childbearing, just like Mama.

Annie was now sixteen and would look after Mama when Betty moved away. She was a sweet child and rushed to help bring in the food for the table.

Before we said grace, Mama wanted us to say a prayer for Papa. She was still grieving, as we all were. Last Autumn, John took me to pay my respects at his memorial monument in St Margaret's Church, Lowestoft. It had done justice to the kindest, most loving father a daughter could want.

Now we were learning to live without him, but he would have relished the sight of my dining table, laden down with beef, ham and goose. Cook had made meat pies in little boat shapes in homage to our naval heritage. Syllabub glasses were filled with a glistening array of quivering jellies and creams.

'All this food for such a small gathering,' Mama commented.

It was true we only numbered five. John's brother was a Lieutenant on HMS *Warwick*, stationed in the Mediterranean. And Alice was in Charles Town, with her husband and Baby James.

'You should have invited young Kitty Gadsden to join us. It would have been nice to have at least one child at the table, even if he is someone else's son,' she added as if we hadn't discussed this.

'Mama, I've already told you Kitty is staying with his Gadsden relatives in Bristol.'

Betty tutted loudly as if she too disapproved of the small party, but they were right. It was a shame there were no children to help us celebrate.

'Any news on Mr Oglethorpe and his Indians?' Annie asked. Since they arrived in England, the Indians had met King George and Queen Caroline at Kensington Palace and had been the talk of the town. I had sent newspaper cuttings to Ralph so he could write about their visit in *The South Carolina Gazette.*

'Nothing very exciting to report, I'm afraid,' John said. 'Oglethorpe's still in London seeking funding from Parliament to construct forts along the Altamaha River, but some of the Lords don't want to antagonise the Spanish any further. The peace is very fragile at the moment.'

'I hear he has some odd ideas,' interrupted Betty, who no doubt had heard such things from Ezekiel Hall. 'He's banned the sale of rum and slavery in Georgia and wants to involve the native Indians in owning the land. I'm not sure he'll be popular with your friends in Charles Town.'

'Well, they seem pleased to have the State of Georgia as a buffer against the Spaniards in Florida,' John retorted, but it was clear he wasn't keen to discuss politics with Betty, who could hold very fixed ideas and seemed to know a lot more that he might have expected.

'James got on well with Mr Oglethorpe on our voyage home, so I'm sure he's not that odd,' I told my sister to keep the peace.

Once we'd eaten dessert, we women retired to the drawing room to play cards and talk about Betty's wedding. Mama was delighted that, at last, one of her daughters was getting married at a proper time and place she could attend. John had no desire to discuss Betty's wedding dress so he made his excuses and retired to his study.

'Don't talk to John about Oglethorpe,' I whispered to Betty. 'He's busy working on his charts for Port Royal Harbour for the Admiralty, but he realises that Georgia might turn out to be more useful and Port Royal will remain a backwater.'

'He needs to get back to sea, if you ask me, instead of hiding away in his study,' Mama said, sternly. 'He needs to get back to full pay. You shouldn't have to live on half-pay for this long.'

John was no longer the dashing Naval Officer she had approved of as her son-in-law. Papa was hardly at home during his naval career and she believed that any naval officer should be at sea, seeking glory, being promoted and earning his wages.

'You know he's on sick leave, and we are managing just fine for money. Anyway, he's busy with the drafts of his surveys, not just in Carolina but all over the West Indies. You should be proud of him.'

She tutted loudly. She would have preferred him to be away fighting the Spanish, which might be dangerous but offered the chance for promotion and prosperity. Sitting in his study drawing charts did not.

'And when are you going to give me a grandchild?' she asked as if I was deliberately holding back to spite her. My return to Stratford had not been the success Mama was hoping for. After seven years of marriage, she had expected me to have several children. Babies that she could bounce on her knee and lecture me about their upbringing. Instead, I was a barren old maid.

I gathered up the playing cards and shuffled them studiously to avoid answering her, but Betty joined in, 'Do you think there might be something wrong with you, Mary-Anne? All those years across the seas in Carolina might have upset your womanly functions.'

'Or the Good Lord might be punishing you for running off to a foreign land when your Papa had told you not to go,' Mama said.

Annie gasped and put her hands over her mouth in horror at the idea that I had lost the favour of the Good Lord. 'Oh, Mary-Anne, I will pray for you every night.'

I'm sure none of my family meant harm but once it had been said out loud it couldn't be unsaid. I was damned for my reckless behaviour, cursed never to have a child.

A silence descended on us. No one knew what to say after that. I lost interest in playing another round of cards and my family soon tired of my company. While Betty helped Mama don her warm coat, I pulled Annie to one side and whispered in her ear, 'Was Papa very upset I had run off to a foreign land? Did he never forgive me? He must have been so disappointed in me.'

She pulled back to look me in the face, 'Are you joking Mary-Anne? He loved you the best of all his daughters. Once you and Alice had left, Betty and I were mere shadows in the home. The only time he was excited was when one of your letters arrived. He was so proud of all your adventures. You were brave and courageous, the fearless son he never had.'

I was so speechless at what she said, I stood open-mouthed while my family took their leave. They walked the short distance through the snow back to their home. I watched them until they reached the corner but only Annie turned to wave.

I returned to the parlour and slumped on the sofa, feeling very lost and lonely. I missed Papa so much. He would have made the day fun. And after all that had happened, all I had done, he had still loved me. He had forgiven me, whatever Mama said. He had been proud of me. I was so overwhelmed by his fatherly love for me that I started weeping uncontrollably.

I really needed John to comfort me, but he and I had drifted apart since we arrived home last summer. I spent time with my family while he shut himself away in his study with his reports and surveys. He stayed up late, sleeping on a bed in his study when he was too tired to climb the stairs to our bedroom. Like wraiths from the spirit world, we circled each other, living, breathing, existing in our own separate dimensions. We had nothing in common, nothing to talk about, nothing to discuss.

I stroked my belly gently and sadly remembered the few times I had been with child. My mother and my sisters were wrong. I couldn't be cursed. After all, Papa had forgiven me and I had conceived two children. Deep down I knew there was nothing wrong with me. And now I was back in sleepy Stratford, where there were no shipwrecks or drownings or other calamities to harm my unborn child, it was surely time to try again. It was worth one last attempt to make John change his mind.

The maid knocked on the parlour door and came in with a cup of bitter, steaming hot chocolate. I liked a cup at supper time, with milk and sugar, a little luxury I treated myself to.

'Shall I take a cup into the Master?' she asked nervously. The servants were careful not to disturb John at work in his study.

'No, I'll take him this one,' I said. 'There's something I want to discuss with him.'

I set the cup of hot chocolate down and ran upstairs to my bed chamber. Somewhere, in some drawer, some cupboard, some chest I had hidden the secret potion, the famous Gentleman's Elixir. The Apothecary had guaranteed it would raise his animal spirits and provide me with all the pleasure I desired. It had worked once on the clifftop at High Bluff and I desperately needed it to work again.

I searched high and low in a frenzy, tossing clothes out of drawers and pulling blankets out of chests. I was on a mission and would not give up. Maybe I'd drunk too many cups from the Punch Bowl, but I didn't want to be thirty and I didn't want this life of an old maid. I knew I had to do something to change things. At last, I found the small phial, hidden in my baby chest under the half-finished layette that Mighells had never worn.

I returned down the stairs and poured a few drops into the chocolate. There was only a small amount left in the phial so I poured that in as well for good measure and then I knocked on the study door.

For 5 years from 1734 to 1739, John was on sick leave from the Navy and spent the time compiling his surveys. In 1737 he forwarded to the Admiralty some remarks on the dangerous errors in public charts and a volume of his own surveys which covered his whole career and included the coasts of England, Ireland, Scotland, the Orkneys, Newfoundland, Galicia, Portugal, the Mediterranean and the Cape Verde Islands. These surveys were never published by the Admiralty.

Letter to the Navy Board from Captain Gascoigne, Stratford, Essex.
30th April 1735

    "Captain Gascoigne is confined by sickness and has been informed by the Master of the Alborough, under his command, that she is to be taken to the wet dock at Deptford for rigging. Asks for orders be given for the Deptford Riggers to assist him in this until his Lieutenant has arrived from Plymouth as he will not have the men to do so."

30

There wasn't time to run away before I heard John shout, 'Enter' and I nearly gave up at his brusque tone. I reminded myself that he was probably expecting one of the maids. I opened the door and peered cautiously around it. John was seated at his huge wooden desk, all his papers, charts and journals spread out in front of him. He could have been in his Captain's cabin onboard the *Alborough*. He'd taken off his jacket, placed his wig on the table and rolled up the sleeves of his soft linen shirt. I felt an overwhelming surge of love for my dishevelled, diligent husband.

He was engrossed in his work, but he looked up and his eyes softened when he saw it was me.

'I'm sorry to disturb you, my dearest husband, but I thought you might like a cup of delicious hot chocolate,' I said as sweetly as I could.

I was shocked at my own subterfuge. No longer the innocent blushing bride. If the past seven years of marriage had taught me anything, it was that I had to take matters into my own hands to get what I wanted. And I wanted John to give me a child.

I put the cup on his desk, just beside his pens. 'Drink up, husband. It will fortify your spirits. For work, I mean, to help you with your drafts.'

'I'd prefer a glass of Malmsey wine to be honest, Mary-Anne.'

He stood up clumsily to reach the bottle that stood half-drunk on his bureau, but his foot gave way and he fell heavily against the desk. As he reached out a hand to steady himself, he knocked over the cup and the hot chocolate spilt all over his papers.

There was mayhem as he rescued his half-drawn charts and I used my petticoats to mop up the thick dark liquid that crept in a disastrous stain over his precious journals. He didn't scream and shout at me, but I could tell he was furious and I burst out crying.

'Mary-Anne, please don't blame yourself. It is I who am the clumsiest person on earth. This blasted foot will still not take my weight.'

I caught my breath in a loud sob. This was not how the evening was supposed to go. The elixir was wasted. My petticoats were ruined. My hopes of marital passion were fading fast.

John limped over to where I was standing and held out his hand. I nervously placed my hand in his. I was expecting an embrace, but he drew me in close as if we were partners in a dance. His bad foot didn't stop us from moving together in a simple minuet. Outside the window, voices were muffled by the thick snow. The firelight and candlelight made the room warm and cosy. It didn't matter that there was no fancy ballroom, no music and no other dancers. We were dancing together and we hadn't done that in a long time.

I nestled my head against his chest. He felt so reassuring and smelled so familiar. I wanted to stay in that moment for as long as I could, but he suddenly let go of my hand and pulled out of his pocket a pearl necklace.

'I meant to give this to you earlier, but I was waiting until your family left. This is my birthday gift to you, the kindest, sweetest person I have ever known. I wanted to show you that I love you and cherish you above all else.'

I lifted my hair and he reached around to fix the clasp at the back of my neck. The pearly white beads felt heavy against my chest and glowed in the firelight. It was the most beautiful necklace I had ever worn. I was grateful for the necklace, truly I was, but right at that moment I needed him to show me he loved and cherished me in quite a different way. I wanted him to give me quite a different gift. We locked eyes and I didn't want to look away. I knew I must speak up or I never would.

'John, I want a child,' I blurted out. 'I want lots of children. Whatever the risks. Please don't deny me the only thing I have ever wanted. The necklace is beautiful, but I want you to give me your kisses and your loving embrace. I want to feel like a wife should. I want you to give me a child.'

There I'd said it! I could see the surprise in his eyes. I had settled into being such a docile, obedient creature. These days I acted more as his nursemaid than his wife. Now I had challenged him and made demands of him. Would he respond favourably or would he walk away, embarrassed by my lack of modesty?

The loud tick of the grandfather clock and the crackle of the fire in the hearth were the only sounds in the room. He didn't say anything but went over to his bureau to fill two glasses with Malmsey wine. He returned to stand in front of me, holding a glass out to me. I took it and we both sipped our wine without looking at each other.

Then he took my hand and raised it to his lips for a kiss.

'Don't say it Mary-Anne. You know what could happen. It's too dangerous. My own mother died giving birth to me. I couldn't risk losing you. I love you so much. My life would be nothing without you here by my side.'

'But other women have children and live,' I pleaded, pulling my hand away in frustration. 'Just look at Alice. She has Baby James. And all the women I visited in Charles Town. They all have their babes at their breast. Even Mama had four children and lives to this day.'

He put his wine down and went over to the window to draw the thick curtains and block out the cold winter evening. When he didn't reply, I carried on, I had to convince him the risks were worth it.

'You know how much I want a child, John. I am sure I could have a healthy child if we were to try again.'

He still didn't look me in the eye but moved to rescue some charts on his desk in danger of ruin from hot chocolate. I got the sense that he was avoiding me.

Eventually, he muttered under his breath. 'Perhaps you could, my dearest, but it's not that easy for me. My illness has laid me low for such a long time and I've struggled to feel desire as a husband should. I've avoided you these past few years for fear of being a failure as a husband. For fear you would no longer love me.'

I'd thought it was my fault we didn't have a baby. Now I realised that John was worried about his husbandly duties. If ever we had need of the Apothecary's potion to stir his desire it was then, but it had spilt all over the desk and there was nothing left in the phial. I was going to have to do this all by myself.

I took hold of both his hands and forced him to turn and face me.

'No longer love you? I have always loved you John, whatever misfortune has befallen us. We have been on an adventure together and dealt with so many adversities. Yet after all that has happened to us, here we are together, a loving husband and wife.'

'Oh, Mary-Anne, I am so blessed to have you as my wife. I have relied on you to care for me through my sickness. I couldn't bear the thought of losing you, but I have been selfish and denied you what you most want.'

'Now is the time to change that, John.'

I had to take the lead and prove to him that we could do this. I unbuttoned my petticoats at the waist and let them fall heavily to the ground. His surprised look showed that he realised we were actually doing this, right there and then. I was shaking with the fear of rejection, but I knew I mustn't stop.

I turned around and asked him to unlace my bodice at the back. With fumbling fingers, he unhooked the laces. I leant forward and shook it off my arms.

I was nervous to take off my chemise. I didn't want him to see my naked body. It had aged so much since our wedding night. Disappointment had taken away the soft curves of my belly, childbirth had made my breasts sag and despair had loosened my skin into folds, but my body reflected what I had survived. I pulled the chemise over my head and stood proudly before him, battered and bruised by the misfortunes of my life, naked bar for the pearl necklace and my silk stockings.

'I'm no longer the young bride you married many years ago,' I said. 'This is what I have become because of all that we have been through. Can you love me as I am now?'

He looked at me for what seemed like an eternity, without saying anything and then he knelt down in front of me and gently removed my slippers and slowly slid my stockings down my legs. He wrapped his arms around my thighs and tenderly kissed my belly.

'Oh, Mary-Anne, I love you so much,' he said, his voice husky with emotion. 'Now, let me give you what you most desire.'

He stood up and roughly undid his shirt, ripping some of the buttons in his haste. I gently moved his hands aside and undid the remaining buttons more carefully. He pulled his shirt over his head and his chest was bare. It carried the scars of twenty-five years of active service on His Majesty's warships. His right hand was twisted and his foot was lame. He was just as wounded and damaged as me.

I took his crippled hand in mine and kissed it gently as if my touch was magic and I could heal it. I placed my other hand on his heart

281

and could feel it beating. It was a good heart. Mama was right, a good heart was the best you can hope for in a husband.

'Do you think you can love me as I am now?' he whispered, looking at me with those spaniel eyes.

'I think that all we have been through has only made our love stronger.'

He pulled me into his arms and kissed the bare skin on my neck, he kissed my shoulder and as he moved lower to kiss my breasts, ripples of excitement made my body shiver. He lifted my chin and his kisses on my lips were gentle at the start, but as I responded he became more fervent. We pulled each other down onto the rug in front of the fire to continue our passionate embraces.

Early evening was not the time of day a married couple should be making love on the rug in the study. At that hour, housemaids lit the candles throughout the house, dirty urchins played in the snow outside the window and hawkers shouted as they sold their roasted chestnuts. The milkmaid herded the cows along the lane, lifting her petticoats high to avoid the muddy snowdrifts. Farmworkers whistled as they hurried home from the fields, their bodies tired and their hands rough. Highwaymen rode out of town to start their night's work on the toll road. Church bells rang out calling the good people to Evensong in the hope they could be blessed.

And we were blessed. As night fell, we lay together as lovers in front of the fire. The curse on my marriage was broken and I was finally reunited in marital bliss with my beloved husband

Our son William was born nine months later in November 1735, healthy, happy and so long awaited. In the next four years, while John was at home on sick leave, we had three more children, John, Mary-Anne and Elizabeth. The children gave John the strength and joy to recover his health and when war was declared on the Spanish Empire in 1739 he returned to active service as Captain of HMS *York*.

While my brave husband was away fighting the enemy on the High Seas, I remained at home in Stratford, running the household, managing the finances and rearing the children, as was expected of the Captain's Wife by my husband, the Admiralty and Society.

In 1739 John returned to active service as Captain of HMS York in 1739 when war broke out between England and Spain.

Letter to Josiah Burchett and Thomas Corbett at the Navy Board
5th May 1742

     Letter asks what rewards should be paid to Captains Candler, Gascoigne and Durell for surveying the coasts of America since 1714. Captain Bartholomew Candler, Commander of the Winchelsea, was allowed 10s a day over the pay of himself and a servant. Captain John Gascoigne, Commander of the Alborough, also received an allowance for surveying the West Indies but Captain Durell has not been rewarded or made an allowance for the survey.
Held by National Maritime Museum: The Caird Library and Archive,

Epilogue – 1741

A loud banging on the front door was the dread of every Navy wife. A messenger from the Admiralty with news of a disaster. A ship captured by the enemy or lost at sea. A husband mortally wounded, an arm or a leg amputated. Or my worst nightmare, a loved one drowned. A lonely death in the cold watery blackness. No marked grave where a body can rest while the soul soars to Heaven. No peaceful resting place for the family to visit. The anxiety of every woman whose brave husband, brother or son was fighting on the High Seas for King and Country.

Of all evenings, this was a foul night to open the door to bad news. A storm had come in from the west, the squalls of wind shrieking through the trees and banging the loose shutters. Heavy storm clouds scudded across the darkening sky, rain battered on the tiled roof and lightning scared the children.

We had run back from the graveyard after laying flowers on Mighells' grave. He would have been nine today. We were glad to be sheltering in the warm glow of the kitchen hearth. I preferred to sit in the kitchen with the servants at this time of day, rather than be alone in the parlour. My four young children sat at the table with me, drinking their warm milk before bedtime. William was nearly six, John a year younger, Mary-Anne was three and baby Elizabeth was nearly two.

A loud crack of thunder overhead made us cuddle closer to give each other comfort. I had a flash of another stormy night when I lay on a lonely grave on a windswept clifftop. I hadn't thought of that night for years. Perhaps the visit to Mighells' grave stirred the memory. I grasped the edge of the old oak table to tether me to the here and now.

'Best not open the door, Mistress,' Cook said. 'There are reports of footpads on the Common these past few days. Who knows what devilish vagabonds might be abroad on a wild night such as this?'

The scullery maid cried out in fear. My children looked at me with wide, frightened eyes. Whoever was out there continued his knocking, insistent that I open the door. I was Mistress of this House, a middle-aged, married woman and I would not allow harm to come to my children while my husband was away at sea fighting the Spanish. When war had broken out between England and Spain last year he had

284

taken command of HMS *Torbay* and sailed with the fleet back to the Caribbean for an attack on Cartagena.

I got up from the table and the children followed me into the hallway. It seemed unlikely that a vagabond would be so bold as to strike loudly on the front door. I had to answer the incessant knocking, even though I was afraid that it would be a messenger from the Admiralty.

William, my eldest son, was the man of the house in John's absence. He offered me his toy wooden sword. It was sensible to be armed, but I looked around for a more suitable weapon. A blue porcelain vase on the hall table brought back another flash of memory. A blue shattered vase lying in smithereens on the floor. Memories I hadn't thought about for years. I shook my head to clear my thoughts and seized the heavy silver candlestick standing next to it.

I slid the bolts and opened the heavy front door slightly to peer through the narrow crack. A tall man in a dark travel cape was standing on the step, looking, it had to be said, every inch a wicked vagabond. He'd been caught in the storm and his clothes were sodden with rain. As he pulled back his hood, I hardly recognised Ralph Wilkinson, my dearest friend from Charles Town. He was the last person on earth I had expected to see when I opened the door.

The thunder and the vase were merely stitches breaking in the fabric of time. When I saw Ralph's face, the whole seam ripped wide open and the ghosts of a past life came rushing forth. Memories came flooding back of a different life, so far away and long ago.

'Mrs Gascoigne,' he said, 'my dearest Mary-Anne, I am so sorry to come unannounced and at such a late hour of the night, but I have not stopped travelling since I left Charles Town six weeks ago.'

I could not imagine why he would have come to my door on a stormy October evening, on the run from Charles Town.

'Ralph, my dearest friend, come in. You are most welcome at any time,' I told him.

'Not so, I fear, with the news I bring.'

What news could be so unwelcome? In a flash, I knew it concerned Alice and I lowered my gaze, dreading to hear what he had come to tell me. Only then did I see the two little boys, one on either side of him. They were clutching his hands tightly and cowering within the folds of his cloak. Both had wild black curls, pale skin and huge dark eyes which looked up at me most pathetically. There was no mistaking they were Alice's sons. Why had Ralph brought them to my door on such a night as this? Where was Alice? I looked past Ralph expecting to see her striding up the path after him, but no one was there.

The three travellers stepped across my hearth and I knelt down to be at the same height as my nephews. I steadied my voice to hide the tumult of questions going on inside me.

'Hello. I am your Aunt Mary-Anne. I am delighted to meet you. The last time I saw you, James, you were but a month old and you have grown quite miraculously. And you must be young Thomas. You're the same age as my son, John. Your mother has told me all about you in her letters.'

I was chattering on. I didn't want to stop. I didn't want Ralph to tell me why he was there and why he had brought these two little boys to my door. I knew what he was going to say and if he did, my heart would explode.

I told the nursemaid to take the two boys upstairs with my children and find them a place to sleep. They looked too exhausted to do much else and we could wait until tomorrow to make the formal introductions to their cousins. They were reluctant to let go of Ralph's hands.

'It's alright, boys,' he whispered to them kindly. 'We have arrived at last. This will be your home from now on.'

The elder boy took his brother's tiny hand and they moved nervously towards the maid.

Ralph and I watched her gather all the children and take them up the staircase. Only when they had gone into the nursery, did I turn and show Ralph into the parlour. I sat down heavily on the nearest chair.

'I apologise for turning up like this, Mary-Anne, but I didn't know where to go or what to do.'

'I think you have done the only thing you could, Ralph.'

I tried to sound calm as if it was just another visit from my good friend, something that happened so many times when I lived in Charles Town.

'I probably should have involved lawyers or notified the officials but I panicked. You have no idea of the confusion in Charles Town at the moment. The city is finished, it will never recover from the devastation. The fire last November destroyed so much of the town and now the fever is running rampant. So many people have died. So many funerals happening every day. It's difficult to find enough people to bury the dead.'

I poured him a glass of brandy to calm his agitation. The horror of what he had seen was still clearly imprinted in his memory and I had no rush to get to the part of his story that involved my sister, as it surely must.

'I have lost so many friends and when I heard that Alice was ill, I wanted to visit her, but I was afraid to leave the house. By the time I had the courage to visit at the end of July, it was too late. She had succumbed to the fever two weeks earlier. Gadsden was very sick in his bed. He would surely follow within days. He begged me to rescue the boys and take them away from there. Most of the household had fled. I found the boys hiding in the nursery at the top of the house.'

'Alice has died?' I gasped. The truth was shocking to hear.

'I can hardly admit it, but yes, I was too late to save her.'

'Was she there? Did you see her? Are you sure she's dead? Could you have been mistaken? We must go and find her.'

I jumped up as if I would go to Charles Town immediately and find her.

Ralph grabbed my hand. 'She's gone. Mary-Anne. There's nothing we can do for her now. Gadsden will have died by now. He had summoned Kittie back from Philadelphia. He'll make the arrangements for the funerals. They'll be buried together in the graveyard at St Phillip's. There's nothing you can do. Please sit down.'

I sat down heavily in my chair feeling quite defeated.

'Gadsden asked me to take the boys to England. He wanted you to look after them.'

'What about Bess and Peggy? Were they still there at the house?'

'Peggy had passed away last summer of the fever. Bess was still with the boys. She hadn't abandoned them, but they were terrified, they didn't know where to go or what to do. I couldn't leave them there. So I took them to my brother's house in town, but his wife wouldn't let us in, in case the boys brought the fever with them. Sarah was out of town, staying at The Oaks. I didn't know where else to go.'

I could imagine Ralph panicking. He'd never had to be responsible for anyone else before, especially two frightened children.

'I went straight to the harbour-side and bought passage on the *Elizabeth,* a merchant ship leaving later that day bound for London. Bess refused to come onboard the ship with us. She said she would seek refuge with Jean McAndrews, but she's the property of young Kittie Gadsden now, so I trust she'll have a good home with him once he returns to Charles Town.'

'No, Bess would not get on another ship, I know that. She refused to come to England with me.'

'It was probably for the best. The passage was very rough and I shared a bunk with the boys for six weeks, the three of us crying and cuddling each other in shock and disbelief. We haven't washed or changed our clothes in all that time. We brought no luggage with us, just the clothes we are wearing. When we disembarked in London, we caught the first stagecoach to Stratford and here we are.'

He fell silent, exhausted by his tale of escape from Charles Town. It was impossible not to pity him. He had acted impetuously rescuing the two children, bringing them across the wild Atlantic to the safe haven that was my house in the sleepy English village of Stratford. How many times over the past two months must he have regretted starting out on this course of heroism?

I knelt before him and took his hands in mine to comfort him.

'Ralph, I am so pleased that it was you that saved them. No one else could have done what you did or shared their grief as you did,' I said.

He looked up at me, relieved that I approved of his actions.

'I couldn't abandon them. You know I always loved your sister. Many times I have wondered what would have happened if I'd taken your advice and married her. They might have been my sons if things had worked out differently.'

The lost dream seemed to deflate him and he sat quietly, sipping his brandy. I told him he must stay with us for a while. At least until the boys were settled. He said he had friends in London and would seek employment writing for one of the newspapers in the city.

I was worrying about Ralph without giving any thought to my own feelings. As I stepped out of the parlour to ask the housemaid to make ready a bedroom and some clean clothes for Ralph, my knees suddenly gave way and I collapsed onto the floor in the hallway.

The reality struck me as if I had been hit in the chest by a club. I fought to breathe, gasping and wailing at the same time. It was not possible that Alice was dead. Alice, my beautiful vibrant sister, so full of life, could never die. Her light which burned so bright had been extinguished as a candle was suddenly snuffed out. The world seemed darker, the shadows longer and my heart broken.

I wanted to run out of the door, cross the ocean and find her grave. I wanted to lie beside it and tell her all the things I never said to her when she was alive. How much I loved her, envied and admired her. I started crawling to the door, but I knew I wouldn't go to her. I had to stay there. There were six young children asleep in their beds upstairs who needed me. My prayers had finally been answered, there were now so many children in my life.

I raised James and Thomas Gadsden as my own. My fifth child, James, was born in 1742 when John came home on shore leave and Ann was born four years later when he retired from His Majesty's Navy as Rear-Admiral in 1746. Six children, the last born when I was 43, took their toll on my frail body and I didn't live to see Ann's second birthday.

By the time my story ended in September 1748, I had given life to six healthy children and love to my dearest husband. I was not just the Captain's Wife but so much more. I was a woman who had laughed and cried, known great sadness and immense joy, lost all hope and realised her dreams. I was a woman who had truly lived.

APPENDIX 1
What happened next to the historical characters

JOHN GASCOIGNE (1696-1753) returned to active service as Captain of HMS *York* in 1739 when war broke out between England and Spain. In 1740 he transferred to HMS *Torbay* and sailed with the fleet for an abortive attack on Cartagena in modern-day Columbia. At the Battle of Toulon off the French Mediterranean coast in 1744, the *Torbay* was one of 14 British warships.

In 1746 John retired with the rank of Rear Admiral. He died on 29th May 1753, aged 57, 5 years after his wife. His was buried at All Saints parish church, West Ham, Co. Essex. In the parish burial register he was described as *"Admiral Gascoigne of Stratford, an old and brave sea commander."*

MARY-ANNE GASCOIGNE (née Mighells) (1705-1748) married John Gascoigne in May 1727. Her first child Mighells was born, christened and died the same day in Charleston in October 1732, but she went on to have six more children, William (1735-1793), John (1737-1750), Mary-Anne (b.1738), Elizabeth (1739-1799), James (1742-1821) and Ann (1746-1808).

She died on 1st September 1748, aged 43, and was buried with her mother at All Saints Church, West Ham, Co. Essex. Their tomb bears the inscription: *"Mrs Ann Mighells, d.1741, wife of the Hon. James Mighells, Vice Admiral of the Blue, and their eldest daughter, Mrs Mary Anne Gascoigne, d.1748, who also married an Admiral."*

ELIZABETH (*"Betty"*) HALL (née Mighells) (1706-1800) married Mr Ezekiel Hall (1694-1748), a merchant in the City of London, in April 1735 when she was 29. They had one son James Hall in 1736, who died without issue. Elizabeth died on 22nd June 1800, aged 94.

In John Gascoigne's will dated 1748 after the death of his wife, he appointed *"Mrs Elizabeth Hall widow of Ezekiel Hall, late of Crutched Fryers in the parish of Saint Olave's, Hart Street, London and Anne Mighells of the same place Spinster (Inmate with the said Mrs Elizabeth Hall) sisters of my late wife Mary-Ann Gascoigne to be Executrixes of this my last Will and Testament and to be restituted by Mr Henry Roberts and Mr James Gascoigne in the care and diversion of the education of my children in consideration whereof (and of my great affection for them) I hereby give and bequeath unto each of them the sum of fifty pounds each to be paid at the end of two years after their taking upon them and continuing to act as my Executrixes."*

ALICE GADSDEN (née Mighells) (1707-1741) became the third wife of **THOMAS GADSDEN (ca.1688-1741),** Collector of His Majesty's Customs for the port of Charleston, in June 1732, aged 25. She died in Charleston on 3rd July 1741, just 34 years old, and Thomas died a month later. Their two sons, James Gadsden (1734-1818) and Thomas Gadsden (1737-1770) were sent to England in 1741 to live with their aunt, Mary-Anne Gascoigne.

ANNE SCHRODER (née Mighells) (1719-aft.1753) was Mary-Anne's youngest sister. She married Mr John Adolph Schroder in 1749 at the age of 30. The Gentleman's and London Magazine carried a notice of the Marriage: "*4 April 1749 Mr John Adolph Schroder, an eminent merchant of London and Hamburg, to Anne, daughter of the late Admiral Mighells.*" In John Gascoigne's will dated 1753, he appointed Mr John Adolphus Schroder as one of his executors.

JAMES GASCOIGNE (1706-1763) was promoted to Commander of HMS *Hawk* and accompanied James Oglethorpe to Georgia in December 1735 with the first two shiploads of settlers. The trustees granted him a 500-acre plantation that become known as Gascoigne Bluff. There he established Georgia's first naval base. He gave up his command in 1739 and returned to England.

John Gascoigne's will dated 1744 mentions his brother, Captain James Gascoigne, "*if said James Gascoigne shall die unmarried or being married leave no male issue*" suggesting he was not married in 1744 and had no children. James died in 1763.

JOHN DURELL (ca. 1700-1748) was Lieutenant on HMS *Tryall* from April 1727 until the ship was scrapped in 1730. He went on to have a successful career in the Navy, progressing to Commander in 1732 and Captain in 1734. He retired in 1742 and died in 1748.

Although there are no naval records for Durell 1722-1726, there is no evidence that he spent those years ashore in Jamaica.

GEORGE ANSON (1697-1762) lead an expedition round Cape Horn in 1742 to attack Spanish holdings in the Pacific Ocean. He captured a Manila treasure galleon out of Acapulco in June 1743 and arrived back in England in 1744, to wide acclaim and great personal wealth. He was promoted to First Lord of the Admiralty in 1751 and elevated to the peerage as Lord Anson, Baron of Soberton. At the age of 51, he married Lady Elizabeth Yorke, aged 23, the daughter of the Lord Chancellor. The marriage brought him wealth and influence, but no children.

There is no evidence that Captain Anson met Mrs Mary-Anne Gascoigne, although they were in Charleston at the same time.

ARTHUR MIDDLETON (1681-1737) was Governor of South Carolina from 1724 to 1729. Middleton was married in 1707 to Sarah Amory, daughter of the Speaker of the House of Commons. He married a second time in 1723 to Sarah Morton. He died in Charleston in 1737 at the age of 56. His grandson, also named Arthur, was one of the signatures on the Declaration of Independence and played an active role in the American Revolution.

Sarah Morton (née Wilkinson) was the widow of ex-Governor Joseph Morton and bore no resemblance to the Sarah in this novel.

ROBERT JOHNSON (ca. 1676–1735) was Governor of South Carolina 1717-1719 and again from 1729-1735. He implemented his visionary township system of settlement in South Carolina. His wife Margaret died in July 1732 and Johnson remained in office until his death in Charleston in 1735. *The South Carolina Gazette* noted that *"the Interest of the Province lay principally at his Heart."* The people of South Carolina knew him as the *"good Governor Robert Johnson."*

There is no evidence that Governor Johnson met Miss Alice Mighells, although they were in Charleston at the time.

CHRISTOPHER ("Kittie") GADSDEN (1724-1805) returned to Charleston when his father died in 1741 and buried him alongside his mother Elizabeth at Saint Philip's Church, Charleston with the Inscription: *"Here lie the remains of Thomas & Elizabeth Gadsden and of many of their Descendants and Relatives. She departed this Life In March 1727. He in August 1741."* There is no record of where Alice was buried by an unsympathetic Kittie.

Kittie inherited the greater part of his father's fortune. He became the principal leader of the South Carolina Patriot movement during the American Revolution. He was a delegate to the Continental Congress, Lieutenant Governor of South Carolina, a successful merchant and wealthy landowner.

Gadsden's Wharf, built by Christopher Gadsden in the 1760s in Charleston, was the first destination for an estimated 100,000 enslaved Africans during the peak of the international slave trade. It is estimated that 40% of the enslaved Africans in the United States landed at Gadsden's Wharf.

All other characters are entirely fictitious and any resemblance to actual persons, living or dead, is purely coincidental.

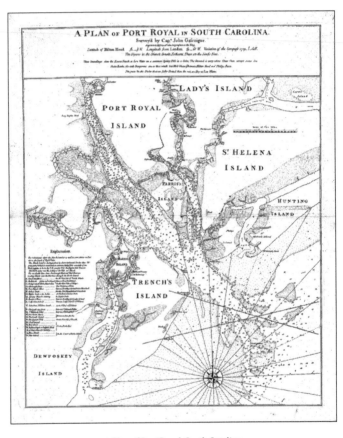

A Plan of Port Royal, South Carolina,
surveyed by Capn. John Gascoigne
Engrav'd By William Faden 1776.

295

APPENDIX 2
Captain Gascoigne's charts

John's surveys in South Carolina were not made into charts during his lifetime, but at the start of the American War of Independence (1775-1783) there were no adequate charts available to the British Navy, which had at its disposal only James Cook's Draught of Port Royal Harbour (1766) and a sketchy chart of the Carolina coast from The English Pilot. Neither was remotely adequate for navigating the region's complex coastline.

To meet demand, the London firm of Faden & Jefferys issued these two impressive charts in 1776 based on "the Surveys of Captain John Gascoigne, one of Port Royal and one of D'Awfoskee Sound." These sea charts were some of the most detailed and accurate of any of the American coastline. Later copies were issued in 1776 and 1790 by Sayer & Bennett.

The mapmaker William Faden said, "This sea chart is one of the most detailed and accurate of any of the American coastline. The immense detail of the hydrography was the result of surveys conducted by Captain John Gascoigne, assisted by his brother James in 1728 aboard the HMS Alborough. He employed the most sophisticated and modern techniques with exacting attention to detail to produce a manuscript chart."

They are recognised as the finest charts of Port Royal Sound available to British mariners at the time and provided extremely detailed hydrographic data, with hundreds of soundings as well as shoals, tides and other information of use to pilots. On land, symbols are used to mark extensive marshlands and the location of several plantations.

These finely engraved maps embrace the coastal region of South Carolina from Port Royal Sound to the mouth of the Savannah River and Tybee Island, Georgia, in the south. Prominently featured is Hilton Head Island (called 'Trench's Island') and 'D'Awfoskee Sound', which is today known as Calibogue Sound. The old name survives on D'Awfoskee Island, now spelled Daufauskie, located at the centre of the map.

These charts must have been eagerly sought after during the War of Independence by British naval commanders assigned to the region, which saw heavy naval fighting in the years 1778-1780. Port Royal Sound was one of the South's finest harbours. Both sides in the conflict believed that possession of the area was of great strategic importance.

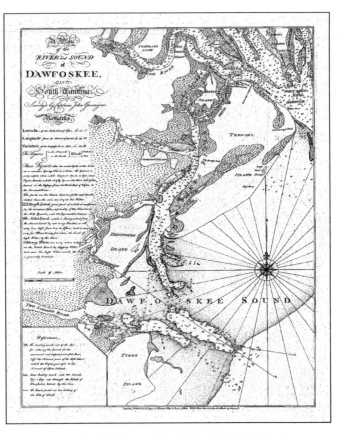

A Plan of the River and Sound of Dawfoskee, South Carolina,
surveyed by Capn. John Gascoigne
Engrav'd By William Faden 1776.

Early in the war, the region fell under the control of the American patriots. On 24th September 1779, at the Battle of Hilton Head, three British ships were set upon by three French ships, allied to the American cause. After a dramatic chase and intense exchange of cannon fire, the principal British ship, HMS *Experiment*, was forced to surrender. The area remained an important base for the American cause and although the British conducted isolated raids along the coast, it remained in the possession the American forces until the end of the war.

Resources

This novel was based around the original handwritten naval logbooks of Captain John Gascoigne on HMS *Tryall*, HMS *Greyhound* and HMS *Alborough* which I read at the National Archives in Kew and the National Maritime Museum in Greenwich.

A great number of books and websites were invaluable for my research life into the 18th century, but special mention must be made to:

"*Dr Johnson's London: Everyday Life in London in the Mid 18th Century*" by Liza Picard

"*Building Charleston: Town and Society in the Eighteenth-century British Atlantic World*" by Emma Hart

"*Three Decks - Warships in the Age of Sail*" - a comprehensive web resource for researching naval history: *https://threedecks.org/index.php*

On a visit to Charleston I visited the many museums and historic houses dating back to the 18th century, explored the harbour and discovered the trail to the High Bluff at Hog Island (now called Patriots Point).

Thanks to Cindy Rinaman Marsch for her Manuscript Assessment and to Curtis Brown Creative for the helpful advice given on various writing courses. Thanks also to my family and friends for their unwavering help, support and encouragement.

Printed in Great Britain
by Amazon

20525279R00174